EVERNIGHT PUBLISHING ®

www.evernightpublishing.com

Copyright© 2019

Katherine McIntyre

Editor: Melissa Hosack

Cover Art: Jay Aheer

ISBN: 978-0-3695-0048-9

ALL RIGHTS RESERVED

HYPNOTIZING BEAT

DEDICATION

To all the lovely oddballs and outcasts, this book is for you.

HYPNOTIZING BEAT

HYPNOTIZING BEAT

Discord's Desire, 2

Katherine McIntyre

Copyright © 2019

Chapter One

The nightmares happened almost every night.

Trevor tried to excise those flashbacks of the past from his skull, but the moment sleep stole him, the memories returned. He'd wake up in a cold sweat to stare at the top bunk Kieran and Liz slept in, half-believing the iron bars of his cage still surrounded him.

Trevor lit a cigarette as he stalked along the sidewalk of a street still blazing with yellow and red neons even at three in the morning. That was Las Vegas, an entire city of insomniacs like him. And with the two-week stretch of shows Liz had booked for their band, Discord's Desire, they'd be full up on the energy they siphoned from humans for a while. This city reeked of sex and desperation, the exact things that fueled their ragtag crew.

He sucked in the first drag of nicotine, which flooded him in a quick sweep, because he needed somewhere to channel this nervous energy. A couple of drunk girls stumbled past him, their loud, carefree laughter echoing into the streets. The shadow lengthening from the alley ahead had him slipping his hand to his waistband for his knife.

The Venetian stood out nearby, all faux and muted elegance compared to the gaudy pinks of the Flamingo or the smack-you-in-the-face monolith of Treasure Island. He just wanted a stiff drink, quick-like.

Ever since the Lotus Garden incident where he'd run into Tymarch Alberich, the very man who enslaved him all those years, his nightmares had increased a thousandfold. The active bounty the asshole placed over his head didn't help either. Avoiding the Otherworld didn't cut it any more.

Ky would kill him for escaping in the night like this. Trevor tapped the ash from his cigarette, the flecks drifting by in the late-night breeze. Their lead singer took overprotective to Mount Everest levels, especially since he got all official-like with their booking manager Liz. Trevor hadn't escaped one set of chains for a new one, however well intentioned.

Trevor rolled his shoulders before he entered the Venetian, which pulsed with energy even now. Balls clinked, buzzers rang, and shouts and cheers resounded through the place while folks gambled away their money and sanity. The moment he stepped inside, the smell of sweat collided with heavy cleaning solution, and he flicked his cigarette behind him to career onto the pavement. Cocktail waitresses bustled through in tight tees, carrying full loads of drinks to tables filled with the latest brand of douchebag. With the summer storm attitude that descended, Trevor wasn't in the mood for chatting with anyone.

He dodged past the machines blaring at him and

flashing their neon lights almost as shamelessly as the broads stripping down on the dozens of stages lining the Strip. The bar stood out in the center of the casino, a fake-marbled attempt at elegance so ostentatious it hurt. Nothing in this realm compared to how the Otherworld's raw, organic growth collided with innovation. Besides, Vegas was tits straining out of a low-cut top and mascara thick enough to smear. Trevor spent too much time with his own desperation to bother with anyone else's.

He slipped into one of the red-backed seats lining a circular cream bar with tall columns in the center. The bartender appeared faster than a blink, as if he could flash in like a pixie or gnome.

"What'll you have?" the guy asked, looking efficient and trim in his burgundy vest and black slacks.

"Gin and tonic," Trevor ordered, hunching forward to rest his forearms across the cool surface of the bar. Just one wouldn't cut it either. A couple of gazes flicked his way—though he was used to the attention. Even with glamour hiding his sharper than human teeth or the wild, banshee light in his eyes, humans still saw a lean black guy with long spiked hair the color of burnished silver. Add on the black patterned tattoos threaded up his arms and he didn't need his leather jacket or spiked bracelets to stand out.

A group of college age girls giggled from the other side of the bar, trying to flash him looks they deemed seductive. Trevor had received enough of them to become one jaded motherfucker. Unlike Jett and Renn who whored themselves out, Trevor exercised a bit more caution with who he took to bed. After all, no amount of energy he could siphon from a good fuck would fix the hopelessness threatening to choke him every waking day. He spent his time waiting for the inevitable—to end up in a cell again.

The bartender returned with his drink, and Trevor wrestled out his wallet. Before he could pass over his card, the bartender shook his head.

"No need," the guy said. "Lady on the other side of the bar offered to pick up your tab."

Trevor lifted the gin and tonic in a salute. "Cheers." He scanned the side of the bar but didn't catch any locked and loaded gazes. The columns obscured the other half of the bar, where she must've been hailing from.

He sniffed the drink—the crisp scent of juniper wafted his way, though that wasn't telling enough. With the bounty over his head, he sure as a snake didn't trust mysterious drinks gifted his way. Time to pay a visit to the opposite side of the bar—somehow, he got swindled into making conversation whether he wanted to or not.

Trevor hopped from his seat, the weight of his knives at his side giving him some measure of confidence. Already, he could hear both Ky and Liz yelling at him for being reckless while Renn gave a thumbs up in the background. Sure, the whole thing could be a trap with a couple of Alberich's hulks waiting for him on the other end of the bar, but he had vigilance tamped into him after years of being under the bastard's thumb. Besides, he could shock them with a banshee wail and bolt.

The moment he turned the corner, Trevor froze.

She sat at the bar wielding an appletini like a weapon, and the trim black dress she wore clung to her lithe form like it'd been painted on. The neon blue scarf around her neck and matching heels fit her style to a T, accenting glossy chestnut locks pulled into a chignon and sharp, inquisitive eyes that sliced like a knife. The leannan sidhe's pointed ears and elfin features were the only tip offs of her fae heritage, since she could blend even without the glamour veil that kept humans unaware of their kind.

The sight of Danica Maslanka delivered a one-two punch to the stomach, the reminder of the smoking ruin way things left off between them.

Trevor lifted the gin and tonic as he approached. "So, let me guess, poisoned?"

Her plum lips quirked in a pert grin. When they'd first met, he'd found her stunning, but nothing painted someone in shades of ugly like betrayal. "Like I'd be so classless to offer a poisoned drink. I was looking for a way to chat one-on-one, and I figured if I sent an email, you'd ignore it."

"You'd be right." Trevor took a seat beside her. He did trust that she hadn't poisoned the drink—the woman wasn't a killer, she just possessed no ounce of moral fortitude. Like he should've expected more from one of his kind. When Ky's brother Larsen Blackmore targeted the band, sending mercenaries after them six months ago, Danica had showed up with a similar vendetta and they'd joined forces.

Until Ky got kidnapped and Danica ditched. She had Larsen in her sights and nailing him to a cross meant more than saving their lead singer. The last time they heard from her, she hung up on Liz while Ky was the worst sort of screwed. Trevor's blood heated all over again, and he took a sip of the gin and tonic to cool his nerves.

He met her eyes, not betraying an ounce of the bitterness. "What's so important you needed to stalk me all the way to Vegas. Not a close drive from San Fran."

Danica glanced away, her gaze flickering to the columns behind the bar. "San Francisco and I are on the outs. Besides, my staff has always been urging me to take a vacation, so I figured now would be a fantastic time."

Bull. Shit.

"Wouldn't Los Angeles be better real estate for your talents?" Trevor asked. If she wanted to play around, he'd indulge. After all, whatever reason brought her to him couldn't have been a good one. "There's more glitz than talent around here." A leannan sidhe like her fed from artists in the same way Ky and Renn siphoned energy from sex and passion. He just leeched off of the crowds' energy, so playing shows offered the perfect medium.

"And miss out on the chance to grab a drink with legendary guitarist Trevor Arceneaux? Never." She placed a hand to her chest in mock surprise, the sarcasm fluid as a stream mid-storm. He had to give her credit for thoroughness—he kept his last name off the internet, so she must've gone an alternate route to obtain the information.

Trevor took a sip from his drink, the coolness gliding down his throat like relief. Not like he'd reached some state of calm. If anything, Danica's presence hotwired his emergency alarms to constant alert. The woman didn't act without motivation and ultimately placed her agenda above all else.

"How's your sister doing?" he asked. Two could tango along the knife's edge.

Danica's gaze sharpened, if possible. The heartless woman had her weaknesses, no matter how she tried to downplay or hide them. After all—she had never been the one with a personal vendetta against Larsen. Everything she'd done was for the sake of her sister.

"She'd be better if she could get a seat at one of your shows," Danica responded, trilling sweet as a sparrow. "A little birdie told me your show at the Joint tomorrow night is already sold out. When did you boys go from garage band blues to Rolling Stones?"

Avoidance of the highest order—that had been Danica's game from the moment they met her. Too bad for her he'd played the game for as long as he could remember. Whatever roundabouts she took, he'd follow, until he managed to suss out her motivations for tracking him here.

"The bar's set for sleazy in Vegas, and that's the reputation we've cultivated for ourselves." Trevor took another sip from his drink, the icy gin trickling down his throat. Not like the liquor did anything to sate the thread of exhaustion pulling tighter in him each passing day, ready to snap at any moment.

Danica's eyes narrowed. She stared past him, and the back of his neck prickled.

"We're being watched," she murmured, her lips barely moving. She placed her appletini on the bar.

Like he could spend some time by his lonesome without one of Alberich's goons trailing him. Lah-dee-fucking-dah. Looks like they'd be proving all of Ky's mother henning right.

"Follow my lead," Trevor mouthed. He downed the rest of his drink in one gulp, the icy blast mirroring the adrenaline that surged through him with the oncoming threat. He slammed the glass onto the bar and slipped out from his seat. If they wanted to tail him, he'd spent years dealing with the occasional bounty hunter who tried to nab him when he neared pockets of the Otherworld. Now they'd taken their game to the human realm.

Trevor held out a hand in Danica's direction. Her smile remained steady even with the confusion lighting her jade eyes. She placed her hand in his, a slight, soft touch, when he'd been expecting claws.

"Why don't we head up to my room for the

night," Trevor said, his words dripping with intent.

Once Danica caught on, her demeanor transformed. Those lids grew heavy with a scorching stare, and her plum lips curled into a seductive smirk. She draped her arms around his shoulders and sank against him like some fawning fan. Should've figured after the way she'd played them in the past that Danica could slip into a role. Her slim body pressed against his, and she leaned in close enough that her lemongrass and lime perfume lingered.

Trevor wound his arm around her waist, his palm flattening on the small of her back. Her hands traveled from his shoulders to waist in a slow, tantalizing dance as she leaned in. Together, they strode in the direction of the nearest stairwell. He didn't have to glance behind him to feel the intensity of being watched. A lifetime of vigilance made sure the instinct was stamped into him bone-deep.

"We'll get him to follow us to the stairs," Trevor mumbled into her hair, his lips brushing against the silken strands. Even though he hated her guts, something about her lithe body pressed against him traveled straight to his cock. Danica was the sort of stunner he couldn't forget, no matter how hard he tried. She let out a loud, girlish giggle, which sounded nothing like the throaty sarcasm she normally rolled on.

Once they got to the steps, that's when his stalker would act, and he could handle the situation away from the dozens of humans and bystanders who could get hurt in the process. Even if they whipped out fae magic, due to the veil of glamour, all the humans would see was a drunken bar brawl, a common sight in this city. The stairwell door beckoned, feet away.

Danica's fingers curled tighter into his leather.

"When he jumps me, run the other way," Trevor

murmured.

Danica snorted in response. "I'm not some porcelain doll in need of protection," she whispered. "Besides, he could be here for me." Trevor's brows furrowed, but before he could ask, she slipped out of their feigned embrace to tug the door open.

She whirled around and crooked her finger at him, a honeyed seduction in her deep, green eyes. Her expression dripped sex, and his cock throbbed in response. Because now was the time to get horny over a woman who betrayed them, right before some bounty hunter jumped them. He sucked in a deep breath and followed her inside to the stairwell.

The moment the door clicked shut behind him, Trevor pulled out his knives. Danica slipped on a pair of brass knuckles, except these ones were tipped in copper.

"Expecting an Unseelie?" Trevor asked, giving her a sidelong glance. Everything surrounding her appearance in Vegas to the acute way she prepared for the situation spelled trouble.

"Who else would Alberich hire for thugs?" Danica shot back.

The door creaked open.

A couple strolled in, laughing with each other as they wobbled on unsteady feet like they drank one too many martinis on the floor. Trevor hid his blade and slunk toward the wall while Danica tucked her knuckles out of sight. She brushed her body against his, following with a throaty, pointed laugh to throw the humans off their scent. The couple barely paid them mind as they focused on conquering the stairwell. The door clicked shut while their voices drifted from the flight of steps.

Only a lifetime of vigilance saved Trevor.

A shadow whipped his way at a bullet train speed right as Trevor lifted his blade. Their stalker must have snuck in when the couple opened the door.

Claws met metal in an echoing screech.

The ankou, a long, lanky shadow of a beast, hissed at him. Those rotten teeth were on full display, and his rancid scent slammed in full force, like a cemetery mated with a dumpster. Empty eye cavities glared at him from the creature often dubbed the graveyard watcher, and Trevor steadied his footing, prepared to shove back.

Before he could make his move, copper glinted under the dim fluorescent lighting. Danica's fist collided with the creature's face.

A screech came from the beast as its flesh sizzled under the impact of the copper tips, the metal like acid to an Unseelie. Trevor didn't miss his chance. His knife slipped between the gauzy flesh covering protruding ribs. He thrust deep and dragged the blade across, the skin tearing with the effort.

The claws descended again, snagging his beat-up leather jacket. They ripped into the fabric, and the creature opened its mouth again to let out a cloud of that horrid breath. Except a blackened cloud drifted from the beast's maw, like a chimney puffing oily smoke into the air.

Danica lobbed another punch, this time aiming for the slice he'd created along the ankou's chest. As her copper tips descended, the cloud made her splutter, and she staggered back a few paces.

The cloud spread, the noxious fumes making his eyes burn as tendrils trailed toward him. Trevor closed his lips and plunged ahead anyway. He'd grown so used to seeing in the darkness that half the time he could close his eyes and find his way. His blade snaked out and sank into something solid.

The ankou let out a low hum in anger. "This isn't

your fight," it hissed.

Well, devil be damned.

Trevor peered through the haze, ignoring the way his eyes stung. His blade had sunk straight into the murky stomach of the ankou. As much as he wanted answers, the creature presented an immediate threat. He dragged his blade up until it stopped against the ribs. Blood poured from the opened gash, thick, black liquid spilling onto the floor.

Danica leapt between them right as the claws lashed out again. She dodged the ankou's blow and delivered another one of her own. Even with the remaining mist hanging in the air leaving a residue similar to pepper spray, she ignored the sting, her shoulders heaving with coughs. She slammed her fist into the creature's skull again and again and again.

As fast as the ankou descended upon them, it dropped to the ground. Chunks of skull created a stark contrast amidst the surrounding pool of blackened blood. The janitor was going to have a joyride cleaning this one up—chances are, the glamour would just make the fae corpse look like someone died from alcohol poisoning, passed out in their own vomit.

Danica's shoulders heaved, flecks of the charcoal liquid staining her porcelain cheeks. Her eyes shone with a crazed, desperate light, and she bared her teeth like a wild thing.

He wasn't sure whether he'd ever known her at all. "You owe me an explanation," he said, crossing his arms as he wiped the slick fluid on his soles against the carpeting.

Danica straightened, slipped off her brass knuckles, and shook out her fighting fist. "All right, lasso of truth time. You're not the only one who Tymarch Alberich has a mark on. I'm the latest addition to his hit list, and I want to take that bastard down."

Chapter Two

After that truth bomb, Danica couldn't return to snarky quips behind the shield of a martini glass. Though, the option faded the moment the ankou got the jump on her.

With the way she left things between her and the boys of Discord's Desire, she should be crushed with guilt. Truth be told, she was—to a point. However, Danica had done the moral tango before, and survival won every time. She and her sister wouldn't have lived past childhood otherwise.

Danica brushed the drops of ankou blood from her cheeks, smearing the liquid in the process. Thankfully she'd worn a black dress, so any residual would blend. Trevor gaped at her, and she was tempted to shove something into his mouth just to see what he'd do about it.

"Yeah, that's right. You're not the only fae on the block with a bounty over their head." She placed a hand over her mouth in mock horror. "I know how you hate to share the limelight." Grabbing a handkerchief from her purse, she wrapped up the copper knuckles.

"And your brilliant idea was to band together so we attracted an even higher concentration of his bounty hunters?" Trevor's voice sharpened with distrust—not like she blamed him.

"*Excuse* me," Danica responded. "I thought out of anyone in my rolodex, you'd jump on the opportunity to be free from Alberich. For good."

His dark eyes gleamed with an allure she'd noticed from the start. Intelligence flared in his gaze, the keen, razor sharp sort that always commanded her attention. She gambled on his survival instinct, but she knew a thing or two about the lengths one would go to for freedom.

Trevor extended an arm. "Let's walk and talk."

She looped her arm through his, catching the hickory and leather scent she couldn't get enough of. "And here I thought you hated my guts," she teased.

Trevor cast her a glance. "Politeness doesn't cost a thing, even if I'm offering a hand to the devil herself."

That shut Danica up. What she regretted most about her tactical reroute involving Discord's Desire was how that left her and a certain banshee guitarist. Because from the moment she'd met Trevor, the sparks between them had promised to turn into something explosive—brilliant. Not anymore.

They wove through the Venetian with ease, barely drawing a second glance from the glazed patrons who sat at the machines, staring at the screens. It hadn't taken Danica long to learn how to disappear in a city like Vegas. So many people shuffled through, burning like the last gasp of a candle, and just as many roamed with those flames extinguished like the walking dead. Slot machines jangled, neon lights flashed, and even at four in the morning, the crowds hadn't diminished.

Danica led the way, her vigilance a persistent itch on the back of her neck. She kept glancing to Trevor, the need to talk burning her tongue. He brimmed with a seriousness as black as her morning coffee, so she stayed silent. They walked arm in arm like they might be friends, lovers, anything but the truth. The divide blazed between them as if chalk outlines had been drawn.

Trevor didn't even turn to acknowledge her until they stepped outside the Venetian. Not for the first time, she cursed her lack of friends. Apart from her sister, Danica had acquaintances and temporary alliances. That was how it had always been, her and Lenora against the world. She drank in the sharp, pre-dawn air, even drier out here.

"So, tell me, why should I believe you?" Trevor asked, a careful edge to his tone. He walked with a casual stride, his long legs carrying him so fast she needed to quicken her pace.

She'd struck too many deals in the past to not know where she stood. Deliver the wrong answer here and he'd walk away, no matter how curious he was.

Danica lifted her chin and held his gaze. She hadn't missed the scars along his arms, or one around his neck like a collar. Maybe that's why she'd been drawn to Trevor from the start—because she would burn the entire Otherworld to keep from being caged.

"I might not have loyalty in spades, but I never lied to you the entire time we worked together. My objective was Larsen, because I will go to any length to protect my sister. I apply the same ruthlessness to protecting my freedom." She paused, the bitterness seeping into her words. They'd stopped walking in the middle of the sidewalk, folks jostling them as they bumbled by. Trevor's stare pinned her to the pavement, the scrutiny making her sweat. She held her ground.

"Tymarch Alberich threatens that freedom," she stated. "I looked into your history, Arceneaux. You've got every reason in the world to want him dead, and after the hit he put on you in the Lotus Garden, I know you've been hounded."

Trevor crossed his arms over his broad chest, stretching the fabric of his worn leather jacket. "Better question, then. What do you want from me?"

Danica licked her lips on impulse, but she kept her eyes on the target. "I managed to get intel from a connection of mine who works for him. Apparently, he keeps a certain family heirloom tucked away in this city. However, I'm not fool enough to believe I can march in there and steal it by my lonesome."

Trevor ran a hand through his silver strands before letting out a short exhale. Still, he didn't walk away. Danica counted the small victory. "You're serious, aren't you," he murmured, his rich, deep voice with the Southern twang gliding right through her. The way he scrutinized her, she couldn't get away with her normal backtalk and deflection. Not right now.

She lifted a brow. "If I wasn't serious, do you think I'd be doing this walk of shame? It's not my style in the slightest."

He opened his mouth to respond when his attention fixated to the right.

Danica followed his gaze.

A couple of blocks down, she spotted the point of fascination. Even in Vegas, the group of three gorgeous guys in leather jackets and the tough-ass chick in ripped jeans drew attention. The satyr with the pointed horns, the incubus with those long fangs, and the siren's greenish skin stood as a direct contrast to the human-appearing chick beside them. Not like the crew of Discord's Desire could go anywhere without drawing attention—even with the veil of glamour, their charisma flew off the charts.

Danica wasn't ready for the full reunion tour yet.

She reached out to press a business card into his palm. "Looks like Kieran Blackmore and the Sunshine Gang are paying a visit. Give me a ring sometime and we'll chat."

Danica stalked off in the opposite direction, her heels clicking against the concrete. She couldn't help the glance back to Liz O'Brien, who was the closest she'd come in years to befriending anyone.

Trevor already strode toward his bandmates, and Kieran exploded in a fury of gestures and loud words that tipped off his worry in a heartbeat. Their sort of camaraderie was rare, especially among the fae. Apart from Lenora, no one would blink if she went missing for a few hours, let alone died. As if that didn't sink like a stone in her gut.

Danica tore her gaze away from Discord's Desire. Ahead, the Tropicana's lights blazed orange, the Bellagio's fountains leapt high, and Mandalay Bay loomed, hundreds of windows lit up like a starry sky. The streets swarmed with folks barely clutching their beers, two steps from disappearing into an alley never to be seen again. Despite all the neon lights blazing in desperation, they couldn't hide the ink shadows of every corner and pocket. Danica had seen enough of life to know the truth. No matter how much light shone on a contagion, the rot would pervade until it consumed.

****

Danica hadn't dolled up for a rock show in ages. Her preferred clients were acoustic crooners, artistry and angst seeping from their pores. They tasted delicious. The chunky heels of her boots slammed against the pavement, and she had pulled out a lace-up corset top to pair with the skintight bodycon dress beneath. Spiked bracelets jangled around her wrists, but she couldn't quit her scarves, this time an electric green one.

The Joint was flush with people lining up to enter this secretive show that had been whispered about through the crowds like wildfire. Even if the boys managed to scrub most of their live shows from YouTube, their reputation for raunchy preceded them. Watching the human orgies erupt created its own brand of entertainment, even if she didn't siphon energy from passion like most of the band.

This early on in the night, the strip reeked of booze without the vomit afterbite, and savory scents of roasting hot dogs and greasy burgers wafted out from the small restaurants near-buried under the monoliths beside them. Her skin prickled as she strode through the crowds. Danica had always been vigilant, but the bounty over her head awakened a new urgency.

She flashed her ticket and maneuvered her way inside. With the privacy of the event and the high security keeping out strangers, this was the prime opportunity to meet with her contact. Besides, she enjoyed watching the boys play. The raw charisma and sexuality offered a potent brew, and with humans and fae alike writhing about in the crowd, she could have her cloak and dagger convo in relative peace.

How they'd booked and filled a show this large was beyond her, since the boys weren't a household name in the slightest. Liz had a knack for attracting the right crowds at the right time though, and if anywhere could accommodate the 'Most Depraved Show on Earth' then Vegas would be the place. Voices filtered around the entryway, the spark of excitement bouncing from person to person as folks stepped to coat check or lined up to enter the arena.

Apparently, the selling point hadn't been Discord's Desire, but the sheer secrecy of the show. Questions buzzed through the air from everyone around her. Who was playing tonight? What sort of twisted would they see? Excitement flared in every gaze, and Danica's lips curled in amusement. With the way Discord's Desire stirred a crowd into orgies, these folks wouldn't be leaving disappointed.

She stepped inside the arena, neon blue lighting glowing down upon her. Danica made a beeline for the bar. The sheer numbers of people pouring into the seats and the floor in front of the mainstage made her nerves dance. Anywhere in this crowd, Alberich's men could be lurking. Once upon a time, before the hunters declared war, Alberich wouldn't have sent bounty hunters out into the human realm. Fae conducted their warfare in the Otherworld, as was proper, keeping a reasonable distance from the human realms.

However, then the hunters had emerged from their anonymity, humans born with the ability to see through glamour, and families trained on every way to disarm and kill fae. A whole bunch of Buffy the Fae Slayers. When the hunters began to leave a trail of corpses, their former rules ceased relevance.

Most of the barstools were taken, though a large, conspicuous purse inhabited one. Danica lifted a brow as she neared. The owner of the purse was a petite woman with pale green skin, the exact yaksha she searched for. Glamour would shade the sharp fangs and the glowing gold eyes of the woman who perched in the barstool, a flared black dress accenting the emerald shade of her skin.

"Marisa Kincaid, you foxy minx," Danica announced from behind her.

Marisa swiveled around in her seat, a martini glass in hand. "Danica Maslanka, it's about time we convened in person." Her dry tone offered the antidote to the nerves brewing inside Danica, and she took a seat beside the yaksha. The bartender roved her way, so she placed an order for a rose martini.

Danica settled in her seat, elbows behind her on the counter as she faced the stage. The boys had already started their prep, Kieran testing out the microphone while Trevor fiddled with his amps. "How's the family doing?" she asked Marisa, as a professional courtesy of course. Her brother Leo Kincaid happened to be the co-owner of Alberich's company, so Danica had always maintained her friendly relationship with his sister.

Marisa cast her a sidelong look. "You know I wouldn't be here if Leo wasn't fed up with his partner. Not with the continent-sized bounty over your head."

Danica shrugged and accepted the rose martini from the bartender with a wink. "I signed for a loan with him, not a life sentence. He wasn't just going to repo my business but demanded I pay the rest of the loan off as one of his menagerie. I'm nobody's pet."

Marisa lifted her martini glass in response as the first thrums of music rolled through the arena. "Here, here. My brother has found the practice repulsive, and we've been looking for a way to get out of our ties with Alberich for a long time. Unfortunately, you can understand with the way our businesses are connected, we can't dive into that morass on our own."

"Which is where I come in," Danica murmured. She'd known from the moment she spoke to Marisa that she'd be the point person in this escapade. If everything went tits up, she alone would pay the penance. This wasn't her first rodeo around the Seelie circuit.

"Your work in outing Larsen Blackmore for his crimes was the tipping point in Leo's decision. If you were able to maneuver a higher-echelon Court shark like that, he believes you're ready to take on his partner."

Danica sipped at her rose martini instead of answering. Marisa had nothing to lose in this endeavor, and she had everything. Backed into a corner like this though, she wasn't flush with options. Her gaze lingered on the guitarist of Discord's Desire. He didn't have many options either, and from the intel she'd gotten, Trevor knew firsthand what being Tymarch Alberich's pet looked like.

Kieran stepped to the microphone. "Everyone

ready for the best show you've seen all year?" he asked. The crowd, brimming with anticipation of the unknown, responded with screams that shook the rafters. "We are Discord's Desire," he growled, the sound reverberating through the venue.

The effects of his voice dropped onto the crowd like a pheromone bomb. All the humans in the audience paid *close* attention in the wake of the lead singer's silken announcement. Danica had watched this party train before and knew any minute it would be pulling into Bone Central Station.

When Trevor's fingers drifted across the guitar strings and the first sinful note pierced through the crowd, the sound ignited the crowd into a frenzy. She found herself sitting up and paying attention to the careful way he plucked the chords as he led the intro of their opening song. The concentration on his face was pure, almost unguarded compared to every other interaction with him. The tender way he caressed the guitar, how he strummed the strings to his whim made her regret even more how the cards had played out between them.

Jett's bass notes threaded in, and Renn followed with the slow, seductive percussion as the band began one of the songs she'd listened to quite a few times in the past. Already, humans in the crowd had begun to make out, finding partners to grope and grind with. Next, the clothes would start shedding, and they'd be privy to one hell of a spectacular orgy. Any fae in the audience who fed off this sort of mojo would be in for a feast tonight.

She kept close eye on any of her kind—after all, Alberich's men could be anywhere.

Danica glanced over to Marisa, who sipped her martini with the chill of Captain Cold. Drinks with big names in the Seelie Court stuck her neck into uncomfortable territory, but the bounty pushed her in this corner. If she could nab Alberich's treasure and use it to buy her freedom, she would. Danica figured Leo Kincaid had his own plan for the most-likely illegal item as a way to get his business partner out of the picture.

"I'm in," Danica said, taking another sip of her rose martini even though her gaze never strayed from the stage. No matter how desperate she was, she wouldn't let those feelings show while sharks swam in the water around her. "Give me the when and wheres and I'll make it happen."

"Glad to hear you're entertaining such a lucrative venture," Marisa responded, her lips curled with a serpent's grin. The emphasis on 'you're' was crystal clear, the hands-off way upper echelon fae dealt with everything. Marisa had originally handled her contract with Alberich's company and remained Danica's contact through all of this. When this recent shit hit the oscillating fan in the wake of the impending hunter war, fae started gathering resources like weaponry. Of course, that spurred Tymarch Alberich's sudden desire to call and collect on her debt.

"You know me." Danica sighed, raising her glass in salute. "Always up for a challenge." She settled against the bar, ignoring the moans that filtered through the audience, the limbs waving around, and the heavy grunts and thuds as people got rowdier. Despite her survival abilities, she couldn't pull off a heist on her own. The success of this venture revolved around convincing one man to take a risk on her again.

Her eyes landed on Trevor, who bit his lip as he thrummed away at the guitar, a sheen of sweat on his forehead. Under the neon blue lights, his silver hair glistened like ice, tamed into spikes for the show. He rocked back and forth, cradling the guitar as the melody poured from his fingertips. The boys dominated the stage, Renn thrashing around at the drums, Jett thrusting with the bass, Kieran leaping from one part of the stage to the other, and Trevor grounded the movement and melody with his indomitable presence.

The crowd writhed and screamed, some in excitement and others in ecstasy.

When the power cut, plunging the arena to pitch black, the screams turned to terror.

Chapter Three

One minute, the melody entranced Trevor, and he plucked at the strings like an extension of his soul. Part inspiration, part muscle memory.

The next, darkness descended upon the stadium. His fingers still plucked the strings, but those electric chords all silenced in the wake of the power loss. Kieran's voice trailed off at the chorus with the mic cut, and even though Renn banged the drums out of frustration, the sound wasn't booming through the arena.

"What gives?" Renn shouted over to them right as the screams began.

Cram thousands of people into an arena and shut the lights out on them? Instant recipe for pandemonium. He knew better than to believe this was an accident. Trevor's hand went to the switchblade he always carried at his waistband. The lights of smartphones created a glow through the arena, like dozens of fireflies bouncing around as everyone in the crowd tried to figure out what had happened. The flashing lights betrayed the quick, deliberate movement of human-sized shadows slinking through the crowd.

They weren't touching the humans.

Warning bells clanged in his head. These intruders had arrived for the fae instead, which meant the hunters had upped their game.

"Head backstage," Kieran called, his rubber soles smacking against the stage as he took off in that direction. Liz waited there to watch the show, and their lead singer's protective instincts were the stuff of smothering legend. If they remained onstage, they'd become prime targets for the hunter crusade. Trevor extricated himself from his guitar, placing her on the stage with reverent care before he bolted after Kieran. For most, blurs of shadows and gray filled the stadium, the occasional illumination coming from the thousands of cellphones on flashlight function.

Trevor had a long and sordid past of seeing in the dark. After all, weeks would stretch by trapped in the cage with no hope of release. The grays, the murky shadows would become so clear that the light turned into a blinding, terrible thing. His throat tightened from the old memories. He focused on the darkened smudge of a doorway, on the clatter of nearby feet coming from his bandmates, not the rumble of screams, shouts, and moving feet from the arena below. His boots squealed on the polished stage as he ran.

Trevor cast a glance back before plunging through the doorway. Dozens of hunters wove through the audience, their bare blades catching the neon glow of phones. Any fae who lingered in the crowds would have the nails on their coffins hammered in before they caught the death descending. Not like he could pause and help— some of those fae might be hunting him. Drops of sweat prickled on his forehead, several slipping down his neck.

He hurtled through the door to plunge down the corridor, already a shade quieter. A flashlight sliced an errant beam through the center, courtesy of their band manager.

"Hurry, guys," she called, a strained urgency in her voice. Many folks would be prone to hysterics in the middle of a sudden blackout and hunter attack, but not Liz O'Brien. The woman was made of pistols and pixie spit.

Trevor's heart thumped at an erratic beat.

The screams reverberated from the arena, loud enough the walls quaked. It didn't take long before the frantic element of the screams took on the sharpness of true terror. The fae culling had begun.

Trevor sucked in a sharp breath as his heavy footfalls reverberated up his shins. The corridor stretched out far, but he could already distinguish the limned lines of the door at the end where the starlight shone through. They needed to get out, and fast.

He flicked his switchblade out, the click echoing in the vacuum of a hallway. Renn raced ahead of him, the thump of his heavy stompers louder than the others. Jett brought up the rear, their siren prepared to unleash his voice on any humans who got in their way. Not like their abilities worked against the hunters' immunity to all things fae.

The door flung open before Liz ever reached it.

Once he spotted the slinky silhouette in heels, he knew who waited for them.

"Come with me if you want to live," called the walking, talking pop culture machine. Danica stood in the doorway, brass knuckles on each hand. The shadows sharpened everything fae about her, from the points of her ears to those wild eyes.

Liz skidded to a halt so fast Kieran smacked against her. "What are you doing here?" Liz's voice sharpened with the same caution that tugged at his insides the moment he'd run into Danica again.

They didn't have time for distrust. A horde of hunters infiltrated their show, and if they wanted to escape without a platinum dagger through the chest, they needed to act fast. Trevor pushed past Kieran and then Liz, squeezing to where Danica stood. If he could place faith in anything, it was her will to survive.

"Where are they coming in from?" he asked. He didn't question why she'd shown up—after all, he was in her sights, and she was the most persistent woman he'd ever met.

Danica tilted her head to the unloading lot behind the venue. "We're going to have to scram and give this space some distance until the morning. They're pouring through multiple entrances, and they've already claimed at least a dozen of our kind."

Which meant before the end of the night there'd be members of the Seelie Court here to scrub minds and spin stories. He needed to be gone by then. As renegades who refused to commit to their court, their band wasn't well-liked by fae authorities. Trevor shifted from one foot to the other, anxious to move, move, move.

"Let's get going." Kieran took charge, striding across the back lot toward the alleyways that emptied out onto other parts of the strip. Trevor's fingers itched at leaving his Fender behind, but his guitar wasn't worth risking his life or freedom for. His boots clapped onto the blacktop when the back of his neck prickled.

Someone watched them.

"Watch out," Trevor called, wielding his switchblade. He whirled to the right.

The shifting shadows peeking past the side of the building were the only tip off he got. First one hunter emerged, and then the next, their platinum and copper blades gleaming under the moonlight. The screams pounded through the building, filtering through the open door. The hunters charged, but Trevor wasn't an idling car like the poor bastards caught in the blackout inside— he was soaring across the asphalt at top speed. The pandemic the hunters caused was reckless, the kind that would end in accidental casualties.

He dodged out of the way of the first blade, and Danica slipped in beside him, her brass knuckles clanging against metal. Renn charged the other hunter, ready to slam his horns into the guy. The hunter swerved to the side, his boots clapping on the asphalt. Liz's pistol made a timely appearance, announcing its presence with a click.

When the nearest hunter's blade swung again, Trevor slammed his own knife against the edge. The metal screeched as it clashed. They both jumped back and circled each other, Trevor's grip steady on his switchblade. Before the hunter could swing again, Jett leapt from the side with his boot dagger in hand. The tip sank into the guy's jacket, snagging him where he stood.

"Don't think you can slink out so easily," the nearest hunter spat. He stepped back a pace to watch them warily. He still wielded his knife, and his gaze scanned across them as if he waited for the right moment to strike. Like Blade wannabes or goth club rejects, the hunters wore leather trench coats, stompers, and all black attire.

Kieran stepped to Trevor's side. "You're missing a precious point." He gestured to the knife. "We've got the two of you outnumbered."

"Why attack here?" Liz asked, an edge to her voice. He'd caught the search history on the computer back at the RV for more history on the hunters, any information she could get. After all, she grew up isolated from her own, a fact which, given the war between the hunters and the fae, they were all grateful for. "The humans aren't getting slaughtered in droves," she insisted, a slight shake to the pistol in emphasis even as she kept it pointed to his skull. "Not like you're doing to the fae inside."

The hunter spat on the ground. "There are so many filthy fae infiltrating our realm that a sneak attack is the only way to claim an advantage."

"Who's organizing the hunters?" Trevor asked. No way could their society be capable of this sort of attack without a leader.

"If you haven't heard Darren Andrew's name yet, you will soon," the other hunter intoned, even though he kept glancing to the muzzle of Liz's pistol. Their own hunter watched with a cool gaze, and Trevor had fought by Liz's side enough to know she wouldn't hesitate. "We're not going to stop until your kind is back in the Otherworld where you belong."

Even though Jett's knife remained steady, he glanced at the nails of his other hand. "The lavender beaches are pleasant and all, but the holier than thou attitudes are a buzzkill. I'd give it a C minus. As to where our kind belong, that's a subject for some quality philosophical debate."

The hunter bared his teeth in irritation. Their siren had that effect on folks.

A door slam from the side of the building echoed in the air, and the first of the sirens began wailing through the streets. They needed to scram. Now. Trevor met Kieran's eyes and tilted his head toward the hunters. Danica's gaze pressed into him, but he ignored it.

He shouldn't have.

Before he could make his move, she swung out, her brass knuckles cracking into the hunter beside them. His eyes rolled, and he swayed on his feet for a second before dropping to the ground. The thump echoed through the clearing. The other hunter surged forward, raising his knife to slice. Trevor waited until he got close, and then dipped to avoid the blade. He pivoted around, and his elbow snapped out.

The hunter swung his forearm around to block.

Unfortunately for him, Kieran already moved in to attack. Their band leader's fist blurred as his knuckles slammed into the guy's jaw with a wet thump. The other hunter swayed before crouching to the ground and clutching his jaw.

"Time to go, boys," Liz called out, taking the lead as she started running toward the alleyway. Trevor leapt after her first, his veins buzzing, buzzing, buzzing with that ever-present paranoia of getting caught. The cops didn't offer him the safety blanket they did for most folks—they had the power to lock him up again, one he didn't take lightly.

Danica surged beside him, moving in heels with a grace and speed that defied physics. "You did promise the crowd the most depraved show on earth. I'm sure mass hysteria and murder means promise delivered, right?"

Liz shook her head. "Yeah, try telling that to the venue's coordinator. We'll be banned from the venue from now until forever."

Overfull dumpsters lined the alley ahead, and crinkled Mickey D's wrappers and crushed Starbucks cups marked the territory. The stain-covered concrete stretched out between two restaurants, leading to the busy street ahead. More than a couple of people scanned the skies at the sound of the sirens in case they'd spot something.

His throat tightened. Instead of the huge wave of sexual energy Discord's Desire had begun to consume, they now ran themselves ragged through the streets of Vegas. Mighty kind of those hunters.

He couldn't forget how he'd run and run and run through San Francisco the night Alberich put the official bounty over his head. His feet had gotten so sore they bled, and his muscles turned limp and boneless. His breaths had been choking gasps, and his insides ripped wide open until he couldn't avoid the rotting husk of hate and fear he patched the fractures in his heart with.

Kieran clapped a hand on his shoulder, snapping

him to focus. "Stick with us, brother." The incubus's golden eyes gleamed with understanding. He didn't deserve a best friend like Kieran, but since the man was a stubborn, persistent ass, Trevor did his best to protect their lead singer—most of the time from his own impulses.

Along the Strip, human escapees from the hunter invasion emerged in throngs, most in some sort of disarray or hysterics. Even with the hunters on the loose, many would be focused on escape at this point, because there was no way they could explain themselves to the cops.

Renn's eyes gleamed when he scanned over a pair of girls sobbing on the corner, crouched on the edge of the sidewalk. "Looks like they could use some comforting."

"Have some class," Jett retorted, the siren's careful brow arched in unerring judgment. "Though I know that's asking a lot."

"But I'm hungry," Renn whined, running a hand through his wild tangle of hair as they stalked down the street as fast as they could without drawing attention.

"Eat a fucking burger then," Kieran shot back, heaving a sigh.

Trevor restrained his grin, the normal back and forth of their crew grounding him. By some miracle, Danica remained silent. Her inquisitive eyes soaked in everything, her gaze flitting from their crew to the crowds stepping into the streets. He shoved his hands into his pockets. They continued down the sprawl of the Strip, heading in the direction the Stratosphere, a beacon as the tallest point in the city.

"Care to explain what you're doing here?" Liz called back, not bothering to glance. No one questioned who she was talking to, because the rest of the band harbored the same question.

Trevor's heart skipped. He wasn't sure how his bandmates would react—that is, if she even told them the truth. However, since she'd shown up at the Venetian and dangled her offer, he'd been able to think about little else.

True freedom from Tymarch Alberich.

He almost couldn't process the thought. Yet his heart leapt at the idea of freeing himself from the invisible chains that still wrapped around his wrists, his throat.

"That's some quality hostility, Obiwan," Danica announced, her voice sharp with bravado Trevor had been able to see past from the moment they met. "Better bottle that shit up to hurl at your enemies."

"What can I say? Betrayal brings out the best in me," Liz sniped back. The two had gotten on so well when they first met for a reason—he'd never met a pair of more feelings-averse women in his life. They were almost as bad as Jett. Trevor shot Danica a glance, one she deliberately ignored.

"Hey now, what was that?" Kieran asked, pointing between the two of them. "The shared looks?"

Renn almost toddled into the street when a couple of sorority girls stumbled by in their matching letters shirts, but Jett yanked him by the collar to keep him in line.

Trevor heaved a sigh. Time to paint this picture himself, rather than let Danica splatter color all over the canvas. "Our favorite leannan sidhe happened to find me at the Venetian when I went late night wandering. She made an offer I'm considering. Before you all shout in horror at me about bad decisions, remember one thing. Danica never lied. She might've possessed shitty moral fiber as a friend, but I reckon in business partners the more important thing is being able to take them at their word."

Danica's eyes bored into him, her expression unreadable. For a moment, he thought he caught a flicker of hurt in her eyes, but just as fast, a bright smile spread to her lips. "I'll take that description on my tombstone, please and thank you. If you lot want to commence the personal stoning in a more private place, why don't we find a diner while I spill the deets." Her gaze flickered his way. "My contact gave me the location."

The means to crush his owner, the man who kept the sword of Damocles dangling over him, lay within reach.

What terrified Trevor the most was the depths he'd descend to if it meant claiming revenge.

Chapter Four

The last time Danica sat with the crew of Discord's Desire at a diner, the situation had been a lot chummier. Now, she'd become chum in the water for some pretty cranky sharks. She'd started a tally of the number of glares delivered her way and lost count after the first hundred. The one person who wasn't doling death stares her way happened to be the same gorgeous banshee she'd roped into this in the first place.

She tapped a pen against the lacquer tabletop, soaking in the scents of bacon, the sizzle of grease, and the piping hot coffee that wafted up to greet her. The second the lights flickered out, she and Marisa had aimed for the first exit they could find. Marisa took off for the streets, eager to disappear, while Danica made the fool decision to flag down Discord's Desire and get them to safety. Not like her actions made a dent in their opinions.

"Look, Ky, I'm getting my goddamned burger," Renn said, jabbing his finger at the menu. His gaze lingered on moving targets—any guys or girls who sauntered in looking hungry for something the satyr was proficient in giving.

"Good for you," Kieran shot back, everyone operating a little tenser than normal. Danica wasn't sure if her presence or the fact the hunters crashed their show had them more riled up. She hoped for the latter.

"So, I'm assuming if Trevor's involved, this is concerning Tymarch Alberich?" Liz announced from the other side of the table.

Danica shot her a look. "Discretion, sweetheart, have you heard of it?" she drawled. Danica checked her peripheral for the thousandth time since they sat down.

With Alberich's men after not only her but Trevor, who knew who might overhear. The drunk girls riding the tilt-a-hurl in their seats weren't an issue, but from her vantage point, she couldn't spot the back corner of the diner and the blind spot was making her skin itch like she had hives.

Liz heaved out an annoyed sigh, the hunter's attitude making Danica's chest tighten. She missed being on the same side of a problem, and she missed her short-lived friendship with Liz that had flowed like the coffee in this diner.

"Danica's found a way to take him down," Trevor murmured, coming to the rescue. "We just need to retrieve an incriminating item."

Liz arched a brow. "So, if we find this item, it'll take care of our pest problem?" She elongated the words as she placed her menu on the table. The hunter might be short, but not on sass.

"Exterminator's guarantee." Danica gave a thumbs up. "They want this pest extinguished as badly as we do."

The waitress swung over, a pad of paper in hand and a dour expression on her face. If Danica had to take orders at two in the morning, she'd be donning the same lemonade look.

"I'd love to order the Reuben," Danica jumped in first. Renn ordered his burger, Ky the same with an extra look in Renn's direction. Jett continued with his heroin chic order of a salad and a second cup of coffee. Liz ordered nachos, a fact Danica remembered from when she'd last hung around this crew. Trevor leaned forward beside her to hand his menu over after ordering waffles, and their arms brushed, the touch electric. Otherworld be damned, she needed to get laid.

"Got a sweet tooth, Southern boy?" She couldn't

help flirting with him, it was compulsory. Especially when those dark eyes of his turned molten and crinkled with a languorous smile, a lazy, feline one that could turn predatory in a heartbeat.

"An insatiable one," he responded, his deep throaty murmur traveling straight between her legs. She would need to put a paper bag over his head to ignore how her body reacted to him.

Kieran shot Trevor a look, and at once, the banshee retreated from the warmth and the flirtation, his expression turning as cold as nightstained granite. Well, a dose of pure loathing did the trick.

Danica bit back her sigh, holding onto her cavalier attitude with all her might. She'd earned this. She knew that. Still, her veneer didn't help against the loneliness that crashed in at night, filling her head with voices all while her mouth was duct taped shut. Survival first. That's what she needed to remember every time she cast her long and lingerings over to Discord's Desire.

"One stipulation," Kieran said, holding up a hand. "Sorry, brother, but you're too close to this." He met Trevor's gaze, and the two of them nodded in agreement. "When we find the item, we're the ones who are keeping it until we hand it over. You can be there with us when judgement day arrives, but you've proven we can't trust you not to bolt once you get what you want."

Danica let out the breath she'd been holding. "Deal. I don't blame you guys for not trusting me—I went all Catwoman on you last time around. Look, I'll even be straightforward with you. I'm in this for survival. Our mutual pest happens to own the loan on my company and he's cashing in his chips now. So, I either pay a sum I don't have, or I'm going to be added to his collection of pets."

Trevor went rigid beside her at the term. He

didn't say a word, but his nails dug into the painted corkboard surface of the table. Her heart thundered at the memories of how Alberich had talked to him in the Lotus Garden and how Trevor went berserk in response. She hadn't fought this hard for her freedom to get tossed in shackles.

Liz took a sip from her coffee before meeting her eyes. "Let me guess. He's consolidating due to the war that's descended?"

A forced grin rolled to Danica's lips as she shunted the mind-numbing fear to the backseat. "Always knew you were the smartest of the bunch, Obiwan."

Liz's gaze softened for a heartbeat, and even though a moment later it grew sharper than ever, that was enough. Danica latched onto any hope she hadn't shattered their friendship entirely. The waitress wandered over with the massive tray and began doling out the plates.

Trevor sliced his waffle with a level of precision bordering on ridiculous, each singular square carved out before he ate the pieces. The others dove into their food like coyotes to a fresh kill, but not him. Danica ignored the way her heart warmed at the sight and tried to shove away the details about him she had begun memorizing from the moment they met.

Once she took the first bite of the Reuben in front of her, piping hot and oozing, some of the stress deflated from her shoulders.

Life like hers was a transitory mess of moments, and she seized whatever ones she could.

Even if the crew of Discord's Desire hated her now, sitting around a table with people she liked, and eating a greasy, delicious sandwich at two in the morning after a life-threatening dash from a stadium—well, that was one hell of a moment to savor.

****

Danica stared out the window of her hotel room in Harrah's, looking at all the neons still lit even at four in the morning. She kicked off her pumps and unbuckled the bracelets around her wrists. The shadows clung to the corners of her room, and no matter how hard she tried to turn off the paranoia, she couldn't rid herself of the prickle along her nape. Her air-condition cold sheets seared her bare thighs when she settled onto the side of the bed.

She hated this part of the night the most, where she fell into bed alone with the monsters inside her head. Every moral misstep paraded through her mind on a regular basis, and like always, sleep lay a few hours away.

Her phone buzzed in her purse, and Danica almost leapt out of her bed to get it. This time of night only meant one person.

"Bout time you called, little sis," Danica didn't bother looking at the screen as she answered.

"Were you about to send out a search party?" Lenora responded, amusement in her tone.

"Calling them off as we speak," Danica said, settling against the headboard of the bed and nudging the covers to the side. "You all finished with your shift at the Lotus Garden? Give them your two weeks, Nora."

"And what, follow you off to Vegas?" The click of a door closing sounded from Lenora's end—her sister was probably finishing work for the day.

"Don't knock it. You could strut your stuff for way more pay here," Danica argued. Truth be told, she just wanted her sister nearby where she could watch out for her. Lenora worked under a stage name at Lotus Garden, but if someone dug deep, they might be able to find the roots tangling them together.

"Stop the sweet-talking, sis. I'm not one of your clients," Lenora shot back. "I'm already sold, but I'm not going to pack my bags and ditch a solid gig on a maybe." Danica could hear the grin in her voice, the soft eyes crinkled in amusement and the wry lips twisted in a half-smile. Where Danica was long and lanky, her sister had stolen all the curves and honey-spun hair to accent. Not like their differing looks ever stopped them from fighting over clothes.

"Perfect, then pack those bags up," Danica responded. She'd spent the earlier half of the day checking out the local talent at open mics and soaking up the energy boost, but she'd also secured her sister a job in the process at Kink and Candy due to a mutual connection with the fae owner.

Lenora let out a staged sigh. "Should've figured you had something worked out, Connections Queen."

Danica grinned on reflex, sinking against the stiff pillow that smelled like cleaner. "Is it a crime to want my little sister within walking distance?"

"Winter's breath, yes," Lenora shot back. "You'll smother me in a heartbeat. Level with me, D. What's the reason you're pushing? Don't think I don't know when my own sister is trying to maneuver me."

Danica ran a hand through her tangled strands, staring at the stucco ceiling of yet another hotel. She missed her condo in San Fran, but ever since Alberich started sending bounty hunters to collect her impossible debt, she had to leave her known places behind. Plus, the attacks from the hunters turned the pressure cooker on high in their community, which had been filled with so many fractures no amount of plaster could keep it together.

"I'm on the run," she admitted with a sharp breath. "Alberich's demanding I repay the loan now, instead of the fifty-year period I'd been given, and he hasn't been shy about sending love notes."

Lenora's silence offered the response Danica expected, the dose of sobriety that sliced beneath both of their outer layers.

"You're stubborn, you know that?" Lenora broke the impasse.

Danica snorted, kicking at the crumpled sheet by her foot. "Took you this long to figure it out? Look, he's dangerous, and I think he'd go to any length to get the money, or me, in his possession. Just come to Vegas, Nora."

"I wouldn't miss the chance to strut my stuff in Sin City," Lenora responded, returning to the lightness from before. Danica clutched onto their banter like a lifeline. Her sister chose a different route than business life for this reason. She'd been uncertain about the deal Danica had made with Alberich from the start, but they each picked their own paths. Of course, hers reared up and ruined things for them both.

"See you in a blink, sis," Danica responded, hanging up the phone. She tossed her cell to the blankets as she turned onto her side, staring out the big glass panes placing Vegas on full display. Marisa messaged her the location earlier, and her wheels had been turning ever since. With this, she walked on splintered glass. As much as she'd love to believe that when they found Alberich's secret stash the guys of Discord's Desire would do her right, she had no guarantees.

Danica always existed in a world where the truth was transient and morals were sold to the highest bidder. If she planned on working with the boys, she needed her own bargaining chip in the process—needed to stay one step ahead. Just in case.

The twinkling lights of the city winked at her, all

neon deception and gilt-covered rot. Most days, she moved along like a train on the high-speed rail, but ever since her business got upended and she started this life on the run, she'd been forced to face the silences, that quiet she loathed. And when she looked in the mirror, she was no better than this gutted city with its flashing-lights desperation.

Chapter Five

By the time the sun peeked in through the windows of their RV, Trevor was brewing his second pot of coffee.

With each night becoming more restless than the last, at this rate he would soon be averaging a cool half hour of sleep.

Trevor leaned into the cherry red vinyl seat, the mug of coffee blazing enough to take his hand off. Yet, even that did nothing to sear through the ever-present fear thrumming through his veins.

A creak of the floorboards signaled Kieran's approach, their lead singer wearing nothing more than boxers as he fumbled with a pack of cigarettes.

"If you keep burning the midnight oil like this, I'm going to dub you the Ghost of Guitarist's Past." Ky set to yanking down the window behind the seats. Even though they'd parked in a dump of a lot with a bunch of beater vehicles and sketch neighbors, the desperate neons from the Strip tried their damndest to cut through the early morning grey.

"Who can sleep with the way you and Liz go at it?" Trevor muttered, reaching for one of Renn's crumpled shirts he left strewn all through the floor of the RV. Trevor tossed it to Kieran. "Do us a favor and cover yourself up. The adoring fans aren't here to see the show."

Kieran flashed him a grin, his gold eyes sparking with a new relationship thrill, where everything was sunshine on the Mississippi, and problems were a snap to fix. Not like he could blame his bandmate for the infectious excitement. Kieran had fought hard to win Liz over to the commitment side. Trevor couldn't imagine that sort of closeness with anyone. The thought settled around his throat, the phantom sensation one that lingered through the years.

Ky sniffed the shirt and wrinkled his nose. "Otherworld be damned, did Renn shit on this? You can deal with some skin, brother." He leaned to the window, cigarette and lighter in hand. Within moments, the embers glowed, and the first stream of smoke filtered out. The comforting scent of cigarette smoke had Trevor jonesing for one himself, the coffee not quite cutting it this morning. Not after he'd made the first step toward confronting his former owner in agreeing to work with Danica.

Ky let out another stream of smoke before fixing his dragon's gaze on Trevor. "You know I can't listen to you for shit on this, right?"

Trevor snorted. "Like you ever bothered listening to me anyway?"

Kieran shot him a look. "This whole situation involves the monster who fucked up your younger years and the one woman you've expressed actual interest in for the past decade."

Trevor arched a brow. "Have you been ignoring our entire time on tour together? I've expressed interest in plenty of women over the years."

Ky ashed out the window. "Fucking is different than interested. Don't think I missed the wounded puppy dog way you brooded after Danica pulled her vanishing act."

Well damn if their band leader didn't swing with an aluminum bat. The tangle of things he felt for Danica had only gotten more muddled with her betrayal, which entrenched her in 'avoid at all costs' territory. Potential wasn't something one of Alberich's former pets got to explore. Especially not while his former owner sought to capture him back. Hell of a half-life he lived.

Ky fixed him with a look. "I'll take your steeped silence as a confirmation I'm always right." The incubus's eyes danced with amusement.

Trevor shook his head, a half-smile rising to his lips. He reached out to snag a cigarette from Kieran's pack. "You're an ass. I'd better call Liz here to deflate your ego—someone's got to do it." He lit the cigarette and joined Kieran in leaning up to the window. If Renn happened to wake up, he'd crucify them both. Trevor loosed a stream of smoke, not meeting Kieran's eyes— fucker was too perceptive. "Y'all don't have to get involved in this. It's my problem, and there's no need to drag the rest of you into danger."

Kieran punched him in the arm.

"What the fuck was that for?" Trevor nearly dropped his cigarette.

"None of that self-pitying martyr shit. You know we're not going to drop a chance for you to be free from the bastard's hold at last. I'm just saying those with clearer heads should be calling the shots."

Trevor arched a brow. "Name a time you've had a clearer head in your life. Ever."

Kieran smirked, and Trevor couldn't help the relief that swept through him. When Danica proposed taking down Alberich, he knew in his gut he'd be joining her even if he needed to go without the rest of the band. But he should've known better. Kieran always had his back. He was one of the few people in his life who proved they were worth trusting, and he'd learned the hard way those were rare.

He sucked down the rest of the cigarette and flicked it out the window before settling into the vinyl booth. His coffee waited in front of him, not enough to combat the sleeplessness as of late.

A knock sounded on the door to their RV.

Trevor tensed. Anything unexpected sent his mind to Alberich even with the ever-present hunter threat. Kieran leaned further out the window to catch who approached.

"What the hell's she doing here this early?" Ky muttered, dropping into the seat. His cigarette still hung from his mouth.

Trevor didn't question who he referred to. "I'll get the door." He pushed himself off the booth.

"Of course you will," Kieran responded, an amused note in his voice.

Trevor lifted his middle finger in response as he walked away. His pulse quickening had nothing to do with fear right now, and his conversation with Ky highlighted things he'd wanted to bury. He ran a hand through his stiff strands, a hollowness lingering in his chest like taffy stretched to the point he was going to snap. The second he reached the door, it swung open from a push on the other side.

"Can you guys walk any slower?" Danica asked, striding up the steps. "Please don't tell me the rest of the band is still asleep." The woman dressed like she'd been born into the purple skirt she wore, a crisp white button-down, and her glossy chestnut strands were pulled into a tight chignon.

"Well hello to you too," he drawled, stepping aside. She walked past him, her lime and lemongrass perfume trailing behind her. She paused to glance back and fix him with a mega-watt grin, one of the dozens that never reached her eyes.

"Don't think I'm ignoring you, charmer," she said with a wink, her voice dripping with sensuality. "But we've got work to do if your band's going to be playing on Mandalay Bay's stage tomorrow."

"Hold the phone, what's going on?" Liz's voice came from the other end of the RV. The noise of the front door must've startled her awake, and even in a sleep-shirt with mussed hair, her eyes flashed like she prepared to go to war.

Danica tilted her head to the side. "You guys wanted to move forward on this whole taking down Evil Incorporated, right? Alberich's treasure's not going to steal itself."

"Sure, but that doesn't give you the right to book the boys a gig wherever you see fit," Liz argued, crossing her arms over her chest. Their booking manager's gaze flashed with challenge.

Trevor sat on the vinyl booth and snagged his coffee. He'd need a whole lot for this conversation.

"Are you worried I'm going to steal your gig, Obiwan?" Danica arched a brow, her sharp eyes aimed like a weapon. Liz attempted to hide it, but Trevor caught the flinch at the old nickname. Once upon a time, they'd connected fast, but their friendship ended up being a firework, sizzling the day Danica chose her personal mission over Ky. "Never fear," Danica continued. "Even with the threat on my business, these guys wouldn't provide an ounce of the sustenance I need to keep grooving."

"And what happened to working as a team?" Kieran asked, a careful gleam in his eyes. "I believe that was a part of the initial agreement—we'd be wanting full transparency."

"That's what I'm giving you," Danica countered, her voice cool and her gaze level. Trevor sat back and observed. The woman didn't do anything without a reason, but he'd learned from last time their reasons didn't always align. "You never established you needed your hand held the entire time, but we can make some readjustments if that's a prereq." Her throat stuttered with her swallow, ever so slight but the movement gave her away.

Trevor spread his arms out on either side of the vinyl booth, leaning back. "If you need to cling to those tenuous tethers of control, keep them," he responded, fixing her with a look. "There's one of you to five of us, and this time, we won't make the mistake of assuming you'll do the moral thing. You may be a step ahead in planning, but you can't pull this off without us."

Her mouth thinned for a second before she flashed him an empty smile. "Well, with that radiant vote of confidence, I'm raring and ready to go." His stomach twisted at the sight of her, how she hid behind her mask like she had nothing else to hold onto. Curiosity infiltrated like exhaustion, an undeniable tug controlling him at every turn.

"All right, I'm listening." Liz, the eternal voice of reason spoke up. She settled against the countertop in their kitchenette with her newly purloined cup of coffee. "So, the boys are doing a gig at Mandalay Bay—I presume that's where this item of Alberich's is located?"

Danica offered her a wry grin, those pretty lips twisting in a way Trevor hadn't been able to get out of his mind. Too bad his stomach soured every time he remembered the final phone call and the way things left off.

"My god, I forgot what it was like to work with intelligent people," Danica said, strolling over to the almost depleted carafe of coffee. She helped herself to the chrome mug out drying on the countertop and finished off what remained of Trevor's freshly brewed pot. "Security is tight at Mandalay Bay, and we need the ability to roam where we please without getting the constant shut off. Guaranteed, Alberich will have his own men stationed on the security force to protect his precious cargo."

"Do we know what we're stealing yet?" Jett's voice came from the back of the RV as the siren approached. Unlike the rest of them who sported epic amounts of bed-head, Jett must've either combed his long, dark hair in his cot or put so much product in that his strands didn't budge.

"Not sure of the item yet," Danica said, her eyes twinkling. Bullshit she didn't know. Except if they tried grilling her here, she'd pull the same conversational pirouettes she always did. Trevor tapped his fingers along the backing of the booth. He'd have to confront her in private. "However," she continued, "I was given the specific location of what we're searching for, so while you lot strut your stuff at the Mandalay Bay stage tomorrow, Obiwan and I will be hatching a plan."

Liz heaved a sigh as a tentative grin rose to her lips. "Damn, Danica. You're a cold bitch, but you're hard to hate when you include me in all the fun stuff."

Trevor's mouth twitched in amusement. Danica's dark eyes flared with emotion, and he seized on it, just like he did any signs that more existed beyond the chilled surface she presented.

"And when you guys find the area of the casino we need to break into?" Trevor asked, fixing his stare on her.

A small grin curled her petal lips. "Well then, you and I will be nabbing Alberich's precious item. If anyone can figure out what might belong to him, it'd be the two of us."

The word 'belong' made him internally flinch, but he remained calm on the surface.

"What are the rest of us supposed to be doing?"

Ky snapped. "Knitting cozies?"

Liz's mouth pursed as she fought her grin. "Don't worry, babe. I'm sure you'll be able to find some trouble to get into. We'll be running inference, I presume. I doubt Alberich would have a treasured possession stowed away there without adequate security in place."

Jett sauntered up the rest of the way to greet them, fumbling with the buttons on his shirt. "Or if you're a really good boy, Ky, I'm sure those security measures include hordes of his personal guard set to attack the moment someone tries to fiddle with his stash. Tell me again why this is a good idea?"

Trevor gripped his knees as he hunched forward. "Look, I can handle it on my own if you guys aren't comfortable."

Ky swatted him in the shoulder. "No. When my asshole family started causing problems for me, we all worked together to stop them. Tymarch Alberich is an active threat to my boy here, so there's no way we'll sit back and let that slide." His golden gaze swung Trevor's way. "I trust you'll keep Ms. Maslanka from darting off the second we find ourselves in some real trouble."

Danica arched an eyebrow and pursed her lips, but to his surprise, she didn't snipe back. He hadn't missed how she kept glancing to her phone during the conversation, to the point he couldn't help the uneasy flip of his stomach. Humans and fae alike never inspired much trust from him, and he was determined to not give her an inch, no matter the way those pert lips enticed and the scent of lime and lemongrass lingered long after she left.

Her phone buzzed this time, but she slipped it out with an expert level of control, despite the flicker of interest in her green eyes.

"As much as I'd love to keep watching you bicker

among yourselves, I've got places to be," Danica announced, placing her mug on the counter with a soft clink. "Maslanka Talent Agency won't run itself. Obiwan, I'll send you the information as soon as I get back to my hotel room so you can set-up the rest of the details for the boys." Her gaze honed in on Liz for a minute before drifting his way.

Her green eyes softened, like she offered a brief glimpse of the woman behind the tailored outfits, sharp wit, and even sharper smiles. Need razed through him like a wildfire. He wanted to see her undone beneath him, those chestnut waves splayed across his bedsheets. Just as fast, her mask slipped back into place.

Her heels clicked along the linoleum as she headed toward the door. "See you on the flipside," she called, tipping two fingers in the air before she descended the steps. The door clicked shut a moment later.

Trev's brows furrowed. Jett glanced to him, the perceptive jackass already forming his own opinion based on the curl of his upper lip. Kieran ran a hand through his hair and let out a loud groan that echoed in the silence. Liz slumped behind him. Trevor's fingers tapped a staccato beat along the vinyl cushion. She'd bolted out of the RV too fast.

"I don't buy that she's meeting with a client," Trev murmured.

Kieran's gold eyes flashed with understanding as their gazes met. "We'll handle things around the homestead. Go find out what she's up to."

Trevor's roving fingers stilled. Not like he would get any sleep at this point anyway.

A thump, followed by a clash sounded from deeper in the RV. A moment later, Renn stumbled up to join the rest of them. His hair was a tangled mess, and the man hadn't deigned to wear anything but boxers, placing his hard-earned six pack and hairier than average legs on full display.

"What'd I miss?" Renn asked as he shook the empty carafe of coffee.

Jett heaved an exaggerated sigh. "Just about everything, Sleeping Beauty. Are you sure ten hours of sleep wasn't enough shut-eye?"

Trevor snorted, and he stood. "I'll be back in time for lunch." He strolled to the front of the RV where he'd left his keys and wallet, nabbing them on his way. The moment he stepped outside, the wave of heat smacked him in the face, pure Las Vegas courtesy. Time to find out what sort of trouble had drawn Danica Maslanka away in a hurry.

Chapter Six

Danica stepped off the Strip, ducking into the shade of the flat-topped buildings on either side of her. A subtle pulse of awareness beneath her skin had been present ever since she'd entered the main sprawl of Vegas again. Someone followed her.

She plunged down the narrow streets cluttered with jilted casinos, a couple of off-brand motels, and the sort of sunshine that bleached the streets around her. Whatever tail followed her could confront her in this dingy, shadowed spot. She couldn't afford leading Alberich's men or hunters to her intended destination.

Danica stopped along a side street, the heat plastering her thin button-down to her chest. She leaned against the wall and waited, feigning an attempt to appear ensnared with the azure sky. *Come on, you bastard.* Minutes passed, and not even a breeze swept through. The sun beat onto her tanned skin, summoning obnoxious drops of sweat to trickle down her neck and her back. She cast one last scan over the area before continuing along the road in the direction of Kink and Candy.

At this time of day, blackout curtains were in effect, and few people braved these side streets away from the Strip. If she were anywhere but Vegas, she might believe a zombie apocalypse had swept through the city while she wasn't looking. With the hunters going to war against her kind, who knew—nuclear levels of fallout might be the fate awaiting them all.

Kink and Candy's neons had been shut off, the nightclub looking like a diner waitress by day and high-class bartender by night. Melrose stepped to the door and waved her inside, shutting the door near as fast as she opened it.

Two cars were parked in the lot beside the club. Danica's heart thumped in double time. She cast another warning glance to the street behind her, but nobody roamed across the river of asphalt. She didn't even catch any glimpses from the windows of the surrounding hotels and restaurants. With a sigh, Danica entered the building.

The moment she stepped into Kink and Candy, the AC slapped her in the face and she liked it. The sweat started drying like paste across her skin, a fierce reminder to future Danica that a shower was essential tonight. Melrose stalked through the maze of stacked chairs and tables across the floor, heading toward the stage. The woman moved with preternatural grace, but it was anyone's guess as to why a water nymph would take up residence in the desert. Melrose ran a clockwork crew, and Danica trusted her in the business capacity—which was the extent of confidence she offered everyone.

All except one person.

Lenora hopped off the stage she'd been perched upon and raced over to her, a hurricane in heels. Her long, golden hair hung in loose waves, and her skin had the perfect tan Danica never bothered achieving. She'd shown up in perfect Vegas attire, jeans so short they may as well have been underwear, and a loose, flowing green tank top. Once Lenora's hazel eyes settled on her, the string around her heart loosened.

"Don't tell me you drove overnight for this ol' gig," Danica said, crossing the space between them. "I mean, Melrose is an absolute doll, but she wasn't in dire straits." She winked over to the long-legged water nymph who simply shrugged.

Lenora didn't respond, just flung her arms around Danica and squeezed.

The touch was something she missed in her isolated bubble, the comfort of a connection she treasured more than any other. Danica swallowed hard, not willing to show her weakness for the only person who'd ever given a half damn.

"Shut up, stupid," Lenora murmured into Danica's shoulder. "I wanted to see your sorry ass."

"Remind me why I was excited again?" Danica responded, unable to help her grin as she tugged on Lenora's long strands before stepping back. Her sister served as a reminder it wasn't always a place but sometimes the people who made a home.

Lenora fluttered her lashes. "Because you're a control freak who would've had a silent meltdown for every day longer I took."

Danica smirked, not humoring her sister with a response, because she was right. "So, Melrose, does my baby sister fit the specs of what you're looking for?"

Melrose strode to where they stood, pure professionalism in a pencil skirt and thick eyeliner. "You already missed her strut her stuff on stage. I trust your judgment, Danica—she was hired the moment you vouched for her."

Danica clapped a hand over Melrose's, and they shook. The woman was cool and savvy, the exact type she preferred to work with, but Danica didn't take any chances. Lenora would go by a different name and they were simply "old friends." If anyone tapped into the vein that they were related and Alberich applied some pressure? Well, Danica didn't trust her brethren from personal experience.

"Well, you just let me know the next time you need extra entertainment to draw some newcomers to the club. I'm sure there's someone I'm representing who would be a good fit here," Danica said, the implication floating. Melrose tipped her fingers in a salute as Danica turned toward her sister. "And since you're in town, Lilah, do you want to grab dinner tonight?"

Lenora's gaze twinkled with the fake name, but she nodded in response. "As long as you pick somewhere better than the Thai-Mexican fusion place from last time. The combination plates tasted like dog puke."

Danica didn't bother hiding her grin when she turned on her heel to head out of Kink and Candy. As much as she wanted to stay and talk with her sister, a glimpse had settled the percolating pile of nerves she'd become. Lenora was safe, and at the end of the day, that's all that mattered.

"See you guys later," Danica said, her mind reeling with the ever-expanding list of tasks she needed to accomplish once she returned to her makeshift office at the hotel. She winced when she stepped back into the sun, squinting as the heat blasted against her.

She hadn't got two steps down the walkway before the door creaked open again.

"Danica?" Lenora's voice came from behind her.

"What's up?" she asked, plucking her sweaty strands away from her forehead as she turned around to face her sister.

"Be careful," Lenora warned, her gaze flickering as she viewed the Strip in the close distance. "I started getting bad vibes when I rolled into town, and mine tend to be on point."

"Same goes for you," Danica warned, unable to keep the scrape of seriousness out of her voice. "I don't know what I'd do if anything happened to you." She sucked in a breath, trying to shove away the surge of emotion. "So, go wow your new boss, and then head on over to my hotel room. If you spot anything hinky, don't hesitate to call."

Lenora nodded, her eyes softening. "It's great to see you, sis," she murmured, her voice quiet.

Danica's lips quirked into a grin, and she made a shooing gesture before striding off again. She didn't trust herself to keep the waver out of her voice, and as the big sister, she needed to don the Man of Steel front. The door clicked shut again, and Danica continued down the walkway, heading back toward the Vegas streets she came from.

"Don't tell me you're finding your clients at Kink and Candy now," a low, smooth voice drawled from feet away.

Danica whipped around, reaching into her purse for her copper knuckles.

Trevor looked just as gorgeous as he did this morning, his well-fitting black V-neck tee and sliced up jeans highlighting all sorts of muscles she'd wanted to run her fingers across ever since they met. The sun gleamed across his tawny skin, bringing out the golden undertones, and his silver strands glowed. His arms were crossed, and he leaned against the side of the building, a knowing look she didn't like glittering in those dark eyes.

She shrugged, trying to suppress the way her heart raced. "Hey, I go where my clients want, even if it's the sorts of strip clubs you boys play at."

Trevor quirked a single brow, and she sort of hated him for the sheer amount of cockiness one look could hold.

Danica volleyed an annoyed glare back while a droplet of sweat trickled down her neck. "I suppose you were the one following me here?"

He lifted a hand. "Guilty. Shame you didn't introduce me to Lenora. I was curious to meet the woman so important you'd screw over anyone, us included."

He knew. Somehow, he knew. Her eyes widened, and she grabbed his arm, near dragging him away from Kink and Candy. Trevor moved with her, and they slipped down one of the streets in the shade, which somehow ended up a minimum ten degrees cooler without the overbearing sun. And now that she'd overreacted like an absolute idiot, she couldn't roundabout out of this conversation.

Danica let go of Trevor and stepped back. Something about the man sent her off-kilter, every time. Short tempers, she could deal with. Sarcasm, quietness, aloof, all of those fit in her wheelhouse. However, his somber gravitas reached straight for her heartstrings and tugged.

"Look, I can't have anyone knowing my sister's in town," she murmured, her gaze skating the ground. "Even at Kink and Candy, she's going by a different name, and I'd like to keep her incognito."

His fingers, those long, perfect fingers, skated across her shoulder, and her eyes shot up to meet his. Understanding flickered there. Still, the touch lingered like he'd somehow marked her. "I won't tell." His brows drew together. "You're just trying to keep her safe, and Alberich's reach is far—believe me, I know."

The dryness in the air had nothing to do with the reason she licked her lips now. Standing this close to Trevor was dangerous. This vulnerable prickle at the nape of her neck was new, something she banished long ago when she'd stuffed her pesky emotions into a Pandora's box. She found herself resting a palm on his chest, feeling the smooth, defined muscles beneath the flimsy layer of fabric.

"Thank you." When she met his gaze, the heat simmering there shot straight to her core. Her heart ricocheted in her chest. She was two seconds away from finding out how those sensuous lips tasted.

A car zoomed by, the rattle of the exhaust snapping her out of the moment. Bad Danica. Hands off the band candy.

"Since you're here anyway," she said, tapping his chest before stepping away, "we may as well grab lunch and start Ocean's Eleven-ing this bitch."

His returning smirk looked so delicious she wanted to take a bite. Spending more time by his side was a terrible idea with the way her libido ran wild. She let out a slow breath. Maybe a hate-fuck would get this itch out of her system. She needed to do something. The way her heart fluttered in her chest at the mere sight of him could only spell bad news.

****

Danica took a seat and leaned back into the booth, watching as Trevor scanned the room at least three times before joining her. He'd been jumpy the whole way over, as if he expected Unseelie bounty hunters to leap out of every door they passed. Not like she blamed him. Ever since Alberich put the mark on her back, she'd been paranoid too.

A quiet murmur filtered through Grenada Central, the elegant hush that came along with these sorts of places. While her kind tended to stick to fae-owned bars, right now she wanted to be as far away as possible from them. This quiet café featured wide, sprawling windows that displayed the dusty hues of the Red Rock Canyon in the distance, a beige booth stretching the entire length of the restaurant, and wire-rim two-seater tables spaced at reasonable intervals.

"I don't think this place caters to my kind," Trevor murmured, casting a casual glance to dressed-for-success individuals scattered all through the room.

Danica grinned, showing teeth. "What, gorgeous

rockstars with attitudes? Of course they do, babe. Now, calm the fuck down and order up—I picked the corner booth for a reason. I've got a clear view of the entire place." His shoulders didn't go down in the slightest, and a frown creased Danica's forehead. She let out an exhale. "Okay, switch seats with me."

Trevor lifted his brow.

"Before you protest," she cut him off, "it's clear you don't do well with your back unprotected. I'll survive. So, switch with me." She wasn't a fan herself, but she'd come to trust Trevor's twitchiness in regards to Alberich. Her vigilance had just begun, whereas his had been bred and perfected over the years.

She marched over to his seat, which he'd evacuated fast for the booth, and she settled into the wire-rimmed chair, mustard yellow cushions accenting the beige around this place.

"My fault for underestimating your perception," Trevor said, mouthing a 'thank you' to follow. Somehow, the hatred in his eyes had already dimmed, the acidity in his tone lessened, and while it didn't slice across her skin like a bare blade, the intensity in his gaze threatened to burrow deeper. She'd take the lashings any day.

A waitress swung by, and Danica ordered a club sandwich post-haste, the metric ton of coffee she'd drank eating away at her stomach. Trevor stuck with a burger, which she'd seen him order medium-well at least half of the times they went out. She was paid to notice the details, but with him it felt personal.

"So how long's it just been you and your sister?" Trevor asked before tipping back the glass of water.

Danica arched a brow. "My folks are still kicking. Climbing their way up the social hierarchy claws first."

"That wasn't what I asked." The intensity in those

umber eyes socked her in the gut. She'd always kept her surface conversations a moving target, but he slammed right through them with the force of a bulldozer. For some reason, the understanding laden in that gaze had her believing maybe she didn't have to peel herself apart to explain how her upbringing brought her to trust one person alone.

The man who was once kept as a pet by Tymarch Alberich might know how she felt.

Her throat tightened, even when she plastered a fake smile on her face. "It's always been the two of us, ever since we ditched the arranged marriages our folks set up." Her words came out caustic even as she tried to soften them, her grin sharpening into something vicious. "I will not be bought or bartered with, by anyone."

The slow nod he gave in response caused something inside to curl tight and release, like she'd been wrung out. The waitress swung by with laden plates, his burger dripping with grease and cheese onto the plate while her club sandwich was pretty as a picture. She wasn't hungry for any of that anymore.

Trevor was getting too close. She needed to get this man out of her system before she wandered any deeper into this maze. "Don't know about you, but I'm in the mood for something else," she murmured, levelling him with her gaze. Danica didn't hesitate in taking whatever short-term thrills could sate her. In the transient life she led, she needed to grasp every opportunity when it arrived.

Trevor's brows drew together, but she didn't miss the way his sensuous mouth quirked. "I think you're forgetting I still don't trust you."

Danica stood from her seat and offered her hand. "Trust doesn't have a thing to do with this, gorgeous. I'm not going to lie about the attraction there—and based on the hungry looks you've been passing my way, it's mutual. So, hate me if you want, but I think we both need to indulge before we drive ourselves to distraction."

Trevor looked at her for a moment, and Danica's heart lodged in her throat.

She'd been rejected before—this shouldn't matter. Except, somehow, it did.

His fingers laced through hers, and Trevor rose from his seat. The weight of his palm against hers settled the churning in her stomach. The heat blazing in his eyes scorched away any other thoughts, and her core clenched at the liquid desire there. She tightened her grip in his to take the first steps forward.

Time to erase distractions.

Chapter Seven

Trevor had fucked his way through a sea of groupies before, and he took new flings into the RV on most show nights. Yet, he'd never felt this thrumming in his chest that plucked at him from the moment Danica extended her hand. They'd slipped, unnoticed, into one of the swanky bathrooms in this joint, a private stall.

He wasn't blind. Once they'd plunged past the superficial thorns and deeper into the woods, she'd pulled the one avoidance technique left in her arsenal. However, she'd been telling the truth about one thing— the attraction had become flash powder between them, waiting for the match to drop. And the sooner they dealt with this lust, the sooner he could return to loathing her with a clear mind.

She let go of his hand when they entered the bathroom, a fluorescent overhead blinking on.

He shut the door behind him with an audible click.

The moment he turned around, Danica's mouth met his. She tasted honey sweet with the sharp sting of coffee, and he slipped his palms around her chin, cupping her cheeks to draw her closer. He'd been imagining how those pert lips would feel from the day they'd met, but the reality was far, far, better, a silken glide he could easily become addicted to. He kissed her again and again, backing away to tease, baiting her to lunge in for more.

His hands traveled lower, around her slim waist, her slender hips. Her graceful curves were mesmerizing. Even with the fabric separating him from her soft as a whisper skin, her heat and the way her body curved against his stoked his hunger. He'd risen to attention the moment she'd taken his hand, and by the time she slammed into him inside the stall, his cock was stiff as a board.

Danica reached for his belt, but he moved her hand away.

"If we're doing this, we're doing it my way," Trevor murmured against her mouth. "Think you can handle that, cher?"

"Not if you're going to talk me to death," Danica challenged, those green eyes flashing with heat.

A grin quirked his mouth. "I planned on putting my mouth to a different use."

She bit her lower lip, and the way she sank against him with her arms twining around his neck was the sort of irresistible he couldn't refuse. A moment before, she'd been all flames and steel, yet now she grew as pliable as heated honey. He could spend a lifetime trying to unravel this sheer enigma of a woman. Trevor slipped her violet skirt up her thighs, and a moment later, he shunted her panties to the black-tiled floor.

The second she kicked them off, he lifted her to the porcelain sink. Her skirt hiked, putting that gorgeous pink pussy on clear display. His cock throbbed at the sight, and he kept his palms braced on her thighs even when he sank to his knees like a monk in benediction. The coolness from the tiles seeped into the frayed holes at the knees on his shredded jeans. His fingers curled into her muscular thighs, and he spread her open wider.

Danica perched on the sink, the heels of her palms digging into the porcelain on either side of her.

He bit and sucked his way up her inner thigh, enjoying the sting of her heels scraping against his upper back. The woman splayed out before him was sheer perfection, and he planned on enjoying every second with her. When his tongue touched her clit, she let out a moan that thrummed low in her throat.

Trevor began working her clit with his mouth, slow, sensuous licks that had her arching as she threw her head back in mindless abandon. She tasted sweet and tart, and he kept returning for more. His grip tightened on her thighs, nails digging in. He devoured her, harder, faster, until her breaths came out in soft pants. The fluorescent light pounded down on them, washing out the rest of the room, but from his vantage point, she couldn't be more gorgeous.

Every bead of sweat on her forehead was highlighted, the way her tongue darted out to trace her lush lips. Strands of her chestnut hair escaped her pin-perfect bun, the sort of disarray he'd been desperate to drive her to. Her button-down plastered to her chest, outlining those perfect tits of hers. He drove his tongue inside her, causing her breath to hitch before he licked and sucked at her swollen clit.

"Winter's breath, Trev," she gasped, her knuckles almost as white as the porcelain sink she gripped. Her heel dug into his shoulder, but he didn't budge an inch even with the scrape of pain. Instead, he lapped at her faster, sucking at her clit until she clapped a hand over her mouth to muffle the scream erupting from her. Her thighs tensed with the spasms of her orgasm, and she closed her eyes. Bliss drifted across her features, her mouth parting, her lashes fluttering, and her arms trembling in the wake.

He pushed himself from the cool ground to grab her hand and help her off the sink. Even her legs shook, so he kept his hands around her hips to steady her.

"Bend forward, sweetheart," he murmured, his lips brushing against her ear.

Danica let out a low moan and turned to face the sink again, her skirt still bunched around her hips.

"Already?" she murmured. "You're a sadist." She thrust her ass back to grind against him, causing his breath to catch in his throat.

His cock strained in his jeans, and the sight of her bare, soaking core was enough to do him in. "My job here's not done until you're an incoherent puddle, got that?" he responded, undoing his belt with a snick that echoed in the quiet of the room. His button flicked open, zipper ripped down, and a second later his cock was out. Danica ground against him again, this time, her bare ass against his length delivering such a pulse of desire that he bit his lip until it bled.

Danica leaned forward, gripping the sink she'd just sat upon. Her head bent down, and small strands of hair plastered against her nape. Splayed out before him like this, he could see the straps of her black bra beneath the pale, creased button-down she wore, the devastating slope of her hips, and the curve of gorgeous breasts he was dying to grip. However, the way she continued to tease him by brushing against his length had his attention front and center.

He gripped her hips tight and guided himself to her core until his tip brushed against all her slickness. The mirror in front of them reflected how she bit her lip, and the sight of standing behind her nearly sent him over the edge. Her lashes shuttered, but the glint of her seductive green eyes contained the brilliant cleverness that ensnared him from the start. Even now, while he entertained designs at control, she wrested strands back with her own wiles.

Trevor rested one hand on the small of her back and gripped her hip tight with the other as he began to slide in. Even with how drenched she was, he pushed an inch into her at a time, a tight fit. He strained at the seams, need ramming at him with an increasing intensity the deeper he sank into her. The rising pulse in his chest, his cock, begged to bury to the hilt inside her and slam into her sweet heat until they'd reached oblivion.

He sank into her the entire way at last, and a ragged gasp escaped his throat.

The way her skirt bunched around her hips, her long legs stretched in front of him, everything about Danica was straight out of his fantasies. Except someone like him might touch the flames but would never get to keep the blaze. Trevor began to move inside her, slow at first, and each time he thrust forward a soft sound escaped her throat, one he wanted to imprint in his mind forever.

As he picked up tempo, his fingers found themselves wandering to her bun. He pulled the band free, and it snapped to the ground. Her chestnut strands cascaded down her back, and he wove his fingers through them until he gripped tight. Trevor gave a gentle tug, and when a moan slipped past her lips, he yanked harder.

He thrust faster into her, a droplet of sweat tickling as it trailed down his chest. Each lunge forward had his balls tightening, bringing him closer to release. He'd been ready to blow the moment she took his hand, and the skin to skin sensation between them pushed him to the precipice.

He tugged on her silken strands and rammed into her hard enough to shake the sink she gripped. Each time he sank in, their skin slapped with a delicious sting that brought him nearer. The sight of her in the mirror dosed him with desire, her green eyes glossed with lust, and her breath coming out in short pants that fogged the surface. In this moment, the past didn't exist between them. Fears for the future vanished from his mind. Even the ever-present thrum of paranoia faded away in the wake of the thunder building in his ears, the pressure increasing with every thrust.

She bit on her lip to muffle her cries as he rammed into her like he chased after something, faster and faster with each stroke. Her core tightened around him in the spasms of her orgasm, and that pushed him over the edge. Danica sagged forward, clutching the sink, and Trevor thrust in one more time before sweat broke out on his forehead. Bliss rolled through him in sanguine waves. He let out a shaky breath and spilled into her.

Trevor closed his eyes, savoring the release.

They stayed still for minutes, hours—time was inconsequential. Their ragged breaths cycled through the air, weaving together in their own melody. Trevor pulled himself out, moving slowly as he tested the steadiness of his legs. He hadn't come like that in far too long, the intensity of their collision leaving him shaky in the aftermath. Her lemongrass scent drifted through, mingling with the sticky heat and the lingering sex in the air.

Danica straightened from her crouch against the sink, and she tugged her skirt down her shapely thighs. A crooked grin quirked her lips. "I'm guessing our waitress thinks we skipped out on the bill at this point."

"That, or there's a line forming for people who actually need to use the bathroom," he responded with a soft smile. He zipped up his jeans and hooked his belt back into place.

Danica snatched her panties from the cold tile and tossed them in the trash. "Hey, we needed to use the bathroom too." Her grin was infectious, and Trevor couldn't help the amusement warming his chest. "I've got a clearer head already."

He ran a hand through his hair, combing back a couple of stray strands before he straightened his shirt.

Danica had composed herself, her hair coiled into a bun again, her button-down less wrinkled, and the twinkle back in her eyes, like she wasn't just glazed from her own release.

Danica reached for the door handle but paused to glance to him. Their eyes locked, and the gravity should've abandoned ship. They'd gotten the quick fuck out of their system and pushed through all the desire clouding their brains. Except the glimpse of her loneliness, the brief pause of hesitation there tugged in his chest.

"Great business transaction," she said with a wink before slipping out through the door.

Trevor didn't follow her out, not yet.

He stared at himself in the mirror, the darkness in his eyes growing with every passing year. One of these days, he wouldn't even know himself any more. Even as they'd fucked, Danica kept her mask tight to her chest. Maybe that's why he kept feeling the inexorable pull toward her, the need to see her exposed and real.

If she could still be found beneath all the avoidance, all the quick grins and easy smiles, maybe there was hope for him too.

Chapter Eight

Danica spent the next few days in a blur, coordinating the Mandalay Bay show with Liz while spending as much time with Lenora as she could swing. Apart from a couple of clumsy Unseelie tails she ditched by swerving into alleys, she hadn't been attacked.

Of course, the lack of action made her tenser than ever.

Danica tugged at a stray curl from her ponytail as her heels clicked on the pavement. Mandalay Bay gleamed down, the massive structure blackened by night and highlighted with columns of pale yellow lights. Palm trees swayed in front of the building, and the ever-present chatter of the Strip buzzed all around her. Her bag weighed heavier than normal, one of her larger purses loaded with more than the average wallet, make-up, and tissues arsenal.

This one held copper tools and a few platinum weapons she couldn't touch but wouldn't hesitate to use in a last resort situation. Hunger coiled deep in her gut, something no amount of food would slake. Any normal day, she got her fill from meetings at her Talent Agency, being able to siphon off her gifted clients while she helped build them up in the world. Operating from her laptop while on the run might keep her business afloat, but it didn't do anything to sate her sidhe side.

She reached the entrance of Mandalay Bay, the neon towers looming over her like monolithic spires of a castle. Thousands of windows glittered across the span of the hotel and casino, a myriad of dim, bright, and lack of light. Out of all the casinos on the strip, this one contained the highest concentration of fae—not shocking, since the place was owned by Jeremy Myanmar, a well-known kelpie.

Danica sucked in a deep breath. *Easy, girl. Just get in, steal Alberich's treasure under locked guard, and get out to march up and blackmail the same man who put your life under risk. NBD.* She tugged on her curl again, the skirt of the black dress she wore swishing around her thighs. She needed easy movement, which her normal business suits wouldn't accommodate.

Danica stepped inside, the A/C prickling across her skin in contrast to the lingering heat, even at night.

Liz stood in the atrium of Mandalay Bay waiting for her. Already, she caught the greenish-blue hue of the water nymphs who strolled through, and the selkies wore their pelts over their shoulders. Not like the humans saw those details—to them, average folks strolled by, wearing everything from suits to sweats.

"Long time no see, Obiwan," Danica called out, crossing the marble flooring between them. Feigned elegance beamed from every overwrought ceiling fixture, and the patterned tiles had been polished so hard she could see her reflection in them.

Liz tipped her fingers in a salute and strolled over, the picture of punk in her shredded black jeans, black tank top, and spiked collar.

Danica couldn't help how her gaze strayed to the empty space beside the hunter, or the hopeful bounce in her chest that fast deflated.

Trevor was supposed to be out of her mind by now. That was the whole point in their extracurricular bathroom activities. However, the past couple of days she kept catching his hickory and leather scent. She could still feel the way his big hands had gripped her hips and how his long fingers curled into her skin.

It hadn't helped that the banshee gave her one of

the best orgasms of her life. Sort of difficult to forget the way he'd wrung her dry. Even though she'd attempted all business afterward, it took every ounce of her composure and focus. She just wanted to melt into her bed, or better yet, take him along for the ride.

"You sure heading to the fae watering hole's a good idea?" Liz asked, once Danica reached her. "I'm pretty sure if Alberich's guys are in there, they'll be gunning for you first."

Danica lifted a finger and touched Liz's nose. "Come on now. Do you think I'm amateur hour here?" Liz wrinkled her nose and gave Danica an arch look, which made her bare her teeth in a wider grin. "First off, we'll be in a public sphere for the Seelie court, which will give my evil ex-lender room for pause. Secondly, Alberich's men stationed here are guards, not bounty hunters. We're there to figure out how to get them to leave their post."

Liz heaved a sigh but slipped an arm through Danica's. "Joy. Well, let's get rolling to Poseidon's Lounge, where drink's pretty much off limits for me." They strolled down the bright corridor, high, carved arches leading the way through Mandalay Bay.

"Let me guess, Kieran put up a fit in case strange fae tried to trick you into owing them a favor?" Danica grinned. "You know I can always buy you a drink."

Liz arched her brow. "Yeah, like I'm going to get myself indebted to you. Sorry Maslanka, but you're still on my shit list."

Danica's smile never left her face as her heart crushed a little. Even the obvious attraction between Trevor and her had been tainted by her actions. Just once, she wished she could afford morals, that it wouldn't cost her those she held dear, or her freedom.

"Damn, you saw through my dastardly plan," she

responded, snapping her finger. They headed downstairs, bypassing the never-ending clink of machines that rang from the casino. "Are the boys heading on soon?" Probably better she wasn't watching the show. If she sat through a performance of Trevor's talented fingers strumming away at his guitar, she wouldn't be able to stop herself from seducing him again.

"They'll be strutting their stuff on stage any minute now," Liz said. They wandered through the maze of chic restaurants in this darker section of Mandalay Bay, closer to their infamous shark reef. As much as this place oozed glitz and glamour from its pores, the humans missed out on Poseidon's Lounge, the most swankified joint in the place.

The entrance was an unassuming glass door, one her kind would be drawn to in a heartbeat, yet humans would never notice. Liz's shoulders tensed the closer they got to the entryway.

"Hey," Danica said, tugging at Liz's arm. "I know you had to fight mother hen Kieran to come here with me, and I don't blame him. I abandoned you guys when Kieran was hanging in Jessa's coffee shop of horrors, and that was a shit thing to do. I won't abandon you to a horde of fae here. We'll either get out together, or not at all."

Liz pursed her lips, her freckles even clearer under the fluorescent overheads. "I want to believe that." Except she clearly didn't. Still, Liz's shoulders relaxed the slightest fraction, and Danica would take anything she could get.

They strode through the glass door, which led to a darkened corridor featuring neon blue lighting that rippled like water. Each step echoed as they came closer and closer to the pocket into the Otherworld. This one emptied into Seelie territory, with Poseidon's Lounge square in the center of the underwater realm. Even in the desert, the water fae found their escapes.

Danica's nerves buzzed at this point. By her lonesome, she would use every literal weapon in her arsenal to survive—her abilities weren't much use in a fight. However, this time, Liz was by her side, and if anyone happened to target them ... well, she hadn't been lying. The idea of screwing over the Discord's Desire crew made bile rise in her throat. The air shimmered around her when they stepped into the Otherworld midway through the tunnel. It formed a slick coat over her skin, like jelly, and then vanished in a blink as she stepped into the other side.

The sign for Poseidon's Lounge buzzed in blue neons at the end of the hallway where two selkie bouncers stood guard on either side of the entrance.

Danica flashed them a grin before striding through the swinging double doors while Liz kept her gaze focused ahead. Between her status on the bounty hunter shit-list and Liz being one of the hunters her kind warred against, their team-up was a cocktail of danger. However, word on the street was Mandalay Bay's fae staff kicked back with a beverage here, and the multitude of side entrances headed to almost every sector of the hotel casino.

They stepped inside, and Danica hid her smile as Liz's jaw dropped. Cerulean water stretched out all around them, the rippling surface backlit to cascade throughout the restaurant. A thick, translucent casing was all that separated them and an endless expanse of water. Chances were, this restaurant had been carved straight into one of the many seas throughout the Otherworld.

Fish of every shape and size darted overhead and around the sides, but they weren't the only creatures swimming in this sea. Mermaids drifted along, their iridescent scales glimmering while they cast curious glances to the denizens inside. Kelpies, selkies, and any other patrons who'd slipped out the back door also swam through these waters, gliding by. Polished black tables and two seaters stretched across the ivory tiled floor, and every manner of Seelie fae filled this place from a sulking naga along the bar to the gaggle of succubi at a table, kicking back with martinis.

Even though Liz would never let the uncertainty flicker on her face, the hunter moved a touch slower, caution gripping her limbs.

Danica stepped forward, leading them to the open seats along an expansive fish tank bar filled with a rainbow assortment of jellyfish. A barnacled, distinguished man in a black suit slung the drinks, his grey skin the consistency of mottled slate.

"Are you sure you don't want a drink, Obiwan?" Danica murmured as they took their seats. "They make a killer mart-indebt-ini."

Liz rolled her eyes in response. "Your sales pitch is impeccable."

The bartender sauntered over.

Danica made a drink motion with her hand before pointing to the gin amidst myriad bottles of different liquors, some that shimmered, some ethereal and not quite liquid.

"What'll you have?" he asked, reaching for the stacks of glasses kept in the drawers framing the fish tank bar.

"Gin and stardust." While she had well adapted to life amongst the humans and preferred their realm most of the time compared to the wilds that comprised the Otherworld, she still appreciated some indulgences.

Liz's brow lifted. The boys of Discord's Desire veered away from most fae-centered businesses because the lot of them hadn't pledged their patronage to a side, so this was new territory for the hunter.

The bartender placed her drink in front of her, and she handed over the coin they slung here. Most Otherworld business operated on barter, favors, or the occasional precious metals since the exchange rate to dollars had gotten obscene as of late. The drink glittered before her, a miasma of shifting silver suspended amidst gin. Danica took a sip, and joy burst through her like a live grenade, sparking all the way to her fingertips and toes.

"Maybe I'll try a sip," Liz said, craning her neck to get a better look at her cocktail.

Danica's lips twisted in a grin, and she passed over the drink. She missed this camaraderie with Liz, or hell, anyone. Operating by her lonesome had its disadvantages.

Here at the bar, they had the best viewpoint, and Danica scanned for the posh and pressed uniforms of those working the floor of Mandalay Bay.

The look on Liz's face when she took the first sip was priceless. Her hazel eyes got impossibly bigger, and she placed the drink on the bar with reverence. "I want to drink that for the rest of my life," she said, tugging on the end of her ponytail. "Think Ky can nab me more?"

"Come on now, your boy would pluck the moon from the sky if you asked," Danica said, circling the pad of her finger around the rim of the martini glass. "Let the rest of us seethe in envy of your epic love."

Liz snorted even as her gaze landed on the back part of the bar. It led to another long corridor with a stretch of doors, some heading to a pressurized chamber and out into the sea beyond, while others led back into Mandalay Bay.

"It's more like lots of great sex and fighting over

toothbrushes or who used the last of the coffee and didn't brew another pot." Liz's fingers tapped along the glass surface of the bar while she continued to scan the room.

Danica glanced to the entrance a couple of times, her nerves amplifying with every passing second.

Liz's gaze snapped her way. "With the scorching glances you and Trev keep passing each other, I'm surprised one of you hasn't immolated yet."

Danica pursed her lips, trying to hide the amusement crinkling her eyes. They'd immolated all right.

Liz's mouth opened as her too-perceptive gaze put together the pieces. "No, you didn't. When?"

Danica tipped back another sip from her drink, but even stardust couldn't compete. Warmth stirred in her chest at the memories of what had occurred in the restaurant bathroom between her and Trevor. "A few days ago. Figured we'd both get it out of our systems so we could focus on the task at hand."

Liz lifted a brow, disbelief painted on her expression. "Let me know how that works out for you. I've never seen Trev interested in anyone longer than a single night, and even after you fucked us over, he's still looking your way."

Danica swallowed, hard, casting an errant glance toward the table of different fae in their uniforms, all sitting back with multi-colored pints. *Focus on the task at hand.* Liz's words seeped in through her barriers, feeding the stupid core inside her that dared to hope. She thought she'd stamped it out years ago, but she'd always been a stubborn bastard.

"Nice try, Obiwan, but we both know I'm pretty much a Terminator when it comes to relationships." Danica cracked a lie of a smile before she drained the rest of her drink dry. She set the glass farther along the counter, which shifted with the rainbow jellyfish drifting by.

Her gaze flickered to the front entrance. Any minute now.

The bartender approached, tilting his head toward the drink, but Danica waved her hand to dismiss a refill.

Liz shrugged, picking at one of the holes in her jeans. She continued to scan the room. "I used to say the same thing, but some people are worth the risk." The serenity in her voice was one Danica envied. She'd clung to her mantra of survive at all costs to the point the hollowness stained her soul more and more with every passing year. One of these days, she'd cease to exist.

Danica brushed her fingers over the handles of her purse, stifling the urge to root around and pull out her weapons. The staff who lounged in the back table glanced around the room on occasion, their careful eyes narrowing in on the selkie, dripping from his swim who took a seat at the bar or the succubi cheering at their table. A couple of times, the gazes rested on her, but she offered a winsome grin when their eyes met, feigning flirtation.

Liz's brows creased. "What's got you so twitchy?" she asked, reaching into her own pocket for her platinum-tipped switchblade she must've picked up after the mess with Larsen.

Danica's heart pounded in her ears, the pulse deafening at this point.

Any minute now.

A creak sounded from the entrance, followed by a shout that echoed down the corridor. Danica straightened in her seat. The bartender and a couple of the other patrons sat up, paying attention to the sudden clamor.

"We've got to go. Now," Danica whispered as she rose from her seat, keeping her movements casual.

Liz's brows furrowed, but she didn't argue. The girl's survival reflex kicked in almost as fast as her own. Together, they headed in the opposite direction of the entrance, toward the side doors lining the back of the bar. Danica had never been scoping them out to get to Alberich's treasure. The escape doors were for them.

For this very moment.

"Obiwan, we'll find you a bathroom, since you can't seem to hold your liquor," Danica announced as they walked along.

Liz clapped a hand on her shoulder and gripped tight, feigning a stumble. The dig of her nails gave the warning though. Liz expected an explanation, ASAP.

Another shout sounded from behind them.

Danica didn't turn around, didn't glance back, just headed for the one exit that would dump them out near the stage where the boys played. Glass shattered in the bar, and growls, shrieks lit the air.

The hunters had arrived.

Chapter Nine

Trevor strummed away at the guitar, his fingers racing across the strings as if he could lose himself in the motions. For these precious moments, the anxiousness wasn't prickling under his skin, and his insides weren't being stretched and stretched until they snapped. His bandmates surrounded him, neon lights flashing around, and drops of sweat pricked his brow. He coasted away on the sound.

The crowd writhed throughout the auditorium, most of them in some stage of undressed. Shirts and skirts littered the floor. Ky's voice tended to stir the crowd into orgies, and with the way Renn channeled his lust-inducing abilities into instruments, every pound to the drums increased the fervor. Jett's siren song channeled through his fingertips as he plucked away at the bass. Out of the guys, Trevor was the only one who didn't need to feed off sexual energy but instead just the frenzy of the crowds. His true purpose when he started the band with Ky had always been the protection of ever-changing locations.

His fingers danced across the guitar strings as he scanned the audience, unable to help the amused grin lifting his lips. His ego would like to think people came to their shows for their stellar music, but he was well aware of the reputation they'd garnered. Not like he cared. He'd take any excuse to continue this life on the road with the only people in the world he'd learned to trust. Each note that poured out of him was a reminder that no matter how dead he sometimes felt, he had a pulse on something real. Something alive still existed.

His brows furrowed. Amidst all the humans who

were making out, groping, and touching each other, a lone figure strode through, untouched by their melodies. One of their kind.

Not like it was uncommon for fae to show up at their shows—Discord's Desire had the reputation in the Otherworld too. However, they were in a fae-owned hotel, and men in Alberich's pocket wouldn't miss the opportunity. He couldn't turn off his vigilance no matter how he wanted to surrender to the flow of the music.

The figure in the crowd snared his attention, turning to look at him.

Trevor almost missed the next chord.

He knew those eyes.

The man in the audience barely stood five feet tall, his hair wild and wispy, and his clothes threadbare, scuffed at the knees. He had knobby joints, sickly green skin, and dark brown eyes that belonged in woodland cabins—not locked away in Alberich's prison with him.

Jared Cragsmire was a brownie, a fae meant to tend to the home and hearth, but Alberich kept him as a personal slave like so many others in his collection. Crags had been an ally on some of his darkest days, but when the opportunity to escape arose, he stayed.

It wasn't coincidence he wandered into one of their shows. Only one man could've sent him.

Repetition and practice alone had Trevor finishing out their final song with no missteps.

"Thank you everybody," Ky called out, his voice rising to the rafters of the place. "We are Discord's Desire!"

At that, the sound cut out, and he slammed his mic back onto the stand. The crowd roared in response like a living, magnificent beast. Trevor's fingers left the strings, and he gripped his guitar tight. His calves twitched, the need to bolt into the audience and confront

Crags warring with the need to run, run, run, until he found some remote stretch of the world Alberich hadn't reached.

The lights dimmed, and Ky slapped a hand on his shoulder. Their lead singer always rolled on a high after a show, filled by adrenaline and all the lusty mojo he'd been absorbing from the audience.

Trevor near jumped out of his skin at the touch. He clutched his guitar tight.

"Are you okay, brother?" Ky's brows narrowed, and his hand didn't budge from Trevor's shoulder.

"Saw a familiar face in the audience," Trevor murmured, scanning out in the crowds for another glimpse of the brownie. He'd lost Crags. Devil be damned.

"Alberich?" Ky asked.

Trevor shook his head. He unhooked his Fender to break down like the rest of the guys. They were just the openers, so the next act would be sliding in to set up in no time. He was headed toward the back of stage, guitar in hand, when Danica and Liz skidded into view.

Danica's shoulders heaved, strands of her hair plastered on her forehead, and her mouth hung open as she panted. He couldn't help but recall their bathroom excursion. The memory was a punch to his chest and a pulse to his cock. He hadn't seen her in days, but he'd be lying if the leannan sidhe hadn't floated through his mind at least a half dozen times every hour. So much for eliminating distractions.

Their eyes met, and for a moment, the electricity between them was all that existed.

"Hunters infiltrated Poseidon's Lounge," Danica announced, the news splashing through the room like a bucket of ice water. "We need to hustle."

"She's leaving out the major point that she's the

one who called them," Liz said, irritation a red-hot brand in her voice. "Which would've been great to know beforehand."

"You knew what you needed to," Danica responded. "I happened to do a little pickpocketing after we faced off with those hunters at the Joint, made a few calls on their cell phone ... bada bing bada boom."

Trevor bolted forward to the two of them, but Kieran outpaced him, almost crashing into Liz headfirst. He threw his arms around his girlfriend all while in motion, hauling her forward with him. Trevor's chest twisted tight, the ugly curl of jealousy. More often than not lately, he'd been indulging in the forbidden of imagining what having that sort of permanent connection might be like. As if someone could believe he was worth more than an object or would stick around to give a good goddamn.

"I thought we were working together?" Kieran emphasized, throwing a glare back to Danica even as he continued down the corridor. "What part includes wreaking havoc on Mandalay Bay?"

Trevor met those clever green eyes, and he couldn't help the bark of laughter that escaped him. "She was the only one in danger, Ky. Liz was safe, and now we have the entire fae community focused on self-preservation, not stopping us from getting into the vault." His fingers itched to reach out and close the space between them as they continued to race along the hallway toward the storage section backstage.

Danica's petal lips curled into a wry smirk. "You know my methods, Watson. Now let's nab us the rat bastard's hidden treasure."

"Wait up, guys," Renn called from the back. Jett slunk beside them with effortless grace. Meanwhile, Renn almost tripped over his own combat boots as he stumbled to follow.

"We're going to leave you to get eaten by the hunters," Jett muttered, running fingers through his dark strands.

"We're not zombies, J," Liz called. "The slow one isn't going to stop the horde because they're taking time to wine and dine." They hustled through the storage room backstage and out the exit door. Trevor left his guitar in the back room, his fingers brushing across the surface in a lingering stroke before he continued on. They could come back and retrieve their instruments later.

Danica kept pace with him, heels clacking on the linoleum and with her proximity, he couldn't help the gravitational pull of his gaze to her body. It didn't help that the way the black dress clung to her curves made him want to pull it off with his teeth. Her green eyes flashed when they met his, heat flaring between them. Business transaction, his ass. Now that he'd tasted her, he craved her like the strings of his guitar.

His skin prickled as they neared the exit. Crags roamed the audience out there somewhere, searching for him.

"Are you ready for this?" Danica asked, her piercing gaze and the pointedness in her voice like a stiff shot of Jager. The woman spun subtle in a layered web, each phrase containing more than she let on.

Trevor's lips quirked in a grin. "A little bit of larceny's all a part of the rockstar mystique, cher."

She clasped her hands together as they entered the main sprawl of Mandalay Bay, the bright lights reflecting off the marble flooring. "I've always wanted to swim with the sharks."

Liz spun around to face them. "So, are the next steps of the plan in action?"

Danica nodded. "We're going to need one hell of a distraction to break into the shark reef. The pocket into the Otherworld is midway through the tank." She cast a glance to him. "Hope you're ready for a swim."

Trevor jammed his hands into his pockets and slunk next to her. If it meant freedom from Alberich, he'd swim through a sea of platinum or let loose the howls he'd been suppressing for far too long. After being used for his death predictions day after day, he'd swallowed the wails until they burned in his throat, until his chest felt like it would combust. They might be an intrinsic part of him, but his death wails had been exploited for so long he couldn't disassociate the scream with the gleam in Alberich's eyes as he demanded to know the next to die, another person on his list to exploit.

"We're the distraction?" Renn asked, loping behind them with a puppy eagerness. "Does that mean we can set something on fire?"

Jett passed him a level look. "We're distracting, not destroying."

"You ruin all of our fun," Ky teased, his gaze dancing even as he cast a look to Trevor. Understanding formed a current between them. Danica wasn't to be trusted, no matter how her green eyes pierced right through him. When they nabbed Alberich's hidden treasure, he'd be the one keeping hold of it.

They continued through the hotel at a fast clip, his adrenaline pumping from the show and from seeing the old ally he'd been locked up with for years. As of late, the nightmares, the memories, snuck back into his life more and more, descending with cemetery seriousness. A couple of security guards marched past them, walkie-talkies lifted even as they kept their terse voices quiet. The chaos in Poseidon's Lounge must've already slipped into this realm.

"You sure you don't want a snack beforehand?" Danica asked, her kitten heels clicking on the tile beside them.

His gaze settled on her, and his tongue darted across his lips before he could help himself.

Danica glanced away, but not fast enough to hide the tinge of pink dusting her cheeks. "Look," she said, thrusting a hand out to the rest of the room as she avoided his eyes. "Restaurants and food stands by the dozen. Don't want to find out you're hypoglycemic in the middle of the extraction and have to carry both your fainting ass and our quarry."

A grin overtook him. Rarely did anyone get the jump on Danica Maslanka, and he'd savor this delicious moment while he could. Even though Liz and Kieran strolled ahead, Liz lifted her brow and delivered a look to the two of them. Apparently, Ky wasn't the only one who sussed out his magnetism toward the leannan sidhe. Living in a cramped RV with the rest of the band left few secrets and even less privacy.

Unlike most aquariums, the entrance to the shark reef in Mandalay Bay blended in with the rest of the tan hotel walls. The neon Shark Reef sign and emptied ticketing line were the remaining indicators of an exhibit, nothing like the stunning glass tunnels inside showcasing the cerulean expanse they kept some of the oldest predators contained in. Even with the late hour, this was Vegas, and enough visitors strolled through this sector to need a distraction, given the throngs of guards on high alert.

Besides, he still hadn't figured why Crags was in the audience.

"All right, guys, kisses and farewells here," Danica said, placing her hands on her hips when they neared the closed door. "We're going to be sneaking in, and you need to make sure Alberich's goons aren't lurking in the distance trying to trap us inside. With any luck, we'll be in and out quick as a flash."

Jett shot her a sardonic look. "You just sentenced yourself to a maelstrom of problems right there. Luck is never, ever on our side."

Trevor snorted. He and Jett were cut from a similar cloth, and while they didn't do care and shares on the regular, their bitter brand of cynicism was born from experience. "Well that's why we'll be counting on you lot to dole out your usual brand of chaos. Should send any wayward problems running for the hills." He tipped his fingers forward before joining the leannan sidhe.

Danica tucked her large purse into one of the wall recesses along the edge of the food court and slipped out of her heels before waving a hand across it. "There, glamoured. I'll pick that up later." She nodded toward his feet. "Better kick yours off too."

Trevor tugged his boots off and left them in the corner beside her purse before sidling up to Danica.

She stepped to the door. A small purse dangled from her wrist, and she pulled out what looked like a wallet. The moment she tugged out the first slim tool, he realized she'd come far more prepared than he had. Considering the extent of information they'd been given was show up, play a show, steal a thing, and run, he'd been hoping she had done some comprehensive planning.

"I'm guessing you've got something in mind for when the interior alarms go off?" he asked, pointing to the blinking light on the wall inside.

Danica pursed her lips and delivered an arch look. "Have you met me? My contingency plans made a brood of babies, and I've got a whole rabble of contingency nuggets knocking around my knees."

Trevor shook his head and patted her shoulder.

"You do you, sweetheart. I'll be here to scream at whatever nonsense hauls our way."

She blew him a quick kiss before bending down to pick the main lock.

He should be watching the perimeter and not that perfect ass, but he remembered how it felt to grip those hips and ram into her. Besides, Ky let Renn loose in this posh food court equivalent, so elephants in china shops and all that jazz. Their drummer whipped out his pipe, and the melody was beginning to incite the passersby to a frenzy. The quick, staccato tone inspired rage from anyone who heard it.

It also didn't help that Renn rushed into the first fight that broke out to headbutt one of the guys. Another man dove in to try and pull him back, and the fight spiraled outward from there.

"Follow me," Danica said, tugging open the Shark Reef's door.

He cast one last glance to the fast exploding scene as Ky let out a wild laugh and leapt into the fray, fists swinging. Liz and Jett patrolled the perimeter, their level heads the best damage control anyone could ask for. With a smile, he closed the door behind him and plunged into the darkness of the closed entrance. A steady beep filtered through the room.

Danica flipped open the outer casing of the alarm, and out came another tool from her pseudo-wallet. His fingers twitched at the lack of motion. He was dying for something or someone to pop their ugly mug into view, so he could contribute. Danica snipped one of the wires, and the beeping stopped.

"I'm supposing you know the best way into the shark tank as well?" Trevor murmured from behind her, rocking on his heels.

"Obviously," she responded, amusement in her

tone. "You're here to carry the heavy stuff."

He followed her deeper, their bare feet not making a sound along the carpeting. It was dark as pitch in here, but Trevor didn't fumble. He'd spent too many years in the blackness of the hateful room where Alberich kept his trophy fae.

Danica whipped out her phone and guided them through with her faux flashlight. The fragile beams glided across surfboard keychains hanging off stands, and shelves were lined with plastic knick-knacks and stuffed sharks. Apparently, they carved their way through the gift shop.

"So, what's the real reason you wanted me along?" Trevor asked. "Because I'm not green enough to buy the heavy lifting excuse."

Danica didn't look back or even stop her stride, but he could feel the tension settle in the air between them. "Because you're the only one who wants this as badly as I do," she murmured, her voice lower than normal. "I've spent my entire life living on the edge for my freedom, and I won't succumb to life as one of Alberich's pets."

Her voice rang through the darkness, resonant as a bell. The words lingered afterward, the sort to stick to his skin. She was right to choose him, because he wouldn't stop until they nailed Alberich on charges at last. He'd spent so long starving for hope that he'd clutch onto this offered crumb with all his might.

Danica stepped to the door and lifted her hand. The air grew heavier with the same mojo she had worked before they'd entered the Shark Reef. "Part three hundred and sixty-eight of my plan. I'm just casting a little glamour so any cameras they've got installed on the tanks don't pick up our entrance. Let's do this."

Danica pushed the door open, and Trevor's breath

caught in his throat.

The shark tunnel surrounded them, a saturation of cerulean, and shimmering lights streaming through. The glass stretched in an arc around them, placing the wide array of sharks in the exhibit on full display. The creatures moved with sanguine grace, a chilling, primordial look in their eyes as they drifted past on either side. Bumpy coral sprawled in every direction, and a myriad assortment of anemone and aquatic plants swayed in the ever-shifting water. This exhibit didn't just house one or two sharks—far more swam above and around as they strode through the tunnel.

"The tank we're swimming in to get to the rift to the Otherworld—it's not this one, right?" Trevor asked, masking the hesitation that thumped in his chest.

Danica whirled around to face him, her bright eyes alight. Mischief laced her features, the sort spelling imminent trouble. "Of course it's the one filled with dozens of sharks," she responded. "It wouldn't be any fun otherwise."

Devil be damned, the woman was insane.

Chapter Ten

The expression 'would rather get eaten by a shark' had always been figurative for Danica until today.

The adrenaline hadn't stopped coursing through her veins from the moment the hunters invaded Poseidon's Lounge, and the hungry look gleaming in Trevor's eyes sure as hell wasn't helping. Around them, sharks glided by, separated by the glass barrier. Soon, there wouldn't be one at all between them and these apex predators who had been killing for as long as her kind.

Except a fight against a shark was fierce, furious, and final. A fight against Tymarch Alberich would be unending agony trapped in a cage. She only needed to glimpse at the ghosts in Trevor's eyes to understand that.

After they bypassed the shark tunnel, Danica directed them toward the employee area, since they'd be entering where the divers did. She'd memorized the layout of the shark reef when she'd been assembling the plan, every piece laid in place. Marisa Kincaid had given her the general location, but that was the most the woman could assist without stamping into the muck herself. Of course, if she and Trevor got their heads ripped off by sharks, the Kincaids wouldn't want any repercussions falling on them. Typical fae politicking.

As they headed across the shiny linoleum of an employee lounge, the stairwell beckoned with the scent of the water and brine.

"What are the merits of just nuking the place?" Trevor asked behind her. She didn't need to look to feel how the man buzzed with nerves.

Danica strode past the staff lunch tables and steel kitchenette, heading toward the staircase. "Because the way to destroy Alberich isn't about slinging punches. You've got to play by the rules of the fae court, babe. If he's not savagely destroyed in the eyes of his peers, his legacy will continue."

"Remind me to never get on your bad side," Trevor muttered.

She opened the door to the diver's tank, offering a rare overhead view of the exhibits most patrons strolled through. The surface of the cerulean water glimmered under the overhead lights, and the air grew damp and cool from the one point three-million-gallon shark exhibit. No bigs. The coral reefs jutted throughout the display, clearer near the surface and murkier in the lower depths. The sharks, multi-hued fish, and probably some weird bacteria she couldn't pronounce waited for her down there.

As they strode up to the grating of the diver's tank, the reality settled into her like an avalanche. This was a real test of survival, stripped down and brazen compared to the hundreds of fae functions she'd waltzed through and the deals she'd cut to keep from getting married off. Her heartbeat pulsed louder and louder by the minute, and the chill from the water settled onto her skin.

However, she wasn't afraid.

Danger didn't terrify her like confinement.

Danica would fight her way through a shark tank and bloody her hands in any manner to keep from getting weighted down either from a figurative chain or a real one. Trevor's hand settled on her shoulder again. She glanced to him at last. She'd expected panic from the man at the insane endeavor before them, but all she found was a steady gaze back.

Trevor arched a brow and glanced to her bare feet. "Good thing you didn't wear your heels—the sharks would've gobbled you up first."

Danica snorted. "Nice try, he-who-wears-stompers. I would've sprinkled shark bait and kicked you in to give myself a swimming head start." She stepped forward onto the cold metallic grating. If anything helped the reality of what they attempted sink in, that did. Trevor wiped his palms on his ripped jeans.

Danica flashed him a grin and lifted the small waterproof bag that dangled from her wrist. "And I've got the essentials on me here. Told you I planned for this." The sharks swam by at what seemed like a leisurely pace, but their constant movement made her skin prickle. She looked up to catch Trevor's gaze and couldn't pull away. His dark eyes were too mesmerizing, reflecting the same livewire tension she felt. They both staved off the inevitable, their nerves woven through every word that passed their lips.

"So ... where's the pocket to the Otherworld?" Trevor asked, hooking his thumbs through his belt loops as he forced his gaze toward the tank.

"Just a quick swim," Danica said, pointing into the tank. "Somewhere between here and the anchor down there."

A large coral structure spanned out before them, the fish and sharks drifting through the large holes. Seaweed and anemone swayed in the drift of the water to a gentle rhythm. At the bottom of the tank lay a massive anchor, partially buried. It appeared close, but Danica knew better than to trust her eyes. She squinted, trying to catch a glimmer in the water, an oil slick stain, any sign of the Otherworld that might be visible to her. However, the overhead lights glancing off the surface obscured her view.

"We don't know where the pocket is," Trevor said, the words hanging in the air between them. Any moment now, her nerves would desert her. This was madness, and they both knew it. But desperation drove her to insane lengths, and she wouldn't back down now. Not when they were this close.

"One way to find it," she responded, walking to the edge of the white metal grate. The sheer amount of water thickened the air around her, and goosebumps traveled up her arms. She could hold her breath longer than a human, but not that much more. If she kept needing to surface for breaths, the sharks would get them. Great buffet of options right now. Her toes hung over the edge, so close to touching the water.

Do or dive time.

Danica sucked in a massive breath and jumped.

She launched into the water like an arrow, the cold water surrounding her at once. Her eyes took a moment to adjust to her newfound terrain of crystal blue and roving predators. The bubbles took even longer to clear as she kicked her way forward, unwilling to pause to get her bearings for even a second. She didn't have that sort of time. The water surrounded her, the pressure gluing to her skin, her chest, her throat. Danica thrust her legs back to propel herself through the blue expanse even faster.

Two blacktip sharks flicked their tails, and their noses tilted in her direction. Fuck.

Her body adjusted to the water pressure as she continued to swim deeper and deeper. Her limbs lost the initial heaviness and motion came more naturally, even with the prickle of fear stabbing her in the neck. She focused on the massive anchor nestled at the bottom, trying to ignore the small crimson fish floating by her and the sandtiger shark that swam around the bend on the other side of the reef. With multiple sharks already taking notice, if they decided she made an interesting target, she couldn't compete against their constant movement and sheer speed. As it was, she'd struck their curiosity.

Her chest strained. She wanted to inhale so badly. The pressure of those inquisitive stares burrowed into her all the more.

A moment later, bubbles flooded above, trickling down to obscure the view, and the whoosh of the shifting water rippled out. Trevor entered the water behind her. The banshee cast a large shadow, but his entrance drew more attention than hers. The black tip sharks swished their tails as they veered closer, those primeval eyes honed in on the current intruders in their water.

Danica's throat burned. The subtle need to take a breath began to squeeze her chest. Not now. She kicked down, swimming faster and faster toward the bottom. Each stroke took far more effort the lower she descended, like she'd strapped weights to her arms and legs as she swam. The sandtiger decided to investigate, gliding through the water with insidious ease. Unlike the black tip sharks who wove in larger circles around her out of curiosity, the sandtiger swam toward them head-on. She couldn't stop now. Damnit. Not unless she wanted to resurface for a breath.

Danica's heart slammed, hard enough to pop right out of her chest. The shark zeroed in on them.

Those teeth would rip her to shreds.

She forced her focus ahead to search for a glimmer, a wrinkle in the water that would only be visible to fae. Her gaze snagged close to the coral reef. Something seemed off right before the structure, but it was either a trick of the eyes or a hazy mark shifted to a shade paler than the rest.

She had to take the chance.

Trevor's long legs had him swimming beside her

within seconds, but in those seconds, the sandtiger shark gained on them, faster, faster, faster. Unlike her slow movements in the water—the kicks that fell short, the overhead swings like she plunged through mud—the shark sliced across the space with terrifying efficiency. It moved like a butcher's knife through butter. Panic gripped her by the throat, uncontrollable spasms, but she couldn't stop. Not now.

The coral reef lay feet away. Feet away and they could escape the sharks.

Except two more sandtiger sharks wound around the massive coral structure with the symmetry of hunting partners.

The sandtiger veered close enough for her to spot the gold flecks in those ancient eyes and the darkened scars ripping up the flesh along its snout. The maw was massive. One bite would shred right through her leg. Kick. Kick faster. Danica clawed through the water like a berserk beast.

Even if the sharks were fed on a schedule and used to divers, that didn't take the wild out of an animal or the urge to hunt out of a predator. Her throat burned, the need for a breath pulling her apart at the seams.

Trevor darted ahead, his movements erratic. The swish of his long legs caused him to burst farther down. He must've spotted the same wrinkle. They both raced for the spot near the base of the coral reef.

Danica kicked faster. Calm abandoned the building the moment she dove into the tank. Bubbles blurred around her, but that wouldn't stop the shark. She needed to get to the pocket in the Otherworld, now.

The sandtiger shark veered around her, so close she could reach out and touch. Its unblinking gold eye gleamed. The jaw opened, placing those teeth on clear display, tons of jagged, messy razors that would shred her to pieces.

Too close.

Her heart pounded harder, harder. She needed to breathe. Her chest burned so badly her mouth begged to open even if she'd only swallow water. Her ribs spasmed, and her throat squeezed tight.

Trevor swam in front of her, stretching out his hand for the coral reef feet away.

In her peripheral, the black tips swam closer and closer, their spurious circles from earlier morphing into a straight line.

Five sharks and two of them. They'd be sunk.

That is if she didn't pass out first.

Her head swirled, and her chest burned. She needed to breathe. Holy hell, she needed to breathe. Her feet kicked, and her small satchel smacked against her arm as she swam.

This close, the murky ripple grew clearer. It had to be the pocket to the Otherworld. Trevor reached out, and his arm disappeared. Instead of vanishing into it, he whipped around to face her. His brows drew together in concentration, and his shoulders braced like he was about to fight.

Not the fucking shark.

Danica didn't dare to glance. She didn't dare look back. She shot toward the ripple.

A foot away.

One of the sharks slammed into her leg.

The force rocked her to the side. Her mouth opened, and the tendrils of air she clung to left as water flooded in. Pain followed, like someone smacked her with a baseball bat. Trevor reached out for her hand, and she seized it, barely able to do much else. He tugged her into the ripple. Danica turned her head in time to see the teeth snap.

Those jagged teeth snagged onto her leg. Trevor moved too fast. Before the shark clamped down, he yanked her forward.

One moment, they existed in the tank in Mandalay Bay where a sandtiger shark was ready to maul her. The next, they tumbled into cool, damp, darkness.

Air exploded into her chest at the same time her leg rioted in pain. Danica slumped to the ground, grabbing hold of her calf to stave off the flow of blood. The teeth only grazed, but already the wound throbbed with a large scrape from the shark's attempt. Trevor's quick acting was the one thing to save her from losing a chunk out of that leg. Her shoulders heaved with the breaths begging to enter her lungs, and she slumped in a ragged silence on the rocky ground of what appeared to be a cavern.

Trevor sat next to her, his long legs splayed out as he leaned back, propped up by his elbows. "Let's never do that again," he muttered, casting her a sidelong glance.

Danica forced a grin, despite the way her leg throbbed. It could've been far worse. "How do you think we're getting out of here, babe?"

He arched an eyebrow, and his sensuous lips curled into a grin. The man was far too pretty for his own good. "We'll find another way."

She pulled her satchel off her wrist and opened it. The waterproof bag contained all her survival basics—including a swath of gauze.

Trevor snorted. "Is there anything you haven't prepared for?"

Danica wound the bit of gauze around her leg, and her jaw clenched on instinct when she tugged tight to staunch the flow of blood. Darkness surrounded them, and the stale, musty air made her think they must be somewhere underground. "Hey, I take my Girl Scouts seriously," she said, trying to ignore her throbbing leg and the acid fear at the flash of the shark's eyes and those ragged teeth. She wasn't about to argue with Trevor about finding a different route out of this realm if possible.

He let out a long stream of breath and pushed himself up to sit. "Well, we've thwarted casino security and a tank full of sharks so far. My guess is we'll be tangling with a mutant rhino guarding Alberich's treasure next."

Danica shook her head, a real grin rising to her lips. She sat forward, her breath reaching a normal, cyclical pace. "Was that an actual joke from the ever-broody Trevor Arceneaux?"

He lifted a finger to his lips. "Shh, I'll lose my mystique." Trevor pushed himself from the ground, and Danica couldn't help but watch the smooth motion. She zeroed in on those powerful muscles with the way his wet clothes glued to his skin.

He leaned forward and offered a hand. "Come on, let's head deeper in."

Danica accepted the assist up, his big hand engulfing hers. A shiver ran down her spine at the memory of those broad palms wrapping around her hips. A flush traveled through her body. *Focus, girl.* The whole purpose of their bathroom sesh was to avoid the distraction of his gorgeous eyes and to forget the feel of his velvet lips on hers. Yet she still held his hand. His dark eyes crinkled with amusement as she pulled herself away.

Danica ran a hand through her sodden strands as she walked forward, leaning on her good leg. She tugged out the pocket flashlight from her survival pouch and cracked it on. The quavering silver beam glided across the cavern floor, all slate and gravel like she expected. She shone the light deeper in, revealing a tunnel.

"One way forward," Danica said, leading the way toward the tunnel. Trevor matched her stride as they headed farther inside. From here on out, she had no clue what awaited them, and nerves prickled under her skin.

They entered the tunnel, which narrowed down from the vestibule they'd landed in.

Danica hadn't taken two steps forward when a rumble sounded behind her.

She whipped around, too late. Rocks cascaded from behind, creaks and crashes as they filled in the entrance. Trevor stood beside her, and they both stared in horror as their one escape route closed off.

Danica's grip tightened around her bag as choking dust rolled toward them. As the rocks filled in the cavern behind them. "Well, I didn't prepare for this."

Chapter Eleven

Trevor watched as their guaranteed exit disappeared in a rain of loose stones and debris.

His skin prickled at the sight. He couldn't even broach the idea of remaining stuck in this pocket of the Otherworld, otherwise the panic pounding in his chest would spread out and infect him. He'd crumple like their avenue of escape had. Alberich kept him locked in a cage once—he couldn't stand if he'd just entered another prison.

"Let's keep moving," he said, leading the way farther into the tunnel. He only hoped Danica didn't notice the too-fast way he moved as she followed behind. Her lips pressed tight together, and she kept glancing toward the closed-off exit, as if the stones might tumble out of the way or better yet, vanish. Each inhale of the stale air tightened his throat a little more.

She moved in closer as they strode forward down the narrow tunnel, slate surrounding them on all sides. If he wanted to avoid claustrophobic spaces, this wasn't the place. Danica flashed her light up, down, and around.

"You know, I've got some choice words for Marisa when we get out of this," she muttered. "She made it sound like we'd pop right into some vault in the Otherworld, not a cavern filled with Indiana Jones traps. If a rolling boulder's about to come careening down the tunnel, let it take me now."

Her chatter soothed his nerves, even when he could hear the undercurrent of an anxiousness that mirrored his. The sound of her voice, the rhythm, or even just knowing someone was there with him—all of it settled him. He wasn't isolated behind bars. The impulse took him, and he reached out to slip his hand in hers.

Danica opened her mouth, looked at him, and then closed it. She didn't tug her hand away. The feel of her silken skin against his gave him the grounding to calm down as they continued along the darkened path. Her hand was cold from the water, but he'd begun to warm up, so he gripped hers even tighter. Danica's small flashlight allowed them to see steps in front of them, but the darkness farther ahead swallowed the fragile beams.

"You knew Alberich for years," Danica said, continuing to talk as if chatter could combat the oppressive shadows ahead. "What would he be hiding? I don't even know what the hell we're looking for in here."

"And I'm guessing you hate every second of not knowing, Control Queen," he murmured.

"Bingo. Marisa can set herself on fire for holding back this information," Danica grumbled, her grip on his hand tightening as they walked along.

"Don't like a taste of your own medicine?" The words slipped from him before he could help himself.

Danica's gaze flashed his way, slightly visible due to the flashlight's beam. "Guess I deserved that one." Her voice sounded smaller, almost as breakable as the silver ray from the flashlight, and Trevor swallowed, hard, at the response. "It's not like I'm not tired of the bullshit manipulation in the fae courts," she continued. "I just can't extricate myself without all those connections forged and deals made wrapping around my throat until I suffocate."

His thumb brushed across the pulse point in her wrist, the motion coming across tender. As much as she'd hurt them before, she had never lied. And the more he got to know Danica, the woman beneath all the smooth lines and sharp smiles, the more he understood how she'd always been trapped by circumstance, fighting to stay afloat. He couldn't keep crucifying her about the past.

"So, you throw yourself into a shark tank, instead," he responded, offering an olive branch. "Seems like a solid strategy." Her eyes gleamed in the low light of the flashlight, and he caught the curve of her lips with a grin.

At this point, his bare feet protested the scrape of the stones along the cavern floor, and cave dust coated the soles. Not for the first time, he wished his combat boots weren't lying on the floor of the food court back in Mandalay Bay. Though, even if they could've, he still didn't want to head back the way they came. One dive in the shark tank was enough for this lifetime.

"This tunnel better end soon," Danica complained, thrusting the flashlight forward as if the beam might reveal more than the nearest few feet before them. "Who knows, Alberich could've hid something in the walls and we missed it."

Trevor shook his head. "The man's too flashy for that. If he's ever entering this chamber to check in on his quarry, he'll want this place to be aesthetic perfection. We're looking for a centerpiece." The knowledge twisted in his gut.

He'd done the same with his pets, long ago. Trevor's cage hadn't been on the floor but an elevated pedestal, one of the many in a ballroom filled with glittering chandeliers and polished marble flooring. One that lay neglected most of the time, while they sat in the dark.

A steady drip echoed from farther down the tunnel. His heart sped in his chest, and he quickened his pace through the corridor. Danica strode along with him, her focus riveted to the darkness sprawled ahead. The echoing plunk offered hope that something existed beyond the surrounding slate and inkstain shadows.

Danica directed the flashlight back and forth in front of them. The pads of his feet scraped against the rough surface of the stone, and his elbows snagged on several uneven bumps that jutted out. The farther they strode down the tunnel, the more gasps of gray filtered in at the end, followed by shards of aquamarine and citrine light spilling in from the round exit.

"Think he hooked up some electricity around here?" Danica asked, an amused grin on her lips. Even in the face of insurmountable danger, nothing would stop the woman's mouth from running.

"Didn't you hear? He's got a whole sound system set up too—this was an elaborate ruse to get a private show from the guitarist of Discord's Desire." Even as he said the words, the lightness flaked away to reveal the corrosion beneath. He'd been forced to play again and again and again, not the guitar, but his voice, as his banshee abilities got used and abused.

Paces away from the exit, the cavern ahead of them sprawled out in greater detail. Danica pulled her hand from his to skip ahead, closer to the entrance. Like he had expected, Alberich chose a masterpiece of a cave to house his hidden treasure, a slice of the best the Otherworld could offer. Ocean blue stone descended from the ceiling in hexagonal stalactites, and likewise, the stalagmites stretched up to greet like a jaw, the colors shifting and rippling of their own accord. Fairy lights beamed between the stalactites as the pixies of all shades of gold and blue bounced their way through the cavern.

"You weren't kidding about this bastard's ego," Danica muttered, rifling a hand through her wet strands. "I mean, I should've guessed since Alberich Industries' main building is pretty dick-shaped, but this is just ridiculous."

They stepped into the cavern, each sound echoing through the expansive space like a circular arena. The ceiling stretched so high it grew impenetrably dark above, and water stretched across the center of this place like glass. The shallow pond reflected the dancing fairy lights as well as the beautiful blue stalactites, even while the striated stones contributed their own gentle hues. Somewhere, amidst all this glitz, Alberich's treasure waited to be stolen.

Trevor strode ahead of Danica, wandering past several large columns of hexagonal stone of varying height in a golden hue that glittered under the shifting fairy light. His fingers traveled along the cool, smoothed surface. That gilt stone surrounded the pool of water like the rim of a bowl. With its central location in the room, he had a difficult time believing the mystery item would be hidden anywhere else.

He stopped in front of the water and stared out across the glittering expanse. It stretched to the size of a small pond, but based on the easy visibility to the bottom, the water would come up to his ankles and not even close to his knees. He gazed out across the length, searching for some ripple in the water, or some glittering catch beneath the surface.

Danica slipped beside him, craning forward to peer into the water. "So, what's your guess, guitar boy? Think it's in the middle of this muck? I'm happy to go splashing in the kiddie pool after our dive through Shark Central Station."

Trevor lifted a brow. "Come on now, I've been relegated to guitar boy?" He couldn't help the grin that rose to his lips. He'd love to chalk it up to her leannan sidhe charm, but he'd met plenty of her kind. Danica could effortlessly make him laugh, her brand of sharp wit and weird something he doubted he'd ever tire of.

"Yep," she responded. "Better pull out the stops to wow me if you want a bump up on the nickname list." Danica gripped the golden stones framing the pond as if she prepared to launch into the water.

Unease filtered through his veins. It couldn't be this easy.

He placed a hand on her shoulder. "Wait a minute. Let me try something first."

They must've triggered a trap on the ground before when they first walked into the tunnel, and he didn't trust this to be sitting out unprotected. However, they couldn't have been the first to ever attempt stealing Alberich's treasure. He sank deeper into himself, watching his breaths while they cycled slower and more evenly. Even though his abilities were as natural a part of him as his limbs, he'd isolated himself from them ever since he escaped his prison.

The last time he'd exercised this one was when Ky went missing. If any trauma or violence had occurred here, he could tap into the past memories. Trevor reached down and brushed his fingers across the water before closing his eyes. The surface rippled, and the icy chill of the water hit his fingertips. Echoes reverberated back at him.

The scene unfolded like a black and white film, shuddering and faint behind his eyes.

A redcap stomped through the water, sending cascades splashing across as he went. He neared closer and closer to the center where a single mirror lay nestled at the bottom. Even with a flashing glimpse, the mirror imprinted in his memory, circular, with an intricate metal frame and patterns carved across the surface. Trevor didn't need to know the wording to understand that an item of power lay at the bottom.

The redcap leaned forward, one step closer, and

then reached. His foot landed on a thick striation in the rock below, circling the mirror. The off-colored band appeared a natural part of the mottled bed beneath the surface, but when his foot touched the band, the water bubbled. In the blink of an eye, the once crystalline water blackened and the redcap began to scream.

The liquid had turned to acid.

The substance corroded his leg, and even when he tried to splash a couple of steps forward, soon the limbs dissolved into the water, skin melting away. He continued to dissolve bit by bit, first the legs, then the torso, until those undulating screams silenced, and the redcap dissolved into the inky pool.

Trevor yanked his hand out of the water like he'd been burned.

His throat dried in the process, and as he looked at the glistening surface before him, all he could see was the shadowed memories of the inkspill of acid that spread throughout to devour the intruder whole. Even if they bypassed the initial trap, who knew what other ones Alberich stationed beyond the perimeter to protect the mirror once they lifted it from its spot.

"Are you okay, Trev?" Danica asked, placing her hand over his. The touch startled him, as did the sheer amount of relief that rushed through in response. He hadn't expected that sort of comfort from the woman, but in this place they only had each other to rely on.

"Yeah, just wanted to make sure we wouldn't die a grisly death the moment we stepped into the pool," he muttered, running a hand through his thick strands to give them a tug. "Because, that's happened here before—I'm sure more than once."

Danica tapped a finger to her lips, like he needed any more reason to stare. "I forgot that's part of your banshee mojo. What a handy trick."

He cast her a wan glance. "I don't do tricks. I'm not a circus performer," he started when she put up a finger and winked.

"Yet you get on stage and strut your stuff every night, so, point to me." She grinned and pushed down on the golden stones in front of them, lifting herself to the edge. "What am I dodging?"

"We're looking for a mirror in the center, beneath the surface of the water." He pointed to where it lay, clear as sunlight to him now. "Whatever you do, don't step on the surrounding band that blends with the stone—it triggers some bad times ahead."

"Right," Danica said, pushing over the edge to dip her feet into the pool. "Don't press the uh-oh button." She strode forward, each step cautious and her gaze sharpening on the stone beneath the surface. The pixies bounced above them, ignoring their presence. Their lights flickered on and off, and the occasional threads of their chatter echoed through the air.

Trevor pushed himself in, wincing as he dipped his bare feet into the water, as if it was the acid he'd seen corrode the redcap. Whenever he used his ability, the images and sensations lingered like they were a part of his own memories. The silt washed off his feet in the water, drifting to the bottom, and the cold slithered from his feet up.

By the time he strode forward, Danica had already made it halfway across the pool. His heart leapt in his throat at how far she'd gotten without him. Trevor forced down a deep breath as he continued to wade through. The crisp scent of metal tickled his nose from the surrounding towers of hexagonal stone, either from the clusters protruding out or the veneer that had attached itself.

"What's Alberich doing collecting mirrors?"

Danica called out. "The asshole's vain enough as is. He doesn't need the encouragement." Some of the water splashed when she waded through a deeper patch that came up to her calves. The sound caused his hands to ball into fists on instinct. Who knew what other traps Alberich had set up. One wrong step, one wrong movement and they would die in this cave.

As he stepped closer, he got a solid look at the thick colored band in the stone surrounding the mirror. Even knowing what to avoid, his breath caught in his throat.

"I'm going to hang back a couple of feet," Trevor said even as he placed one foot in front of the other, deeper and deeper into this pool. "If we need a quick escape, I can tug you forward, and we'll vault to the edge as fast as possible."

Danica snorted. "I see how it is. Dangle me in front of the danger. It's okay, guitar boy, I won't tell anyone you were scared."

A grin curled his lips despite the way his heart thudded. He didn't trust there not to be another trap if they removed the mirror. "Terrified," he responded, bracing his shoulders. He could reach out and grab Danica, but they had a couple of feet to cross before reaching the other edge of the pool.

Danica slowed when she got closer to the mirror. Her paces grew measured as she inched nearer, zeroing in on the shift in the colored stone under the surface of the water.

Trevor wanted to pluck them both out and run. Every step of this heist had been fraught with hurdles—this wouldn't be any better. His firsthand knowledge of Alberich's vindictiveness painted his insides with a slick paranoia.

She tipped forward, avoiding the massive band of

color by a few inches. One sneeze, the slightest askew move, and this entire pool would turn to acid. The breath snagged in his throat. Trevor reached out on instinct, his fingers tensing. Any second, she'd make the grab. He'd tug her out as fast as possible.

Danica bent at the hips and plunged her hand into the water, the skirt of her black dress sodden. She tilted her head to the side, and her cheek skimmed the surface when she wrapped her fingers around the mirror.

Trevor forgot to breathe.

Danica plucked the mirror from its resting place beneath the water. She tugged it tight to her chest and stumbled back several paces. Even as she moved fast, she avoided the thick colored band in the stone below. She had retrieved the item, but his chest still squeezed tight.

Danica's gaze met his, and he took a step forward, reaching out to grasp her hand.

The water beneath them remained crystalline, merely disturbed by their small rippling movements. Silence stretched through the cavern for a moment, as stale and laden as the surrounding air. Trevor's heart skipped a beat. Danica broke through the quiet, sloshing toward him until her hand rested in his. He gripped tight and moved.

They had taken several strides forward when Trevor made the mistake of looking up. The pixies no longer bounced around, the lights frozen as if in suspension. A deep rumble sounded from above, one that rolled through the entire cavern like a crack of thunder. The stalactites trembled, quaking with ominous intent.

That's when the first one dropped.

On the far right of the cavern, the stalactite plummeted to the ground. The crash splintered through the expanse, and as if a spell broke, the pixies began darting in every direction possible. Trevor met Danica's eyes.

"Run."

Chapter Twelve

Danica wasn't an idiot.

She didn't think they'd just be able to pluck the mirror from the ground without facing some sort of consequences. However, she had expected something more along the lines of mutant fishman or unleashed beasties—creatures they could physically fight and kill.

If she tried to fight with the descending stalactites, the massive hunks of stone would most definitely win.

She clutched the mirror tight in one hand, and Trevor gripped her other one, yanking her forward. Together, they raced across the pool, sending cascades of water in every direction. Droplets splashed against her cheeks. She glanced left, right, all around this room for somewhere, anywhere, to run.

Iridescent dust rolled down from the ceiling in choking waves, and the whole structure trembled above them. Danica coughed, trying not to inhale any that swept their way. They needed to find another exit than the tunnel they came from—otherwise they'd be trapped. Trevor squeezed her hand and loped ahead with unexpected fluidity.

The steady lights illuminating the room grew erratic as the pixies darted out of the way from the descending stalactites, which turned the ceiling into one big rave party. Another of the columns trembled, this one to the far right of the cavern. An earsplitting creak echoed through, then the massive hunk of stone dropped. Any one of these could crash down onto them. They'd be dead before they could take another breath.

Her heart slammed in her chest, and her mind

spun, but her gaze didn't falter from the corners of the room swathed in shadows. They needed an escape, now. Trevor vaulted over the edge of the pool first, tugging hard on her arm to bring her sailing along with him.

Danica almost slammed into his back when she landed. Her bare feet hit the ground so hard reverberations traveled up her shins.

Darkness encroached in every corner, but they didn't have time to investigate. Logic took over.

"Aim for the opposite side we came in," Danica shouted, sprinting forward.

"Already on it," Trevor called back even though he didn't halt. They raced across the cavern as fast as they could manage, her bare feet scraping against the stone until they'd grown numb to the stabs and aches. She gritted her teeth, clutching the mirror tighter as they hurtled forward.

Another creak sounded through the cavern, and her heart leapt in her throat.

The massive stalactite dropped.

Right in front of them.

Splinters of stone flew in their direction, and the choking dust coated her throat, making her cough. Danica's brain froze, shock striking her like lightning. Even with the spray of pebbles and debris before them, Trevor didn't stop. He rushed forward, veering around the column in their way as the stone crumbled to the ground. *Survive, survive, survive* pounded a marching beat in her mind, replacing the steady pump of her heart until it was all-encompassing.

Shadows along the far wall stretched even longer without the pixies lighting the ceilings, and she struggled to discern anything with the way her vision shook while she ran.

Details. Focus on the details.

Danica raced faster, her calves pumping as she caught up with Trevor, rushing side by side with him. Dust coated her skin already slicked by water and sweat, and her breaths came out in ragged gasps. The edge of the cavern veered even closer, but she only caught more of the walls stretching to the ceiling and formed from impermeable stone.

A creak sounded, this time from far behind them. Another stalactite wobbled then dropped. The thundering crash followed and too fast, the screech of grinding stone echoed. The entire cavern quaked, the pebbles at her feet trembling. A boom erupted through the cavern, and Danica's breath snagged in her throat. An entire section of the ceiling had fallen to the ground, the rubble crushing anything underneath. The more of the stalactites that dropped from the ceiling, the more sections of the cavern would disintegrate with it.

They were so screwed.

The edge of the caverns lay feet away, but all she could see was an unending sheet of blue stone stretching toward the ceiling. Alberich must've come here before. Since no one had ever stolen the item and escaped alive, this place would've remained undisturbed. Danica tugged her hand from Trevor's and stopped still.

He whipped around to face her. "What are you doing?" he snapped, his eyes flashing. "We need to run."

Danica shook her head. Instead of wasting her time staring holes in the walls, she scanned the ground. Her pulse hammered so loudly it was a miracle she could think let alone breathe. She seized on the patterns in the stone and cavern floor like her life depended on it. Frankly, it did.

The gravel and cave dirt stretched out, disrupted by the stalagmites casting longer shadows to the ground, but she ignored them, sweeping her gaze across the surface. One section looked worn down, a slight, intermittent scuff across the surface.

"Follow me," she commanded, bolting forward and not looking back. Trevor would follow—the man possessed the same levels of self-preservation she did. She kicked up dust, running for the trail and hoping beyond hope she hadn't imagined the details. Her vision blurred as sweat stung her eyes, and she swallowed stale air, more and more dust coating her throat by the second.

A tremble from above stole her attention. One of the massive stalactites in the center shook, a hingepin of this cave. Any moment, it would fall, and when it did, the others would follow. They'd be buried by the gravel and rock until their shallow breaths ceased and they faded away, never to see the light again.

Trevor raced alongside her, his chest heaving.

Danica stamped to the faint scuffs along the ground, not daring to look ahead in case she'd led them to a false end. Hope twisted tight in her chest, like overstretched, fragile glass that could shatter at any moment. She soared along the worn ground, following the only trail she'd found.

They reached a large stone crag that jutted forward, attached to more impermeable wall. Danica's insides plummeted. All she could do was stop and stare. They would die here, buried alive. The pixies who hadn't already gotten crushed in the quakes flitted around, searching for holes in the stone high above to escape through. Bile rose in her throat, and she wanted to lash out, her fists balling on instinct.

"This way," Trevor said, grabbing her hand again to pull her forward. Their connection was the one thread of sanity that remained.

The large column in the center of the cavern quaked. They'd run out of time.

He led them past the crag, closer to the wall. Not like that would help. Except the moment they whipped around the opposite side of the crack, a crevasse wide enough to walk through emerged, one obscured from direct sight. The footprints continued up to it.

A breath caught in her throat. Trevor tugged her forward even as her steps faltered.

The central stalactite let out a groan that resounded through the entire cavern, and the air trembled. The massive structure gave one last shudder before it dropped.

Danica plunged into the darkness behind Trevor, squeezing through the seam in the stone. She hadn't taken one step inside when the large pillar smashed to the ground. The sound reverberated through the cavern until it hurt her ears, and dust rolled out in every direction. And that wasn't the only thing to fall. Seconds later, large chunks of the ceiling descended. Rubble splashed into the pool and crashed over the cavern floor, enough to destroy anything in the way.

They both halted to watch the destruction hail from on high, as the once stunning room that glittered like jewels turned into iridescent heaps of rubble and broken stone. Half of the lights snuffed out as the pixies vanished. The ones who remained darted around so fast their rays flickered across the ground in erratic bursts.

"Come on, let's keep moving," Trevor said, snapping her to the present. Navy rocks surrounded them on either side, close enough she couldn't stretch her arms out in full. She followed him as he strode farther into the inky depths, one cautious step at a time. Even though crashes and rumbles sounded behind them and the stone above and around hummed in response, they continued forward. This had to be the way out. Danica couldn't accept the alternative.

Her breaths began to grow more even as she focused on putting one foot in front of the other. They groped along jagged walls in the dark, but the passage didn't widen or divert, leaving them one pathway to follow.

She clutched the mirror to her chest, as if reminding herself why they dove headfirst into this danger. The chaos they'd left behind in Mandalay Bay felt lightyears away. "Hope Alberich doesn't mind we did a little redecorating," Danica said, needing to hear a voice out loud, even if it was her own. While they left thunderous quakes behind them, the oppressive silence ahead didn't reassure her.

Trevor snorted. "I think that's going to be the least of his problems when he discovers his sparkly mirror's been nabbed."

Danica pulled the metal-framed treasure to her chest, feeling the cold curves through the fabric of her dress. "I'd give my right nut to know what sort of trouble this is going to cause him."

"Easy to say when you don't have any to give away," Trevor responded, his pace slowing when grays infiltrated ahead. Danica placed a hand out before she crashed into him. Instead, her palm rested on his back, and she should've snatched it away, but she couldn't bring herself to. He slowed even more, as if he wanted it there too. She could feel the heave of his breaths, the heat of his body, and the faint whiff of leather she caught filled her with relief and desire at once.

The end of the narrow tunnel came into view, the gray of an area growing brighter by the second. Trevor stepped ahead faster, and the connection between them broke. Danica pulled her hand back, curling her fingers into a fist before she dropped it to her side.

Trevor ducked in first, but Danica slipped in right

after to a cavern far smaller than the last one. The light came from lichen and moss that glowed silver and clung to surrounding slate stone.

Danica stood still for a moment, soaking in the room. Round. Almost perfectly round, like the space had been carved out with an ice cream scoop, and a silence pulsed through the place.

What stood out the most was a lack of exit.

Danica sucked in a sharp breath. "Well, fuck me sideways," the curse came out a moment later. "Don't suppose there's a magic button to push in here to levitate out?" Even as the jokes spilled from her lips, her chest squeezed tight and panic descended.

Trevor staggered forward, one step, then another, and he lifted his hand for a moment as he seemed to grasp the air, like he tried to pluck a solution from it.

Danica took a step forward across the cool floor to stand beside him, but the moment her gaze flickered his way, her heart twisted.

His eyes normally crinkled with a casual grin or glowed with the serious aura he projected, but right now, they were wide and filled with terror. His anxiousness flooded the air, this buzzing, frayed thing. She wanted to reach out and touch him, but he may as well have had a forcefield with the way his shoulders squared.

"Trev," she said, keeping her voice level, despite the jig her own heart performed. At first, he didn't look her way, staring straight out to the opposite end of the cave, frozen in his own mind. Frozen in the past. Danica swallowed, hard. Of course he'd have a problem with this. For years, he had suffered the same fate she was fighting to avoid.

"Trevor Arceneaux," Danica tried again, this time lacing her words with steel. He looked her way, but his haunted eyes sucked the breath from her lungs. The man always appeared impermeable, skating on the same slick surface she had. However, the past had its way of leaving permanent marks.

She took one step closer to him, and then another, her motions slow and deliberate. Even as he stared at her, he wasn't here. He wasn't in the cavern with her but launched back to the horrors of his past. If she didn't pull him out of this, they wouldn't be going anywhere. Her chest squeezed tight. Not like they had somewhere else to escape.

Danica reached out to thread her fingers through his. She half-expected him to rear back or lash out at her, but instead his hand curled around hers. "Let's sit for a beat," she said, taking deliberate steps toward the other side of the cave. "We can figure out a plan, talk a little smack on Alberich." She led him forward to where the lichen glimmered along the side of this impenetrable cavern. She crouched, tugging him with her, and together they sat on the smooth ground. Danica stretched out her legs, but she hadn't pulled her hand from Trevor's, as if the connection helped her as much as it helped him.

His breaths came faster, but the panic in his gaze subsided, replaced by a desperation she'd grown far too familiar with. His mouth formed a thin line, and she was certain the past still held him in manacles. Right now wasn't the time to confront that bullshit.

However, one thing would command his attention.

Trevor never asked her—out of anyone she'd met, he understood the need to keep the past secret—but his eyes always questioned. Always searched. She sucked in a sharp breath and stared at the mirror she clung to, as if the reflection mocked her.

"You know, it's just been my sister and I since we came of age in the Courts," Danica started, casting a brief glance to Trevor. He still hadn't responded, and he didn't look her way, but the light squeeze to her hand gave all the indication she needed. "Lenora was the sort of gorgeous to attract suitors and interest before she ever should've, and I could charm my way through a crowd, so neither of us had ever worried. However, our parents were as hungry as the Blackmores."

"Court tends to bring out the worst in people," Trevor murmured, the first words he'd voiced since they entered. The warm timbre of his voice rolled through her like honey, a relief she hadn't known she needed.

"My parents decided to arrange our marriages for us, because let's face it, we can be far behind humans on that front. They wanted the bargaining chips to guarantee our social success, and we were too young to break out on our own." Danica's heart clenched tight when she looked up at the cavern ceiling, unable to focus on the way Trevor might react. Unable to deal with the judgement of having ever been small or vulnerable.

"I'm guessing you escaped," Trevor responded. Good, he was engaged, which meant he might begin to ground himself. All it took was ripping her scars wide open. She could stop now and should—except she didn't.

"Not at first," Danica continued. "Lenora didn't want to go, and there was no way I'd leave without my sister. So, they introduced us to the haggard gentlemen we were meant to wed the moment they could sell us off. Monsters in the truest sense of the word, both of them. And I planned our escape, whether Lenora wanted to or not. But … I was too late."

The moonlight had dripped into the room back then, shining over the pale face of her sister as she walked in. Her dress was torn, bruises the color of nebulas across her arms, around her wrists.

Lenora's eyes, those beautiful, luminous things

that reflected the sunlit skies had darkened.

She had failed. She failed her sister once, and she swore, never again.

Trevor's thumb swept across her wrist at the pulse point, drawing her to the present. Her eyes burned, and she hated herself for the weakness. Danica forced an unsteady breath in.

As if the cork had been popped after far too long, the words kept flowing from her. "I took Lenora away that night. We barely had enough to survive on, plus our parents cut us off once they found us missing. So, we took odd jobs and lived amongst the humans, doing anything we could to survive. Lenora worked as a dancer while I ended up fast-talking my way into enough circles until I found funding for my Talent Agency. However, that's what got me into this mess in the first place, since Alberich's now coming to collect."

Too fast. She'd divulged too much too fast. Danica gasped in a breath, the vulnerable prickle across her skin causing her to glare into the floor beneath them. She couldn't bring herself to look at Trevor. Otherworld be damned, she didn't want pity.

Those long fingertips, the ones she had dirty daydreams about, brushed along her chin. Danica looked up at him. Trevor didn't say anything, but his eyes glowed with a hearthfire understanding that scorched right through her. His breathing evened, and his hand no longer trembled.

Danica's chest hollowed, as if someone clawed at her insides and scooped them out. They should be looking around for an escape, a distraction, anything. However, she could as much tear herself from Trevor's gaze as she could escape a hurricane.

The weight of what descended between them sent a new flush prickling through her, and part of her begged to run. But she had nowhere to go. Danica remained here with the weight of her past by the side of the one man who might understand, and she found she wanted him to.

"You did enough," was all he said, his fingers stroking her chin. He stared at her with a wonder she didn't deserve.

Her throat tightened, and tears pricked at her eyes.

Trevor leaned in, mere inches between them. The heat from before returned as strong as ever, but this time the fire strengthened into an inferno she couldn't escape from. Not like she wanted to.

Danica closed the space between them and kissed him.

Chapter Thirteen

Trevor had lived a long time, but he hadn't dared believe he'd ever see the stripped down and unplugged version of Danica Maslanka. The woman behind the false smiles and fast words had a depth etched on her bones from all she'd survived. Her loyalty might belong to her sister above all, but he couldn't help but admire the ferocious strength of it. She was like Ky in that aspect, their devotion a trait he'd learned to appreciate after years without a single soul in his corner.

When her green eyes darkened, her breath hitched, and she looked his way, he couldn't help but close the distance between them. No words could express his admiration for what the woman had survived and how her words, her confession, touched something deep inside he'd buried away. She'd reached out when he needed her the most to rescue him from the memories that froze him from top to bottom, the ones that twisted his insides like a car wreck.

He'd leaned closer, needing to connect in whatever way he could.

Danica moved in first.

The moment her lips brushed his, Trevor's libido sparked to life and thoughts of their surroundings and their current predicament were forgotten. All that existed was the two of them. His fingers wove through her tousled brown hair, the strands out of place for once. Even with the water they'd swum through, cave dust already re-collected on their bare feet and printed into their clothes, yet the scent of lime and lemongrass still clung to her. His mouth watered as he deepened their kiss, slipping his tongue into her mouth.

He stroked it into her with each kiss, as a low moan rumbled from the back of her throat. His grip on her hair tightened, the strands dried and soft against his palm.

Danica wound her one arm around his neck while she pressed her other hand to his chest, the heat reaching him through the still-damp layer of fabric. His cock stiffened at the way she crashed against his mouth again and again, filled with the same hunger.

The first time they'd come together, the collision had been a flame flashing bright they both thought would flicker out. However, what burned between them now held weight. This grew into a mounting bonfire with no end in sight. She gasped for breath, and he closed his mouth around hers a moment after, as they surrendered to the endless game of back and forth between them.

Danica's fingers slipped to the buttons of his shirt, and she flicked them down one by one.

Trevor shrugged out of his shirt, and he tugged at the hem of her dress to slip it up and over. Her bra followed suit a second later, and he swallowed hard. The sight of her bare breasts and perky pink nipples illuminated by the silver lichen dosed him with such intense lust he wanted to slam her to the ground and take her now.

Danica licked her swollen lips, and he couldn't help but watch the trace of her tongue, mesmerized. Their eyes met, and gravity descended between them.

This wasn't a quick bathroom fuck to get rid of some excess desire. Whatever unfolded between them here and now, this was real. Trevor wanted her like he'd never allowed himself to want anything before.

Her fingers traveled down his flat chest, and Danica took her time tracing each ridge, each dip and divot as they dropped lower, and lower. Her mouth quirked in a half-smile, and when she looked up at him again, pure wickedness flashed in her eyes. She gave him a light push to the chest. He rolled with the motion, sliding onto his back, elbows crooked to prop himself up.

"Perfect view from here," he murmured, his gaze traveling up and down. A mere scrap of fabric kept her from being entirely nude. He cracked a grin, with a glance to her panties. "It'd be even better if I took those off with my teeth."

A light blush skated across her cheeks, and she leaned overtop him. Her fingers snapped open the button of his jeans, and the snick of the zipper echoed through the cavern. He sucked in a sharp breath once he caught the intent in her gaze. Trevor shimmied the pants down, kicking them off to the side.

Danica prowled to him, zeroing in on his stiff length which lay stark between them. His throat dried. The sight of her had his cock pulsing. She hovered overtop it, her pink mouth mesmerizing. She dipped down to lick the tip. The moment her tongue touched his cock, he may as well have been struck by lightning. Danica trailed her tongue along the length, tasting him, exploring him with a torturous attention to detail. His hands balled into fists by his side, and his breaths came out faster.

Once her hot mouth wrapped around his erection, all other thoughts obliterated from his mind, and a moan slipped from him. She worked him at a rhythm that had him surrendering to the bliss that rolled all the way through. His balls tightened as she bobbed up and down on his length, strands of her hair slipping to her shoulders, and those pink lips the stuff of his fantasies. Her gorgeous breasts moved with each stroke down, and his breath came out in pants all too fast. The tightness coiled in him, reaching the point of pain. He was going to blow if she went any longer.

Trevor reached down and stroked his fingers through her hair, tugging back. "If I'm given the choice, I'd rather come inside you, cher."

Danica pulled off of him with a pop, her mouth glistening. "Too bad, I was just starting to have fun." Her green eyes gleamed like sin.

He reached out to wrap his hand around her neck, guiding her forward over his body. Trevor needed to capture her mouth, now. She slid against him, wearing that stupid scrap of fabric. He snagged the elastic and pulled it down with a snap. His hand slid in place of the flimsy scrap a moment later, and he salivated at her soaked folds. Trevor slipped two fingers inside her and leaned forward to press his lips against hers.

Danica let out a shuddering breath against his mouth, one that traveled right to his cock. He pumped his finger insides her tight pussy as he continued to kiss her, enjoying how she melted against him. The tips of her nipples brushed against his chest, and the sensation made him want to drive deep inside her, to feel her tight heat around him.

Her breath came out in rasps as he drove his fingers in faster, and her core clenched around them. Trevor drowned in the honeyed taste of her mouth, the weight of her pressed against him, the fact she was gloriously real and here with him. He wasn't trapped alone.

"You bastard, just fuck me," Danica murmured against his mouth between gasps while he continued to drive into her.

A grin spread on his lips when he pulled back from kissing her. His erection grew painful, pulsing to the point of distraction. "You sure?" he responded. "I could keep doing this all day."

"And I could slit your throat," Danica muttered before her breath caught in her throat, and her thighs clenched around his hand. Her lashes fluttered shut for a moment, and a flush stained her cheeks as she lapsed to silence. Her core pulsed around his fingers when she came, the look of bliss on her face something he wanted stamped into his memories. A deep laugh rumbled in his chest as he slid his fingers out of her.

Danica opened her eyes again, a satisfied breath escaping her lips, one that thrummed like pride inside his chest. She moved with deliberateness when she rested her palms on either side of him and lined her dripping core with his cock. The air tensed between them as she met his eyes again. They faced each other, freed from their masks. Their time in the cavern had scraped them both raw, and at last, he witnessed the woman beneath her slick smiles and the charms of her trade. She was breathtaking.

Trevor slipped a hand through her hair and leaned up to kiss her. As their lips met, she lowered herself onto his length, inch by excruciating inch. She glided across his cock like silk, and the moment she slid to the base, a guttural groan escaped him. Her heat squeezed him tight, and he thought he might lose his mind.

His hands settled on her hips, and he began to rock forward. Her muscular thighs brushed against his, and they clashed together at every stroke, the skin to skin pushing him closer and closer. He and Danica found a rhythm fast, a constant chase and retreat as they thrust together and pulled back. Each glide into her caused his balls to tighten and his breath to hitch in his throat. Her nails dug into his shoulders, and he tensed his hold around her perfect hips, ones he wanted to sink his teeth into.

The hard floor pressed into his back, and the

stones scraped skin while they rocked back and forth, faster and faster with the rhythm they found. They moved as naturally as his fingers to guitar strings. The way her core pulsed around him as she squeezed him tight with every thrust brought him closer to the edge.

Trevor tilted to the side, bringing her with him. They rolled across the ground, almost colliding with the wall until Danica lay flat on her back. The sight of her there beneath him, her breasts rising and falling with her shallow breaths, that pink, fuckable mouth open, and her green eyes glazed with lust had him panting with desire. He pinned her wrists on either side of her as he adjusted their position, his thighs closing in around hers.

"Trev, I'm close," Danica murmured, the words breathy.

He nodded and began to pump inside her, thrusting harder and faster than before. Moans came from her lips as he continued to chase the pulsing in his veins, his chest, his cock, until need pounded in him like rolling thunder. She wrapped her legs around his waist, and he ignored the bite of the stone against his knees while he rammed into her again and again and again.

Her cries reverberated around the cavern, and his breaths echoed in response, sweat prickling across his forehead. Droplets glided down his back, tickling as he rocked into her harder and harder with every thrust. His jaw clenched. The need grew unbearable as he reached the precipice. Danica's clit smacked against his skin when he rammed in to the hilt.

A sharp cry came from her, and her core thrummed around him. He continued driving into her as her head tilted back, eyes closed and a mesmerizing expression on her face as she came. The sight of her and the way her pussy pulsed around his length brought him over the edge with her.

His gaze flashed brilliant white, and his cock kicked as he spilled out inside of her. Trevor's limbs shook in the wake of his orgasm, even though his grip around her wrists never loosened. He sagged forward to collapse on top of her, crushing his mouth to hers. Their sweaty skin was slick as they pressed against each other. He kissed her in a lazy, languorous way while the bliss of his release reverberated through his body.

They lay together for seconds, for an infinity, the soft puff of their breaths echoing through the closed cave. Trevor didn't dare move, the feel of her lithe body beneath his while they lay joined like this something he wanted to remember. He'd entertained plenty of enthusiastic bed partners in the past, but none ever reached to the heart of him like Danica. Those girls had sex with the guitarist of Discord's Desire. Danica had sex with him.

"Oh, you know, just smother me," Danica mumbled from beneath him. "Not like I need to breathe."

A laugh slipped from his throat, and he pushed himself up to give her space. Danica's green eyes twinkled, and a flush lit her cheeks. His mouth dried at the sight of her. She swallowed, hard, and glanced away. This thing that unfolded between them moved too fast, too quickly. Dizziness swept through him, and Trevor pulled out of her. He rolled to his side, toward the wall.

Except the rough surface never scraped his skin. He kept going.

His heart slammed in excitement as he groped in the dark around him, fumbling forward into something his eyes didn't believe.

"Trev?" Danica's voice came out sharp while she glanced around, her eyes not landing on his even as he stared right at her.

He crawled forward in her direction, past what

he'd perceived to be the cavern wall. Her brows furrowed.

"You vanished..." She trailed off, her eyes troubled, as if hope cost too much.

His chest pulsed with adrenaline, and a giddy grin rose to his lips. "Put your clothes on," Trevor said, tugging on his jeans. "We've got an exit to find."

"Make up your mind," Danica drawled, "because a moment ago you couldn't wait to get them off me." Despite her comment, she slipped on her dress, then her shoes. His stomach twisted tight when he glanced her way. Whatever transpired between them—he didn't know if this was the beginning or the end after they left the cavern.

He slipped his shirt over his head, but before he took another step forward, Danica approached.

She pressed a kiss to his lips, the sweep of her mouth a reassurance. As fast, she pulled away. "Come on," she said, flashing him a blinder of a grin. "Let's find a way out of here."

Trevor took the lead, heading toward the part of the cave wall that had been illusion. He was kicking himself for not having thought of that earlier. Of course, Alberich would place one more hurdle to keep any intruders from getting out with his mirror. Danica picked the coveted item up and clutched it tight to her chest. He held a breath. The moment they returned to Mandalay Bay, to Vegas, there was nothing to stop her from running off with the mirror to save herself. He wanted so badly to believe she wouldn't do that, but she'd turned on them once before.

He plunged past the cave wall into the darkness, and a moment later, Danica flickered her flashlight on, the dim beam cutting into the depths. Up ahead lay a door.

"Well, shit." Danica's voice echoed through the chamber. "Go figure it was here all along."

Trevor ran a hand through his hair, the thick strands dried at last. His palms itched, and the words leapt to his mouth before he could help himself. "I better take the mirror then."

He may as well have plunged a platinum knife through her chest.

Danica's gaze darkened, and she almost stopped mid-stride. The easy camaraderie froze between them, and the shift made him regret those words at once. If he hadn't said anything, Ky would've, because at the end of the day, taking Alberich down was the aim of this entire endeavor, nothing more. Even if the woman who strode by his side left an indelible mark on him.

"Of course, as per our agreement," Danica said, pivoting to face him. The coldness in her tone broke him. They'd shared something real, and he'd let his fears creep in and ruin it. She stared him down, lifting her chin as she handed over the mirror. Devil be damned, he'd messed this up. He hesitated when he wrapped his hand around the mirror, but Danica had let go, leaving him behind as she headed for the door.

He needed to say something, anything, but the words gummed in his mouth. As much as he wanted to make the leap of faith in her, life had snatched that naivete from him a long time ago. Trevor heaved a sigh and followed behind, trying to ignore how his skin prickled with guilt.

Leave it to him—he'd sabotage deeper connections every time. He'd been broken to the point that grasping at true happiness was hopeless.

A shimmer gleamed around the door, the thickness in the air signaling they'd reached a pocket in and out of the Otherworld. This time, they were looking to get the hell out. Danica strode to the exit and grabbed the handle. She didn't even look back at him before she yanked the door open. The mirror weighed heavier than ever in his arms.

When the door opened, the clink and clang of slot machines rang into his peripheral, a lifetime away from this cavern in the Otherworld they'd roamed through. He followed Danica through the doorway, and the air frizzed around him as he strode past the pocket, back to the human realms.

They'd stepped out onto a side lounge overlooking the main casinos in Mandalay Bay, this sector tucked out of view. Trevor glanced at his bare feet. They wouldn't be able to trek through the sprawl of Mandalay Bay without attracting attention.

He hadn't taken a single step forward when a familiar figure approached, the knobby-kneed brownie he'd last spotted in the audience of their show.

Jared Cragsmire.

Chapter Fourteen

They had only walked paces out of the Otherworld exit when an unknown brownie stepped into view. Based on the way he glowered at them, he wasn't here to offer a polite escort out of the casino.

Danica gritted her teeth. Her feet were bloodied and bare, her limbs throbbed, and she needed to find an open mic show to tap some energy like no one's business, because hers was zapped. To make matters worse, all her weapons lay back in the bag she'd tucked in the food court.

Trevor's shoulders tensed, and his brows furrowed. "Crags, what are you doing here?" he asked. Based on the tension in his voice, their association wasn't old bar buds.

Danica didn't let her guard down. She began inching to the side away from the wall. The guy didn't pack on the heft and stature of a redcap—quite the opposite. If she got the chance to dart past him, she'd seize it. Except Trevor now had the mirror, and she couldn't leave him or her bargaining chip for freedom behind.

"Do you need to ask?" Crags stepped forward, knives gleaming in both hands. "You're not going to make it past here, Trevor. Hand over Tymarch's mirror and I'll spare you."

A caustic laugh rolled from Trevor's throat. "On a first name basis now? Next you'll tell me you're sucking his cock every night."

"He's a good master," Crags responded, those thick brows tugging together with his frown. "If you'd stayed instead of escaping, maybe you could be enjoying a comfortable life instead of this desperate on the run business you've been about."

"If I had stayed," Trevor growled, something deep and animalistic in his voice, "I would still be in the cage, waiting in the dark for hours until the next time the bastard needed to use my abilities."

Bile rose in Danica's throat. She'd heard stories of what life was like for Alberich's menagerie, and she knew they didn't have picnics and afternoon tea, but the words from his lips with that expression on his face cemented the terror deep inside her. He had suffered more than anyone—human, hunter, or fae—ever should.

"Look, just hand over the mirror," Crags responded, a tension in his tone that set Danica's nerves on edge. "I'll overlook your outstanding bounty—both of yours. You can stay on the run."

Trevor lifted his brow. Even though Crags arrived armed with knives, there were two of them and one of him. She'd weather some cuts if it meant escape. Trevor glanced to her, the same understanding gleaming in his eyes. Getting the mirror out was worth the risk of charging the brownie.

"I wouldn't run," Crags continued, those dark, gimlet eyes sparking with a knowing light. "You won't get far before Alberich's employees arrive. I sent them the alert, which means they know you have the mirror. Even with the chaos brewing out there, they understand the brand of loyalty he commands."

"Sure, fear and terror leave such wonderful memories," Trevor drawled, rolling his shoulders. He took one step forward, then another.

Danica's mouth dried, but she strode forward with him. They were definitely going to run. If more of Alberich's men were on their way, they'd only get this chance. With the bounty over both of their heads, if they got outnumbered, they'd end up dragged back to Alberich's museum of fae oddities, a fate she feared worse than death.

Crags tensed, wielding his knives as he braced for them.

Trevor glanced to Danica, and she nodded. Go time.

Before they could take another pace forward, four figures whipped around the corner. Her heart lodged in her throat, and she prepared to make a mad dash to the pocket of the Otherworld, anywhere but surrounded and captured by Alberich's men.

Until she caught sight of who had appeared.

Ky led the charge, his blades flashing, and Liz trailed behind him with her trusty Beretta already aimed. Renn charged in headfirst, his horns barely visible with the way his wild hair whipped around.

A breath of relief escaped from her, so strong she could feel it prickle under her skin. Crags turned around with his blades in hand, but at the sight of Ky charging for him and Renn close to follow, he leapt to the side, cringing as he lifted his arms to cover himself.

"About time you assholes appeared," Ky called out, slinging an arm around Trevor's shoulders and tugging him forward.

Liz reached out with one hand and grabbed Danica's, all while she aimed her Beretta at Crags who wasn't making any attempts to stop them. Instead, he kept glancing for the door. Her hazel eyes crinkled in warmth, a look that shot right through Danica. "You left me with that rowdy bunch and took our voice of reason with you. Renn terrorized the entire Food Court until a riot broke out at the Cinnabon."

This was the camaraderie Trevor fought for, this family who protected each other. She hadn't realized the full weight of how much she missed Liz's friendship until now.

Danica flashed a grin in return as they raced forward, past where Crags cowered. They didn't have the time to waste in knocking him out, and in a way, she almost pitied the man, this cringing, broken thing. Yet she also feared what he had become, direct proof of the damage Alberich could inflict.

"We've got to get out of here in a flash," Danica said as they raced forward to join the guys who already took off down the corridor. "I want shoes and a shower, stat, but Alberich's men are also on their way."

Ahead of them lay the Orchid Lounge which overlooked the main floor of the casino where small two-seater tables and chairs were stationed across the posh, patterned carpeting. At least a dozen couples hung out with drinks, having private chats which they were about to rudely disrupt.

"Rockstars coming through," Renn screamed, his voice reverberating through the lounge as they raced forward. "Make way, make way." As they raced forward, the patrons swiveled around or stared to see what caused the ruckus.

Ky let out a whoop, continuing forward with a skip in his step. "If you haven't heard of Discord's Desire yet, you're in luck!"

Liz shook her head, an amused grin quirking her lips before she snagged her hand from Danica's, lifting it to her mouth. "They're playing at the Park Theater tomorrow night," she called out. "Don't miss one hell of a show!"

A broad smile ripped across Danica's face. Rule number one of working with rockstars: embrace the chaos. Using their status made for the perfect cover. Even if no one knew who the hell Discord's Desire was, the crowds always expected drunken shenanigans and spectacles from band guys. Danica hooted and hollered behind Renn, the sound ripping from her throat in one freeing torrent. They continued to make their way through the main floor of the casino. Already, some of the casino security circled the perimeter, but human attention wasn't an issue.

Even though she attempted carefree and casual, Alberich's cronies could be anywhere here, waiting for the moment they stepped out of the public eye. Once word traveled down the branches to Alberich that they'd succeeded in absconding with his mirror, he'd be relentless. Even though she still didn't have the slightest as to what they toted around, the sheer amount of obstacles in retrieval meant this was way beyond any of their pay grades. Leo Kincaid better have some answers forthcoming.

So far, with the band holding onto the mirror, her connection to the Kincaid family remained her one point of leverage to keep them from running off and cutting her out of the process. Her stupid, hopeful heart kept telling her they weren't like that. They weren't like her. However, Trevor asking for the mirror had hurt.

Just for once, she'd wanted to indulge in the fantasy of having someone who cared—someone to wake up next to and share a cup of coffee with. Except he'd never trust her, not after the way she'd screwed his band over, and that was proof.

Danica made a pointed effort to avoid looking in Trevor's direction as the band continued to shout and laugh while tromping through the casino. Easy enough with the way Liz looped an arm through hers and they skipped together. Despite the pulse of fear from the impending arrival of Alberich's men and how her mind and heart wrung dry after her time with Trevor, a giddiness bubbled inside her amid the chaos.

"If you think this is crazy, wait until you see their live shows," Danica shouted out. A laugh spilled from Liz beside her, and she couldn't help how her heart squeezed tight.

The bright lights of the casino shone down on them, and most of the patrons didn't bat an eye at the way they scampered through. The folks at the tables focused on their bets, and others glazed over in front of slot machines. Danica's skin prickled nonetheless. She was waiting for the pointed gazes, the tails she was sure would follow. The door lay so close.

All they needed to do was make it through.

They'd accrued quite a few casino security tails at this point, ones who followed them the entire way until they'd reached the edge of the patterned crimson carpeting.

"We've got to get out, now," Trevor murmured, a note of urgency in his smooth voice.

Shit. He must've spotted Alberich's men.

Ky nodded, even though his wide grin hadn't dropped once. Jett slunk behind them like a specter, scanning their surroundings while the noisemakers tromped in the front. The entrance lay up ahead, all glass doors reflecting the globe lights shining from above.

Danica quickened her pace.

She hazarded a glance behind her. Behind them in the casino, a group of at least ten redcaps wove through the crowds. Oh, fuck. This group of artists and lovers wouldn't stand a chance against big beaters like them.

"We've got to run." As the words left her lips, she launched herself forward. Danica ran barefoot across the marble flooring of Mandalay Bay's entrance, leaving streaks in the process. She didn't give a damn. They needed to get out of here, fast.

Liz surged beside her a moment later, followed by Trevor on her other side. Of course, the survivalists raced quicker than the rest. A shout came from behind them, probably from the cabal of security they'd accumulated throughout the casino.

Three of the redcaps had already caught attention and surged through the crowd like linebackers after a football.

Danica's legs groaned at the punishing pace she set, vaulting toward the doors as fast as possible. Shouts and murmurs sounded around them, but she ignored them all, focusing on her goal. The redcaps would outrun them. The thought burrowed in her mind and dwelled, burning the reserves of the little energy she had left.

She skidded to a halt in front of the doors, almost smacking in front of the glass panes. A second later, she grappled with the handle and vaulted through into the smog and deadening heat of Vegas. The six of them burst out through the entryway, Trevor and Jett last. The banshee balled his hands into fists as he opened his mouth, an unearthly wail stuttering as it ripped from his throat, like his voice was stifled from disuse. Jett let loose a sonic scream at the same time, the sounds so shrill and loud she winced.

The redcaps stumbled, stunned by the ferocity of the sound blasts, and the humans either gaped or passed out.

"Hurry." Trevor rushed in behind her, his hand brushing against her shoulder.

Danica allowed herself a single glance before bolting forward as fast as she could.

One glance was enough.

Already, the handful of redcaps had begun to recover from the stun. The others veered in closer, cutting across the polished floor. Their eyes almost glowed, and their taut reddened skin displayed the muscles they'd use to snap their bones like kindling.

They needed to be out of here ten minutes ago.

Danica raced across the pavement, smooth and glossy to reflect the yellow lights that glowed against the eggshell exterior of the hotel. Palm trees hovered in every direction, but none of them would make for good hiding spots.

"Any of you know how to hotwire a car?" Danica called back, her breath coming out shallow as she raced forward, closer and closer to the crowds who wandered to and fro on the sidewalks of the strip.

"Not fast enough that we'd dodge Alberich's rent-a-fae's," Liz responded, running neck and neck with her. Trevor loped ahead, even on bare feet. She didn't miss the frantic look in his eyes, the desperation of a rope circling the neck before it tightened. Not now. Not when they were so close.

The lights of the Strip flashed in full swing this late at night, a patchwork of neon so loud it drowned out the pitch sky. Danica raced past Mandalay Bay's fountains and sprawling landscaping toward the sidewalks teeming with people. Except this time, blending into the crowd wouldn't cut it. Redcaps were faster, and once they caught a scent, they'd follow it until they claimed their quarry.

From behind, the clap of footsteps reached a rising crescendo, the group of fae growing loud as thunder.

Even though her breaths slipped out ragged and her feet bled at this point, Danica ignored the throbbing to vault forward.

A familiar creak and groan sounded amidst the chatter from all the people wandering around. Danica glanced to the road. The Deuce approached from farther down, the double decker buses that flowed along the strip. The neon location scrolled across the top bar, and the bus veered ever closer. If they could just move fast enough.

"Catch the bus." The command ripped from Danica's lips as she rocketed forward, faster. They needed a second. Just a second.

Danica whipped around, lifting her hands as she faced the oncoming redcaps. She thrust every ounce of energy she could summon into crafting an illusion quick as a snap.

"Look, it's Brad Pitt," she called out, pointing to the redcaps who raced their way. "And George Clooney." At once, the surrounding humans whipped their heads in the direction of the beasts rushing toward them.

The one thing she could count on was for humans to chase after celebrities. She pivoted around and bolted forward, even as the murmurs turned into excited shrieks behind her and the pounding of more and more footsteps echoed around them.

The bus pulled to the curbside, and the double doors opened with a creak. A couple of people stumbled out, and a few slipped in to board. Closer, closer. All six of them raced forward at top speed. They needed to be in the bus before it headed off. The familiar rumble echoed through the area, sending a jolt of panic through her.

"Wait," Trevor called, racing past her as he almost vaulted for those steps. Growls lit the air from farther behind them—the redcaps.

Trevor reached the doors first, slamming his hands on either side as if that might stop them from closing. He leapt up the steps, and Danica launched herself in after him. They garnered an irritated look from the bus driver, a hunched over old guy who wanted to peel away before now. Ky fed a bill into the meter to pay for their fares.

Now, now, now.

The redcaps raced closer, the whole horde of them locked in on this bus. A growing crowd of humans rushed up to or around them, hopefuls looking for an autograph or to snap a selfie.

The bus driver let out a grunt and shut the doors. His brows furrowed, and he slammed on the gas, the Deuce bus groaning as it launched forward down the Strip. Danica grabbed hold of the nearest pole, almost sagging against it in relief when they glided by the approaching redcaps, who were already surrounded by their adoring 'fans.'

Thank everything for surly bus drivers.

"Let's find a seat," Jett suggested, stepping in as the voice of reason amidst all of this madness.

Danica's chest rose and fell with staggered breaths. She wanted to sleep for the next century, after she took a scorching shower. The other patrons on the bus looked away from them fast, no one wanting to make eye contact and have a seat-mate.

Danica slipped into the first open two-seater, but to her dismay, Trevor slid in beside her. Like they hadn't gotten enough confusing signals from their time together in the cave. They were hopeless anyway—neither would ever be able to break the cycle of their paranoid survival tendencies to pursue anything real.

Jett and Renn hadn't been seated for two minutes before Renn slumped against him. The satyr's mouth hung open when he began to snore, and Jett let out a belabored sigh before he stared at the ceiling. Ky and Liz leaned against each other as well, their foreheads touching while they murmured together. The sight of how far they'd come since she first met them made her heart twist with envy.

Discomfort prickled her skin as she glanced to Trevor. Even though he was dirty and bedraggled from their time in the Otherworld, his sensuous lips, those soft, serious eyes that crinkled when he grinned, and the strands of his silver hair drifting across his forehead made her breath catch in her throat every time she glanced at him. His intense gaze settled on her, and she swallowed.

She wanted to hate him. She wanted the flare of attraction to have flickered out after the way she stung when he'd taken the mirror back, the one he now clutched tight to his chest.

"Hey, D," he murmured, his silken voice ensnaring her. God, she hated and loved the nickname from his mouth. "I wanted to apologize. You've done everything to prove you can be trusted so far, and I should. I really should. It's not your fault I've got years of damage fucking with my head."

"You and me both, babe." The words slipped from her lips. "Look, it's better you guys have the mirror anyway. Strength in numbers and all that."

Trevor cocked an eyebrow. "You don't think after we escaped a pack of bloodthirsty redcaps you're going to be heading off to the hotel by your lonesome?"

Danica bit her lip. His concern burrowed inside her cold, black heart, as if it hadn't desiccated years ago. "Like your RV's not crowded enough already? Who knows what travesties that couch of yours has seen."

"Who said you'd be sleeping on the couch?" he responded, the heat in his voice flushing through her from the inside out. He needed to stop being so attractive. It had become a serious problem.

"I don't want to hear your sex noises until the wee hours," Kieran whined from behind them, poking through the seats to interrupt.

A laugh escaped Danica as Trevor shot him a glare. "Like I haven't suffered on the bunk underneath while you and Liz don't even wait for me to fall asleep before the creaking begins," he responded.

"We could always turn it into a competition," Liz shot back, a wan smile on her face. "See who comes first."

Trevor tilted his head back and stared at the ceiling, letting out a groan. Not like she didn't catch his slight grin. His fingers slipped through hers, and he gripped tight.

"You're on, Obiwan," Danica cracked back, an amused grin rising to her lips. The bus continued to chug along down the Strip, more people getting on and off as they went. She squeezed Trevor's hand a little tighter. Despite the way they joked around, if they'd been in danger from Alberich before, it was nothing compared to now. And with the way her heart had begun to lurch every time she looked at Trevor, she wasn't sure what terrified her more.

Those chains wrapping around her body, or her heart.

Chapter Fifteen

Trevor emerged from the shower a new man.

After the sheer amount of cave dirt and sludge that came off him, he felt like he'd shed his skin. Danica waited out with the rest of the band who gathered by their kitchenette and vinyl booth, putting the coffee machine through the motions again. Sleep wouldn't come any time soon, no matter how thin he was stretched from insomnia. His gray tee clung to his chest with the layer of dampness lingering post-shower, and even his jeans glued themselves to his thighs.

Danica looked up at him first, and when their eyes met, he couldn't dismiss how his chest tightened, like he'd tripped and hadn't stopped falling. He didn't know where they stood in the slightest or what their future held, if anything at all. However, he was done denying how he felt. She'd solidified a place in his heart, no matter how crumbling and fragmented it might be.

"Cast some mojo on the RV while you were drowning in the shower," she said, leaning against the wall.

"Oh yeah?" He arched a brow as he stepped closer.

She grinned, one of those that made her green eyes light up like sunshine on a meadow. "I may not have a lot of useful abilities, but anyone coming with intent to harm is going to find themselves subtly distracted to look elsewhere." She lifted her phone. "Sent Kincaid a text, too. The plan is to meet with him tomorrow, and then we'll press the destruct button on Alberich.

Jett leaned over the surface of the mirror,

continuing to scan it over. "I should know what this is," he murmured. "But every time I veer close, my brain keeps skipping like a scratched album."

Trevor let out a breath. "So, we've got to survive a day with this nuclear bomb on our hands, right?" As someone who'd experienced Alberich's persistence, he didn't trust leaving the mirror alone for a second.

"I need grease in my system if we're going to be taking shifts with this thing," Ky muttered, running a hand through his dark hair.

Liz hopped down from her perch on the countertop. "Well, it's five in the morning. Perfect time to hit up Mo's." She didn't wait for the others, taking the first steps toward the front of the RV.

Trevor reached out to offer a hand up to Danica who pursed her lips.

"What's with the gentleman routine?" she asked, cocking a brow. "Are you planning on slitting my throat later?"

He rolled his eyes. "Heaven forbid anyone show a bit of decency with you." He glanced to her feet, which were no longer bare. "New shoes?"

Danica flaunted the black pumps she now wore with a band tee and black skirt. "Obiwan let me raid her wardrobe. Apparently, we're a similar size, which is information she should've never given me."

The rest of the band already launched themselves out of the RV by the time she and Trevor locked up. They lingered paces behind the others who tromped across the lot to Mo's, the nearby diner with even more red neons added to the mix. This time of day, the first streaks of magenta sprawled across the horizon. No matter how jaded he'd become and no matter how much futility he'd drowned in over the years, he couldn't resist the pinpricks of hope infiltrating with the new dawn.

For the first time since he escaped, Alberich wasn't this looming, impenetrable force. They now possessed the button to cause his destruction, and he still found himself barely able to believe they'd accomplished as much as they had. And it was all due to Danica Maslanka.

She strode next to him, her gaze focused on the diner ahead. Strands of her still-damp hair glued to her neck, even with the way she'd pulled it back into a loose bun. He couldn't forget how her long legs wrapped around him, but even deeper burrowed the vulnerability in her emerald eyes when she'd told him about her past with her sister. She'd been as isolated as him—at least, until he'd met Kieran and they formed Discord's Desire.

"So, how long do we want to tango around this?" Trevor asked. He knew the way she'd respond, how she'd find some diversion to slip into, but he needed to at least try. Even if she shattered him in the end, he'd already been broken beyond repair anyway.

Danica gave him the side-eye. "Around the fact you'll never be able to trust me? Or that all this A+ chemistry is going to waste on two perpetual avoidance cases?"

He blinked. That hadn't been what he'd expected, but something shifted between them in the cave, like the rocks descending from the ceiling—when one began to fall, the others were soon to follow.

"Look, what happened between us in the past is that. My trust issues were a problem before you ever entered the picture," he murmured. "I spent so many years locked away, a mere object to that monster, so my reflex response is to run. To escape at any cost. Yet, for the first time in my life, I might be able to learn something new. If we succeed in taking Alberich down, there's no one I'd rather try with than you." He was fully clothed, but in the moment he may as well have stripped bare. Trevor avoided Danica's eyes, unwilling to deal with the surefire rejection he'd find there.

She'd made her point clear—neither of them could swing something like a real relationship. Yet Danica unlocked a part of him he had believed buried forever. She'd unearthed the battered footlocker where he'd kept what little hope remained, and no matter where their tour ended, he would always be grateful for that.

"You're assuming I'm capable of more than surface." Danica kept her voice light, but an underlying fragility dwelled there, like her attempt would crack at any moment. He met her eyes, and for a moment he caught the fleeting gleam there of the girl she'd buried away the day she escaped with her sister. "You'd have better luck romancing a Terminator."

His throat tightened. She was distancing again, and he only had himself to blame. He'd seen the way she'd begun to unfurl, yet when he implied she couldn't be trusted by asking for the mirror, a winter frost snapped in overnight.

They lagged behind the others who'd already reached the front door of the diner. He caught the nod Ky gave him before the band leader stepped inside, gesturing for the others to follow.

"Then let's at least indulge in this A+ chemistry while it lasts," he murmured, reaching down to twine his fingers through hers. Words might never convince her— she'd used them as weapons for far too long—however, he couldn't deny their skin sparked at a simple touch. He tugged her forward, and she came willingly, pressing her palms against his chest. She smelled fresh and clean, the pure, intoxicating scent of lemongrass.

When Danica looked up at him at last, her evergreen eyes were vivid, clear, like the real woman existed there beneath all her deflection and hurt. He leaned down to capture her lips in his. The kiss was sweet, a heady swirl of desire and longing as he sank into it. Her fingers curled into his shirt. He wrapped his hands around her waist, drawing her in tight. Even with the desire she sparked in him and how he'd love to take her here in the parking lot, an ache had grown in his chest every time they came together, like it might be their last.

Maybe he was delusional in believing he'd ever be able to hold onto any real sort of relationship. He'd spent his life being used like an object, whether in Alberich's grasp or the dozens of beds he bounced into. With them, he was numb, safe, and he didn't have to feel this desperate yearning. This pain.

He pulled away from the kiss, but neither of them moved. They stared at each other in the hush of early dawn, their chests rising and falling in tandem.

Danica glanced to his chest, as if she'd burn a hole through it. "When this is all over, I think I might be wanting to take a road trip. See how a band operates firsthand, you know?"

His heart caught in his chest. Trevor ran his fingers through her hair, and a slow grin rolled to his lips. "You know, I was saying to Liz we could use a bit of a PR boost. Think you know anyone who'd fit the bill?"

Danica gave him one of her blinder smiles, but this time, her eyes twinkled too. She took a step away from him even though she left her hand twined in his. "I happen to know the perfect person to help. Now let's get some grub." She took the first steps toward Mo's to follow the rest of the band and brought him along with her. "After fighting off sharks, dodging stalactites, and a vigorous fuck, I need sustenance."

As if on cue, Trevor's stomach rumbled. She wasn't wrong—even though the exhaustion stretched him thinner, his appetite had reached a pulsing point. He grinned, following her up the steps and toward the glass doors. Even if they couldn't admit anything out loud, something had shifted between them. Something real.

****

Playing this show tonight was either their worst or best idea.

Liz had booked them another big venue at Park Theater but on a low traffic night and opening for a small-time band. Not like that would stop the hunters swarming the city or Alberich's endless cavalcade of henchmen. With any luck, maybe the two groups would take each other out in the process and leave them alone. Trevor stood on the stage, tuning his guitar as the band rolled through sound checks. Danica and Liz waited for them in the audience. Their spot in the upper rows gave them a good vantage point, and they'd have extra security watching out for them.

He plucked a few strings, listening to them hum beneath his fingers. Ky stood at the mic, rocking back and forth with the stand as he gave it a test. Jett strummed at his bass, the strokes reverberating through the room despite the heavy curtain in front of them. Renn did a drumroll, moving fast for the hell of it while he burned the energy that coursed through all of them.

They took a massive risk betting on Alberich's unwillingness to try anything too public. However, if they waited at the RV, no matter what flimsy glamour Danica had cast, eventually creatures smarter than the redcaps would wise up. For that reason, they hadn't tucked away the mirror anywhere back there. No, they'd brought it right on stage, hiding the mirror beneath Renn's drum rig. If Alberich wanted to snag the item from them, he'd have to breach all sorts of Court etiquette and go for a publicized grab.

Besides, after the incident at their last show, venues as a whole had tightened security throughout the city. They were banking on that today, since they still hadn't figured out the mirror's significance. If Kincaid gave Danica the information, she wasn't divulging it.

Trevor skimmed his fingers over the strings. Not like he could ignore the tension if he wanted to.

"So, what's with the moon eyes you've been making at Danica?" Jett asked from behind him.

"Forget moon eyes, they're already getting down and dirty." Ky stepped in, his eyes gleaming in amusement. This was punishment for the grief they'd all given him over Liz. Trevor heaved a weary sigh despite the warmth flaring in his chest.

"At least someone's getting action here," Renn grumbled. "Since our last show got rudely interrupted, I'm surviving off of that threesome a couple of days back."

"Poor baby," Jett drawled. "Like you don't get laid enough on the regular."

"I know *I* am," Ky jumped in, amusement and a hint of pride in his voice.

"We all know you are, brother," Trevor responded, strumming the strings of his guitar a little harder. "The RV isn't big, and I drew the short end of the stick in being your bunkmate. Instead of prying into my sex life, why don't we get ready for this show we've got to play."

"Look who's getting grouchy," Kieran responded, stepping up to the mic. "Must be getting serious between you two." A grin played on his lips, and he flipped the microphone on with the obligatory "Testing, testing, one, two, three."

Screams sounded from out in the stadium, enough to warrant a large crowd. Renn let loose on the drums, drawing more shouts and hollers from the audience, and Trevor baited them with a couple of soulful plucks from his guitar. A gravity settled over him, the same one that always did when they played—for him, it was the closest he'd come in his life to peace.

Here on the stage, he was as free as he'd ever be, playing the songs they'd spent years on while he lost himself to the music. When he'd lived as Alberich's prisoner, he'd never imagined a future for himself, let alone one like this.

The announcer came over the speaker, giving them their cue.

Ky glanced to him, their lead singer's energy infectious. A massive grin spread across his face, exposing those sharp fangs.

The curtains swept away, revealing an arena of seats filled with people, one that would soon become another orgy with the way their shows tended to go. The lights shone down on them and undulating screams pounded loud enough to reverberate through the air. Kieran took the lead, in his element as inveterate showman.

Trevor waited, his fingers poised on the guitar as he prepared to play. They'd gone over the Vegas setlist dozens of times, the songs familiar ones with a few new jams woven in. Truth be told, the humans would be coming to their shows even if they played hurdy gurdys and yodeled, because they couldn't resist the lure of a siren's song, not when combined with the lust-filled strains of a satyr and an incubus.

Blue lights glided across the audience, pivoting over to them as they circled in arcs.

Show time.

Trevor began to play, addicted to the initial moment when the audience hung on the first notes breaking through the silence. He strummed away, and Jett's low bass joined in, followed by the bump kick of Renn on the drums. The audience watched, rapt, as if their breath caught in their throat. And then Kieran's voice descended.

The tension in the crowd ignited once the incubus's silken voice glided over the sound system, and the arena grew twenty degrees hotter.

Trevor's fingers glided across the strings from memory while he played in sync with his brothers. Most of the time, he glazed over when he played, not focusing on anything but the strings beneath his fingers. The audience grew hazy, and besides, most of the horny fuckers down there would turn this into a Pay Per View session fast.

However, tonight his gaze skated across the crowd.

Even though Liz and Danica were higher up, he caught sight of them at once, given the cluster of human security nearby. The distance between didn't matter. He could catch her eyes on him from the opposite side of a stadium, the inquisitiveness there holding him spellbound.

For the longest time, he'd played guitar for himself. He'd spent so long being used by Alberich, unable to grasp onto even the slightest bit of control, so when they'd started the band, he'd latched onto these moments. The instrument was his to command, and in a way, playing healed parts of him he hadn't realized were broken.

Yet tonight, as he stared out at Danica in the audience, his fingers strummed the strings even harder, as if somehow he might convey how he felt through song. How she inspired him to push past his own limits. How she made him hope maybe they could overcome, together. Because tonight, he played for her.

His heart cracked open on the stage as he played the songs like he'd found them for the first time—like the old chords somehow became new. He couldn't look away from her, unable to explain the gravity between them or this draw that kept him coming back to her every time. If she ended up ditching him once they turned over the mirror, he'd be closed for business for a long time.

The song ended, and the crowd stood, half of them screaming at the top of their lungs and thrashing about, while the other half began making out with each other. A few more songs into the set and the clothes would start coming off.

Danica stood from her seat, severing the connection. She leaned in to murmur something to Liz and pulled her purse with her. Trevor's brows furrowed. What was she doing?

Renn kicked up the initial beat of the next song, and his fingers followed the strings even as he watched out into the audience. Danica stepped past Liz and headed toward the security guards. That wasn't a part of the plan at all. Out there, he couldn't protect her—none of them could.

Except he was tethered to the stage, playing the guitar as the audience screamed and cheered. All while Danica disappeared.

Chapter Sixteen

Danica should've been sitting back and enjoying the show. And with the sensual look in Trevor's eyes as he plucked the strings, she had every reason to enjoy watching the dexterity she got a front row seat to yesterday.

Yet the second her phone buzzed with a text, she couldn't explain the way her nerves followed suit. She opened the text, the words glaring at her as her fingers and toes went numb. Melrose from Kink and Candy had hit her up. Lenora never showed for her shift.

Discord's Desire launched into a new song, and the folks around them were getting frisky and loud, sloppy sounds coming from every direction. Ducking out now plunged her straight into treacherous waters with Alberich's men in full battalion mode to search for the mirror—she knew that—but she couldn't risk anything happening to her sister. She just couldn't.

"Obiwan, I've got to jet." Danica leaned in close to Liz.

Liz's brows furrowed. "What's going on?"

"Family emergency," she murmured, her heart thumping in overdrive. She hoped and prayed Lenora had found some better gig, even though her sister was as regular as the post office. If she didn't show up for work, something had happened.

Liz pressed her lips tight. Not like she needed to worry about anything since their bargaining chip against Alberich lay on the stage with the boys. Liz reached out to squeeze her hand. "Stay safe." Those hazel eyes gleamed with concern Danica didn't deserve.

She swallowed hard and nodded. This crew was

one of a kind with their genuine care. Anyone would be lucky to consider themselves part of this family. She cast one last glance to the stage where Trevor poured his heart out. The masterful way he played each chord plucked straight to the core of her. She could sit here for the next century spellbound by his performance, but if something had happened to Lenora, she'd never be able to forgive herself.

She'd failed her sister once. Never again.

Danica swept through the aisles, maneuvering through the thick of the half-dressed crowds rather than sticking to the cleared sidelines. With this many people, trying to pick out Alberich's hired men was an impossibility. She only hoped the boys would steal all their scrutiny, leaving her the ability to sleuth out undetected. Within minutes, she'd made it up the aisles and Danica stuck to the shadows as she headed for the neon glow of the marked side exit.

Her heart lodged in her throat with every step forward. She wouldn't even bother going to Melrose's place, instead heading to her hotel room where Lenora was crashing until she nabbed her own. She should've checked in on her sister yesterday. Otherworld be damned, she should've headed to the hotel instead of the band's RV. Worries surged like the tide as she fought the urge to run the rest of the way to the exit, and any minute, Danica would drown.

Lenora needed to be okay. She had to be.

****

Thirty times.

Danica tried her sister's phone thirty times on the way over to no avail. Every time, the beep of the start of Lenora's voicemail recording widened the hollow pit in her stomach. Her palms had begun to sweat, imprinting on the back of her phone. She should've kept a better eye on her or hired some form of security. Bringing her to Vegas wasn't enough protection, not while Danica had been off frolicking in the Otherworld to nab the damned mirror in the first place.

Danica reached the entrance of Harrah's, the white letters glaring on the overhead globe as she approached. Sweat glistened across her forehead and soaked into the band tee she'd borrowed from Liz. She checked the screen of her phone again, but no calls snuck in during the two point five seconds she hadn't stared at it. The moment she stepped in through the sliding doors, the air condition blasted at her, pasting loose strands of hair to her skin.

Danica's throat dried. All she could see was the night Lenora staggered into her room, tears staining her cheeks and abject terror in her eyes. Danica had sat and held her for hours and hours as Lenora didn't utter a word or even a sob. The silence had spread like a stain until the darkness near consumed them both. After that night, she never wanted to face the quiet again.

All around her, the hotel bustled with tourists wearing visors and gaudy Hawaiian shirts, mixing with the business professionals who strolled by in pressed Burberry suits and fitted Versace dresses. Her shoes scuffed against the polished cream floor reflecting the bright overhead lights as she tried not to run the entire way to the elevator. Lenora needed to be there. The alternative wasn't something she could broach. Not now.

Danica jammed the button, the ding of the elevator reverberating through her. If she could just transport up, she would. Not to mention, she could avoid the crawling sensation that plagued her from the moment she'd left Park Theater on her own. When she rolled with the Discord's Desire crew, they had safety in numbers, but out by herself again, her paranoia mounted to unreasonable levels. Every glance her way was poisoned, and every longer than average shadow became a threat.

The elevator doors opened, and she launched herself inside. Before anyone else could approach, Danica tapped the 'doors close' button. Her heart raced as she waited for those metal doors to shut with a click. The breath didn't escape her throat until the elevator surged up.

The panel of mirroring mocked her when she leaned against the back of the elevator. The circles under her eyes needed cover up, and her hair rarely slipped into this messy-bun state of distress. Liz might be comfortable roaming around in casualwear, but Danica donned her make-up and neat clothing like armor to face the day. Her current look was 'spat out by a hurricane,' and she hated how her inside turmoil reflected out.

The elevator shuddered when it came to a halt on the eighth floor, and the doors opened again. Danica fumbled for her key card as she vaulted off the elevator. She raced down the hall, almost slamming straight into a housekeeping cart parked in front of one of the rooms. Her door stood out at the end of the corridor, and the need to open it warred with the fear of what might await her. Because if Lenora wasn't there, she knew—*she knew*—who had taken her sister.

Her palms grew so slick she almost dropped her key card as she lifted it to the door. Her hands trembled when the light switched from red to green.

The hotel door swung open.

Danica took one step in, and then another. "Lenora?" she asked, her voice scraping hoarse with the fear she could no longer contain.

No one responded. As she bypassed the narrow entryway to step into the room, the worst of her fears descended. It was empty.

Except, her neck prickled like she'd been shocked.

Danica whipped around toward the bathroom in time for the door to creak open.

A short, familiar man stepped out from the tiny bathroom, the fluorescents washing out his sickly green skin even more. Danica's heart plummeted. Jared Cragsmire, one of Alberich's cronies. His appearance couldn't spell good news for her.

"About time you showed," Crags said, running fingers through the wisps that constituted his hair. His gimlet eyes shone with amusement. "I thought you'd be in far earlier than this to check on your sister."

"Where is she?" Danica asked through gritted teeth.

"She's safe, for now," Crags responded, slapping one of the hotel towels over his shoulder, as if it were part of his attire. "However, her continued survival depends on you returning the mirror to us."

Oh hell.

Of course. Of course it would come to this. Danica flexed her fingers, unable to feel them. Crags watched her with an intense knowing that crawled beneath her skin. She hated it almost as much as she now hated him.

"I don't have it," she said, her mind racing so fast she couldn't catch up. "The item's out of my hands."

Even as the bullshit spewed from her, Crags passed her an incredulous look. Despite the brownie being half her size, right now his shadow loomed larger than ever with the control he'd seized. Alberich had kidnapped Lenora. Bile rose in her throat. The monster took her sister.

"Then get it," Crags responded, his tone as cold as the tundra. "Alberich expects the mirror to be in his hand by the end of the day tomorrow, or the next time you see your sister, it'll be her corpse."

Words dried on Danica's lips. All the excuses, the pleas, any clever roundabouts died there. She faced the stark reality that the monster who haunted Trevor, the one who hunted her, had taken Lenora. Alberich would follow through on his threats. She'd already witnessed the results of his violence.

"Where?" was all she could manage.

Amusement gleamed in Crags' eyes, a confidence she hated. "The Fremont Hotel and Casino. Enter in through the red door on the side—you can't miss it."

Danica opened her mouth, all the normal words she employed vacating the premises. Her sister was in Alberich's clutches, and it was all her fault. She'd signed the deal with the sidhe devil in the first place. Then she stole his mirror.

"See you tomorrow." Crags tugged at the towel over his shoulder, leaving it there as he strode toward the still-open door to her hotel room. Danica's fingers twitched. She should fight, should scream, should throttle him. But her efforts wouldn't make a difference. He wasn't the one holding Lenora hostage, simply conveying the message. She stood as still as the marble statues through Caesar's when he exited, bringing the door shut behind him.

The moment the click of the door resounded through the room, whatever energy kept her standing abandoned her. Danica sank to the floor, her knees slamming onto the gray carpet. She tried to breathe, but every one snagged in her throat, her chest straining to the point of pain. Heat pricked at her eyes, and she sagged forward, her nails curling into the carpet before her.

If she betrayed the band again, there would be no second chances. She wouldn't just be screwing over their one shot at escaping Alberich's grasp. She would also be continuing Trevor's sentence to a lifetime on the run.

But Lenora.

Her sister was technicolor when everything else had been filmed black and white, and she'd been protecting her for as long as she could remember. Lenora might be stubborn, impulsive, and a bit of a brat sometimes, but she was the one person who gave a damn if Danica lived or died. She was the one who reached in and touched her heart even after she'd tried to shut everyone else out.

Lenora had suffered too much at the hands of her betrothed, while she dated Larsen, Kieran's pig of a brother, and now she faced execution.

It was all Danica's fault.

Tears slipped down her cheeks, hot and hateful. She sucked in a ragged breath while the liquid slithered down, staining the dark band tee she wore. Her shoulders shook, hell her entire body trembled in the wake of this news. In the past, she'd remained in control, but ever since she'd allied with Discord's Desire—ever since she began falling for Trevor—her heart fragmented open like she'd never allowed it to before.

Tomorrow, she'd hate herself no matter what decision she made.

Chapter Seventeen

By the time the show neared to an end, Trevor was ready to leap out of his skin.

Each time they ticked another song off the checklist, the temptation to launch off the stage and rush through the audience to look for Danica reared. Ever since she'd stepped out, she hadn't returned, and yet Liz still sat in place watching the show. Sweat beaded on his brow. His fingers swept across the strings at a frenetic pace, part of the rising fervor of this final song but also to channel the desperation that flicker-flashed through his veins. Ky's voice crashed over the audience, but at this point they were too distracted to pay attention.

All across Park Theater, concertgoers abandoned their spots, folks in various shades of undress as they got busy on top, beneath, and against the seats. The security guards long stopped paying attention as they dove into the fray with the others, lust taking the wheel. With the mindless abandon most of the audience sank into, the few who weren't participating stood out even more.

Guaranteed, they were the fae Alberich sent—after all, not everyone fell under Kieran's incubus spell.

They'd be guarding the entrance, and once their band tried to escape out back, an army of redcaps, rakshasa, or even pissed off goblins would be waiting.

Trevor strummed harder at the strings, the song reaching a crescendo he rode along with like the crest of a wave. He glanced to Jett, who nodded, edging closer to the stage. Ky lifted a hand in the air, which to the audience looked like a flourish with the song. Only the band knew the signal.

He finished his part of the guitar, the chords

resonant through the air as Kieran sang the final line, the bass trickling off, and Renn slowing the drum beat until it faded away.

"Now, I know we said that was the final song," Kieran called out, drawing the attention of the audience. "But we're trying something a little different tonight."

At that, Renn rose from behind the drum set, placing his sticks down. From his pocket, he pulled out his set of pipes. Ky tilted his head forward, and Renn joined him as Kieran slid the microphone out from the stand. He'd chosen a cordless mic tonight for a reason.

"Join us in this one if you know the lyrics. Even if you don't, come and dance." Kieran gave the command and walked to the edge of the stage. Trevor placed his guitar down at the same time Jett did, and they both followed their band leader to where he and Renn stood. Without Kieran's lusty vocals churning the audience into a frenzy, the crowd began to pay attention again—which is exactly what they wanted.

Kieran leapt from the stage first, his combat boots booming as he landed. The stage manager here would kill them. Better him than Alberich's men. Renn launched himself off after, pipes in hand, and Trevor sucked in a deep breath before he joined them, Jett following close behind. The force of the landing reverberated up his shins.

Renn's pipes sounded first, the tremulous melody quiet until one by one, the hundreds of people in the audience grew hushed to hear the music. The more humans caught the tune, the more they were ensnared. Some of them hummed to the melody, and others who knew the lyrics joined in, but one by one, they began to rise from their seats and head to the aisles. Kieran and Renn walked side by side as he sang alongside the satyr. The microphone carried the preternatural sound of the pipes, ones that manipulated emotions as easily as breathing.

They would pied piper their way out of this show.

Trevor lifted his hands to clap to the beat of the song they played. Jett flashed him a grin, the siren's dark eyes filled with his sardonic brand of mischief. Jett joined in on the harmony of Kieran's vocals, and Trevor opened his mouth a moment later, singing loud enough for the mic to pick up.

No matter how they danced up and down the aisles to bring more of their audience trailing behind them, Trevor's focus never left the exits. He could pinpoint every single fae in the audience, as well as the ones lingering by the exits accidentally-on-purpose.

Even with the nerves running up and down his arms and legs like flame, Trevor allowed himself to grin and laugh with his bandmates. It was hard not to with the ridiculous way Renn piped, headbanging up and down to his own music. Or how Kieran fondled the mic like he owed it a favor. Even Jett dove into the fray, sneaking his own brand of misheard lyrics into their song, pickle instead of fickle, or heartbroken as Hoboken. Trevor lifted a hand to help project his voice, unleashing a couple of wails of his own—just not the banshee sort.

They reached halfway through the aisle when Trevor caught three goblins inching closer to them, trying to wedge their way past the throngs of humans. He reached forward to tap Kieran on the shoulder.

Ky didn't look back but nodded. "Come on, you slackers! Join us," he called, beckoning the humans to surround them. He launched into the lyrics as at least a dozen more of the audience members squeezed into the aisles to the point they could barely move forward without jostling elbows. The human buffer alone kept Alberich's assholes off their backs.

Liz was nowhere to be seen. Good.

Neither was Danica. The thought slammed into his chest like an airbag in an accident, but he didn't stop singing along with the rest of the band while they wove their way through the crowded aisles. Guaranteed, they'd be banned from ever playing Park Theater again.

More humans leapt in to join them, the temperature rising a thousand degrees with the surrounding crush of bodies, like they'd jumped into the middle of a mosh pit. Once they'd gathered more of the audience, Alberich's cronies stopped inching forward and instead headed for the doors. His switchblade weighed heavy in his pocket. If it came to a straight-out brawl against a horde of heavyweights, they were screwed. Their band could handle the occasional bar scrap and had even held their own against the one-off bounty hunters Kieran's brother had lobbed at them, but an entire crew of pros was another story.

They'd reached the end aisle and headed toward the double door exit. Oh yeah, Park Theater management was going to *hate* them.

"Let's keep this party going," Ky called out, strutting his stuff with the mic and performing hip gyrations that would make Prince jealous. Renn continued to play his pipes, his hair flying around with the way he thrashed. The simple melody reached a frenetic pulse, drawing as many people as possible. He could only carry this on for so long—not like they could take the massive entourage through the streets of Vegas and back to the RV.

Trevor marched up the aisle, the exit sign glaring at them as they got closer and closer. Elbows jostled into his ribs, skin pressed against his, but he needed to keep his eyes on the sign. Otherwise claustrophobia would rear its ugly head again. He couldn't afford a breakdown here and now.

Jett leaned in close. "Ready to run? Renn's huffing and puffing like he just deep throated a monster cock the last half hour."

Trevor snorted, even though, the siren wasn't wrong. Any moment, Renn's throat would dry, the magic would drain him too much, and he'd need to stop.

The exit sign lay feet away.

Kieran threw his hands in the air. "Thank you for being a fantastic audience," he called out through the microphone. "We are Discord's Desire." As he shouted their send-off line, Trevor's muscles tensed to run. Ky didn't need to look back to give them a signal—they all understood.

Renn stopped piping.

All four of them ran.

Sweat dried on his skin when he raced through the doorway into the ticket sales atrium, which held about a dozen people milling around.

Half of them were fae. All those fae turned to look their way the moment they burst into the foyer.

"Run," Kieran commanded, as if they needed further prompting. A rakshasa loomed, the skeletal wraith sweeping across the floor at an inhuman pace. Next, the venom spit would follow. Trevor's legs burned from the abuse he'd put them through the day before, and only the strain of a short nap carried him.

He almost slammed into the glass door, his hands smacking against the metal bar to shove it open. The cooler night air swept over him as he burst out of Park Theater, rushing into the crowds. He raced toward the palm trees lining the edge of the walkway where it spilled onto the street. The next part of the plan hinged on timing, otherwise they'd be fighting Alberich's merry band of assholes.

His shoe snagged on one of the bricks, and he almost went flying. Trevor used the momentum to vault forward. All too fast, the edge of the pavement came into view, spilling onto the road. Headlights glided by with the same intensity of the neons scaling the tall buildings of the Strip. He squinted as he stared the cars down.

Jett leapt after him, skidding to a halt that sent pebbles flying, and Renn scampered behind. Kieran brought up the rear to make sure the rest of them got out. A skeletal beast lurked close, all hooked claws and shadows—the rakshasa. Trevor reached for his knife, right when Jett opened his mouth to let out a stunner of a shriek. When Trevor had used his pipes yesterday, it had been the first time in a long while, his wail simultaneous relief and remorse.

The rakshasa pivoted out of the way of the sound, those talons rising as the beast prepared to strike at Kieran. Spittle flew, hissing as Ky dodged, and the acidic stuff landed on the ground.

Trevor bolted forward, his knife out. Kieran whipped around, his hands balling into fists. From farther back, two redcaps approached, moving with the speed their taut muscles afforded.

Jett let out another shriek, this time, right in the way of the rakshasa. The creature raced after them, a hiss coming from its throat when the forked tongue flicked out. Before the rakshasa's talons swept down like a scythe, the creature froze as if encased in ice. Kieran didn't hesitate, ramming his head into the rakshasa's gaunt torso. It toppled over, but already, the stun wore off. Before the rakshasa could spew venom again, Trevor landed in front of them. He dropped to his knees and dragged his knife across the creature's gnarled throat.

Blackened blood dribbled across his fingers. Kieran's hand clapped onto his shoulder, drawing his attention to the two linebacker redcaps racing their way, jagged teeth dripping crimson. Their pale skin showed more veins than the average human, and their muscles bulged like they'd stepped up for a bodybuilder competition. Redcaps were the best mercenaries-for-hire, and Alberich had the cash to spare.

Renn charged forward, fists swinging, and his horns directed straight for the redcaps rushing their way.

"Your rental chariot awaits, boys," Liz called from the roadside. She pulled up in a black Civic, the tires screeching with the force of her stop.

"Time to go," Kieran said, lunging forward to grab one of Renn's arms. Trevor snagged the other, and together they hauled him toward their getaway car. Renn stumbled backward as all three of them raced to avoid the big, burly redcaps fast closing the space between.

Jett slid into the passenger's seat, and they'd left the back door open. Trevor gritted his teeth, ignoring the strain in his chest and the ache in his calves. He vaulted forward faster. His grip tightened around Renn's arm, even as the satyr tried to wrest himself out to pivot around—or fight, he never knew with Renn.

One of the redcaps reached forward, those massive hands groping for a hold. Trevor swung his other hand around, the one clutching the knife. He had teeth of his own. Blood burst from the slice as the redcap yanked his hand away. Before the redcap could lash out again, the wail burned in his throat, begging to be unleashed.

Trevor opened his mouth, and the sound reverberated from it, shaky at first until the wail pierced loud. The redcap stumbled back, and he seized the seconds even as his throat pulsed and his heart ached.

"In, get in," Kieran called out, almost tuck and rolling into the backseat of the car. The force of his movement brought their fucked-up daisy chain with him, Renn first, and Trevor following.

He hadn't even landed on the backseat when the car rolled forward. Perfect timing too. A fist slammed onto the trunk of the car, crushing the metal.

Trevor landed hard against Renn who squeezed in the middle. He whipped around to fumble for the door handle. The redcaps raced along with the car, even as Liz picked up speed, and those large hands groped out. If they grabbed the car door, they'd take it right off. Trevor surged forward to reach the handle, and he launched his full weight into tugging the door shut. He landed against Renn and Kieran, crushing them into the opposite side of the car.

"Seriously, man, lay off the steak dinners," Renn groaned, elbowing Trevor in the side. Liz raced them down the road, fast enough the redcaps couldn't hope to keep up any longer.

Kieran leaned between the two front seats to press a kiss to Liz's cheek. "I'm guessing you got the goods?"

"You know it, babe," she responded, a sensual stroke to her voice. Kieran's eyes glimmered in amusement. Trevor couldn't help the twist in his chest. Their easy affection made him yearn like nothing else.

"The mirror's in the trunk. I hauled it off while the staff was doing the equipment break down. We'll have to head back later to grab your gear." Liz swerved into the next lane, her eyes never leaving the road even as Kieran bit down on her ear. Jett swatted him, a look of annoyance creasing his brow.

"Where's Danica?" Trevor asked, unable to keep the question restrained anymore. Ever since he'd seen her take off at the beginning of the show, the need to know burned beneath his skin with a growing intensity.

Liz chewed on her lip, those hazel eyes looking troubled. "She said she had a family emergency and ducked out."

Trevor's veins turned to ice. The only family she gave a damn about was Lenora.

Jett glanced to him, dark concern in his eyes. "Is there something we need to worry about?" he asked, his voice light even as caution danced across it.

Trevor swallowed the burn of an immediate response. Of course, they had no reason to trust Danica—they hadn't shared the experiences in the caves or seen how she interacted with Lenora. The woman's living, beating loyalty lay in her sister. If Alberich threatened Lenora, he wasn't sure what Danica would do.

"You guys just keep hold of the mirror," he said, guilt churning his stomach. He wished he could say she'd choose them this time. However, after everything she'd been through, the way she'd fought with her sister to survive, and the guilt she carried, he couldn't offer those definitives. "I'll talk with Danica."

Liz zoomed across the freeway despite the weight packed into their too-full Civic. He would head to Danica's hotel once they returned to the RV and find out what happened. With the main targets painted on both of their backs, they were the ones in the most danger right now. This was the worst time to go it solo.

Renn elbowed him in the side as the satyr shifted around in the middle. Trevor leaned harder against the side of the car to stare out of the window. He might physically be here, but his mind raced to the most remote depths of the Otherworld. At night, the Vegas skyline was like nothing else, a crammed stretch of neon desperation that strained like his own heart. Every peak and display screamed louder until they were all drowned out by the consuming night sky.

Liz turned onto the off ramp and wheeled into the RV park they camped out at. Even though this lot had been their home the past couple of weeks, right now the asphalt stretched out like a pool of ink ready to drag them under.

A rare quiet descended through the car when they approached their on-the-go home.

A figure sat out front of the RV, leaning back in one of their lawn chairs. Her hair was coiffed into a low bun, and she'd gotten changed out of the rocker tee she'd been wearing before, into a polka-dotted dress that fit her form all too well.

The tight cord inside him loosened at the sight of her. Danica was safe.

Chapter Eighteen

The relief in Trevor's eyes when he stepped out of the car was a slap to the face.

Danica stepped from her perch on their lime green lawn chair and strolled up to the crew who spilled out of the Honda Civic they'd crammed into.

"False alarm," she announced, flashing them her best PR smile, even as her chest tightened. "Lenora was late getting to her shift at Kink and Candy, and Melrose sounded the alarms. We're all square now." She forced herself to meet Trevor's eyes with a steadiness she didn't feel. Ever since she'd gotten the news about her sister, the earth ceased to exist beneath her feet.

"You missed the encore of a lifetime," Liz said, her eyes gleaming in amusement. "Park Theater's never seen entertainment like that."

Questions about the mirror leapt to Danica's tongue, but she swallowed them back. Most of the band didn't trust her, and the worst thing she could do was rouse suspicion. Her stomach churned. No matter how many scenarios she ran through, every mental simulation ended badly. Either she abandoned her sister, or broke Trevor beyond repair. Either way, she'd become a monster.

"We'd better pack into the RV," Kieran said, striding to the door. "We have a long night of driving ahead of us."

Danica's throat dried. The last thing she wanted was to be stuck in an endless cycle on the freeway with this silent terror draining her dry of rational thought.

Trevor stepped closer and wove his fingers through hers. His hickory and leather scent surrounded her, and she took her first full breath since she'd gotten the text at their concert.

"We're going to step out for a bit," Trevor said, casting a glance to her, the knowing in his eyes making her heart twist.

"Is that safe?" Kieran asked, his tone sharp and his golden gaze wary. "You two are the ones with the bounties on your heads."

"Which is why you'll be drawing attention by looping around Vegas in the RV and protecting the mirror," Trevor pointed out. "If Danica and I are anywhere near that thing, we're just going to concentrate all the focus."

"Don't worry," Danica interjected. "I'll keep your boyfriend safe. I've been told I can talk people to death, and I plan to weaponize that skill against my enemies."

"Hate to say it, but they've got a point," Jett said, loping past them. The chains hooked to his pants jangled with the motion. "The end goal is getting the mirror to Kincaid tomorrow, and if we can draw even a little distraction away from us, the effort will be worth it."

"I'll play it safe, brother," Trevor said, giving Kieran a pointed 'got this' look.

Kieran lifted his brow. "If you wanted to slip off to fuck, you could've just said so." A wicked grin spread on his face a moment later, so wide his fangs slipped out.

Trevor let out a sigh.

Danica snorted even as she squeezed Trevor's hand. "Please, like I need your permission." No matter the way she joked around with them, desperation pulsed in her veins, a hollow ache filling her chest. The more camaraderie she felt, the darker her world turned, because she'd reached the last rung of the ladder. No matter her choice, Alberich won.

"Well then, if you all don't mind taking your

business and leaving it out of mine, we'll be heading off. If we run into trouble, I'll call," Trevor announced. At that, he leveled a look at Kieran. "Don't wait up."

Liz let out a wolf's whistle, exploding in throaty laughs a moment later before she headed for the door of the RV. "Have fun, kids."

Renn clapped a hand on Trevor's shoulder, a wide grin rolling onto his face as he strolled off to follow Jett and Kieran inside.

Danica's pulse pounded, the weight of the situation dropping onto her like a cement block. With just her and Trevor, she couldn't avoid the vulnerabilities that seemed to surface around him or the way the air thickened with tension. She couldn't avoid the yearning in her chest either, a constant dagger that tore more pieces of her away by the minute.

When his gaze settled on hers, her breath hitched in her throat. Those dark eyes gleamed like coffee, with a warmth she didn't deserve.

"Hope you don't mind the judgment call there," he said, brushing his thumb across her wrist. "I saw the flash of panic and thought we could use some time away from our merry band of misfits. Besides, I've got plenty in mind to distract you."

Her tongue dried. His sensual tone stroked across her, as did the heat in his gaze. Danica squeezed her thighs tight. She wanted him like every ice cream stand she'd passed when she'd first set on the run, broke and unable to even afford meals let alone indulgences. A collision so raw and real it would leave marks on her for a lifetime. Just tonight, she'd do something stupid and selfish. She'd pretend for a single moment they had a future. Like this beautiful, searing potential that unfurled between them could grow into something lasting.

Danica's lips twisted into a grin. "If you're

talking about the coaster in the middle of the Strip, been there, done that. Not worth the hype."

He rolled his eyes and tugged her hand as he began walking. She needed to move twice as fast to keep up with the way he booked it from the RV. Apparently, she hadn't been the only one with a bad a case of the jitters at the thought of being stuck in a confined space while under threat.

She swallowed hard and quickened her pace to catch up with Trevor as they strode across the asphalt. The words stuck in her throat, but she forced them out anyway. "Thanks, Trev." Her skin prickled at the real admission but watching his Adam's apple bob in response was worth the discomfort. "If we're going on a date tonight though, I'm picking where we go."

"Oh, it's a date now?" he asked, his voice light with amusement. A mere day before, she would've drank that down like hot chocolate, but right now the warmth burning in her chest hurt all the more.

She sucked in a breath. One night, and then she would do what she had to.

"You betcha, babe," she responded, heat flushing through her as their gazes met. A boldness gripped her by the throat. "I'm planning on wining and dining you, then fucking you senseless."

The curl of his lips into a sensual smirk was the only encouragement she needed.

****

The top of the Stratosphere placed the entirety of the Las Vegas Strip on crystalline display. Danica took her seat at the intimate two-seater in the restaurant, the quiet thrum of jazz music and chatter helping calm her nerves. Over the years, she'd become proficient in compartmentalizing, and she utilized the skill in full force now. She sucked in another breath. Stay present.

Stay here.

Trevor sat across from her, looking some sort of gorgeous in the amber lighting. He leaned back, those long legs stretched out in ripped jeans and his leather jacket slung over the seat. He watched her with affection she couldn't deny any longer.

They'd ordered Chardonnay and steamed clams that came out fast, and she lifted her glass in salute.

"To taking down a veritable asshole tomorrow," she murmured. He clinked his glass against hers. They locked eyes, and the air left the room. His intensity held her suspended every time. It made her want to stay.

Trevor ran a hand through his silver locks. "I reckon I'll have to revise my whole future," he responded. "I always figured I'd be on the run from him for the rest of my life."

"And what's that future going to hold for you?" Danica's heart hurt so bad it spasmed in her chest. No matter what she chose tonight, hers went from as expansive as the view up here to a nothingness that wrapped around her neck like a noose.

He reached across the table to thread his fingers through hers. "You, if you want this," he said, his voice hoarse. The man she'd met had always been aloof, all confidence and competence. He was the guy sitting in the corner with a wan smile and a wisecrack. She never thought she'd get to see this vulnerable shade of him, and as their fingers touched, her breath hitched and her eyes burned.

Enough of the denial, enough with the roundabouts in the conversation, and enough skating on the surface. Trevor was the first man she'd ever met who made her want to take the leap. Who made her yearn for something real.

"Yeah, I really do," she responded, quieter than

intended. A flush crept to her cheeks, and she tipped back the rest of her glass of wine in an attempt to cover up the way she ached.

"You know, I escaped Alberich over a decade ago," he said, staring into his glass like he'd lose himself in it. "Back then, I couldn't trust anyone. Every strange face was going to turn me in, back to him, and my brief stint of freedom would be over. Even when I met Ky and we formed the band, I lay awake most nights, waiting for them to betray me."

"Sounds familiar," she responded. She lived that way, apart from Lenora. Every other soul on the planet would sell her out to the highest bidder.

His sad smile melted his eyes. "It took years for me and a lot of stubbornness from Ky to begin to trust again. I still have a hard time. When we first met, you sparked my interest from the start—I'd be lying if I said otherwise."

"And then I shattered the trust," Danica said, gripping his hand. Her throat squeezed tight. If she screwed Trevor over now, she would shatter him. There wouldn't be any coming back from that—ever.

"I want to trust you, cher," he responded, gliding his thumb across her pulse point.

"But you just need time," she finished. Time they wouldn't have. She offered a grin that hurt, and those shards drove deeper into her heart. "I trust you, Trevor Arceneaux, and that's good enough for me right now. You take all the time you need."

The liquid heat in his gaze rolled through her. The intensity held all the emotion they'd both avoided, pretending their wounds were hate. Acting like they both weren't falling hard.

"You're one of a kind, D," he murmured. "Gorgeous and witty are just perks, but I've never met anyone with your singular brand of loyalty. Your sister's lucky to have you."

Otherworld be damned. If that didn't just sucker punch her then and there. She drew in a shaky breath, not bothering to hide the way his words affected her.

"I may not give a damn about a lot of people, but the ones who are mine, I'll defend with my life," she responded, the statement sinking into her marrow. She stared at Trevor, near trembling at the relief his touch brought as his thumb stroked across her wrist, at the curve of his sensuous lips and how they sparked her desiccated heart to life. Somehow, he'd become one of those people to her, someone she'd come to rely on. She hadn't lied when she confessed her trust in him—he'd earned it with her from the start.

She was the one who lied. She stabbed people in the back, screwed them over, and left good folks out to dry so she and Lenora could survive.

"And you're one of mine, Trev," she murmured, staring out the window. Outside, Vegas stretched out with thousands of glittering lights, as if the city waged war on the stars above. If she stared into those mesmerizing eyes, she'd lose what resolve she had left. The heat prickling behind her eyes would unleash, and everything she held back would come spilling out.

"We'll get through this together," he said. "You won't be alone anymore."

Her throat tightened. That was everything she'd wanted to hear since she was a little girl, ever since she and Lenora escaped her parents' clutches. Danica had been fighting, fighting, fighting for the both of them, and the weight grew so heavy it threatened to crush her with every passing year. For once, she wanted to be the one taken care of. Protected.

She tapped the side of her empty plate—they'd

finished the appetizers a bit ago, and the glasses of Chardonnay were both spent. She slipped a couple of bills onto the table, enough to cover their meal. "I don't know about you, but I'm about ready for the final course." Her voice dripped with intent, and as their gazes locked, a hungry, wolfish smile spread to his lips.

"Look at that, turns out I'm still famished," he responded, leaning forward. He pushed himself up from his seat in a fluid motion. The wickedness in his eyes traveled straight between her legs, and she licked her lips in response.

Before she could rise from the seat, she found herself being lifted. Trevor tugged her onto his back, and she looped her legs around each side. The warmth of him pressed into her even through the fabric of his shirt, and those lithe muscles were on clear display, shoulders she wanted to bite. Her arms dangled in front of him as he quickened his pace, carrying her through the restaurant on his back. Giddiness bubbled in her chest, and a laugh escaped her while most of the intimate restaurant gaped at them in abject horror.

"Heavens above," Danica said, murmuring in his ear. "Is Trevor Arceneaux pulling rockstar shenanigans? I thought Renn and Ky were the only ones ridiculous enough to try."

He laughed, quickening his pace to a run, almost crashing into a waiter as he raced for the elevator. The stares of all the dining couples burned into her, but she ate them up and spat them out. She bounced up and down on his back, relishing in his strength, how he held her thighs effortlessly with those corded muscles. He skidded to a halt in front of the elevator and pressed the button. Danica leaned closer to bite his ear, earning her a heavy breath from him.

"Bad girl," he murmured. "Save that for in here."

The elevator doors parted, and she slipped to her feet to join him inside. The second she stepped into the elevator, his hands were around her waist. Trevor pressed her against her the mirror-lined walls. The door clicked shut, and up they went.

Danica's lips met his in a crash, a desperate need driving her. This close, heat burst between them, the air so thick she could sink into it. She bit down on his lip, a copper sting following, and a second later his tongue slipped into her mouth. His fingers curled around her waist, and he crowded against her close enough his erection nudged through his pants, pressing to her center. She panted in response, desire rushing through her like the flu.

The floors continued to ding as they rose even higher.

Trevor pulled back for a gasp of air. "I want to be inside you, now." He slipped a hand into his pocket and pulled out a pick. Within seconds, he had the fire lock turned and pressed the bottom floor—this elevator traveled a long, long way.

He slipped his hand beneath her skirt, bringing it up as he glided his palm along her thigh. The fingers traced right over the swatch of fabric barely covering her. He pressed down, stroking right over her clit.

"Think I found it," he murmured against her neck before those lips traveled up and down the column in slow, sensual precision. Danica let out a low moan tugged straight from her core. She ground against his long fingers, growing slicker by the second until he dragged her thong down her thighs by the elastic. His fingers stroked over her clit again, this time bare, and her breath hitched.

"I need you in me, now," Danica whispered, drawing his face to hers. She cupped the side of his cheek.

"I think I can accommodate," he said, his eyes crinkling with his smooth-as-sin grin. The dim light of the elevator sharpened the shadows of his even features, his skin duskier as the golden hues emerged. His brows curved with wickedness, and the leather jacket of his show attire, the plain grey tee and the ripped jeans, hugged muscles so defined her mouth watered to sink her teeth into them.

Her thumb traced his bottom lip before he descended again, drawing her into the sort of kiss that sent warmth coursing through her like the first sip of coffee. She focused on the sharp, ragged breaths between them and the way her chest heaved, even as the elevator continued to ding while it traveled lower to ascend once more.

She reached down to snag his belt, flicking it open, even as he bit and sucked at her neck, her collarbone, all before returning to her mouth. He tugged on the elastic of her panties before he had them off and flicked them to the opposite side of the elevator. A low growl came from his lips, one that reverberated against her skin.

The snick of his zipper resounded through the elevator, and he brought his cock out. The sheer size made her core throb with a need that pulsed until it grew into a deafening roar. He nudged against her drenched entrance. She leaned against the mirror panel, her skin sticking to the surface as her breaths came out ragged.

Trevor inched inside her, and she lifted her thigh to circle around his, taking every ounce he offered. Drops of sweat beaded across her forehead, and her chest swelled up and down with anticipation. He slid deeper in, and his hands wrapped around her hips as he brought her up against him. When Trevor sank deep into her, Danica let out a moan that resounded through the room and wrapped her legs around his trim waist. He slammed her against the wall, bracing her there.

His lips met hers, right as he began to move inside her.

They were a clash of teeth, skin, and desperation as he thrust deep. His fingers dug into her hips, and he slammed her against the wall again and again, holding her effortlessly. Danica sank into his sheer strength, the heat blistering between them and the ecstasy rolling through every time he rocked inside her. Sweat dripped down her neck, and the bunched fabric of her dress rode up around her thighs.

The elevator continued to ding, ding, ding, as she rode him, as he thrust inside her like they searched for the same thing. Her nails curled into his shoulders, biting past the thin fabric. Trevor's lips met hers again and again as if he chased a fleeting memory. Her chest tightened, and she gasped out a sharp breath. Maybe he did.

Danica closed her eyes, surrendering to the sting of their skin against skin when they smacked together, to the bliss curling around her like a spring breeze, and to the ragged breaths they shared with every kiss.

Her pussy throbbed as each thrust brought her closer and closer.

"Come for me," Trevor whispered in her ear, the silk of his voice her undoing.

She threw her head back, and her core squeezed tight, her vision blanking for a moment. Pleasure so exquisite she could feel it in her teeth took over. Her breath caught in her throat as she sagged in his arms. Trevor continued rocking forward into her until a few seconds later, heat followed as he spilled inside her. Their bodies shuddered together, and for a moment, the only sound was their ragged breaths and the ding of the elevator.

Danica made the mistake of looking up. The way his eyes crinkled when he looked at her, how he pierced past her surface to plunge straight to her heart—she'd remember him for the rest of her life. Her heart stuttered at the sight of him, rumpled clothes and ragged heart, yet he risked all of those fragile pieces on her.

She didn't want to leave.

Chapter Nineteen

Trevor stretched his arm out, but he felt nothing there. He blinked the sleep out of his eyes before pushing himself from his bottom bunk on the RV, which he lay in alone. Last night, he and Danica had fucked their way across Las Vegas between drinks, laughter, and sharing old wounds. Disappointment curled in his chest at the sight of his empty bed, but based on the golden rays creeping in through the blinds, they were already well into the day.

He hopped up and strode to the kitchenette. Jett leaned over the table, studying the mirror and tracing the symbols again and again. Even though everyone else remained asleep, Jett was dressed in his usual button-down and slacks ensemble, his dark hair combed and his thick brows pulled together in concentration.

"Your girl snuck out hours ago," he said, not looking up from the mirror. "Her rustling about is what woke me up in the first place."

Trevor's heart pounded in double time, and he couldn't resist the smile that spread as he sat at the booth.

Jett looked at him, those ice blue eyes crystallizing. "Be careful," he warned. Trevor's chest burned at the statement, but he just nodded. Jett continued, "She's witty, charming, and she may care for you, but the woman's a liar. I know my kind."

Trevor opened his mouth and then shut it. Jett wasn't wrong—they both knew Danica lied and maybe even to him, but the way they'd connected was real. He reached out and cuffed Jett on the shoulder. "Thanks for watching out for me, J," he said. Because at the end of the day, all of Jett's concerns and sharp comments came from a place of worry.

The siren's eyes darkened as a charmer's smile lit his face. "Hush now, we both know I don't dabble in things like feelings or concern."

"Total ice, man," Trevor said, glancing to his phone. No calls or texts from Danica, but the time ticked closer and closer to their scheduled meet-up with Kincaid. He reached down to fire off a text to her before casting a glance at the mirror again. The heavy piece glared at them, somehow still in their possession despite Alberich's attempts. After today, Kincaid would make his move, and if luck was with them, they'd take the impossible monolith down—that part, Trevor still had a hard time grasping.

"First thing I'm going to demand from Kincaid is an explanation of what the hell this mirror is. I know this scrawl from somewhere, and it's been driving me crazy ever since," Jett muttered, slumping onto the table. He pressed his forehead against his folded arms.

Kieran lumbered out from the bunks, sliding a hand through his tangled black hair. His gaze landed on Trevor with the same wild intensity as always. "Today's the day, brother," he said, grinning so wide he revealed his fangs. "Are you ready? You won't have to look over your shoulder at every new place we travel."

Even as Kieran's enthusiasm rolled over him, Trevor couldn't shake the nerves jittering like a wrong chord that reverberated inside. Maybe he'd spent too many years disappointed to hope, but he couldn't shake the feeling something had already gone horribly wrong.

He cracked a grin, more for Ky's sake than his own. "Habits like that die hard. I'll still be the same paranoid fucker you've known from the start."

Kieran peered at the coffeemaker, which had a slim amount left. He pulled the glass carafe out and poured the coffee straight into his mouth. A moment later, he was wiping his forearm over his mouth and had replaced the carafe. Kieran strode over to set his hand on Trevor's shoulder, the heavy weight a familiar one. The hotheaded incubus might not have been his birth family, but he was the only one who'd earned the title.

"I'll summon the troops," he said. "We'd best start getting ready. We've got an important meeting with your freedom today."

****

By the time they reached the Peppermill Lounge, Trevor's heart slammed full force in his chest.

The entire walk over, he'd been waiting for one of Alberich's redcap mercs to jump them, or some shadow to lengthen and another fae to emerge. They ran into a couple of close calls with roaming ankous and had been ducking into alleys and shadows, but they'd managed to blend with the dense crowds every time.

What amplified his nerves was the silence. He hadn't gotten a single text from Danica, and the closer they got to the meeting with no word, the more the pit inside his stomach grew. If she didn't show for this meeting... His mind buzzed. The neon sign for Peppermill Lounge glared at them, even though the flashing lights looked less impressive during the day.

"Where's your girl?" Liz asked when they approached. She nudged him in the side. "I thought she'd be here jawing off and making sure her hard work got delivered into the right hands."

Trevor shrugged, staring ahead to avoid Liz's discerning stare. "She skipped out this morning, but I haven't heard from her since."

"My bet is she's waiting inside," Liz responded, even though her tone didn't have an ounce of confidence behind it.

"Gloating, you mean," Jett piped in, slinking beside them with the grace of a shadow. "I can't imagine that woman doing anything as paltry as waiting."

Trevor snorted, jamming his hands into his pockets. The nerves didn't die down, but Liz and Jett both did their damndest to fight the fight with him. The shadow of the lounge fell over them, at least twenty degrees cooler than walking under direct sunlight out here. Sweat beaded on his brow, more pronounced once he stepped out from under the glowing ball of hate in the sky.

Kieran didn't waste any time—he grabbed the door and entered. Renn swept in behind him, maintaining an unusual level of quiet, probably because he held the mirror. Out of the crew, they'd agreed Trevor was the last person who should be walking around with it, what with the bounty hanging over his head like one of the flashing Vegas signs.

The interior of Peppermill Lounge was all classic kitsch, the vibe he'd expected from Vegas rather than the slick monstrosities along the Strip. Neon lights lined the bar in blues and pinks, and cherry blossom trees craned over the patrons, interspersed between the circular booths. Stained glass lampshades hung from every fixture, and the low chatter murmured through the place with a steady pulse.

"Kincaid's supposed to be waiting for us in the lounge," Kieran directed, striding across the linoleum with purpose. Trevor sucked in a shaky breath as he followed. Once they handed over the mirror here, Leo Kincaid would be delivering the killing blow to Alberich's reputation. Their part to play in this whole escapade would be over, and the waiting game would begin.

Where the restaurant section decked out in all

cool blues and pinks, the lounge created a different atmosphere. Cozy red cushions circled around tables with inky pools in the center, and a vibrant, flickering flame lay in the middle. The fire dancing amid the water was pure Otherworld, and Trevor felt like he'd stepped through the veil, even though they were still smack in the center of the human realm.

Trying to find Leo Kincaid wasn't hard. Few loitered here during the day, and Alberich's business partner leaned back along one of the circular booths, his arms sprawled out on either side. The yaksha had pale green skin and golden eyes the same color as the flames flickering before him. The moment he caught sight of them, his grin revealed sharp fangs and even sharper dimples. Kincaid stood from his seat, towering over most of them from sheer height and broad shoulders that strained the seams of his pin-perfect striped suit. If anyone could give the redcaps a run for their money, it was this guy.

Trevor scanned around the room, and his heart sank. Danica was nowhere in sight.

"About time you arrived," Kincaid said upon approach, his voice low and rich. "I hadn't heard word from your business associate, and I'd begun to worry you were going to stand me up."

Ice filtered through his veins. Once Danica claimed a target, she'd proved to be relentless no matter who got caught in the backlash. From the start, her goal had been to take Alberich down—so if she wasn't at the meeting she'd orchestrated herself, something must've happened.

Liz cast him a worried glance, but he just offered a grim nod in response. They had already arrived with the mirror. They needed to see this through.

"Important thing is, we've got the item you

requested," Kieran said, standing before him with his arms crossed. "So, are we going to deal, or what?"

Kincaid lifted a brow and rapped his knuckles onto the tabletop. "Straight to the point aren't you. Why don't you sit, have a drink, and we'll discuss this like we're civilized."

Renn shrugged and strode forward. "I'll take a drink."

Kincaid scanned him over, his tongue tracing over his bottom lip as he looked. "I'll gladly buy you one."

Renn's gaze sparked with interest, and a wicked grin rose to the satyr's lips. Of course, because in the middle of an important business deal, their drummer was thinking about sex. Trevor strode past them to take a seat on the cushions. If he stood any longer, he didn't know if his legs would hold him up. The moment he'd strode in and Danica wasn't here, the ground vanished beneath him and he was falling, falling, falling.

Kincaid slid into the other side of the booth to take a seat, and Renn followed him, inching in closer than necessary. Renn spread his arms along back on the booth so that his one arm lingered right by Kincaid. When the yaksha CEO who could crush them with a single transaction glanced his way, their intrepid satyr flashed him a sultry smile. Jett inched in beside Renn, keeping an ample amount of distance as he rolled his eyes. Kieran and Liz squeezed in on Trevor's side, both of them flashing him glances like he might bolt at any moment. Their nerves buzzed as loud as his.

Within moments, the waitress jotted down their drink orders and scurried off. Renn leaned in close to Kincaid, murmuring something into the man's ear that had the CEO grinning. Jett's gaze never strayed from the shadows inside the lounge. Trevor brimmed with silence, and he'd checked his phone at least a dozen times since they sat down, the glare of the screen mocking him.

The waitress plunked a whisky on the rocks in front of him, and he didn't wait to start drinking. The smoky liquid scorched his throat, and he downed it faster than normal until the glass lay empty. Trevor plunked the glass onto the table with a click that resounded through the air.

"We've had our drinks," Trevor said, giving Kincaid an arch look. The sooner they left here, the sooner Trevor could head to Danica's hotel room. "So, let's talk this mirror."

Kincaid pursed his lips and lifted his scotch and soda in salute. "Message received, you aren't a fan of pleasantries. Makes me miss our leannan sidhe friend all the more."

Trevor's stomach twisted. That made the both of them. He could imagine her there, chattering Kincaid's ear off, quick, flashy smiles and some witty words sprinkled in their conversation. Danica lived for those types of situations—the PR slickness she excelled at. Meanwhile, he skated on raw, rusted nerves every second Alberich remained free to prowl.

Renn tugged off the rucksack he carried, slipping it between the two of them. "We've got the goods here."

"Now I'd like to know what you plan on doing with the mirror," Kieran interrupted, his golden gaze as sharp as Kincaid's. "What even is it?"

Leo Kincaid pulled up the rucksack and peeked in. His flame eyes flashed in appreciation, and he let out a low whistle. "I had a hard time believing you retrieved this. From everything I've heard, he set some impossible security standards."

"Nothing we couldn't handle," Trevor responded, a glacier coolness in his voice. The man needed to get to the point or he'd reach over the table and throttle him.

"What it is doesn't matter. This mirror doesn't belong to Alberich," Kincaid said, drumming his fingers on the countertop. The firelight danced across his carved features. "However, the owner happens to be in the upper echelons of the Court and would like to know who stole their item in the first place. We're going to give them that intel, including Alberich's official seal on the document."

Trevor crooked a brow. Impersonating an official seal wasn't just a forgery of words—it involved an imprint of the person's essence. This endeavor hadn't been a snap of the fingers for Kincaid. He must've been planning his business partner's demise for some time.

"And what guarantee do we have that you're not going to run with this artifact and sell it to the highest bidder?" Jett asked, ever-present caution in his tone.

"Because I'm giving you this," Kincaid said, reaching into his pocket. He passed Kieran a small oak box with beveled edges.

Kieran lifted the top open with a creak, and his eyebrows rose. "You're handing us your own self-destruct button?"

"You've got my official seal as well. If I don't uphold our agreement, you can feel free to use it however you see fit." Kincaid's smoothness crawled under his skin, but Trevor couldn't argue the fair exchange. If the yaksha didn't follow through, he wouldn't hesitate to screw over the cocky bastard who'd worked with his former master for years. Even if Renn was a hot minute from crawling all over the man.

Kieran shut the top of the box and dragged it off the table. Liz swallowed the last dregs of her JD, and Jett polished off his pint. Trevor was ready to leap out of the booth since he'd already leapt out of his skin. He nudged

Kieran and Liz to push them out, and all three hopped from the seats. Trevor stood facing Kincaid on the opposite side of the flickering fire, watching as the flames danced to an undulating rhythm. Kieran gripped the box tight and lined up beside him, clapping a hand on Trevor's shoulder.

"We'll find her," he murmured. Because of course, Kieran would say that. The man possessed the sort of warm heart most Seelie and Unseelie could only wish for. Jett reached across Renn to offer Kincaid a handshake, ever the polite operator. Renn leaned in, and Leo Kincaid whispered something into his ear, earning a wicked smirk from the satyr. Trevor didn't miss the business card Kincaid pressed into Renn's palm before they exited.

Trevor heaved a sigh. At least one of them had enjoyed this meetup. The rest looked like they'd emerged from an off-tune symphony.

"Pleasure doing business with you," Kincaid called while they headed toward the exit. "I'll let you know once the plan's in motion."

Kieran stuck a hand in the air to acknowledge, offering a brief wave as they stepped up to the thick door.

Once they stepped out into the blazing Vegas sun, Kieran sagged against the wall. "I wanted to punch the fucker from the moment I met him."

"I just wanted to fuck him." Renn shrugged, his dark eyes dancing with mirth. He cast a glance back to the door as if he could X-ray through the walls.

"We know," Jett muttered. "I was ready to place a bucket beneath you to collect the drool."

"Anyone else feel like that was all too easy?" Liz piped up, her arms crossing over her chest as she cast a stubborn look to Ky.

"Yeah," Trevor responded, his hands balled into fists inside his pockets. His throat dried with the panic that descended with every following minute he heard no word from Danica.

"Go, look for her," Kieran said. "We'll grab lunch and meet you back at the RV."

Trevor swallowed the lump in his throat, not able to do more than nod. He took off like the scorching sun set him ablaze as he headed in the direction of Danica's hotel. With every step forward, the dread twisted tighter inside. He couldn't lose her, yet he feared he already had.

Chapter Twenty

The light-up red awnings of Fremont Hotel and Casino blinked and flashed in front of Danica, and in her current state of unease, they made her want to vomit.

Leaving Trevor this morning marked up there on the 'hardest things she'd ever done' list, along with leaving behind their pet Chupacabra and throwing out her lucky pair of Docs. She scratched at her wrists, trying to ignore the chill that slithered through her even in this intense heat. She stepped into the shadows under the main entrance before she followed the length of the building in search of the red door.

She would be showing up empty-handed. Smart plan on her part. The one thing she grasped onto was the slim hope Alberich might be willing to swap out prisoners. Even in the face of imprisonment that terrified her, a life that still haunted Trevor, Danica would volunteer to take Lenora's place.

Every step forward had Danica tightening the lock on the box she'd stuffed any residual thoughts into. Otherwise, she'd be screaming in mindless panic right now. Otherwise, her knees would give out beneath her and the shakes would overtake at the memory of Trevor lying there in the bed when she'd left. His eyes were closed in slumber, the soft swell of his chest mesmerizing. For once, he seemed at peace, like the stained-glass shards of his past had been healed.

Yet she'd pulled away from the hickory and the heat that soothed her own mottled heart. She'd slipped on her heels and marched out the RV toward a future in a cage.

Honks sounded all around from the busy street,

and the crowds crawled everywhere here, murmurs and shouts intermingling with the rest of the ever-present ding-ding-dings of Vegas's slot machines. Danica stuck to the sidelines, skimming her numbed fingertips across the tiled exterior. She scanned for the red door Crags told her about.

Part of her, an ugly, loathsome part, wished she wouldn't find it. That she could return to Trevor and bask in the moments with him, the sunlit corridors she'd spent her whole life searching for.

Yet she'd never be happy if she'd let go of her sister when she needed her the most.

Under one of the big theater style billboards interspersed across the awnings, Danica spotted a small red door that looked like part of the scenery—a utility entrance at best.

Danica's breath stuck in her throat, and her palms broke into a cold sweat. Even though she hadn't given her legs the order to move, she found herself walking in that direction. No one wandered around the door or even glanced at it, one of the surefire indicators something fae this way came. Her hand rested on a rusted old handle, one that looked worn even to her eyes. She bored holes into the door in front of her, frozen.

This might be the last glimpse of the sun she'd get, and she wasted it on the searing rays of a Vegas morning surrounded by throngs of fanny-packed tourists and college age kids slumming through the streets as they nursed massive hangovers. Danica shook her head. Kind of them to give her a stunning sight to remember. Maybe she was better off inside a cage. A tinny, metallic taste bloomed in her mouth even as she swallowed her lies.

Danica pulled the door open and entered.

Rich, perfumed air greeted her when she went inside. The ripple of the veil to the Otherworld tugged at her skin as she took the first couple of steps down the long corridor lined by velvet runners. Globe lights gleamed from metal claws on either side, a taste of the Old World that didn't belong amidst the Vegas glitz.

No one leapt out to greet her while she wandered down the hall, but her skin crawled as if someone stared at her from every shadow, every crack in the wall. Danica quickened her pace toward the end of the hall where amber beams filtered in from an adjacent chamber.

Midway through the corridor, a hobgoblin appeared in front of her.

The creature sidled up a few steps to close the distance between them, the dim lighting deepening the wrinkles in its bumpy skin and highlighting the sharpened, grey teeth. "Danica Maslanka, I'd be happy to escort you to speak with the Master." The hobgoblin's scrunched features shifted when he looked up to her before offering a bow.

"Your master can suck a dick," Danica responded, balling her hands into fists at her side. Her nails bit into her palm, the only indication of fear she let slip. "Let's pay him a visit though. We're overdue for a chat."

The hobgoblin didn't bother shuffling off to take the lead. Instead, he locked eyes with her and snapped his fingers. A second later, Danica's insides churned like she'd eaten a rotten burrito, and they'd landed in what appeared to be a large hall, all oaken rafters and cream walls. A long table stretched the length, and at the end sat a loathsome figure, the man she'd been avoiding all this time.

Bloodred eyes stared at her, Alberich's gaze unwavering. The man was one of the sidhe with myriad abilities at his control, and despite the bumpy ridges along the curves of his face, the slashing arcs of his browline, and the loathsome core of his character, the man exuded pure nobility. His fingers drummed along the top of the massive wooden table, and he sat stiff-backed in a metal-tipped, ornate chair, like the king of his stupid castle.

"You're late," Alberich said, his rich voice echoing through the room. He twisted his metal cuff-links, accents on a gray tailored suit he wore. She'd never seen him in anything but business attire.

"Is it morning?" Danica shot back, passing the hobgoblin as she approached. "Oh wait, it is. I'm still in the clear. If you wanted specifics, you should've given them."

Alberich's lips quirked into a smile, one that made her tense. This was the man she'd be bartering her sister's continued existence with. It was best not to anger him.

"Then I presume you did at least catch the memo on what I want returned?" he said, pinning her with his stare.

Danica lifted her chin to stare him square in the eyes. If he wanted to keep her as a pet, she'd make him regret this day. After all, few had learned how to be as obnoxious as her. "I couldn't get it from them," she said. Her voice didn't tremble.

Alberich's brows furrowed, but the wan look on his face didn't alter. "So you arrived to what purpose?" he asked.

"You gave me until today to bring the mirror to you, or my sister's life was in jeopardy," Danica responded, her nails biting into her palms so hard she bled. "I'm here to offer a trade. Lenora's life for mine. If you're going to try and use one of us as leverage, I'm the better option."

"Come now, Danica. I thought you were a

smarter girl," Alberich near purred, those bloodred eyes glowing. He didn't stand from his seat, but he lifted two fingers and gestured. "I might consider bartering with a business associate, but my dear, you not only owe me money but also the prized possession you stole."

Danica took a step back from the table to bump into something solid.

She whipped around and looked up. A redcap loomed over her, and he grinned wide, his teeth crimson and dripping with former kills. He wasn't the only one who'd approached during their brief conversation. A rakshasa, another redcap, and an encantado strode forward, their shadows falling over her. Even with her hands balled into fists and the weapons she'd stored in her pockets, the sheer stature, venom spit, and vicious claws outclassed her.

"What, afraid to chip your nails, Alberich?" Danica called over even while she searched for a gap between the wall of creatures. Anywhere to run.

This idea had been terrible from the start, and it just got a whole lot worse.

Alberich didn't even bother to look her way, his gaze on his lacquered claws when he gave the order. "Capture her."

Danica bolted on instinct, her calves squeezing tight as she shot off toward the nearest door. The clap of heavy footfalls resounded through this room. Her heart jackhammered in her chest, and she rushed as fast as she could. No time to contemplate any other exit strategy.

The encantado slithered across the floor, veering in front of her so fast she almost tripped. The second cost her.

The redcap stepped behind her, his shadow falling first, before his fist descended. Her vision went black.

****

"Wake up."

A voice sounded above her.

Danica clutched at her head, fighting the heavy throb in her skull, like she'd downed a couple of bottles of whisky before bed. She blinked, her vision hazy at first as her eyes adjusted to the dim room. This place smelled like citronella, polish, and a deeper tang she couldn't identify at first. Her nose twitched with familiarity. Blood. Oh, joy.

A familiar face hovered over her, with deep-set hazel eyes and her usually smiling mouth in a frown. Her long golden hair hung down her back, messy strands escaping from what was once a tight braid. Lenora.

"Funny meeting you here, Nora," Danica mumbled, a wave of relief crashing through. The mere sight of her sister hit her better than the first sip of coffee in the morning, warmth saturating her from the inside out. "What's the free breakfast like? Does he offer room service?"

Lenora snorted and squatted in front of her.

Danica pushed herself from the slump, realizing cold bars pressed into her back. She patted herself down, checking her pockets, but Alberich's mercenaries hadn't been idiots. They'd taken her weapons.

"At least the bastard locked us up together," Lenora muttered. "You shouldn't have come for me, D. He's just getting what he wants."

"Not everything," Danica muttered, staring at the bars overhead. The cage they sat in was tall enough for them to stand and lay down in but didn't offer much more space. The short proximity she could wander made her skin prickle. She wouldn't survive long trapped in here. Danica leaned toward her sister and lowered her voice. "At this point, I'm relying on the boys in the

Discord's Desire to pull through and praying Kincaid's good on his word."

"What did you steal?" Lenora asked, slumping next to her. Even though Danica's stomach twisted in guilt at seeing her sister behind these bars, Lenora hadn't swung an accusatory glare or comment her way once.

"Just some mirror in his treasure trove," Danica said, wrinkling her nose. She never got the time to sit and figure out the significance of that item, but it had gotten him riled enough to send wave upon wave of mercenaries after them. Not like he couldn't afford them. Her gaze drifted past the bars to the rest of this massive ballroom. More cages lined the marble flooring, most of them elevated on wide pedestals. Fae hunched inside, sleeping, curled into the small space they'd been given. Some stared, while others ignored them. All contained a haunted look in their eyes she recognized.

This must've been the room Trevor spent years and years imprisoned in.

She was surprised she hadn't voided the contents of her stomach yet. Danica gripped the bar beside her tight, the coldness imprinting into her palm.

"Whatever you stole, forget kicking the hornet's nest—you took a flamethrower to it," Lenora said, tugging on the end of her braid. "I had been heading out for work when they cornered me."

Ouch. Danica opened her mouth, but her sister fixed her with a glare.

"Don't you dare apologize," Lenora warned. "It happened. You've bailed me out of so many bad situations in the past, and we both know why you agreed to take a loan from Alberich in the first place. If I have to hear your guilty conscience for the next century, I'm taking us both out."

Danica closed her mouth, grinned, and gave

Lenora a gentle shove. "Fine, you caught me. This was all an elaborate plan, so I could keep a better eye on you."

"You might want to see a shrink for those attachment issues." Lenora's lips twisted into a wry smirk. "It's getting creepy, sis."

The creak of footsteps pushed her to sit upright and look around. After all, the long strides meant someone moved outside of a cage. A shorter figure crossed the ballroom, one she recognized by the knobby joints and the pale green skin, the same cowering creature who had plagued them since the Mandalay Bay show.

"Come to gloat, Crags?" Danica called over. She had been hoping Alberich would mosey on in so she could spit in his face.

Crags didn't respond at first, his caterpillar brows furrowed fiercely as he approached.

Danica locked gazes with him, refusing to look down. If they wanted to cage her, she'd make their lives hell.

"Why didn't you bring the mirror?" he asked. The hesitation in his voice scraped her awareness, a genuine confusion from the brownie slave.

Danica shrugged. "Truth be told, maybe I could've used the Discord's Desire crew and nabbed it out from underneath them. However, I've already done too much to them. I've become someone I hate. If I took Trevor's freedom away from him, I doubt even my sister would still love me."

Lenora shrugged. "Not like I'd have much of a choice. But I'm proud of you for making the right call here."

Crags stepped to the bars, his fingers skimming over the surface as if he remembered them well. From what Trevor told her, they'd both resided in this hall in separate cages. Where Trevor had rebelled and claimed his escape, earning a life on the run, Crags' loyalty earned him a place in this house outside of the cage— still a slave.

"I just don't understand," he murmured. Seeing the soft shade of this creature, the hunched-over brownie clarified in her mind like he hadn't before. He was small, terrified, and not built for a life on the run. For him, this had been the only option. Hating him would be easy— after all, he'd been running Alberich's errands for far too long. But the loathing would be misplaced. Alberich had imprisoned them. Alberich was the one they needed to take down.

Danica placed her hand on one of the bars and looked him in the eyes. Oftentimes, she hated her abilities. Unlike a redcap who was effectively a killing machine, or even an incubus who could soak up energy from any sort of passion—including a fight—Danica's abilities allowed her to inspire. Not like she could whip out 'inspiration' when an Unseelie merc had razor sharp teeth and claws.

Yet here and now, maybe she could do something.

"I showed up today empty handed, because I believe in what we're doing," Danica said, concentrating as she tapped into the honey-sweet inspiration she dabbed upon any artist or musician she strode paths with. The act of using those abilities bubbled up inside her like liquid sunshine, like the first note of a heartbreaking melody. Her skin prickled in response to the emotion that emerged, the sort she often pretended didn't exist for her.

"That mirror is the one thing that can take Alberich down, and granting freedom for every soul caged in this castle is worth a little self-sacrifice. Took me a long time to learn, but the lesson stuck." Her words resonated more than normal, and Lenora's eyes crinkled with amusement at the realization of what Danica was doing.

Crags shook his head, those dark eyes gleaming with fear. "He'll find a way around it. He always does."

Danica reached out, her fingertips brushing against his. He snapped them back, but she'd already done the deed. In a single touch, she'd conveyed the jolt of bravery he might need to stand tall here, even after he'd been crushed more with every passing year. What he did with that gift was up to him, but Danica had to try. She had fought her entire life, but what she did best, was inspire.

"Not this time," she intoned, a seriousness in her voice traveling deep to her bones. Maybe, in the secret heart of her, she believed her own words. "This time, he's finished. I bet my life on it."

Chapter Twenty-One

Trevor texted Kieran after searching Danica's hotel room and her normal haunts in this city to no avail. He headed back to the RV. When he'd checked in at Kink and Candy to find out Lenora was no longer employed there because she hadn't shown for work two days in a row, his marrow turned colder than the winter realms in the Otherworld.

Alberich must've taken Danica's sister. The family emergency hadn't been a lie, but the sunset smile and relief on her face was. The entire night they'd spent together—she must've known it'd be their last.

He thundered across the asphalt toward their RV, bringing his storm cloud with him. They'd handed over the mirror to Kincaid, and supposedly, cinched Alberich's impending destruction, but at what cost? If he knew turning it in would sentence Danica and her sister, he would've returned the mirror to Alberich and stayed on the run for the rest of his days. He'd survived so far, but he wouldn't be able to surface above the water if he discovered he'd lost her for good.

The darkened windows of their RV glared. Trevor loped to the front door and opened it. Silence greeted him, meaning he was the first of the band to return. When he stepped inside though, his nose twitched from the scent of lemon polish. Trevor climbed the steps and entered. Inside lay the same RV as always—the booth they lounged in, the kitchenette they cooked their weird-hour meals at, and farther in the back, the bunks and bathroom.

His brows furrowed. Something was off in here, but no signs leapt out at him.

He took another couple of steps forward, his fingers gliding across the surface of the wall. Not an ounce of dust. The sink full of dishes had been cleaned and put away into the cabinets. The windows sparkled. None of their crew ever did this sort of deep-cleaning, and in all his time spent on this RV, no matter how they'd tidied, the place had never reached these levels of neat, organized, and polished.

Someone had broken into the RV.

Based on the lack of overturned tables and the sheer cleanliness, he could easily figure out who.

Trevor wandered over to the kitchenette, the counters now free from grease stains and the normal gunk gumming into the cracks. Since the mirror already rested in Kincaid's eager hands, Trevor wasn't worried about anyone trying to break-in, not if the brownie wanted to do them a favor by cleaning their place.

His gaze landed on a square of white paper in the center of the counter. All it contained were a few simple lines.

'She turned herself in. Fremont Hotel and Casino.'

The confirmation he'd been searching for slammed into him like a car crash. Trevor leaned over the counter, his palms digging into the edge and his breaths coming out ragged. Danica was in the hands of that monster. Something tightened in his chest, a keen understanding he'd been missing. He might not have been able to trust her due to past deceptions, but she was a woman of actions—this one spoke volumes.

It reaffirmed what had grown between them, how when Danica truly cared about someone, she would sacrifice everything. Even though she might lie to protect herself or others, she was honest about what mattered.

They both understood what destroying Alberich

could mean. How so many others would find the liberation he fought every day to preserve. And even Crags had come to realize that.

The door to the RV creaked as Kieran tromped in, followed by Liz close behind. Once they caught sight of him, they both stopped in their tracks.

Liz's brows furrowed. "I don't suppose you went on a cleaning spree…" She trailed off as Jett slunk up the steps. Renn was nowhere to be found, so the satyr must've made a detour along the way. Trevor didn't have to wrack his brain long to figure out who Renn had stopped to visit.

Trevor lifted the piece of paper, but the words dried on his tongue.

Liz marched forward and snagged the note out of his hands, scanning the contents. When she looked at him, her eyes widened in horror. "Danica turned herself in?" Liz asked, her voice small. Apart from him, their band manager was the other one who'd grown closer to the leannan sidhe, and the other one who'd been hurt at her initial betrayal. Despite her reluctance, Liz must've warmed to her once more. "Trev, what happened?"

He leaned against the kitchen counter, and Jett strode by him to pluck a handle of Jack Daniels from the cabinet.

"Take a sip," the siren said, understanding in his dark eyes. "You look like you could use it."

Kieran paced up and down the aisle, his gaze glued to the ground as he brimmed with the same anxiousness that descended on all of them.

Trevor lifted the bottle to his lips and took a swig. The golden liquid burned as it traveled down his throat. Even though the warmth couldn't permeate through his panic, the whisky scorched his mind clear. "Alberich must've threatened her sister over the mirror," he said.

"The family emergency was real."

"She was in the RV with us for most of the night. The mirror sat right there on the table," Kieran said, glancing at him. "Why didn't she take it?"

Liz exchanged a glance with Trevor and nodded. "Because her feelings for Trevor are the real deal." Liz walked over to place a hand on Kieran's shoulder, if only to stop his pacing. The admission out loud made his skin prickle, made him feel so vile, desperate, and afraid in a way he'd almost forgotten he could. He wanted to say something, anything, but he'd never be able to communicate the maelstrom within.

He wanted to do one thing so, so badly, but he could never ask the rest of them to go along with him. It was suicide.

Kieran's gaze softened when he locked eyes with him. "If she's in Alberich's clutches, we can't just leave her there."

Trevor's heart broke right then and there. Warmth soaked through him from this family he called his own, like entering home after wandering in the winter woods for far too long. He might not be able to ask, but Kieran always knew. Trevor trusted their band leader to make the hard call every time.

Kieran snatched the paper out of Liz's hands. "I mean, fuck, the who-what-where's pretty much already all out there waiting for us. And the mirror's in safer hands than ours, so we don't have to worry about Alberich getting it in his clutches."

"Sorry, but doesn't this reek of a trap to you?" Jett interjected, the siren operating as the devil's advocate—his normal role.

Trevor rifled a hand through his hair. "Crags is loyal to Alberich, so yeah, I don't know why he'd be giving us this information. He stayed behind when I escaped, even though I offered him the chance."

Kieran shrugged. "Sure, maybe he's looking for us to show up with the mirror as a trade, but that's not what we're doing. We'll sneak in, set off all his fire alarms, and nab Danica in the chaos."

Liz let out a sigh and grabbed the handle of JD, taking a swig. "Who let you make the plans? That's a terrible one."

Jett stared at the ceiling. "This just seems like a suicide mission. We're neck-deep in this as it is."

"You don't have to come," Trevor responded, with a little more force than intended. Guilt corroded his insides for not realizing what Danica was up to, for getting the guys into this mess with Alberich, and for being such a coward that all he'd been able to do these years was run. "This is my fight, my problem."

Jett leveled him an arched eyebrow look. "Enough of the pitying martyr shit. You know I'm with you regardless. I'm just saying there are ways of handling things, and this sort of situation begs for an exit strategy."

Liz sat at the table and plunked a mug of cold coffee in front of her. She looked at all three of them. "Well, what are you waiting for? Let's get started."

****

The hours ticked by, each one making his nerves buzz even more. In the stranglehold of his panic over Danica, rushing to Alberich's manor to save her seemed the obvious move. However, in the dizzying haste, he'd ignored the barbed claws that place sank into him, how he bled every night from the nightmares that dragged him from his sleep.

Trevor had taken to standing outside of the RV to chain smoke. The smog drifted from his lips as fast as he could spew it.

The manor. He hadn't returned there since he escaped, all those years ago. Back then, the entrance had been in a different location, but places in the Otherworld always shifted.

If he closed his eyes, he could still feel it.

Cold steel bars against his back.

Air thickened with despair.

The raw throb of his throat after screaming on command.

Bile rose in Trevor's chest. He sucked down another drag from his cigarette, spilling the smoke into the night sky.

The RV door creaked as Kieran hopped out to join him. "Everyone's almost ready," he said. "Pass me a smoke, brother?"

Trevor handed him a cigarette, and as Kieran lifted it to his lips, he lit the end. Their band leader donned his beat-up leather and had pocketed enough weapons between his waistband and boots to make him rattle if one of the massive redcaps decided to turn him over and shake. Not like Trevor didn't have his own at the ready—he just didn't know if he'd ever be prepared to face the manor and that man, even if they'd come up with as good of an exit strategy as any.

Trevor flicked his stub onto the asphalt. As much as he wanted to let all the fears inside him come pouring out, the moment he opened the faucet, he wasn't sure he'd be able to shut it again.

"So, what are you going to do with your freedom?" Kieran asked, the careful edge to his voice drawing Trevor's attention at once.

Trevor arched a brow. "What freedom? Your insane optimism in the face of impossible odds is admirable, Ky. Chances are, we'll either end up part of Alberich's collection or bloodstains his brownie crew will be mopping off the marble floors."

"Your ever-present cynicism aside, what are your plans?" he asked, persistence still there.

Trevor met Kieran's gaze, knowing what his friend was fishing for. "Don't do me the disservice of asking if I'll leave. I may have started this band with you as a way to stay on the run, but I love playing, and this band is my family. I've never known a home like the one we created, and I won't give that up for anything."

Kieran nodded, looking away from him on purpose, as if the asshole could hide his eyes getting glassy. Ky let out a stream of smoke and stared at the night sky glittering with more lights than Vegas could hope to compete with. "Good," he said, his voice thick with feeling. "That's good."

Trevor's anxiousness stuttered for a moment, and warmth permeated through to the part of him that had grown so damn Arctic. He cuffed Kieran in the shoulder. "Don't worry, we're all going to die tonight anyway."

Ky rolled his eyes, and Liz and Jett strode out of the RV to join them. Renn trailed close behind, the bruises clear around his wrists and along his neck. He'd shown up at the RV looking like he'd gotten fully worked over, and the wry grin and glint in his eyes told everything—not like it was long before he started in on all the unwanted details.

"Our levels of co-dependency are teetering on the unhealthy range," Jett drawled as he picked his fingernails with the edge of one of his throwing knives. "I mean, we sing together, live together, and eat together. They fuck together," he said, jerking a thumb at Liz and Kieran, "and we've done a bit too much fighting together as of late. I'm just saying, let's skip doing the whole six-feet-under thing together."

Kieran shook his head, finishing his cigarette

before Renn could pluck it from his fingers. "You lot are so morose. We're just going to rile up Alberich's manor a little, cause some chaos. If anything, that's our specialty."

"Your words," Liz said, pointing a finger to him as she strode by. "Come on, boys, we have a leannan sidhe to save."

Trevor pushed up from the side of the RV and loped behind her. His heart was a hummingbird inside his chest, and his mouth turned to sandpaper, but his legs were moving forward. Each step brought him closer and closer to his old master's manor, the place where he'd spent years behind bars, enslaved in a cage.

Yet each step brought him even closer to grasping at the freedom that had eluded him for so long.

And each step brought him closer to her.

Chapter Twenty-Two

Danica kicked the bars for the dozenth time in the past couple of hours. Not like they budged in the slightest, but if she didn't try, she'd be liable to burst out of her own skin.

"If I knew you were going to be this annoying, I would've requested a separate cage," Lenora muttered, leaning against the bars. She stared at the ceiling far out of their grasp. "I can feel the reverberations every time you do that."

Danica leveled a stare at her sister. "Then don't lean against the bars like you've been languishing in a cell for the last century."

Lenora lifted a brow as well as her finger. "What spacious section am I to get my jazzercize on in? This miniscule corner, or that one?" To prove her point, Lenora slumped even farther, edging her sneaker out to knock against Danica's ankle.

Danica sighed, tracing the bar with her fingertip, searching for any type of nicks or weakness in the metal. No one had come to visit since Crags appeared, and she warred between wanting them away versus needing someone else to swing by lest she go insane. Besides, if a guard got close enough, maybe she could dig her nails into their carotid.

"Just chill for a second, D," Lenora said, kicking her in the ankle again. "It won't kill you."

Danica crossed her arms over her chest. "When in the history of our relationship have you ever seen me chill?" She slumped beside Lenora, giving her sister a willful glare. "I've got to figure a way out of here."

"Good luck," rasped a spriggan from the cage

nearest to them who was a mottled mixture of grotesque and wild, like many of the Unseelie. His eyes gleamed gold, and his long legs and arms were twisted branches, which he hugged tight to himself in the small cage he sat inside. "Most of us have been here for years, some decades. Alberich keeps a tight clench on his toys."

"I'm no one's toy," Danica responded on instinct, even as fear clutched her heart with icy fingers. Right now, she clung to gossamer strands of hope that Trevor and the others delivered the mirror to Kincaid. That the CEO would even uphold his end of the deal. So much hinged on trusting others that a graveyard chill settled deep in her heart with the realization. Alberich had locked her up. She had become part of the menagerie.

"Ignore him," Lenora responded, elbowing her in the side. "We have more important things to discuss."

Danica heaved a sigh, combing her fingers through her coiffed hair. In a little while, she'd be as bedraggled and worn as the others in here, all her niceties of living free stripped away. "What's so important?" she asked, swinging her gaze over to her sister. Even though Danica spent her entire life protecting Lenora and getting her out of trouble, she recognized her little sister did the same in her own way.

Lenora had always protected her heart. Her sister drew her out when Danica threatened to turn as brittle as the autumn leaves.

"I'd like to know who's snared your interest enough to take a risk on them," Lenora responded. "I know you too well. Someone in this band must be important to you. Otherwise, you would've found a way to nab the mirror and run."

Danica let out a reluctant breath. She hated to think of herself as that self-serving, but Lenora was right. Unless someone managed to navigate the hedge maze she hid her trust behind, she could double cross with the best of them. The moment someone navigated through to steal her heart though? Well, only two people in her life had managed to thus far.

"The guitarist," she murmured, staring at the bars above them. "He's the one I initially approached when I got into trouble, because he used to be here, in these cages." Admitting it out loud prickled her skin with vulnerability, but if she could share this with anyone, it would be her sister.

"Alberich kept him locked up?" Lenora asked. Her sister's eyes held a soft warmth that made Danica's insides twist.

Talking about Trevor poured battery acid on an open wound after the way she'd escaped in the morning without telling him. Chances were, her disappearance corroded every good memory he still had of her.

"Yeah, for years. He was here for so long it did irreparable damage on him," Danica said, remembering the haunted looks in his gaze and the vigilant twitch of his muscles at the slightest sounds. Only a few times had she witnessed him unencumbered and free, and she treasured all of them. She glanced to her sister, her throat tightening. She and Lenora would end up scarred like that. If all of her well-laid plans shattered like glass in a storm, the way they inevitably would, a life in captivity would ruin them both.

"I'm so sorry," Danica mouthed, her words coming out a whisper. Everything she'd been holding back came rushing to the surface, those weathered boards splintering as they broke. "I did this to us."

Lenora's hand settled over hers, and she squeezed tight. "We've been running ever since our parents sold us off, D. I'm just glad I'm not here alone." Her sister should've been crying, should've been terrified, but a serenity descended around her, damnable calm. Danica had sat with her through so many tears, had stroked her hair and held on tight. Yet today, their roles reversed.

A couple of hot tears streamed down Danica's cheeks, ones she hated. She was the big sister, the one who needed to remain steel strong. But being around Lenora had that accursed effect on her of drawing out the emotions she'd buried tight. She hadn't allowed herself to cry from the moment she left Trevor behind and hadn't allowed herself to grieve the sentence of the locked away life she'd spent a lifetime trying to avoid.

She wiped the liquid away, rubbing it out of her cheeks as if she could erase the fact she ever shed a tear. Danica ran a finger along the cold bar beside her, drawing in the chill as she evened her breaths.

"Hey, if he's good enough for you to fall for, guaranteed he'll be busting down these doors to get you back," Lenora said, hope shining in her eyes that Danica could no longer feel.

"Yeah, or he'll check in with his common sense and realize he needs to be as far away from this place as possible." She yearned for Trevor to come as much as she feared his return to these loathsome halls.

"Okay, Pessimistic Polly, we're going to languish in these cells for the next century, and then die miserable deaths. Happy now?" Lenora shot back.

"Overjoyed."

The whisper of footsteps from the other side of the ballroom drew her attention at once. With the waning day, chandeliers cast low-light throughout the room, bringing shadows to the fore. Mirrors along the walls reflected so many bars from the cages where she and the other fae were displayed like statues. From across the patterned tile came a figure that made her blood pressure spike on sight.

Whatever murmurs coursed through the ballroom shut off like water from a faucet. Tymarch Alberich marched in, the shadows carving into the forest green hue of his skin, deepening the crimson of his eyes, and amplifying the cruel lines of his face. He headed toward them, which could only mean trouble.

Danica pushed herself from the ground to stand in front of the bars. "About time you paid me a visit," she called out, baiting the bastard. "I make a pretty miserable pet. Need to be fed about sixteen times a day, or I'll just pass right out."

"Where's the mirror," Alberich said upon approach, disregarding her comment.

Danica shrugged. "We all have our hardships. You, a missing mirror, me, being stuck in this damned cage. Life's not fair."

His brows narrowed. The eyes reflecting back at her were the same red as the blood he'd spilled, far too many bodies to count. Danica lifted her chin and thrust it forward. She should be quaking in her heels, but he'd done the worst by sentencing her to this imprisonment. Any other threats fell like dried petals to be crushed underfoot.

More footsteps sounded through the ballroom as three of his redcap thugs approached, the weight of them causing the crystal drops on the chandeliers to tremble.

"I'll give you one more chance," Alberich's voice carried menace that didn't sink beneath her skin. "Where's the mirror?"

Danica lifted a hand and waved it around three turns before she flipped her middle finger up. "Your guess is as good as mine, buddy. Does the arrival of your goon squad mean I get to go on a walk?"

Alberich didn't answer. He nodded to the redcaps who'd accumulated around their cage, already beginning to unlock the door. Her heart pounded harder, but she cast a look to Lenora, trying to convey all the bravery she could muster.

Before she could say another word, meaty hands shot into the cage to pull her out. She stumbled forward, the redcaps tugging her across the polished tiles of the ballroom. Alberich strode ahead, his gaze focused as he ignored her existence. This disregard was one of the ways he broke his prisoners here. As she crossed this massive ballroom, the hollowed stares of all the different fae in cages burned into her. The pity in their glances chilled her like a winter's day.

The redcaps pulled her through one of the side doors, and they entered an ornate hallway, peach lighting glowing with a rustic hue. Landscape paintings decorated the walls, and a paisley carpet stretched the entire length. Alberich marched in the lead, heading straight for a door at the end of the hall, one painted crimson with a dull iron knob. The mere sight caused her skin to prickle, like it was an office plucked straight from the far reaches of her nightmares.

Her mouth dried, but she opened it anyway. "How often do we get to go on walks in this joint? I didn't get the full rundown on pet protocol when you guys gave me the super warm introductory meeting. Do we get extra treats if we perform tricks?" Even as the sarcasm rolled out of her mouth, it coated her tongue in bitterness.

"Winter's breath, you're mouthy," the redcap behind her muttered, giving a push forward.

She almost lost her footing—not like it mattered with the vice grip Thing 1 and 2 had on her wrists. "I was lucky enough to inherit the gift of the gab, so I figure it better be put to use."

"We'll loosen your tongue soon enough," the

redcap at her side responded, his teeth glinting when he revealed a jagged smile.

Danica maintained a grin when she looked at him, even though her stomach twisted. Before she could say anything else, Alberich already opened the door with a resounding creak and entered. Her fingers threatened to tremble, but she willed them steady.

The redcaps pushed her into a simple room, all concrete floors, walls, and ceiling. A couple of bulbs hung overhead, casting paltry beams in here, and a single chair sat in the center of the room. Her heart plummeted to the floor at the sight. The metal chair featured a lot of mottled and shiny spots where they must've taken chemicals to clean the surface.

Within seconds, they dragged her over, which was fine by her, because her legs didn't seem to want to work anymore.

"So, we're resorting to torture now?" Danica said, forcing herself to speak. At this moment, talking kept the overwhelming, writhing darkness at bay. "Ever since I entered this manor, it's been one new experience after another. First, my stay in a cage, and now we're entering the torture part of boot camp. I'll be ready to take on the whole Otherworld after this retreat."

If anything, her words had them slamming her into the chair that much harder. Danica's palms began to sweat, and they bound her wrists to each of the chair arms. Her nails settled against pre-carved grooves in the metal, ones that didn't instill her with confidence of making it out of here alive. The light over her highlighted all the dirt streaks along her forearms, the slight pebbling of goosebumps, and the white of her knuckles as she gripped tight.

"Since you can't give an answer the civil way, we've been reduced to this route," Alberich said, rolling up his sleeves, as if he might do any of the dirty work here. Danica soaked in the room, the big workstation at the end, featuring far too many drawers, the scuffs in the floor from where this chair must've slammed or been dragged around—anywhere but the monster who'd hurt so many people.

A shadow coated her as one of the redcaps stepped before her, his meaty fingers wrapping around her pinky. Danica's heels dug into the concrete when she reared back, but there was nowhere to go. She was strapped to this chair.

"Where is the mirror?" Alberich repeated.

Rage bloomed in Danica, something raw and furious, a blaze she couldn't contain. "Your guess is as good as mine," she forced out, keeping her tone level.

The redcap bent her finger back, until—

Snap.

She saw white, but when she dropped back into her own body, that's when the pain arrived. Her teeth hurt at the sheer agony rolling through from such a tiny spot, and her stomach spasmed. Bile rose in her throat, but she choked it down. Her finger screamed, the nauseating pain reverberating all the way up her arm.

A knock sounded on the door.

Alberich strode over to greet a selkie dressed in all-black butler's attire. Danica blinked the liquid out of her eyes to get a better sight. She could barely force herself to swallow while the two of them murmured in a low exchange. Alberich let out a sharp breath as he turned toward the redcaps, keeping his hand on the door.

"I need to attend to some business. Kylar, you stay to keep watch over her. Samuel, Liere, follow me. We'll continue this later."

With that, the other two redcaps departed after him, and the door clicked shut, the sound echoing around the room.

That left her with the redcap who'd just broken her finger looming over. His mouth twisted in a wide smile, one revealing those jagged, jagged teeth. Danica was going to be sick.

Chapter Twenty-Three

Fremont Casino and Hotel was in full swing this time of night.

Trevor led the approach toward the jangling sounds of the slots as people gambled away everything from their pennies to life's savings. Overhead, a large tunnel stretched the entire length of the street, neon lights shifting above in even patterns, all fuchsias and sapphires. The crowds had grown so thick around here they could barely take a couple of steps forward without jostling someone else's elbows. Trevor carved through with purpose.

When he'd lived in Alberich's manor, the entrance had been in a different part of the globe, but he knew what to look for. The red, rusted door that looked like a utility entrance.

"Are you sure we should be marching through the front door?" Liz leaned in to ask him as they sliced their way through the crowds.

"No other way to get in," Trevor responded, scanning the walls of the casino. With all the flashing overhead lights of the red overhang and the big screen between the words Fremont and Casino, distraction came easily. Jett slipped past them to weave through the throngs of drunk assholes with a skill he envied. The siren could stealth like no one else.

Jett veered toward the right side of the casino, and Trevor quickened his pace, smacking errant elbows and arms out of his way. Most of the crowds milled outside with drinks, laughing and chatting. The people here floated on the ease of vacation, so far away from the nerves prickling his skin, the alertness in the back of his throat, and the slight sickness past memories brought with every step closer.

From along the side of the wall, Trevor caught sight of the door. While the rest of his body screamed to stop, his legs carried him forward faster. Panic clawed at his throat, but he'd already committed himself to the task, even if it sank into his stomach like a peach pit. They were going to march into Alberich's manor and find Danica. If he was truly lucky, they might escape alive.

If he wasn't, he'd end up behind those bars again.

He passed Jett, his gaze focused on the door as he walked with a purpose the others would have to just follow. The grim reality of their endeavor coated his bones in lead, and each breath he took in sliced like razor blades. The blinking lights, the chatter, and pinging bells all faded into his peripheral. All that existed was his former prison.

Trevor reached the door too fast. He wasn't ready, and yet, his hand gripped tight on the knob like he might turn it.

"We're behind you," Kieran announced, his presence and familiar voice grounding him. "Let's go ruin Alberich's fancy manor."

Trevor tugged the door open, even though his throat tightened. Each breath came shallower than the last. Darkness stretched before him—at least until he crossed the threshold to the Otherworld.

Danica waited inside, and she needed help. Time to stop running and to face his fears.

Trevor sucked in a deep breath and entered.

The threshold to the Otherworld rippled around him, binding like plastic wrap across his skin as he strode inside. At once, he entered a familiar hallway, a presence that marched across his shoulders like millipedes. He scuffed his muddy boots on the velvet runner traveling the length, taking small satisfaction at the smears he left. Trevor's hands balled into fists as he continued down the hall, waiting, waiting, waiting. Any moment, one of Alberich's retinue would appear, either to fight them off or escort them forward—in entering his abode, they'd essentially rang the doorbell.

Footsteps clattered behind him.

Trevor didn't even have the chance to spin around before Renn charged past, his boots slamming against the polished floor and his head down, horns pointed. Kieran galloped by a moment later, letting out a giddy whoop before he leaned over to smack one of the paintings on the wall. It teetered to the side, almost crashing to the ground.

Jett surged beside him, his hands slipping into his pockets. "This is your fault, you know," he murmured, casting an irritated glance to the way Kieran and Renn gallivanted down the hall. "We could have left them behind, but no, we had to bring the two loudest people in existence."

Even though his nerves buzzed to the point he could barely hear anything else, Trevor couldn't help the grin twitching on his lips. "Alberich knew we'd arrived the second we stepped through the door. Might as well make a little noise."

"Come on, Jettsy," Liz said, slipping her arm through his. He wrinkled his nose at her nickname, the disgust clear by the curl of his lip. "Let loose," she continued, her hazel eyes glittering with amusement. "Have a little fun."

These halls should've terrified him. They should've paralyzed him faster than a strike of lightning. Yet, surrounded by his friends, his family, and his home—these people gave him the bravery to keep going.

To laugh, even in the halls of his old prison.

A crash sounded ahead, and Trevor whipped out a dagger.

A porcelain vase lay in splinters on the floor while Renn stood beside it, lifting his hands in clear guilt. Kieran continued racing past him, arms flailing out and the huge grin on his face revealing his fangs. They'd reached the center of the hallway at this point.

His shoulders relaxed a fraction—at least, until his gaze traveled to the end of the corridor.

Two naga emerged, slithering in their direction at top speed. The snake-like creatures whipped around their tails behind them, claws flashing on their extended fingers, and serpentine gazes unblinking. Trevor didn't open his mouth to call out—he bolted forward. Liz and Jett took the cue. Not like he needed to worry about Renn or Kieran who always brimmed for a scrap.

The air shifted behind him.

Trevor skidded to a halt before whipping around. A hobgoblin blinked into existence, teeth bared and dark eyes screwed tight with anger. He recognized those eyes. That creature had been in Alberich's retinue for longer than he'd been caged. His heart slammed hard in his chest, a mix of adrenaline and terror at the sheer sight of his face in this place. Trevor slashed forward with his dagger before the creature could even open its mouth. The hobgoblin stumbled back, and his dagger missed the lumpy, mottled skin by an inch. Trevor lunged in again, closer this time.

His dagger sliced against the hobgoblin's shoulder, biting into flesh. Green liquid trailed along his blade where it cut. Before Trevor could dart away, the hobgoblin exposed its teeth and launched forward to rake with its claws. The tips snagged against Trevor's sleeve as it dragged down. However, he loomed over this creature who had once been a blight from his past.

"I'm not in chains now," was all Trevor said as he lunged forward again. His blade made a neat slice across the hobgoblin's throat. The creature stared at him for a single moment, frozen in time, until liquid poured from the open wound. Alberich's crony let out a gurgle as he staggered forward, groping with those clawed hands.

The hobgoblin hit the floor. Trevor spun around. Liz and Jett continued on, launching themselves into the fray against the two naga Kieran and Renn fought. As much as their gang pulled the Scooby Doo run more often than they fought, Kieran made bar brawls his business, and Renn liked to ruin things for fun. With Liz standing back and firing her platinum-tipped bullets into the fray, the naga didn't stand a chance.

Liz pumped another bullet into the one closest to her, and Kieran lunged in to throw his arms right around its neck. The naga writhed around, whipping back and forth, but the incubus who had ridden his fair share of mechanical bulls in bars held on tight. Liz aimed another shot, this one straight for the gut. As the slug burrowed in, the naga reared back, almost throwing Kieran off.

"Hey," he shouted to Liz. "Don't get me killed in the process." His arm wrapped around the creature's neck, and a snap followed.

"Then don't make it so tempting," Liz called, a grin on her lips. Trevor skidded to a halt in front of them right as Renn thrust his horns into their naga's stomach. Jett slipped a knife in on the other side, his hand flickering with the speed he peppered the cuts. Blackish blood poured out of them, and Renn wrinkled his nose when he pulled away, flecks of the blood matting his hair and sprinkling across his cheeks like freckles.

"Let's keep going," Trevor said, his heart an accelerated thump-thump-thump in his chest. "Follow me." After all, he knew these halls like the strings of his guitar, no matter how hard he tried to forget them. Down the right turn lay Alberich's personal corridors, but they were looking for the left. That route, they'd find the ballroom where Alberich kept his menagerie.

The scent of lemon polish lingered in these halls, making him want to gag. He led the others through the narrow corridor, trying to ignore the way his fingers were still sticky with the blood of the hobgoblin. More would follow.

They hadn't gotten paces down the one hallway when the clip of footsteps came from farther in.

Two redcaps whipped around the corner, followed by a face he saw in his nightmares. The same arrogant features twisted in a sneer. The same blood-darkened eyes. He even wore a similar tailored suit to the ones he always donned during Trevor's time here.

Tymarch Alberich.

Trevor's heart stopped cold in his chest. This was the man who'd turned him into an object. This was the man who'd kept him behind bars for far too long. This was the man who'd darkened his future until he'd fumbled blind out of this place and continued to do so for years after. His palms broke into a cold sweat, and he forgot how to breathe.

Both groups skidded to a halt at the sight of each other. However, the seconds their eyes locked gave Alberich the advantage.

"Rally to me," Alberich called, projecting his voice down the hallway. Any moment, the other mercenaries would come rushing to his aid. The man employed more fighters than the King, and he had the cash to ensure their loyalty.

Kieran rushed past him. "Looking for another black eye, Alberich?"

Trevor hadn't forgotten about the encounter in the Lotus Garden when they'd last seen Alberich. He'd lost control and began mutating into the form he rarely used. Kieran had stood up for him then, even in the face of an entire casino full of Unseelie who wanted to claim the bounty Alberich put over his head. At once, a similar transition took hold as his limbs stretched longer, his skin greying to the ash of a cremation. Within seconds, he towered over the other bandmates.

Liz cast him a nervous glance, but she nodded.

Jett slapped him on the back. "Go get him, bruiser."

Trevor soaked in their support, and he bolted forward, chasing after Kieran. He hadn't gone a couple of steps before the clamor of others approaching rose from behind.

"Keep going," Jett called out. "We've got this covered."

Trevor surged forward, the force of his steps reverberating up his shins. His entire body vibrated with unspent tension—like this, he became death in the breeze.

A call bubbled in the back of his throat, and for the first time in years, his screech erupted from his throat with the full fury of his kind. The scream reverberated around the halls, rattling the paintings along the walls and resonating through his entire body to his bones. The sound undulated until his throat dried and his body ached as he poured every last ounce of energy into the wail. It trailed off, the echoes carrying through the corridor. The sound soaked into the very stones of this place. His gaze hadn't left Alberich once as he let out a death cry.

For the first time, his former master's eyes reflected true fear.

Kieran crashed into the first of the redcaps, his

fist cocked and sailing toward the big bastard's jaw. Trevor reached for his knife, pulling the still wet blade out as he swerved toward Alberich who'd begun backing away.

Before Trevor could let his blade swing, the other redcap stepped in the way. The steel trap of a hand wrapped around his wrist, and the guy yanked him forward. He was all limbs at this point as he staggered past the redcap, trying to stay steady on his feet. The redcap pivoted around, and his fist popped right into view.

Too fast to dodge.

The redcap's fist slammed right into his solar plexus. Trevor's vision tunneled for a moment, and the breath flew out of him. He wheezed, unable to draw in air as he sagged down. All he could do was toss his hands up in defense. The fists thudded against his forearms when he tried to force a breath. His chest felt like someone dropped a stick of dynamite inside.

Trevor stumbled a few paces until the first breath splintered through him and his vision returned to normal. The redcap already charged for him, sharp gray teeth bared and dripping in crimson. Trevor dodged out of the way by an inch.

A shout came from behind him, followed by the bark of Liz's Beretta. He chanced a single glance back. Two rakshasas, another redcap, and another naga arrived on the scene. Jett, Renn, and Liz were doing their best, but these brutal professionals had the odds now.

The redcap's fist veered toward him again. Trevor ducked out of the way, another close call. His heart slammed in his chest. He moved around at an accelerated speed in this form, his longer limbs allowing him greater reach. Amid the chaos, Alberich vanished, which was just like the cowardly bastard. He'd always leave the bloodstains and bruises to those he paid to protect him.

Some thread in Trevor's chest snapped, an urgency driving him to the offensive. Alberich couldn't escape again. Not after everything he'd done. Not after Trevor risked his freedom to return.

The redcap's fist sped his way again, but this time he stayed still. Before the punch landed, Trevor snapped out and gripped the guy's wrist. He yanked forward, pulling the same move the redcap had on him—except, he followed through. The second the redcap stumbled forward, Trevor's knee slammed him right in the chest.

Before the redcap could recover, Trevor's fists thudded into him again and again and again. He moved like a machine, unable to dispel the images thundering through him of the endless nights where he'd stare at the bars above him and hoped. Or the nights those hopes died and he'd floated through on a cloud of numbness, hours turning into days turning into years.

He focused on the redcap before him, only to realize blood covered his fists. Trevor continued punching, even after the guy's eyes had rolled into the back of his head.

Trevor let the redcap drop, and he hit the ground with a thud. Kieran wrestled around with the other redcap, limbs whipping around as both of them took their fair share of lumps. Liz fired at the encroaching naga, doing her best to dodge out of the way as the creature slithered closer to her. Renn and Jett stood back to back, fighting against the two rakshasa and the redcap determined to make their lives miserable.

More footsteps thundered from the direction they'd entered.

Trevor's heart plummeted to the tundra depths of Winter's Realm.

"Devil be damned," scraped past his lips as he whipped around to face whatever new threat approached.

Three centaurs appeared at the far end of the hall with matching grim expressions. The King's cavalry had arrived.

Chapter Twenty-Four

The seconds felt like hours, and who knew, maybe they were. Danica stared down her prison guard who strode back and forth in front of the door, getting more restless as time passed. Her pinky throbbed with a distracting pulse that had her clenching her teeth so hard she tasted copper.

"You know," she said between her gritted teeth, "if you loosened these bonds, we could get ourselves a nice game of cards going while we wait. I've been known to play a mean game of pinochle."

The redcap glowered at her from where he waited by the door. "If you don't shut up soon, I'll do the trick for you," he muttered. "We've got duct tape somewhere around here."

Danica's mind started whirring into overdrive, sparked to life by the statement.

"Come on now, and miss out on the pleasant sound of my voice?" she continued, goading him on. "You wouldn't deprive yourself of that, now would you? If you like, I've got a half dozen limericks memorized. I could recite them."

The redcap let out a grunt and stalked toward the desk. Her heart pounded faster in her chest, but she continued. "There once was an old man in a tree, who was horribly bored by a bee."

The redcap marched forward, duct tape in hand and a doomsday expression on his face. Her breaths sharpened as she waited. Closer. This might be her one shot.

"When they said, 'does it buzz?" she continued. A foot away.

The redcap leaned an inch away from her face, fiddling with the duct tape. "He replied yes it does," she said, right as she slammed her head forward. Her skull thwacked against his with a thud that echoed around the room. Danica used the force to tilt her entire body forward, sending the iron chair tipping. She rocked back, and then vaulted forward again, right as the redcap clapped his hand to his temple.

The iron chair came crashing forward with her still strapped to it, as the entire weight crashed on top of the redcap. The wind rushed out from her chest, and her head conked against the floor with a force that made her wince as the chair tumbled off to the side. The redcap pushed himself from the floor, blood smeared across his face and several cuts accumulated along his arms.

Danica leaned against the floor. Fuck. She'd exhausted her one mode of attack, and now the big bastard was pissed.

"Then some more bullshit about a bee," she finished the limerick, testing the restraints around her wrists. Still on tight. The redcap loomed over her, his shoulders heaving with rage, and a sickening glow in his eyes. He bared his teeth as if to display what would be sinking into her flesh in mere minutes. She tensed her calves—they'd made a mistake when they didn't bind them.

The second he came close enough, she'd at least get a final kick in before he ripped her to shreds.

His shadow careened over her. Sweat trickled down her neck, dripping to the floor. Her pinky throbbed something fierce, a reminder she couldn't even form a fist right now. Her calves twitched at the ready.

The door flung open with a resounding bang.

Danica faced the wall, so she couldn't see who'd entered. "Alberich, if you do happen to find the mirror, you can shove it right up your ass."

"D?"

The voice made her heart stop still. She had to be dreaming. The redcap's shadow shifted away from her as he approached the intruder. From behind her, all she could hear was the shuffle of footsteps, then the thump of fists to flesh. The snick of a blade being drawn. Danica shifted from side to side in the seat, trying to rock the chair over in the other direction.

She needed to see if he had arrived.

A low grunt sounded, followed by the scrape of shoes on concrete. Danica got the chair rocking back and forth, trying to use the swing of her legs to bring it teetering over to the other side. She got closer, enough that it swayed up to clang down on the concrete again. As the two fought out of view behind her, she continued funneling every ounce of energy into swinging the chair around. Each time she got the chair to swerve higher, she tugged at the restraints around her wrist, trying to loosen the bonds more and more.

Finally, Danica got enough momentum. The chair swung around to the opposite side and her with it. As she crashed to the ground, her head bounced against the concrete, again. She tasted blood at this point. The cords around her wrists had loosened enough to almost pull her hands from them, even though her wrists chafed. As she pulled at the fraying bonds, she glanced to where the redcap fought.

They moved too fast to gauge from her floor-level vantage point. Yet she knew that voice. She kept the memories of what he'd said to her in his silken tone buried deep in an impenetrable part of her heart. Danica focused on rocking her wrists back and forth even though the cords scraped across her sensitive skin.

Blood sprayed against the concrete in front of her,

and Danica froze.

The redcap swayed on his feet before crashing to the ground. The thud as he hit trembled through the whole room. A second later, his opponent crouched in front of her.

As soon as her eyes met his, it didn't matter if his form was stretched out and gaunt like the time in the Lotus Garden, or that his skin had turned ashen—she knew that soft, haunted gaze.

"I've got you," he said, bringing out his blade to free her from the cords. His presence was a warm blanket on a winter's night, and a breath of relief shuddered from her. As he slipped those large hands around to help her up from the toppled chair, she sank into his embrace, drawing in the scent of hickory and leather, of him, amidst the tinny blood. By the time she straightened with him, Trevor had returned to a normal height, and his skin transitioned back to his normal golden brown.

Danica leaned against him, her legs shaking so hard she could barely stand. He braced her with his hands wrapped around her waist, and it wasn't a minute before his lips found hers. She kissed him with the force and fury of everything she'd restrained all this time. Trevor had come for her. She'd taken the leap, and he hadn't let her down. Heat stung her eyes as she savored the sweet taste of him, as she forgot the bitterness of her fear and basked in the sharp joy of the adoration she felt for this stunning survivor of a man.

Danica could keep kissing him forever, mesmerized by the rhythm he whispered on her lips, a motion that carried the words they both couldn't communicate. However, her sister remained in a cage, and if Trevor had arrived, the rest of the band must be here too, stirring up chaos.

When she pulled back, he stared into her eyes

with this searching, worried look that broke her heart.

"Hey," she murmured, running the fingertips of her good hand along his cheek, his chin, needing to feel the smooth touch of his skin. His palms felt like fire through the flimsy layer of clothing, and she willingly burned. "He didn't ruin me. Just don't touch my pinky."

Trevor lifted her damaged hand, scanning over the mutilated pinky. Danica winced at the movement. His expression darkened with a rage that belonged to drunk-driving accidents and lonely screams down dark alleys.

"Alberich's going to die," Trevor growled, even as he remained gentle with her hand, helping lower it back by her side.

"How the hell did you guys make it past his dozens of hired heads?" Danica asked, her brows furrowing in confusion. Their band was meant more for bar brawls than fights against mercenaries.

"Kincaid must've delivered on his deal," Trevor said, weaving his fingers through the ones on her good hand as he tugged her towards the door. "The King's men showed up searching for Alberich. They want to lock him up, which means we're running out of time if we want to get to him first. While I can hope we ruined him for good, who knows what Kincaid pulled, or what Alberich might be able to buy his way out of. I can't risk that monster living another day."

"Ditto," Danica said, following him when they exited the room. Her gaze drifted down the hall to the ballroom she'd been dragged from. Lenora would still be inside there, but if fights broke out all around them, her sister would be safest behind bars right now. "Where do you think he would've gone?"

"He's looking to escape unnoticed," Trevor said, his jaw thrust forward and those dark eyes flashing with determination. "There's only one place he'd be heading."

Before, she'd felt hope ripped away like roots from the ground, but as they strode down the hall hand in hand, it all rushed back. Resolve flooded through her, the drive to fight—not just for her sister, but for her own future, one that would contain Trevor Arceneaux. He led them in a different direction than the ballroom, a left hand turn along one corridor, and then a sharp right.

"Thanks, Trev," she murmured beside him, squeezing his hand.

He didn't look her way, but he nodded in response. "We're going to have a long talk when we leave here about the fact you lied about your sister getting kidnapped. And then I'm stealing you away for the next century or so."

Danica swallowed hard, her throat tightening with emotion. As much as she hated the vulnerability that emerged around her sister and Trevor, they'd both earned their places in her life a thousand times over. "Yeah, I deserve that."

"Don't think I didn't understand what you did though," he said, his voice softening, even as he focused on guiding them down the hall. "I trust you, D."

She sucked in a sharp breath, annoying liquid rising to her eyes. When she was done here, she'd remove her tear ducts so the traitorous bastards couldn't pull this shit on her. "I trust you too," was all she could manage. To the two of them who'd spent their entire lives avoiding attachments, who'd been burned bad early on, trust meant more than love. They passed the open door of a kitchen, the bright fluorescent light spilling out onto the hallway. Danica tugged on Trevor's arm. "Where are you leading us?"

"The servant's entrance. It's meant to keep the lowly members of his staff out of sight and out of mind," Trevor said, his long legs in undulating movement as he quickened his pace. "It also makes the perfect place to escape unseen while the King combs his manor."

Up ahead, the corridor ended at a massive silver door.

As they approached, Danica's nerves simmered, then boiled. Her pinky throbbed, her heart ached, and conviction tightened her throat. When they arrived in front of the door, they came to a halt. Danica leaned forward, pressing her ear against the cool surface. From inside the room she could hear light shuffling, the scrape of footsteps.

"Well, someone's inside," she mouthed, meeting his eyes.

Trevor may as well have been vibrating with the way the air around him buzzed. His gaze sharpened, and his breaths steadied, a pulse she could feel between their locked palms.

She met his gaze. "No stupid risks," she whispered. "We're both making it out of here alive."

His lips narrowed into a thin line, and for a moment, her heart lurched like she'd slammed the brakes. Except he then squeezed her hand tight and nodded before pulling his away. Trevor rested his palm on the knob.

He tugged the door open.

Unlike the other opulent rooms in this manor, the mudroom featured slate tiles along the floor, plain russet walls, and a stack of wooden shelves lined with a cluttered mess of tools and bags. Coats hung from a rack, an array of muddy shoes beneath it, leaving streaks along the floor. A large eggshell-white door lay on the opposite side of the room, and two figures approached the exit, one dressed in his finest on-the-run suit, the other half his size and hobbling along.

"Take another step forward and I'll bury this

dagger into your back, Alberich," Trevor called from the doorway. He aimed the blade in hand, his forearms tensed and ready.

Both Alberich and Crags froze mid-step.

For the first time since she'd met the man, he wasn't surrounded by a crowd of cohorts set to do his bidding. No, those cronies barred the way between the King's men and his escape.

"Come and face me, Alberich," Trevor said. "I won't stab a man in the back, even if he's no better than naga spit."

"Crags," Danica warned as the brownie turned around first. The hunched over man stared at her with resonant terror glowing in his beady eyes. "If you want to survive this, step away. This man isn't worth saving." She had his attention, so she rolled her dice. "The King's men have arrived. If he isn't dead by our hand, they'll kill him next."

Slowly, Alberich turned around to face them.

His mouth was pinched, and he kept his chin thrust forward as if it might shield the fear gleaming in those crimson eyes. Even in the wake of his obvious dread, his brows bled nobility, and his posture remained in that rigid aristocratic stance. Alberich reached to his side for whatever weapon he hid. Guaranteed, the man hadn't attempted to flee without any.

Trevor strode forward, keeping his steps even and his dagger pointed at Alberich in case the man tried to bolt for the door. His gaze swept over his former master while his lips pressed in a calculating twist.

Danica didn't want to fight Crags, but if he leapt in defense of his master, she wouldn't have the choice. She clenched her fist, following close behind Trevor. After a mere day of Alberich's treatment and the countless justifications she'd made in the name of survival, she understood the brownie more than she wanted to. As their eyes met, years of the same fear reflected back. He tilted his head in the slightest of nods.

Trevor stood mere steps away from Alberich, who hadn't budged.

That's when Crags leapt onto Alberich from behind, the brownie's dark eyes wild. His mottled nails sank into Alberich's throat as he attempted to strangle his master. Crags' gaze locked onto Trevor's.

"Here's your chance," was all the brownie managed to squeeze out before Alberich grabbed him from behind. His eyes were desperate, pleading even as the poor creature winced. Alberich latched around Crags' neck and gave a vicious twist.

The snap rang audible through the room.

Chapter Twenty-Five

Trevor could only watch as the life blinked out of his former cellmate's eyes.

For years, he'd been disgusted by Crags, his cowardice, and the fact he remained with Alberich even after he had been offered an escape. However, in watching the fragile life snuffed like a twig crunched underfoot, Trevor understood.

Edge-of-a-precipice terror had kept Crags in line, yet in his final moments, he'd shown more bravery than Trevor did all those years running. He'd sacrificed his life to offer them the chance for retribution.

Trevor was closing the distance between them before Alberich's hands ever left Crags' neck.

Bile rose in his throat. His hands began to shake. Free. Free, free, free. The first night after he had escaped, he crouched in the alleyway, long legs pulled to his chin and repeating the word until it scraped against his tongue. Until it rasped in his throat like the resonant hum of his banshee's wail. Until it burned in his chest like a first new breath, like he was reborn.

Crags dropped to the ground, a crumpled heap where once the man had been sharp, those eyes inquisitive. The brownie lay slumped on the floor, his years of service, all the loyalty not amounting to a second glance from the monster who murdered him. No more. Trevor would not let Alberich ruin any more lives.

Alberich stood a foot away, lowering his hands.

Trevor's knife hadn't lowered. The pointed tip of his blade still aimed at his former master's skull. However, if he tried to play safe by hurling the knife, it would give Alberich precious few seconds to run. Trevor couldn't waste Crags' sacrifice. He closed the distance between them and swung his executioner's blade down.

Alberich didn't have the time to race out of the way. He dodged back, but the tip of Trevor's knife snagged into the man's fancy suit, ripping right through the crisp lapels. Trevor tugged his blade back. Alberich groped for his side and pulled out a gun. This close, he couldn't miss.

Trevor thrust forward with the knife again, right beneath the ribcage. The tip sank in, past fabric, past flesh even as Alberich tried to swerve back.

Alberich couldn't pivot and shoot, so he fumbled for the trigger. Danica dove in to smack the man's wrist, forcing him to readjust. The leannan sidhe darted back out again, circling and waiting for another opening. Trevor wouldn't stop. Not now. Even if the man shot him right in the gut, he would keep attacking until Alberich fell with him.

Trevor's other hand curled into a fist, and he let it fly. His knuckles slammed against Alberich's jaw, sending the demon reeling. He didn't shake it out. He swung his fist again.

When he'd sat in the cage, Alberich had loomed. His presence stretched throughout this manor until it suffocated. Even after he'd escaped, the man's influence, the pawns his money could buy had the same effect—the shadow that stretched five times as large as the man itself.

However now? This man was shorter than him, less muscled. When you took away all the money and influence, Alberich didn't loom. He cowered. The wet thump sounded through the room as his fist landed home again. Again. Again. The pistol dropped from Alberich's hands to clatter onto the floor as the cruel sidhe bastard tossed his hands up in defense.

Trevor thrust out with his fist, and when Alberich's arms lifted to cover his head, that's when he swung with his blade.

The dagger sank deep into his former master's stomach, and Trevor dragged it across with a sickening squelch. His blood spilled out, along with other fluids that dribbled from the open slice. Alberich staggered back, groping at the open wound like he tried to hold himself together as he looked at Trevor. The wound was a death sentence as sure as Trevor's wail had predicted. They both knew it.

"How … could you?" The words slipped from him, a confused helplessness in them. "You … belong … to me."

Trevor kicked him square in the chest. The man toppled, blood staining his once-pristine suit. Those crimson eyes flickered open and shut. "I never belonged to you," Trevor said, looming over him. "None of us did."

Alberich curled up on the floor, clutching his stomach, as if he could stop the pool of blood fast pouring out from him. Trevor didn't budge, holding his dagger aloft even as it dripped. Alberich's gasping breaths turned to wheezes, until—nothing. The hand gripping his stomach went slack, and those crimson eyes clouded.

Trevor stared at his former master, the man who haunted his nightmares for years. He should feel triumphant. He should feel joy. Yet all that swept over him when he stood over the broken body of the man who had terrorized him was the hollowness of a cemetery. Blood coated the bottoms of his boots, but he didn't budge, unable to look away from the monster who'd caged him for so many years lying dead on the floor.

He should feel safe—yet the ever-present

paranoia dwelled in his veins.

Danica slipped her fingers through his, her touch reaching straight to the heart of him.

"You did it," she murmured, squeezing his palm tight. Trevor dropped his dagger, the metal clattering on the floor. He pulled her forward, drawing her tight to his chest. She leaned against him like she belonged there. Killing Alberich didn't give him the satisfaction he had imagined through the years. However, the scent of lemongrass and the affection gleaming in Danica's green eyes caused his heart to stutter. Like the first bud unfurling after an eternal winter, he felt hope.

"None of that matters," he said, resting his chin on her head. "I've got you. That's the reason I came here."

A couple of wet spots bloomed on his shirt, but he didn't comment. He'd let her keep her pride.

Danica let out a shaky breath. "So, the conversation we had at dinner the other night," she said, diving right into the deep end. She looked up at him, even though her eyes had grown a little glassy. "Are we doing this?"

Trevor dipped down to capture her lips in his. The feel of her in his arms, the honeysuckle taste of her—he basked in these things even as he stood surrounded by the broken bodies of Crags and Alberich, blood leeching into the floor. This kiss was new, gentler somehow, more real in the wake of their threat eliminated. It was a promise.

He broke away, and a grin spread across his face, one he could feel crinkling the corners of his eyes. "I want you, Danica Maslanka. I want you more than I've wanted anything in my entire life. So yeah, if you're game, we're doing this."

She stepped to her tip-toes and pressed a brief

kiss to his lips. Her gaze glittered when she pulled away, a mischievous smile on her face. "I'll have you regretting this in days," she said. "You know I'm a talker, right?"

Trevor arched a brow. "Do you see who I live with, cher?"

"Fair point," she responded. "I'll have to up my attempts in the face of competition."

Her eyes kept meeting his with a shyness he'd never seen before in her. After they'd spent so long dodging around their feelings, he could barely believe they'd reached this point. Devil be damned, after so long running, he could finally stop. Trevor's throat tightened, and he pulled her tight to his chest, letting the gratitude wash over him like warm rain.

They had survived. They survived, and now he could live.

Footsteps sounded from the end of the hallway, drawing their attention to the door.

Trevor leaned down to snag his dagger off the ground. If they were Alberich's hired men, they had no more reason to fight—no one would be paying them. However, he didn't want to risk it against those who lived on a shoot first, talk later approach. Danica's shoulders tensed. The echoing sound of the footsteps grew louder and louder. Whoever approached must've spotted the open door.

Jett burst through the door first, followed by one of the centaurs.

Trevor lowered his dagger, and relief filtered through his veins. "Problem solved, J," he called out, tilting his head in the direction of Alberich who lay lifeless on the ground.

Jett shook his head, true panic alight in his eyes. "Yeah, you haven't heard what Alberich did."

Trevor's stomach dropped. The siren rarely let his

fear show. Jett gave him a subtle look, which he soaked in. The stunt Kincaid pulled must've caused some upset.

"You killed Tymarch Alberich?" the centaur asked, his hooves clipping on the floor as he passed Trevor and Danica to observe the body.

"In self-defense," Trevor claimed, as if that might matter.

"Good," the centaur said. "The traitor was either going to die here, or at the hands of the King."

"What did he do?" Trevor asked, playing dumb. In a way, he didn't have to—while he might've stolen the mirror, he still didn't know the significance of the item they'd handed over to Kincaid. Danica played it cool, not even glancing to him. Whatever they had done, based on the panic in Jett's eyes, he sure as shit wasn't going to own up.

"He had stolen the accords between the Seelie and Unseelie," the King's centaur said, his dark brows furrowing and his gaze filling with a cold fury. "If that wasn't crime enough, he returned the mirror. Broken."

"What does that mean?" Danica asked even as horror descended in her eyes.

The accords had been the rules set for their kind for centuries. They were the laws they stood by and the reason it wasn't open poaching season between Unseelie and Seelie. Why they needed to act in the shadows. No one knew how the untenable laws were created or enforced, apart from the kings themselves, but those who violated them felt the weight of the old as bone magic.

Trevor's jaw dropped. "The accords are broken."

The King's centaur gave him a grim nod in response. "The Seelie and Unseelie magic in the words carved onto the mirror enforced the accords throughout the years, bound together in an ancient spell. We're hours, days away from the sort of lawlessness most of us have never witnessed. In our worst hour—when the hunters bang at our doors and invade our spaces—we will descend into pure bedlam."

Kincaid had known. The cocky bastard had smiled at them, used them to steal the item, and then did the deed in Alberich's name. Trevor had been living outside of the fae community for so long the change wouldn't impact him—at least, not at first. However, anyone who dwelled in the rigid Court system was in for an upheaval akin to a World War. For the King, this was the worst timing, but for any revolutionaries? With the hunters stirring up chaos, one rebel had seized the perfect moment.

Now Trevor understood the panic in Jett's eyes as clear as the freeway late at night. Kincaid tied their fates with his. If they wanted to continue their existence, no one could ever know they were the ones who stole the mirror from Alberich—that Kincaid broke it.

The one man who could contest the statement lay dead on the ground.

"If you don't mind, I'd like to set my sister free," Danica announced. She emanated poise and coolness, snapping back to focus like the shock never hit her. "Alberich had her kidnapped so I'd come for her, since he placed a bounty over not only my head, but Trevor's as well." He could kiss her for covering their tracks.

The King's centaur nodded. Already, his focus had departed from them, and he trotted forward to examine Alberich's body further. "Do what you'd like. We're going to have to report to the King his enemy is dead."

"Let's go," Trevor said, placing a hand on Danica's back as together they headed for the door and out of that bloodstained room. Jett loped close behind them, buzzing like a maniac. It wasn't until they strode halfway down the hall that Jett whipped toward Danica.

"What did you do?" he mouthed, fury flashing in his gaze.

Her lips pressed tight together, and she shook her head. "I didn't know what the item was either."

Trevor's grip around her waist tightened as he stared Jett down. "Neither of us knew."

Jett ran a hand through his dark hair before letting out a sigh. "Well damn. Then we all got played. Ky and the others headed deeper into the building to look for you guys."

"We're getting Lenora out of the cage," Danica insisted, a heat in her voice he understood far too well. "He kept his fae locked in the ballroom."

Jett nodded and began to stride past them. "I'll collect the rest of the band, and we'll meet you there." Within seconds, the siren launched off at a jog, probably wanting to run far and fast away from the centaur back there. Not like any of them could escape the truth of what they'd become complicit in.

They set off down the hall after him at a quick pace.

Danica looked up while they walked, those liquid eyes flickering with concern. "I'm sorry," she said. "If I knew that's what he had in mind, I would've never worked with Kincaid."

Trevor shook his head. "Don't apologize. While I didn't like his lack of transparency, I won't be shedding any tears over some chaos ripping through the Courts. I've witnessed firsthand the corruption our kind can achieve with the system we had. It wasn't working." They turned the corner, closer to the place that held him prisoner for too many years.

His stomach clenched, and he waited for the dizzying nausea to descend. However, Danica tightened her hold on his hand, squeezing tight when they approached the double doors. She was the tether he needed to fight the memories, something real and tangible to grasp onto.

Trevor stepped forward and opened the doors.

The ballroom looked the same as ever, all marble floors, delicate chandeliers that cast shadow and light in the same breath. The sterile environment washed over him. His heart accelerated, and the panic clawed at his chest.

"Breathe," Danica said, tugging him forward, deeper into the room. Even though she led the way, her palms had begun to sweat. She glanced back, meeting his gaze. "If you need to hang back, I understand."

Trevor sucked in a deep breath, and then another. Even though the panic squeezed him tighter and tighter until his breaths shallowed, he floated above it as if his mind detached from his body for the time being.

"No, let's do this." He strode in along with her.

"Don't suppose you brought a lockpick?" Danica asked as they stepped closer to the cages. All eyes zeroed in on the two of them, most of the faces unfamiliar. Many of the ones who'd been imprisoned alongside Trevor had eventually found a way to take their own lives. The gilt edging on the wall, and the paintings along the far reaches of the room were ones he'd memorized. These tiles, he didn't just feel them beneath his soles, they plucked a chord deep inside him, one that sent terror rushing through anew.

Trevor pulled out his lockpick. "Yeah, I came prepared to bust you out."

Even if he hadn't spotted the honey blonde hair of Danica's sister, he could've gauged where Lenora was by the beeline Danica made toward her. They reached the cage within seconds, their footsteps echoing through this vast room. Everything echoed here, especially memories.

"You're okay?" Lenora's voice held a thickness, and her lip trembled as they approached. Those glossy eyes filled with tears.

Danica nodded, but he didn't miss the way she shifted the hand with her broken finger behind her back. Instead, she gave her sister a bright grin. "Ding-dong, the megalomaniac asshole is dead."

Trevor stepped up to the lock and slipped the pick inside. Lenora's gaze glittered, first from tears, which fast turned to curiosity as she stared at him.

"Is this the guy?" she asked Danica.

"Yeah," Danica responded. The softness in her voice stroked his heart. He didn't think he'd ever get sick of hearing vulnerability from her, the way she let him in past her mile-high walls when so few did.

He cracked open the cage door and tossed the lock to the ground with an audible clang reverberating around the room. "You're free, Lenora."

The word resonated in him like the last note of a song. Free. Everyone in this room would be free.

While Danica threw her arms around her sister, Trevor's legs already carried him toward the others locked away. With quick twists of the pick inside those padlocks, soon, more doors to cages opened. Soon, more fae stepped out from their confinement, some, for the first time in years.

Even though his brain had numbed with the overload of everything that happened, of being here in this place, Trevor moved swiftly through the ballroom. One by one, he set all the fae free, even if the motions grew mechanical and his mind numbed. Footsteps pounded around him, low murmurs and the sound of weeping. Sometimes, they'd throw their arms around him in a fast embrace, so overwhelmed at taking those first steps outside of the cage. Other times, they shuffled off without a word, too broken to respond.

Yet if someone as broken as him could begin to heal, they had hope too.

Kieran entered the ballroom first, followed by Jett, Renn, and Liz, their footsteps louder than the rest. Ky caught sight of him and waved at once, gold eyes flashing as he directed the others over. Renn stomped through, scuffing the marble floor, and Liz fired off a salute to Danica who strode forward with Lenora close behind. A bright smile plastered onto Danica's face, one that finally reached her heartbreaker green eyes.

Trevor stood in the center of this ballroom that had broken him, but as he soaked in the faces of these people he loved, the ones he cared about so deeply, he took in one, real breath. For a single moment, his feet settled on the floor again. Fae rushed around him, heading for the doors as fast as they could limp or run, fae who he'd set free.

Alberich's reign of terror had ended.

At last, Trevor could start his life.

Chapter Twenty-Six

By the time Trevor stumbled out of bed, Danica had already drank three cups of coffee and busted out the laptop to respond to company emails. She glanced to him from her perch on the booth inside the band's RV. His silver hair was mussed, and he didn't bother tossing on a shirt, giving her a perfect view of those sculpted abs, and the v that carved into a trim waist. He'd slung a loose pair of jeans on and fumbled with his belt when he approached.

Danica licked her lips at the sight of him, her libido revving like they hadn't spent the last week fucking in every available place they could find, preferably outside of this confined box on wheels. A week had passed since the confrontation with Alberich. A week since both the Unseelie and Seelie Courts descended into mass panic after their accords had dissolved.

Trevor slumped into the seat beside her, still blinking the sleep from his eyes. "Don't you ever rest?" he asked, even as he slung his arm around her shoulders, pulling her tight to him. The possessive way he clung to her every chance he got was something she didn't realize she'd love, something she'd lived without for all these years, never understanding what she missed out on.

"I'm a robot," she responded, continuing to finish her email. "We just get plugged in for a few hours. Sleep is for you weak bags of flesh."

He snorted and stole a sip from her cup of coffee. "Is Lenora staying in Vegas for a while?" he asked.

Danica nodded, signing the email and sending it off. "Once I explained the situation, Melrose hired her back. It's a lucrative spot for her here, and she won't be too far from my main office in San Francisco." Danica passed him a pointed look. "Let's be honest, if I stayed in the RV 24/7, I'm certain someone would slit my throat in my sleep, most likely you. Besides, we're both the independent sort."

He leaned in to press a kiss against her temple. Winter's breath, the affection was addictive. "I'm not arguing," he responded. "You've got a business to run, the same as we have our tours. As long as you don't mind the occasional visitor at your San Francisco office."

Danica grinned, the sort she felt deep in her chest. "And I'll be joining you on some of those tours when I feel like working remote. You'll be stuck with me for this next stretch."

"Perfect," he said, before stealing another sip from her coffee.

Danica grabbed her mug from his hands. "You keep drinking this and there'll be nothing left. There's more in the pot over there." His deep, rumbling laugh vibrated against her, and she couldn't help her smile in response. She gave his chest a gentle thwack. The scent of hickory and leather drifted over her, and she took a deep inhale. Even though she'd spent a long time bouncing from place to place, staying light and superficial, she recognized the scent—home.

The RV door creaked open. Jett and Liz scampered up the steps followed by Kieran and Renn. As they'd each gotten up in the morning, they left the RV to finish their last-minute stops in Vegas, whether a quick grocery run or grabbing more razors in the CVS. Today, they were leaving for the next stop along their tour, down to Phoenix, Arizona, and Danica would be traveling with them.

"I smell fish," Kieran complained as they

tromped up the steps.

"It's all that pussy you're missing out on by being monogamous," Jett retorted, hauling the overfull plastic grocery bags up the steps. "Some of us have more refined palates."

"Seriously? Seafood is disgusting." Kieran grabbed the offending package of tilapia from Jett's stash.

"Then don't eat it, babe," Liz responded with an exasperated sigh. "Maybe the rest of us want fish."

"I put up with the lot of you sneaking smokes," Renn pointed out. "I think you can handle a single night of seafood."

Kieran made gagging noises and marched his way to where they sat at the booth. Danica snorted and shared a glance with Trevor. Ky's intense gaze shot their way.

"And you two—I haven't gotten any sleep this past week," he said, fixing them with a glare.

Trevor cocked a brow. "Payback, brother. I've been bunking under you and Liz for far too long."

Danica ran fingers through her combed and coiffed strands. "The lot of you are so codependent a therapist would throw her clipboard out the window. I don't know how any of you deal with this arrangement long term."

"Tell me about it," Liz said, leaning against the counter. She cast a glance Danica's way, her hazel eyes twinkling in amusement. Somehow, after everything that went down the past couple of weeks, the rift between them had healed. Warmth burned in her chest like cinnamon schnapps at the camaraderie this bunch brought. At the hope for a future she'd found in Trevor, a refuge from this cruel, chaotic world.

Jett rapped his knuckles on the counter once he finished packing away their groceries into the mini-fridge and pull out pantry. "Does anyone need any last-minute things before we head out? This is the final chance."

"Yeah, I could use a break from the sound of your voice," Kieran muttered, in a peach of a mood.

Jett flashed him a vindictive grin. "Acid jazz, it is." At that, Trevor, Renn, and Liz all groaned in response.

Kieran shrugged. "Your drive, your choice."

Jett lifted a hand in salute as he headed up front. A moment later, the RV rumbled to life, the thrum of the engine traveling across the floor. Anticipation hummed in her veins, more of a jolt than the dozens of cups of coffee she downed during the day. For so long, she'd been on the opposite side of the window, watching cozy scenes. When she'd first met the crew of Discord's Desire, it had been like that, seeing this comfortable crew bicker like kids while she skated on the superficial.

The Otherworld might be in uproar, Kincaid might have disappeared for a while, and she might be on the road, but this time, she wasn't alone.

Danica was traveling with the crew of Discord's Desire. With the man she loved. Their gazes locked, and even though the words stuck in her throat, she'd save them for whatever private time they could carve out. Not like it mattered. She saw the love shining when his dark eyes crinkled in affection. She felt that love with the way his long fingers stroked across her back, a mere touch from him making her shiver.

Renn snagged the last of the coffee from the pot, causing protest from Liz, and a fight broke out anew as the two argued over who was the last one to brew. Danica rolled her eyes and settled against the booth, curling into Trevor's warmth. The RV creaked, and then Jett jammed on the pedal, causing the behemoth to shoot across the asphalt.

She stared out the window at the lot that had been their home base during the crew's stay in Vegas. They passed the other RVs camped along the stretch, the couple of cars filtered amidst them, and with a mighty rumble, they set onto the freeway. As they launched onto the highway amidst the cars, trucks, and unending expanse of gray, Danica's heart grew lighter and lighter in her chest. A giddiness swept over her, one her life of guarded responsibility hadn't allowed.

However, she was here with Trevor, with this crew, with a brand-new life set out before her. And today? They were going on an adventure.

The End

www.katherine-mcintyre.com

KATHERINE MCINTYRE

EVERNIGHT PUBLISHING ®

www.evernightpublishing.com

Practical Dharma

Pragmatic Strategies for Everyday Challenges

Jeffrey C. Fracher, Ph.D.

ISBN: 979-8-213-08237-6

Library of Congress Control Number: 2022918465

Author photograph by Melody Robbins Photography

Image: Flaticon.com

Book Cover design by Ogsaint

Formatting by Atticus.io

Serenitysanghapublishing™

www.serenitysangha.org

serenitysanghacville@gmail.com

Contents

To my beloved, Kay, for the gift of her in my life.

And to all my students, and the members of Serenity Sangha, who have been my best teachers.

And, finally, to my teacher, Lila Kate Wheeler, who has been my perfect guide.

Chapter One

Introduction

"The seed of suffering in you may be strong, but don't wait until you have no more suffering before allowing yourself to be happy."

—*Thich Nhat Hanh*

We all suffer. No one in this life is spared.

Yes, life is also rich, wondrous, joyful, mysterious, and exciting. But that's another book.

While the extent of one's suffering may differ in intensity and quality it cannot be avoided. We suffer externally due to life circumstances but most of our suffering is internal, hidden, and private. Why is this true and what can we do about it?

Much human suffering is inevitable—sickness, loss, old age, and death. With what a brilliant young man discovered 2600 years ago in what is now Nepal we can understand the causes of our suffering and change our relationship to our suffering and, thereby, reduce it.

My practice of Buddhism has been positively life-changing in ways I could never have imagined. I cannot express how deeply grateful I am for the radical transformation in all aspects of my life since embracing Buddhist practice. My study of Buddhism over the years has convinced me that though he lived over 2600 years ago the Gautama Buddha was the greatest living psychologist the world has ever known. His understanding of the human condition's vast complexity has been unrivaled by anyone since that time.

The teachings of the Buddha are referred to as the *Dharma*. Simply put the Dharma consists of the path that the Buddha taught to reduce suffering. The Buddha purposely avoided metaphysical and unknowable ideas and focused on practical teachings which lead to the end of suffering.

The Dharma offers specific tools beyond psychotherapy to deepen our connection to ourselves and others, find joy and wonder in our lives, and reduce our suffering. The Buddha's teachings are ancient but they apply to our daily lives whatever the circumstances. Practical Dharma is just that—useful and relevant—no matter what your life situation. To support the creation of more happiness for ourselves we need to focus on the positive in our lives, not just what is wrong. If we fail to take advantage of the tools of Practical Dharma actively and intentionally we will continue our dysfunctional patterns resulting in persistent suffering.

Throughout I refer frequently to the *practice* by which I mean the implementation of the combined and overlapping tools of the Dharma and modern psychology, the integration of which I call Practical Dharma.

This book is a narrative compilation of thirty of my best-received talks on aspects of Buddhism that I have offered to my students over the years. In addition to practicing Buddhism for 30 years, I have been teaching Buddhism and Buddhist practice for the past ten years since completing an intensive 2-year Buddhist teacher training program. I practiced as a clinical psychologist for over 44 years during which I worked in many inpatient and outpatient settings including many years in full-time private practice and as an adjunct professor at four universities. My work provided me with many opportunities to explore and address human suffering.

Over the years of my profession as a psychologist, I learned and refined a range of methods to help my patients manage their symptoms such as depression and anxiety which improved the quality of their lives and relationships. But elements were missing which left both me and those with whom I worked feeling incomplete about the therapeutic outcomes.

When I undertook the study and practice of Buddhism I knew I had discovered the missing elements of my clinical work. The combination of a modern psychological theory and the ancient teachings of the Buddha fit together like a lock and key. Practical Dharma has resonated strongly with my meditation students over the years.

Buddhist teachings added a spiritual element to my clinical work. But most importantly they added a larger more spacious context for understanding the human experience, especially that of suffering which was not always available in my therapeutic work. Most schools of psychotherapy offer to alleviate suffering which is an impossible goal. Practical Dharma aims to change our relationship with suffering while acknowledging its inevitability.

My aspiration and primary motive for teaching Buddhism and Buddhist practice are to share the wealth of the teachings that I have experienced in my own life. For ten years until early 2022, I was president and a senior teacher in a large Buddhist community. More recently I started a small group at the request of some of the members of my former community. I am pleased that my teachings continue to resonate with my current group of students many of whom asked me to commit them to writing. Thus the idea for this book was born.

This is not a book on formal Buddhism or psychological theory nor is it an attempt to be complete in exploring either approach. Instead, it offers selected tools that provide practical and accessible guidance on improving one's life. It attempts to present the more salient and pragmatic of the Buddha's core teachings, augmented by the methods of modern clinical psychology, as I have integrated them over the years in both my psychotherapy practice and my own life.

You do not have to be or become a Buddhist to benefit from these methods and strategies. I have intentionally avoided discussing Buddhism's obscure and metaphysical aspects as they tend to be inaccessible and unnecessary for implementing Practical Dharma.

Let me add a few words about the application of the tools and techniques of Practical Dharma. We all have busy lives and often it is all we can do to make time for daily meditation practice. We do not have time to focus on the nature of reality or other digressions into the esoteric aspects of Buddhism. Nor will doing so change our dysfunctional personality patterns—the unhealthy or unproductive ways in which we suffer. We must address our patterns directly. For example, I may be someone who always blames others for my unhappiness—I am unwilling to accept my contribution to my suffering. Or, I am someone who often flies off the handle in the form of temper outbursts at others. These are the type of recurring tendencies that Practical Dharma addresses.

I am a pragmatist. I want to know what works and how to apply it. Together Buddhist teachings and modern psychology offer a hands-on approach to addressing the things that trigger our suffering. What drew me to a specific approach to psychology and Buddhism is that they provide prescriptions to reduce our suffering and live more joyfully in the gift of this life. Alone, Buddhist practice may not affect the shift I am talking about. Combining Practical Dharma with the methods of modern psychology creates a broader framework for addressing these patterns.

When I practiced psychotherapy I often treated people who developed deep insights into their dysfunctions but never implemented those insights to change. They could not make their lives and relationships work because they would not confront their dysfunctional relationship patterns. They understood where they habitually ran into problems with others such as reflexive defensiveness or being highly controlling, yet they failed to take the steps available to change. As a result, they made little or no progress in alleviating their suffering or that of those around them. If we do not use the insights and tools at hand to inform our patterns in daily life what are we achieving other than possibly stress reduction?

Embracing Practical Dharma in our lives is no quick fix. It is effortful, challenging, and requires a strong commitment. We in the West want instant transformation and instant gratification because we are culturally impatient. Practical Dharma is not that path. There is no quick fix for the struggles we face in our lives. Relief does not just fall in our lap. We must cultivate it, work at it, and pursue it as it is an active, engaged, ongoing process.

Practical Dharma is not psychotherapy. Nor is it a substitute for psychotherapy when it is indicated. Nonetheless, the Dharma combined with modern psychology offers specific tools to deepen our connection to ourselves and others, find joy and wonder in our lives, and reduce our suffering. If we fail to, with intention, implement the tools of Practical Dharma we are spinning our wheels.

The Buddhist path is an active, engaged one. It is not passive, where transformation happens simply from meditating every day. We must work at it daily with intention. It requires patience because progress on the path is incremental. The path is a challenging one with no panacea but the rewards are immense, as has been confirmed in my life. I hope you will undertake the journey.

Chapter Two

Buddhism 101

"A man is not called wise because he talks and talks again; but if he is peaceful, loving and fearless then he is in truth called wise."

— The Buddha

Siddhartha Gautama, the founder of this path was not a divine being. When asked, "Are you a God" he answered, "No." When asked, "What are you?" it is written that he said, "I am awake."

Like you and me he struggled and experienced the pain of suffering in his life. By learning directly from his own experience he discovered that he could live with more joy. Each of us can also. Through direct experience, he became an awakened human being and a beloved teacher whose wisdom has stood for 2600 years.

Buddhism began with the life of its founder who was born sometime in the fifth century BCE in the foothills of the Himalayas in what is now Nepal. While we refer to Gautama as the *Buddha* the word Buddha means awakened one. Gautama was not born with this title but achieved it over his lifetime. The Buddha is seen by Buddhists as an enlightened human being given that he saw through to the reality of existence and taught others how to escape suffering in life.

Though there is disagreement as to whether Buddhism is a religion in the traditional sense, I do not consider Buddhism a religion as it is non-theistic. There is no deity to worship. Instead, it is a spiritual path and a philosophy of life. The person of Buddha was none other than a normal human being with the same challenges and struggles that we all face. We do not worship him. Instead, we see him as a role model and brilliant teacher whose life and teachings we embrace and seek to emulate. He taught a path to a fully engaged life. He offered means that promise reduced personal suffering and full engagement with life.

Because the practice of Buddhism is non-theistic it is compatible with other faith traditions. Many who embrace the Buddha's teachings do so in concert with their primary faith be it Christianity, Judaism, Islam, or any other religion. Some who practice Buddhism are agnostic or atheists. All are welcome to avail themselves of the Buddha's teachings and one does not need to be a Buddhist to benefit.

A review of the more essential fundamentals of Buddhist practice includes:

- The Four Noble Truths (the foundational teaching)

- The Three Refuges (also called The Three Jewels)

- The four *Brahma Viharas* (Heavenly Abodes)

- The Three Poisons (the sources of most suffering)

- The Lay Precepts (ethical guidelines)

- The Ten *Paramis*, or Perfections (virtues or aspirations)

We will briefly review each of these in this chapter and the next.

The Buddhist canon or collection of his teachings and commentary was not committed to writing until hundreds of years after the Buddha's death. Before that, the teachings were transmitted as an oral tradition and memorized by generations of monks. The written teachings and commentary are deep and vast and beyond the scope of this book. I am offering a limited slice of the collected teachings which I consider most pertinent to Practical Dharma.

The Four Noble Truths

For those not familiar with Buddhism we begin with The Four Noble Truths, the foundational teaching of Buddhism. They include the identification of the primary problem of living (the truth of suffering), the cause of the problem (the truth of the cause of suffering), the means of solving the problem (the truth of the ending of suffering), and the eight steps to address the problem (the truth of the path that frees us from suffering).

- The First Noble Truth: The Buddha begins by telling us that life involves ongoing suffering ("*dukkha*"). He did not mean simply physical pain nor did he mean that life is constantly and unremittingly awful. Instead, he noted that suffering includes everything from minor dissatisfactions and day-to-day annoyances to significant losses, including our mortality, and that of all that we love.

Suffering primarily results from the temporary nature of all experience. We suffer when things go away. Buddhism is often criticized for being too focused on suffering. However, the focus on suffering is in the interest of reducing suffering so that we can experience joy once the impediments are removed.

- The Second Noble Truth: The *Pali* word (Pali being the language spoken at the time of the Buddha) for the cause of suffering is *"tanha."* This Second Noble Truth in the Buddhist canon has been translated variously as grasping, clinging, thirst, craving, greed, and desire. The Buddha taught that we can never be satisfied by looking for our happiness in external events, possessions, and relationships, all of which are fleeting. We become frustrated when the world does not conform to our expectations. All phenomena are temporary so our efforts to hold on and make them permanent are futile. This teaching is one of the Buddha's most brilliant insights and is as relevant today as it was 2600 years ago. Once we can engage with life without trying to hold onto and control everything we can experience true joy and emotional freedom.

I often use the example of getting the newest model of smartphone. When it first comes on the market I think about it, get excited, and count the days until it arrives. Once it is in my hands I experience excitement and happiness but soon the novelty wears off and it is just another phone. The joy that I experienced was fleeting. If obtaining shiny new objects is the source of my happiness I must move on to get the next new thing as any satisfaction is temporary. The process is endless and sustained happiness is elusive.

- The Third Noble Truth: The solution to our suffering is called *"nirhodha,"* which tells us that we cannot force ourselves to stop clinging and grasping to temporary phenomena. The circumstances that cause us to grasp and cling remain. We must apply the roadmap that the Buddha offers us, in the form of the Noble Eightfold Path, to free us from the cycle of suffering in our lives.

- The Fourth Noble Truth: The last of these Four Noble Truths, *"magga,"* is the Buddha's treatment for the illness of suffering. Called the Noble Eightfold Path it includes eight practice areas to free us from the bonds of suffering. It is comprehensive and covers every aspect of our lives.

Unlike many other faith traditions, Buddhism does not ask us to take anything at face value or simply by believing a doctrine or reciting a creed. Instead, it gives us clear pragmatic strategies and areas of focus. The Buddha cautioned his followers not to take his word for the validity of his teachings. He taught that we must implement them and see if they work. This is the path that we walk as we apply his teachings.

The Noble Eightfold Path

The eight components of the Noble Eightfold Path are listed below. They are variously referred to as wise, right, or skillful to indicate that their pursuit will lead to reduced suffering and greater happiness. They are grouped into three baskets: moral conduct, mental discipline, and wisdom.

The first basket consists of the three components of moral or ethical conduct:

- Right Speech is refraining from harmful speech such as lies, gossip, slander, rudeness, abusive speech, and the like. Careless speech is also to be avoided. My late mother used to say, "If you can't say something nice about someone, don't say anything at all." Unbeknownst to her, she was following the Buddha's teaching on Right Speech.

- Right Action is aspiring to engage in behavior that is non-harmful, honorable, ethical, and promotes peace.

- Right Livelihood is making one's living in a way that does not bring harm to people or other sentient beings. Our livelihood should be characterized by honesty, fairness, and a high moral standard.

The second basket contains the three components of mental discipline:

- Right Effort is aspiring to avoid what the Buddha called "Unwholesome states of mind," meaning those characterized by evil, immorality, and hostility.

- Right Mindfulness is the factor that addresses our meditation practice. It directs the cultivation of mindful and present-moment awareness during formal meditation practice and in daily life. The Buddha instructed us to be mindful of four objects of meditation: our bodies, our feelings, our ideas and concepts, and the activity of our minds. The practice of Right Mindfulness includes noticing what is occurring moment-to-moment and discerning our responses to what is arising.

- Right Concentration is the practice of developing one-pointedness of our mental activity. We are invited to focus our awareness on one physical or mental object such as the breath. There are advanced absorption practices known as the *Jhanas* which fall under Right Concentration but are beyond the scope of this book.

The third basket contains the two components of wisdom:

- Right View or Right Understanding is to see clearly

the path of practice and cultivate an understanding of the steps necessary to progress on the path. With Right View, we clarify and set our intention for how we want to live our lives.

- Right Intention is the determination or resolve not to cause harm or ill will and to practice renunciation. Renunciation in this context does not mean asceticism or adopting a monastic lifestyle. Rather, it means letting go of old dysfunctional habits and beliefs.

There is a vast literature on the Four Noble Truths and the Noble Eightfold Path for those who seek a deeper understanding of this profound teaching. I encourage you to pursue a greater appreciation of Buddhism which is beyond the scope of this book by utilizing the references at the end of the book.

Reflection:

- What about Buddhism sparked your interest in learning more about it? Reflect on which areas of life where you would like to experience less suffering.

Chapter Three

Buddhism 102

"The thought manifests as the word: the word manifests as the deed: the deed develops into character. So watch the thought and its ways with care, and let it spring from love born out of concern for all beings."

—*The Buddha*

In this chapter, we will delve more deeply into additional teachings from Buddhism that are an important part of the Practical Dharma approach to reducing suffering in our lives. Again, this is not a comprehensive overview of the vast Buddhist teachings.

The Three Refuges

The Three Refuges in Buddhism are *Buddha, Dharma*, and *Sangha*. We refer to them as refuges because they offer us a haven from the slings and arrows of daily life. They are a shelter from the storm that is this life and are also referred to as The Three Jewels or The Three Treasures. These serve as anchors when we are inundated with the challenges of daily living. We have a home in the refuges.

- Refuge in the Buddha does not mean that we view the Buddha as a deity. The person of Buddha was a normal human being with the same challenges and struggles that we all face. We do not worship him. Instead, we see him as a role model and brilliant teacher whose life and teachings we embrace and seek to emulate. He taught a philosophy of life and offered a path to meet the human journey which promises reduced personal suffering and full engagement with life.

- Refuge in the Dharma, often referred to as the *Buddhadharma*, includes the teachings and wisdom of the Buddha; all the suttas and discourses accumulated over the centuries that guide us in addressing our suffering. The Dharma instructs us to see life as it is, not as we wish it to be. The wisdom of the Dharma is life-changing and priceless, available to anyone. Refuge in the Dharma is having faith in the teachings and trusting that the teachings will positively impact our lives.

- Refuge in the Sangha, or community, is affiliating with others on the path. Sangha is extremely important. The Buddhist way is a challenging one and the support of others is essential to our commitment and progress. Opening ourselves to others with vulnerability and honesty is a check on our ego and self-absorption as doing so encourages humility. We come to this practice because we are suffering. Being with a community of others who acknowledge their suffering, and sharing it, aids our progress.

The Three Poisons

The Buddha taught that there are Three Poisons or unwholesome states: greed (desire, lust), hatred (anger, avoidance), and delusion (ignorance). These are the source or root of all unwholesome mental states. I believe that most of the world's ills and suffering originate from the Three Poisons.

Greed is the primary factor in the planet's destruction and much human misery, hatred fuels violence and warfare, and delusion allows us to deny the reality of the suffering all around us including our own.

Our lives are filled with suffering and misery because of the Three Poisons. They cause us to make unskillful choices, engage

in dishonest and harmful behavior, and behave without moral
or ethical considerations.

- Greed: The ancient Pali word for greed is often translated as lust. We desire things or relationships that we
  believe will bring us happiness. Due to the law of impermanence, the novelty wears off and we are on to
  the next shiny object or milestone. We envy those who
  have things we cannot obtain. The ego is right at the
  center of this poison. "Me, me, me" and "more, more,
  more" are the ego's constant refrains. When my choices
  are governed by the poison of greed I am constantly in
  search of the next novel thing or experience to bring
  me momentary happiness often without regard for the
  consequences.

- Hatred: The second of the poisons, hatred or anger, also
  involves the ego. The second poison is often referred
  to as aversion because we push away or avoid anything
  that will hurt our fragile sense of self—our ego. We
  do not hesitate to hurt others if that is what it takes
  to feel superior. We may feel anger and hatred toward
  those unlike us resulting in prejudice, discrimination,
  and violence toward others. We may look down on and
  dehumanize those we perceive as different to inflate our

sense of worth resulting in warfare, violence, prejudice, and many other ills on a societal scale.

- Delusion: The third poison, delusion or ignorance, is seeing reality as we wish it to be, not as it is. We human beings have an amazing capacity to convince ourselves of anything that suits us or allows us to continue with the same self-serving destructive patterns. Denial is a classic form of delusion. The phenomenon of confirmation bias is another form of delusion whereby we favor information that confirms or strengthens what we already believe and ignores information that does not. Once the bias is affirmed it is very difficult to change. This is especially true within a closed social system or group as is the case in our political system.

As with all unskillful behavior, thoughts, beliefs, and attitudes, we use the tools taught by the Buddha to address the Three Poisons. We cultivate the opposing mental states or antidotes of the Three Poisons: compassion, loving-kindness, and generosity—all sources of peace, goodwill, and reduced suffering in the world.

The Brahma Viharas

Another foundational teaching is the *Brahma Viharas*; four aspects of human nature that are of the highest order. They are variously known as the Four Immeasurables, the Heavenly Abodes, or the Four Sublime States. If we only commit to practicing the Brahma Viharas daily we will make significant progress on the spiritual path improving the quality of our lives and those around us. They are an essential part of Practical Dharma as their benefits are many.

They are:

- Loving-Kindness (*"Metta"):* The practice of Loving-Kindness is the wish for all living creatures to have happiness and to know the causes of happiness. This quality is immeasurable because it is open and limitless and intended to bring care, comfort, and empathy to all. It is without self-interest, selfishness, or the wish for aggrandizement. Loving-Kindness comes from an open heart and is an antidote for anger, ill will, and hatred.

- Compassion ("*Karuna"*): The practice of Compassion is just what the term implies. The Buddha defined compassion as "A quivering of the heart in response to suffering and pain." Compassion fosters connection with others, lessens suffering by fostering understanding, reduces the isolation and stigma of suffering, and opens our hearts. With compassion, we move toward suffering, not away from it. It does not come from guilt. The practice of self-compassion is also included in this practice and is a powerful antidote to the experience of shame and self-loathing.

- Appreciative or Sympathetic Joy ("*Mudita*"): The practice of Sympathetic Joy involves stepping out of ourselves and taking joy in the good fortune of others. It is the antidote for self-centeredness, comparing mind, envy, and jealousy, emotions that cause us a great deal of suffering and separation from others. It is intended to be offered to all living beings, not just those known to us.

- Equanimity ("*Upekkha*"): Most simply stated, equanimity involves the ability to maintain balance amid life's challenges. It is the antithesis of indifference and requires that we let go of attachments, cravings, and clinging. We practice equanimity when we are calm, emotionally or psychologically balanced, and non-reactive, especially when confronted with challenging circumstances.

Our challenge is to live the Brahma Viharas at all times, not just occasionally. They are guideposts of how we relate to others; we direct lovingkindness to all, express compassion toward those suffering, take joy in the success and achievement of others and interact with difficult individuals and situations with equanimity.

The Ten Perfections

The final set of important practices is the ten *Paramis* or Ten Perfections. These values are practiced and cultivated as part of our spiritual path. As with the Brahma Viharas, they bring our practice into day-to-day life. They guide ethical and skillful behavior in our lives. Rather than focus on accumulating wealth or possessions, or achieving status and recognition, we practice them. Each one of the Perfections supports the development of the others in an overlapping and complementary manner.

- Generosity-giving of oneself or one's possessions with no strings attached. Doing so loosens the grip of greed, one of the Three Poisons, and fosters a non-clinging perspective.

- Virtue-cultivating ethics and morality so that we live a life consistent with higher values.

- Renunciation-letting go of whatever binds us to suffering including those things that we grasp or cling to which we believe bring us happiness.

- Discernment-seeing the true nature of life without distortion which cultivates wisdom.

- Equanimity-seeing things clearly, without the influence of the ego so that our choices are not governed by our emotions. It is the "calm in the storm."

- Patience-enduring hardships in our life. Patience will be discussed in depth in Chapter 15.

- Persistence-giving our full energy and commitment and showing fortitude on the path of the Dharma.

- Truth-practicing honesty both within ourselves and with others whatever the circumstances. It is a function of Wise Speech.

- Determination-committing to the path of the Dharma whatever the obstacles that we encounter.

- Goodwill-abandoning ego-driven self-centeredness and understanding that the suffering of others is our suffering.

Note that several of the qualities the Buddha taught occur in more than one category reflecting the degree of importance placed on them in his teachings.

Ethics and wisdom are two aspects of Buddhist teachings that are essential to progress on the path. We briefly touched on ethics earlier in this Chapter One when discussing the first basket of the Noble Eightfold Path: Right Action, Right Speech, and Right Livelihood.

Embracing all the Buddha's teachings, including the ten Perfections and the four Brahma Viharas, provides a strong ethical foundation. Ethics in Buddhism is not mindlessly following a list of rules or commandments. We are not motivated to live ethically by the fear of some nebulous punishment or condemnation. Instead, it is part of the process of mindful awareness and discernment whereby we aspire to live by the values that the Buddha taught that lead to well-being and a reduction in suffering. We live a life that we can feel good about; one in which we do not have to justify our actions and decisions to ourselves or others.

A solid ethical foundation also engenders trust in ourselves and others and contributes to the existence of a robust and supportive community. Our ethics bring awareness to our day-to-day choices and our relationships with others. A simple rule of thumb providing ethical guidance is the Golden Rule found in most of the world's faith traditions, "Do unto others as you would have them do unto you."

There are five Lay Precepts in Theravada Buddhism which also contribute to a strong ethical foundation. Again these are not commandments but guidelines to which we aspire.

They are:

- Non-harming: Abstain from killing living beings.

- Not stealing: Abstain from taking that which is not freely given.

- Avoiding sexual misconduct: Abstain from inappropriate or harmful sexual behavior.

- Speaking truthfully: Abstain from telling lies.

- Avoiding intoxicants or activities that cloud the mind.

Wisdom is considered the heart of Buddhist practice and is grounded in all aspects of our Buddhist path. It is foundational in that we build our practice on a base of wisdom. With wisdom, we see the world as it truly is, not as we want it to be. The third basket of the Noble Eightfold Path is the wisdom basket and consists of Right View and Right Intention.

Wisdom is the antithesis of ignorance, which is the denial of reality, the rejection of the ego's role in our suffering, and nonacceptance of the impermanence of all phenomena. Wisdom is not an intellectual understanding of life and the human journey. Instead, it is experiential as we acquire wisdom through practicing meditation and living our lives more mindfully and successfully. It is developed over time and cannot be taught or learned from a book.

Unlike many other spiritual traditions, faith is secondary to wisdom in Buddhism. The Buddha was a pragmatist who taught that we should pursue the path he outlined and see for ourselves if it reduces our suffering; he did not intend that we take it blindly on faith because he said so. Immersing ourselves in his teachings with understanding and discernment results in acquiring wisdom. Our faith takes the form of the promise that the teachings will improve the quality of our lives.

Each set of the core concepts has been an essential part of my practice of Practical Dharma and greatly informed and improved my daily life. This brief introduction to Buddhism emphasizing Practical Dharma will guide our discussion in the upcoming chapters.

<u>Reflection:</u>

- Of the methods of Buddhism outlined, which of them most resonates with you? Reflect on why a particular aspect of Buddhism may make sense in your life.

Chapter Four

ACT

"If you aren't willing to have it, you will."
—*Dr. Steven C. Hayes*

ACT (Acceptance and Commitment Therapy) is a relatively new approach to therapy that grew out of two earlier therapy schools, a discussion beyond this book's scope. Briefly, ACT is an evidence-based approach that emphasizes the acceptance of our difficult thoughts and emotions rather than avoiding them, a concept consistent with the Buddhist teaching of accepting life as it is, not as we want it to be. The commitment aspect of ACT involves facing our difficulties head-on with committed action, the antithesis of avoidance.

The aim of ACT is psychological flexibility. It is the primary overarching goal of ACT. When we achieve psychological flexibility we accept our unpleasant feelings and thoughts instead of fighting them or feeling guilty about them. With psychological flexibility, as with equanimity in Buddhism, we roll with the punches and remain stable during the storms of life. In ACT, psychological flexibility is achieved by the interaction of the six processes listed below. It is synonymous with mental well-being.

There are six components in the ACT model, all of which are consistent with, or overlap with, the teachings of the Buddha.

- Acceptance: Allowing our inner thoughts and feelings without avoiding them. Acceptance as opposed to avoidance involves fully recognizing and becoming aware of our thoughts and feelings without trying to change them.

- Cognitive Defusion: The process of seeing thoughts simply as thoughts free of the elaborate stories we tell ourselves; i.e., not letting them define who we are. With cognitive defusion, we start noticing our thoughts and becoming more aware of them. Once we can de-identify with our thoughts by simply observing them and not getting hooked by them, they reduce the impact on how we feel, behave, and think about ourselves.

- Self-as-Context: An abstract concept because it is largely experiential. Simply put it involves seeing our thoughts as separate from our actions. It is the noticing part of us. We become aware of our flow of experience, especially thought processes, without attachment to them. With mindfulness and cognitive defusion, we learn to simply observe experience without clinging to it.

- Present Moment Awareness: Using our mindfulness practice to be fully in the present moment. The practice of mindfulness will be explored in more detail in the next chapter.

- Values: Those beliefs that guide us toward Wise Action. We clarify how our values and ethics permeate every aspect of our lives and inform our choices and decisions. As with Buddhism, clarifying our values and ethics cultivates wisdom which is recognizing the reality of life as it is through our life experiences.

- Commitment: A willingness to change no matter how difficult. The commitment aspect of ACT focuses on acceptance followed by an investment in change no matter how challenging.

As with Buddhist practice, ACT emphasizes the importance of seeing clearly and honestly our patterns of behavior and actions, both external and internal, including all the private inner experiences we have: thoughts, sensations, feelings, and memories. Our intention is not to disavow or deny any unacceptable part of ourselves. In ACT terminology trying to distract from, avoid, or rid ourselves of painful experiences is known as experiential avoidance. Avoidance is understood in ACT to be the source of much human suffering as is also the case in Buddhism. We humans have endless strategies to avoid painful experiences, all of which can cause additional suffering. We compulsively shop, we eat too much, we drink too much, we take drugs, we exercise too much, or we spend too much time on social media—the list is endless.

Traditionally, western psychology has held out the promise of normalcy as the goal of psychotherapy. ACT, like Buddhism, validates our suffering and accepts that none of us will ever be free of emotional and relational challenges in our life; i.e., normal. Both approaches emphasize acceptance of life as it is, not as we want it to be.

Throughout my training and career, I have been trained in and practiced many therapeutic approaches to reducing suffering and improving the quality of my patient's lives. In 2000 I was introduced to Acceptance and Commitment Therapy while attending a workshop with Dr. Steven C. Hayes, the primary developer of ACT. I resonated strongly with the underlying theory of ACT and its practical applications. To become proficient I attended many ACT trainings and began incorporating ACT into my clinical work as my primary mode of treatment. ACT has proven to be the most effective approach to reducing suffering of which I am aware, with a short-term symptom-focused approach.

Though I no longer practice as a psychologist I continue teaching ACT to doctoral clinical psychology students at the University of Virginia where I supervise students in their clinical practicums using ACT. Of the numerous schools of therapy I have learned and practiced over the years ACT is most compatible with the teachings of the Buddha. There is significant concordance between the two approaches regarding both theory and practice. Practical Dharma is the synthesis of ACT and the most pragmatic of the ancient teachings of the Buddha.

With ACT we lean into, or accept, our pain so that it does not govern our behavior. We give up unworkable action resulting from unskillful choices. Psychological flexibility as a position from which to engage with life is particularly important when we are suffering or are faced with a painful situation. Otherwise, the danger is that we withdraw resulting in our world of experience contracting and shrinking. When we are highly anxious we create rigid and narrow rules about what is safe, making our world smaller and more limited.

A classic example is a person suffering from agoraphobia who will not leave their home due to a fear of being away from their safe space. In reality, they have a fear of fear. They are afraid of internal physical sensations such as shallow breathing, panicky feelings, and excessive sweating signaling the onset of a panic attack, an extremely unpleasant experience. They are experientially avoiding the internal sensations signally the onset of a panic attack by never leaving their safe space. Only by accepting and being fully present with such sensations and gradually exposing themself to them will the suffering lessen and their freedom of movement increase.

With ACT we frequently use metaphors to bypass the thinking brain which is not always our friend, especially when we try to think our way out of our suffering. One example is called *Passengers on a Bus,* created by Dr. Steven Hayes the developer of ACT.

Imagine you are a bus driver driving your bus. Your bus is full of passengers. Each passenger is a different difficult thought, memory, emotion, or sensation. Many of the passengers are irritable, angry, judgmental, and critical. Some are frightened, self-loathing, or sad. Others are risk-averse. What to do with such passengers? We cannot kick them off the bus as they have paid their fare. We try to make them leave anyway since having them on board is so unpleasant, but they resist and remind you that they paid. Try as you might to block them out they are too loud and insistent making it almost impossible to drive the bus safely. If you close your eyes and put your hands over your ears you cannot drive. The situation appears unworkable and hopeless. Suddenly you realize that there is a solution—accept them despite all their negativity, shouting, and complaining. Give up arguing with them and willingly let them be there. Go about driving the bus in the direction that you want to go, where your values take you, despite the obnoxious passengers on your bus. You do not like having them on board and you would prefer they not be on the bus but you simply accept their presence and keep driving.

The moral of the story is that the passengers represent our unpleasant and painful thoughts, sensations, memories, feelings, and moods. Rather than struggling to get rid of such inner experiences or feeling ashamed of them, we welcome them as nothing more than part of the full range of human experience. We are then freer to live our lives consistent with our goals and values. In Buddhism, this is the definition of spiritual freedom.

Reflection:

- In what areas of your life might any of the ACT practices be beneficial?

Chapter Five

Meditation

"Mindfulness is about being fully awake in our lives. It is about perceiving the exquisite vividness of each moment. We also gain immediate access to our own powerful inner resources for insight, transformation, and healing."

—*Jon Kabat-Zinn*

"McMindfulness!"

Mindfulness has become embedded in our culture in the recent past. A simple Google search makes the point. It is everywhere on YouTube and there are hundreds of podcasts on mindfulness and multiple mindfulness apps for smartphones.

Mindfulness has been monetized in a way the Buddha could not have imagined. Some are making millions of dollars selling mindfulness. It is on the cover of every magazine in the checkout line at the supermarket. Every organization small to large has incorporated it into its human resources offerings as part of our therapeutic culture. It is offered as a cure for everything from anxiety to insomnia to a myriad of physical ills.

Meditation has been separated from its Buddhist roots in the move to popularize mindfulness practice. This separation is not without cost. Without a foundation in ethics and wisdom, mindfulness practice is just another self-improvement technique directed at those who are anxious, those functioning below their potential on the job, and those seeking stress reduction. The practical benefits of this secular mindfulness meditation are touted as lowering stress, decreasing depression, improving memory, and strengthening relationships. While these goals are not without their usefulness they are a limited use of this ancient practice.

Right Mindfulness is the seventh of the eight components of the Noble Eightfold Path and an essential part of the path that the Buddha taught. Though it can be a challenging practice, especially for beginners, it is cultivating awareness of oneself, one's feelings, thoughts, and the nature of reality. The full benefit of mindfulness comes from paying attention to sensations, feelings, thoughts, and surroundings in the moment from a position of non-judgment and acceptance.

For those new to meditation, it may sound mysterious and abstract. In practice, the instructions are relatively straightforward. The benefits may not be readily apparent so it is important to give the practice at least 2 to 3 months before rendering a verdict on your practice of meditation.

With mindfulness comes the awareness of one's true nature and the ability to deal with the feelings and movements of the mind peacefully with detachment and wise understanding. This may sound complex and challenging because mindfulness practice is experiential and not easily described in words. It is not simply the practice of bare attention that the Buddha described though that is one ingredient. The Buddha did not give specific instructions on how to practice mindfulness. Instead, he taught that there are four foci of mindfulness we need to include in our practice.

They are:

- Mindfulness of the Body: This focus includes mindfulness of breathing, posture, comprehension, bodily functions, material elements such as earth, wind, fire, and water, and the impermanence of the body.

- Mindfulness of Feelings: This second focus includes attention to feeling tones, not emotions. Is our immediate experience pleasant? Unpleasant? Neutral?

- Mindfulness of Mind States: The focus is on our state of mind. Does it contain greed, hatred, and delusion, or is it free of these states? Is it distracted? Developed or undeveloped? Concentrated or scattered? Free or bound?

- Mindfulness of the Dharmas: This category is esoteric and beyond the scope of this book other than to say it includes mindfulness of The Five Hindrances which are barriers to our meditation practice. The Five Hindrances are sensual desire, ill will, restlessness and worry, doubt, and sloth and torpor. Mindfulness of the dharmas also includes mindfulness of the Four Noble Truths.

The Four Foundations of Mindfulness that the Buddha taught cover virtually all of our experience including our mental experience which is covered by the fourth category. He asks us to be fully present with all experience as we cultivate new levels of self-awareness. Doing so is the key to freeing us from the grasping and clinging in all areas of our life which causes so much suffering. We set the intention to cultivate clarity about the fullness of our experience.

Mindfulness is an active process; it is not spacing out on life. One of the goals of meditation is to cultivate non-judgmental awareness of the totality of our experience. We are not living our lives on autopilot; instead, we feel connected to our experience. We are not pushing it away if it is unpleasant or clinging to it if it is pleasant. We bring an open-minded curiosity to our experiences as we watch them arise.

Before establishing a regular meditation practice I lived my life largely on autopilot. Day after day, I functioned mindlessly much of the time, lost in unproductive thought about mean-ingless topics. Every day seemed like the previous one regularly interrupted by some manifestation of my suffering or self-judg-ment. I was bored and unhappy and my life lacked joy or rich-ness. Each day was predictable and days flew by with a notable sameness. I took things for granted without appreciating the bounty of life.

My meditation practice woke me up to the pattern into which my life had fallen. I began to pay attention to my surroundings and my choices became clearer and consistent with how I want-ed to live my life. I was no longer a passenger in my journey—I was now the driver. Boredom decreased and more joy began to come into my daily life as I appreciated all the gifts in life. I no longer took so much for granted. When combined with the teachings of the Dharma my daily life started making sense to me and having meaning.

Meditation practice helps us develop greater discernment regarding our experiences and more wisdom about life as it is, not as we wish it to be. Meditation practice is not a means of ridding ourselves of aspects of our behavior or personality that we dislike. Instead, it is a means of changing the relationship with those aspects of who we are. We become less judgmental about ourselves and are more inclined to accept all parts of ourselves with compassion. We begin to see that perfection is not achievable and begin to give up the quest for it.

If you are not currently a meditator I suggest that meditation is best learned in real time with guidance from a teacher. I recommend you join a meditation group, take a class, or avail yourself of guided instructions on the Internet. Below is a brief instruction if you want to begin on your own.

The instructions are straightforward and relatively brief. However, the practice requires discipline and a willingness to set aside time daily. Remember that it is an active, engaged, and purposeful activity—not a time to make a grocery list. Your mind will constantly wander which is what our minds do. We return to our anchor point, typically the breath, each time we realize that our minds have wandered. We always do so with kindness and without judgment.

Find a comfortable sitting posture that is upright and alert in a quiet room. It is best not to have your back supported as you may fall asleep once you begin to relax. Set a timer for 5-10 minutes if you have never meditated. Take a couple of slow deep breaths with your eyes closed. Let your breath settle into a natural rhythm. Do not try to control your breath. Rest your attention on the breath at the tip of the nostril as it enters or leaves the nose. Pay attention to the mind as it wanders into thoughts. This is normal and will happen frequently. When you notice that it has happened, very gently, without judgment, return your awareness to the breath. Continue this practice until the time is up and slowly open your eyes. Take a moment to come back into outward-directed attention. Set aside time each day for this practice. Gradually increase the length of time for your daily meditation until you reach 30-45".

For mindfulness to be other than a means of stress reduction, it requires a solid ethical foundation. All the world's faith traditions, Buddhism included, have such a foundation. The central question is whether we can ever be truly happy if we live contrary to our core values and ethics. This is why we look to the Buddha's teachings for guidance on living an ethical life consistent with our values. The Noble Eightfold Path provides a game plan for living ethically in concert with our meditation practice.

An instruction as simple as "Do no harm" provides guidance on living an ethical life. No such instruction is regularly offered with secular mindfulness. I am not suggesting that anything goes with secular mindfulness. Instead of being explicit about an ethical foundation any such foundation in secular mindfulness is not apparent. While those in medicine, and the helping professions, who use mindfulness in their practices typically adhere to their professional codes of ethical conduct, their ethics are not necessarily accessible to those to whom they prescribe mindfulness.

The Buddha eschewed an ascetic path on the one hand and one of sensual indulgence on the other. He did not ask us to live like monks or renunciants. He fully understood that true happiness was not attainable if we behave unethically in our daily lives or pursue unbridled sensual pleasure. Mindfulness alone is not an antidote for immoral or unethical behavior. It requires the underlying wisdom and guidance that the Buddha offered.

One of the appeals to me of Buddhism is that it does not deal in absolutes as do other faith traditions. It gives us guideposts with which to mindfully contemplate a course of action that is ethical and does no harm. We are not threatened with eternal damnation or other punishments should we fall short in our efforts.

Buddhism is not a judging or shaming tradition. It is loving and compassionate. It accepts our human frailties. As we cultivate these qualities, our ethical foundation is strengthened because we care for ourselves and others. We want to do right. Our participation in a community, a Sangha, further supports our ethical behavior. The Buddha taught a Dharma that was not based on faith or metaphysical beliefs or requirements. Instead, he asks us to take individual responsibility for following the ethical tenets of his teachings. We are guided by the wisdom achieved through our regular meditation practice and our honest discernment of ethical questions in concert with the ancient teachings of the Buddha.

Reflection:

- Have you previously tried to meditate but had no success? Are you willing to try again, possibly with the help of a group or teacher?

Chapter Six

Impermanence

"Man suffers because of his craving to possess and keep forever things which are essentially impermanent."

—*Alan Watts*

Impermanence and acceptance are often taught together because they are so closely related. Without accepting that all phenomena are impermanent, inconstant, or unreliable we are not seeing the world as it is. We are stuck wishing it otherwise which is a sure path to suffering.

One of the Buddha's many brilliant insights, impermanence is central to understanding why and how humans suffer. It is one of the three characteristics of existence that the Buddha taught, the other two being not-self and suffering.

Not-self is an elusive concept for many. A popular misconception is that we do not have an identity. It refers instead to the absence of a fixed, unchanging self that is permanent. It is also the source of the ego we spend so much time and energy protecting and defending. Whenever we say, "I am (fill in the blank)," we are identified with and show our attachment to the idea of a fixed self or ego.

Simply stated, impermanence means that everything is constantly changing including ourselves. The Buddha said, "All conditioned things (by which he meant they arise, persist with alteration for a time, and then cease) are impermanent." It is not impermanence *per se* that causes suffering; instead, it is our clinging to things to try and make them permanent. Acceptance of the universality of impermanence is central to the Buddhist path of reducing suffering. It is a key tenet of the path and underlies all the other teachings.

Acceptance as a practice in both Buddhism and ACT is an antidote to avoidance of seeing life as it is, not as we want it to be. It is a practice that confronts our longing for persons, places, and things to be permanent.

For example, I want my loved ones to live forever or at least outlive me. I cling to that wish and do not accept that I have no control over that outcome. My clinging creates suffering in the form of incessant worry about the well-being of my loved ones. I am so busy worrying that I miss the joy of spending time with them in the here and now. Or, I want my shiny new smartphone with which I am smitten to continue to bring me joy and continuing happiness forever. When the novelty of the phone wears off, as it indeed will, I suffer due to the disappointment of it no longer making me happy and excited. An essential element of accepting impermanence is letting go of fixed ideas about how we want the world to be despite having no control over it.

I grew up in the 1950s when a boy would excitedly collect cereal box tops to send in for the free toy graphically displayed on the back of every box of Kellogg cereal. Once I had the required number of box tops after several months I would mail them in with great anticipation. My longing for the toy to arrive was so great that I could feel it in my body. I suffered from the tension. Every day I would rush home from school and check the mail on the hall table to see if my toy had arrived. I thought about it constantly, and even though the excitement was positive, it was a form of suffering due to its all-consuming nature. Finally, after what seemed like months I arrived home from school to see a package with a return address of Kellogg. Without fail, the toy was a cheap trinket the novelty of which almost immediately dissipated. My suffering then took the form of deep disappointment both at the cheapness of the toy and because my weeks of suffering in the form of my longing were for naught. Such is the nature of our suffering.

In its many forms avoidance of reality keeps us from facing life as it is and from accepting the sorrows of this human life. Whenever we engage in wishful thinking about the status of people, places, or things we invite suffering into our lives.

Humans suffer which can be debilitating. Our psychological pain includes difficult emotions and thoughts, unpleasant or painful memories, unwanted urges, and sensations. We think about them, worry about them, resent them; we anticipate and dread them. We try to get rid of our pain which amplifies it, entangles us further in it, and potentially transforms it into something traumatic.

Humans resist the idea that life is filled with uncertainty. Simply put, we do not like it and try to deny it. Uncertainty about the future makes us anxious so we invent stories, beliefs, superstitions, and religious doctrines to try to reduce the uncertainty in our lives. We try to control the future be it five minutes from now or five years from now. Without accepting that the future is unknowable, and that we have little to no control over it, we engage in fruitless worry and anticipation and suffer accordingly. Letting go and accepting that we cannot know what lies ahead brings a great deal of freedom and reduced suffering in our day-to-day lives.

None of this is to say that we are not resilient or capable of coping with adversity when it occurs. Humans have the capacity for courage, compassion, and the ability to face tragic circumstances. Adversity and uncertainty do not stop us from loving, dealing with hurt and loss, and being present with all of life.

Avoidance of painful emotions and facts are primary sources of our suffering. What is it we do not accept? The list includes our bodies aging, loss of youthful vigor, conflicts with others, past failures or regrets, old resentments, financial stress, and unmet goals to name a few.

As a practicing psychologist, I treated people with phobias and other anxiety disorders. We know from years of research that avoidance of that which is frightening or painful is at the root of anxiety disorders including phobias. When we avoid an anxiety-provoking situation by removing ourselves from it we strengthen the fear; we become more afraid, not less. While avoidance stops the anxiety in the moment, over time it makes the object of avoidance stronger and the anxiety greater. Our world shrinks as we engage in more and more avoidance of what frightens us. In ACT we talk about experiential avoidance which means avoiding not just that which is external but just as importantly that which is internal including thoughts, feelings, and sensations that are painful, unpleasant, or frightening. Have we not all said in the face of something frightening or unpleasant, "I don't want to think about it."

With ACT there is the concept of creative hopelessness which is the experience of seeing that our efforts to fix a problem are only making it worse. For example, recognizing the unworkability of experiential avoidance. It is waking up to the fruitlessness of our attempts to control our inner experiences. This opens the door for our willingness to make room for new possibilities such as accepting the situation as it is, not as we want it to be. We can then let go of what is not working.

So what exactly does it mean to let go? It is the opposite of clinging or grasping to persons, places, beliefs, experiences, or things. It is the acceptance of things as they are, not as we want them to be. For example, if I am stuck in traffic I can curse, fret, and become upset that the traffic is not moving when I have somewhere to be. Or, I can accept that there is absolutely nothing that I can do about the traffic jam. Instead, I focus on relaxing and accepting the situation by focusing on my breathing rather than generating mental messages that frustrate and aggravate me. In other words, I let go.

The most effective ACT treatment for anxiety disorders is facing our fears in what is known as graduated exposure to the fearful situation. This is "psych-speak" for saying that we must face our fears or they will control us. The adage we use in therapy for anxiety disorders and other emotional suffering is, "What we resist, persists." In ACT change requires a willingness and the courage to have our unpleasant experiences. The Buddha understood this over 2600 years ago. He said that transformation happens when "Suffering is known." When we accept and face, or lean into, our suffering—anxiety, fear, and scary places—we can change our relationship to them and obtain freedom. I have seen this in my life and hundreds of times in my clinical work.

One of our biggest challenges is accepting the impermanence of our lives and those we love. The paradox of loss is that it opens our hearts and strips away our protective armor whether we want it to or not. As we open to the experience of loss, accept it and lean into it rather than avoid it, we step into the stream of the experience of loss. We feel a lightening of the load. In ACT terms, we are more psychologically flexible. We are still sad and feel grief but are better able to ride the waves of it.

As our acceptance grows so does our experience of freedom. Of being able to be with what is present in the moment despite the pain of it. Facing that which we want to turn away from with compassion and without judgment is truly a path to freedom.

We shift from a judgmental and controlling stance about our internal experience to a compassionate and accepting perspective. We stop working so hard to repress or avoid that which is painful and understand that doing so only worsens our suffering.

Acceptance, the "A" in ACT, leads to freedom because it makes us more psychologically resilient and more able to embrace all experiences. Emotional rigidity and inflexibility, including fixed ideas about how life should be, cause much suffering. With acceptance, we do not waste energy avoiding things. We are not shut down and emotionally contracted. Rather, we are open to whatever life hands us which results in true freedom. The opposite of not opening to all experience is to constrict, avoid, and deny. With acceptance, we move from resistance to embracing life as it is.

I would like to share an experience of true acceptance of impermanence that I witnessed several years ago. One of my best friends was someone I met over four decades ago. We remained close friends up until his death several years ago. Though we lived in different cities we vacationed with him and his family every summer. Our children grew up together. My friend was very successful in business and lived as full a life as anyone you will ever meet. He traveled the world and climbed mountains; he lived life with energy, passion, and presence. In 2010, after several years of undiagnosed problems, he was diagnosed with a rare form of cancer for which there was no specific treatment protocol available. My friend immediately began an aggressive treatment regimen as he was unwilling to accept that his life would end so early. He fought the disease with every means he could muster. My wife, Kay, and I begin traveling every 3 to 4 weeks to spend time with my friend and his family and to offer support. I spent hours talking to him about his life and his difficulty accepting his imminent death.

I was fortunate to watch his transformation from fighting the inevitable to accepting the reality of his death. It was a profound teaching on letting go and accepting the impermanence of our existence. He relaxed and his sense of humor returned. He could appreciate the gift that his life had been including the people he loved and who loved him. The last time I saw him before he died he was a shadow of his former self. I held him and told him I loved him. He was semi-conscious but I knew that he had heard me. His wife later told us that he died peacefully after we returned home surrounded by her and their children.

My friend's acceptance of the inevitability of his death brought him a sense of peace at the end that was profound to witness. He showed the true meaning of acceptance during one of the most challenging times in our lives. Though my loss was profound I am grateful for the teaching that he provided me.

Reflection:

- Acknowledging the reality of impermanence can be unsettling as we feel out of control. What is your reaction to the teaching on impermanence?

Chapter Seven

Noticing

"You may even have so many thoughts that it seems as if trying to meditate makes them increase, but you are just noticing the previously unidentified extent of your own ramblings. Your attempts at mindfulness are causing you to notice what is happening."

——*Dalai Lama XIV*

An important practice I always include in my teaching is the fundamental activity of noticing. If we are on autopilot and not mindful/noticing our experience we cannot utilize the other tools of our practice. We must seek contact with the present moment.

Once we undertake the practice of noticing, we must develop the habit of pausing when we are in a challenging situation. It is sufficiently important that we refer to it in Buddhism as the "sacred pause."

Noticing is an essential part of being mindful. For example, if I am in a long slow checkout line at the supermarket and begin to feel irritated it is a cue to notice what is going on internally. I pause to pay attention to where I feel out of sorts in my body. What thoughts are arising? What story am I telling myself about the line taking so long? What steps can I take to change my perspective and create spaciousness around what is happening? Doing so creates an opportunity to let go of the self-centered, ego-based, expectation that the line should move faster for me.

The process is not as complicated or involved as it sounds; typically it only takes a couple of moments. We simply shift our attention to the body. Is there tightness or tension? Where in the body? Is our jaw clenched? Can we feel frustration or irritation arising in our midsection? What thoughts are accompanying the changes in our body?

Noticing and pausing open the door to reducing suffering in the form of frustration and impatience from being in a long slow checkout line. Such situations present an opportunity for acceptance of the situation as it is and to let go of our expectations and sense of self-importance. Imagine what it can do for more challenging situations, especially in the relationship realm.

Another critical and related skill is discernment. It is a close cousin of noticing and is the process of differentiating between beneficial and not beneficial choices in whatever context we find ourselves. Discernment involves seeing life clearly without delusion, not as we want it to be. Discernment is a critical step in pointing to where we need to let go of clinging or attachments that cause suffering. It is also essential to our ethical foundation and the development of wisdom.

The Buddha suggested that we seek out wise contemplatives to help with discernment. It is why working with a teacher on this path can be so beneficial. We all have blind spots as we travel the path of Practical Dharma and a wise teacher can help us identify them. Consulting a teacher also helps to tame the ego by reinforcing a position of humility. The guidance of my teacher over the years has been critically important to my journey on the Buddhist path.

The Buddha believed that the search for real long-term happiness could only succeed if we employ discernment in our lives. We have agency over our decisions and choices—we only need to exercise them skillfully. Discernment helps us see if our decisions are wholesome or unwholesome and whether they will lead to more suffering or a reduction in suffering.

While the notion of *karma* in the Buddha's time, a vestige of Hinduism, referred to cycles of death and birth many modern Buddhists have eschewed that notion. For many Western Buddhists, it has been replaced with the idea that our actions have consequences. It is the law of cause and effect, often characterized as "What goes around, comes around." Or, as the *Holy Bible* says "As ye sow, so shall ye reap." When we engage in meritorious acts we reap the rewards of inner satisfaction, extending goodwill to others, and making the world better. The Buddha taught that our actions and choices are impactful so we should be mindful of that fact and use discernment and wisdom to guide us.

Discernment can also help us delay gratification when pursuing sensual pleasure. The Buddha considered sensual pleasure one of the Five Hindrances that hold us back on our path. All Five Hindrances (sensual desire, ill-will, doubt, sloth and torpor, and restlessness/worry) are considered habits of mind disrupting our meditation practice and our progress on the path. Anything that impinges on our senses, what the Buddha called "sense doors," can become a hindrance to our present-moment awareness if we fail to manage it skillfully.

Discernment helps us distinguish between healthy and unhealthy desires. Unchecked desire can become a compulsion or addiction, interfere with our awareness of the present moment, and create problems in our relationships and lives. As we bring discernment to our desires we may find they are tied to ideas about emotional connection, security, success, status, or a need for reassurance. Are we trying to use sense pleasures to fill an emotional void such as sadness or loneliness? If so, we must understand desire as an "itch that can't be scratched." Discernment is the tool needed to make such distinctions.

In my years of practice as a clinical psychologist, I found that desire and craving for sense pleasures were for many people an attempt to self-medicate unpleasant emotional states, an example of experiential avoidance. These include eating when not hungry, casual or compulsive sex, intoxication with drugs or alcohol, compulsive spending, excessive gambling, spending hours on the internet, compulsive exercise, or anything done to excess that takes us out of the present moment. Noticing, pausing, and discernment are the means of more skillfully managing problematic desires.

For example, I am helpless when presented with chocolate in any form. It is comfort food for me. I reach for chocolate when I am tired, sad, stressed, or overwhelmed as a cure for many of my ills. While doing so temporarily distracts me from my unpleasant feeling state, it prevents me from dealing with my mood more skillfully. The feeling state persists. At that moment I am not pausing, noticing, or using discernment; I am stuffing chocolate in my mouth. This is how addiction or compulsion pulls us toward sensual pleasure. Often it is a misplaced attempt to fill an emptiness or manage frustration or other negative emotional state.

With mindfulness, present-moment focus, and being open to all experience, we learn to fill our inner emptiness with awareness, spaciousness, and a sense of connection to everything and everyone. When we become familiar with our tendency toward sensual desire by noticing, pausing, and discernment, freedom only requires looking at desire directly, naming it, and feeling how it is experienced in the body.

If I do not reach for the chocolate but instead bring mindful awareness to my unpleasant mood I have the option to address my mood skillfully. I can then touch into the joy of being present, settled, and concentrated. Sensual desire becomes less and less powerful. The satisfaction and confidence I experience can help me manage the compulsion behind my desire. As we become free of the compulsive desire for sensual pleasure by pausing, noticing, and discerning, we use that freedom to decide wisely which desires or aspirations we will allow to guide our life.

Another aspect of noticing is shining a flashlight into the dark corners of who we are by taking a brutally honest look at ourselves, especially our unwholesome and problematic personality traits and behavior patterns. We are all capable of denying or disavowing the parts of ourselves that we deem to be harmful, unacceptable, or contrary to how we like to view ourselves—the parts we feel ashamed about so deny or hide. Acknowledging them is a complex process as our ego screams "No, no, no, don't make me look!"

I am describing what Carl Jung, the famous psychoanalyst, called "The Shadow Self." He characterized it as composed of repressed ideas, instincts, impulses, weaknesses, desires, perversions, and shameful and embarrassing fears. It is often the wellspring of our reactivity, suffering, and poor choices.

Note that discerning does not involve judging. Judging ourselves in the process of noticing or discerning causes contraction and shame, not freedom and openness.

Reflection:

- Noticing practice requires a significant shift from our usual way of functioning on autopilot. What challenges do you foresee in beginning a noticing practice?

Chapter Eight

Suffering

"There are only two tragedies in this life; one is not getting what one wants, and the other is getting what one wants."

—*Oscar Wilde*

Suffering when we do not get what we want is obvious—but what about suffering when we get what we want? The tragedy then is that it never lasts so we suffer. This is the nature of impermanence that the Buddha so brilliantly described. One of the things that most appealed to me about Buddhism was the acknowledgment and normalizing of suffering in life and the offering of a means to address the suffering. In the psychology field ACT does likewise. In other faith traditions suffering, which is part of the human experience, is typically addressed by the promise of a better suffering-free afterlife. In other words, suffering may be without relief in this life but will be lifted in the next life.

Suffering, both large and small, is everywhere in our lives and we, as humans, engage in various tactics and strategies to avoid it. Unfortunately, we cannot buy, achieve, accumulate, succeed, drink, drug, or have enough sex to overcome suffering. Try as we might to ignore it, avoid it, run from it, deny it, or cover it up with all kinds of activity, distractions, and mental gymnastics—at the end of the day we still suffer. Rarely do we have difficulty with pleasant things other than the fact they never last. We welcome the 10,000 joys of life, for as long as they last, but try to avoid the 10,000 sorrows that the Taoists teach.

I view suffering as one of the most effective teachers on the spiritual path. Suffering calls our attention to dysfunctional aspects of our life so that we can no longer ignore them. It is like a toothache that continues to hurt until we see the dentist. It is a spiritual wake-up call. In my experience, many people find their way to the Dharma as a result of their suffering.

I grew up in a family overflowing with dysfunction. Early in life I unconsciously concluded that if I strived to be perfect in every way—grades, manners, and behavior—I would be rewarded with the love and acceptance that all children need and crave. I believed that being perfect was the way to alleviate my suffering. Upon entering puberty I realized that my strategy was not working. I went in the opposite direction by rebelling against everyone and everything but that did not work either. My suffering persisted if not worsened.

My suffering deepened in early adulthood in the form of anxiety, depression, and dysfunctional relationships. I felt a painful separation from everyone and everything. I felt ashamed as if I was the only one suffering from isolation, loneliness, and alienation. The faith tradition in which I was raised provided no relief nor did it give a perspective to understand or make sense of the suffering in which I was immersed.

Because of my pain, I was highly motivated to find a way out of my suffering, something that psychotherapy was partially helpful in achieving. My introduction to Buddhism and the Dharma completed the search. Once I began a regular mediation practice and a study of the teachings I knew I was on the right path to finding some answers.

In the 30 years since I embraced the Buddhist path, every aspect of my life has been better in immeasurable ways. Once I understood and accepted my suffering, and leaned into it by embracing it head-on rather than running from it, the light bulbs began to turn on.

Accepting that my suffering was the product of the causes and conditions that I grew up with was vital. I was not bad or defective nor needed to feel ashamed of who I was; I was not weak for suffering. My suffering was a gift in my life for as much as I hated it; it brought me to Buddhism and the understanding and relief I sought.

In Buddhism, we embrace our suffering with two outcomes in mind. The first is that by accepting and welcoming our suffering without judgment we reduce it. The second goal is to reduce the suffering of those with whom we are close and who have been subjected to our unskillful and hurtful actions that were a product of acting out or externalizing our suffering.

In the West, we tend to feel guilty and ashamed when we suffer as if we are defective for not meeting the Western ideal of perfection. This is not the Buddhist view. The Buddha's teachings spoke to me as nothing else had—I knew immediately that I had found my spiritual path and my spiritual home. Buddhism provided a framework and context in which my suffering finally made sense to me. It taught me the sources of my suffering and all the things I was habitually doing to perpetuate it. I no longer experienced it as a defect, a failing, or something about which I should feel ashamed.

One of the many things the Buddhist path has helped me see is that I can feel compassion for my suffering. Self-compassion is essential to healing but requires that we acknowledge our suffering without shame. Shame about our suffering forces us to hide, deny, avoid, and disavow it. Compassion for ourselves is a powerful antidote to shame. Our suffering can be a gift that teaches us and points us toward compassion for ourselves and others. I was motivated to become a Buddhist teacher to introduce this path to others because of the powerful impact of the teachings in my own life.

I have deep gratitude for how this path has reduced my suffering. As I say to my students, "If it can work for me, it can work for anyone," provided there is a willingness to commit to the path including regular meditation practice. Participation in a community or Sangha is also critically important. With so many online offerings for community, this should not be difficult.

Thich Nhat Hanh, the recently deceased Vietnamese monk, said, "No mud, no lotus" by which he meant that we try to avoid suffering, or cover it up, because it can feel so bad. Unless we can face our suffering (the mud), we cannot be present and available to life, and happiness and joy (the lotus) will continue to elude us.

Let us take a deeper look into suffering as the Buddha taught. He paradoxically stated that accepting our suffering is a path to reducing our suffering. As I noted earlier suffering is too narrow a translation of "dukkha," the Pali word. It also includes dissatisfaction, uneasiness, anxiety, annoyance, and worry. Suffering is any state of unease that we experience.

Variations of the experience might include not getting what we crave, not getting enough of what we crave, not having our expectations for what we crave met, getting what we want but worrying about losing it, or getting what we crave but becoming bored with it. The list is not exhaustive but gives you a flavor of how varied the experience of suffering can be. The Buddha was even more nuanced in breaking down the experiences of suffering into three categories.

In the first category, the Buddha described the type of suffering that occurs with unpleasant physical or mental experiences. Without fail, our lives will include unpleasant experiences but routine unpleasant experiences are not what the Buddha meant by this first type of suffering. Rather, our aversion to unpleasant experience constitutes this first category of suffering. The origin of this type of suffering is our craving or longing that the circumstances of our lives be different—that the unpleasantness cease.

The situations with which we are unhappy are typically not subject to change. This leaves changing our response to the unpleasant experience as our only option to reduce our suffering. If we accept unpleasant feelings and sensations, be fully present with them, and recognize their impermanence this type of suffering will be reduced. This was a brilliant insight by the Buddha that requires noticing, pausing, and discernment. For example, if I cut my finger it hurts. Physical pain is unavoidable but if I avoid engaging in the mental activity of craving that my cut finger not hurt (i.e., accept it), this type of suffering would not arise. The physical pain from my cut finger will run its course as it is impermanent. The mental anguish only occurred when I responded with aversion to the physical pain. That is, when I longed for it to disappear and be replaced with pleasant or neutral sensations and feelings, an unrealistic craving.

The second category of suffering that the Buddha described occurs when we go beyond simple aversion in response to a negative physical or mental experience and add stressful thoughts about it. This includes judgments, rules, and anxious thoughts and questions. The Buddha brilliantly illustrated this teaching with the parable of the *Two Arrows* from the Pali Canon. He taught that the first arrow which strikes us represents an unavoidable source of suffering such as my cut finger. The second arrow is self-inflicted and is the suffering that we add to the original injury by our mental and emotional reaction to the pain from the first arrow. While the teaching focuses on the physical injury caused by the arrows it applies to all the challenges we encounter.

This type of suffering is also called existential suffering because it is the suffering from simply being alive and knowing that nothing lasts. It manifests as a constant underlying unease and uncertainty about the future with which we must live. It also originates in "tanha" (craving) because our mental activity reflects a wish for things to be how we want them to be, not as they are.

When I could, with mindful present awareness, accept the unpleasant nature of the pain of my cut finger the first category of suffering did not arise. It arose only when I reacted with aversion by wishing for the pain to stop. The second category of suffering was not far behind in the form of second-arrow mental activity such as, "How dumb of me that I cut my finger." "What if it gets infected?" "I have too much to do. I don't have time for this." The suffering here originated from the anxiety-filled stories I concoct about my injured finger.

Several years ago another one of my close friends died. The first type of suffering arose when I felt an aversion to grief. I did not want to feel the pain of it but when I added thoughts such as

"I will be so lonely." "This grief may make me ill." "Who will I do fun things with without my friend," I was in the throes of the second category of suffering. The challenge is bringing these thoughts into conscious awareness, setting them aside, and letting them go. Acceptance creates an experience of spaciousness about the event; it enlarges our perspective. Engaging in the mental activity described changes nothing and only adds to our suffering.

With mindfulness practice (inside or outside of formal meditation) we become aware of whatever sensations or feelings are arising by noticing either from outside stimuli (someone playing drums loudly next door), body stimuli (that painful cut finger), or from our thoughts in response to these stimuli. If the stimulus is unpleasant our mental reaction can range from a simple craving for it to stop (first category) to the mental formations of the second category, such as "If he doesn't stop playing the drums, I'm going to flip out."

As our practice deepens, we can shift our focus from the feeling tone of our experience to its impermanent nature. Seeing the impermanence of all phenomena shows us that trying to control our experience and make it pleasant only increases our suffering. This is where we start letting go of wishing for life to be other than it is in the moment. Achieving this is what I refer to as, "holding it all." We complement the process by employing the

ACT technique of defusion, which is watching our thinking without getting hooked by our thoughts.

The third category of suffering that the Buddha described also originates in craving. While the first two categories occur in response to unpleasant experiences, the third category arises in response to pleasant ones. When we enjoy a pleasant experience we crave for it to continue and we suffer when it does not. The craving is often present during the pleasant experience. We experience underlying displeasure when we are having a good time because it will not last.

I sit on the beach after dinner when we go to Jamaica in the winter enjoying the natural beauty of the island and the breeze off the sea. It is something that I look forward to all year yet I always had a nagging feeling that something was amiss. Over time I realized, thanks to the practice of Practical Dharma, that I was experiencing the third category of suffering that the Buddha described.

The sunset would not last and my focus was on not wanting the sun to set rather than the moment's beauty. The Buddha taught that "Nothing that is impermanent can ever be satisfactory." He understood that the transience of all worldly phenomena can negate pleasant experience.

Our experience of transience can only successfully be handled by coming to terms with the temporary nature of all things and noticing and accepting this fact. Simply put, by wanting permanence we will suffer because we will never get it. Again, we are reminded that craving and grasping underlie all types of suffering because we crave for life to be other than it is.

So how do we manage the types of suffering in our lives? First and very importantly we must become aware of when suffering is present. If we do not notice it we are flying blind on autopilot. This requires mindfulness and discernment because all three kinds of suffering are subtle and often hard to recognize. It requires contact with the present moment that both the Dharma and ACT offer us.

When we feel dissatisfied we must stop and notice our suffering. From that point, we examine our experience with discernment until we find the place where we are not getting what we want or are getting what we do not want. Lastly, we consciously try to let go of this craving and remind ourselves to accept the circumstances of life as they are at that moment.

As with the Jamaican sunset, I first became aware that during a most pleasant experience I felt a bit of unease and dissatisfaction. I then examined that dissatisfaction until I found the source—my wish for that sunset to last forever. Of course, as the Buddha fully understood that could never happen.

By embracing the concept of impermanence I could consciously choose to let go of my craving for the sunset to be other than a temporary phenomenon. Having done so I was free to enjoy, in the present moment, the pleasant experience for as long as it lasted. Too often, however, we are so busy worrying about an enjoyable experience ending that we fail to enjoy it in the moment. To paraphrase a popular bumper sticker "Suffering happens."

Getting to the root of our suffering—this constant dissatisfaction in our lives—opens an opportunity to let go of grasping and craving. When we are not getting what we want, or what we do not want, we can consciously choose to let go of that craving. When we let go of the clinging, even for only a few seconds or minutes, we have a taste of freedom that lingers. Freedom has an expansive, open quality to it. At that moment suffering ceases, which is what the Buddha taught in the Third Noble Truth—that the end of suffering is possible through the abandonment of craving.

The Eightfold Path, and the fourth of the Four Noble Truths, contain the Buddha's complete treatment plan for understanding suffering by abandoning craving. It is the cure for the disease of suffering and the path that offers us the possibility of fulfilling our human potential through the cultivation of wisdom, ethical intentions, and mindfulness. All we must do is avail ourselves of it.

Reflection:

- We often think that if only we try hard enough or achieve enough success we can eliminate suffering in our lives. How does it feel knowing that suffering is an inevitable and unavoidable part of life?

Chapter Nine

Ego

"It's in the act of having to do things that you don't want to that you learn something about moving past the self. Past the ego."

—*bell hooks*

Did you know that the Buddha never instructed us to rid ourselves of a separate self or ego? Neither should we hide behind it or drape it in spiritual language to avoid dealing with our emotional baggage. Our challenge is to develop a healthy sense of self/ego that recognizes its ever-changing quality and frees us from fixed ideas about who or what we are, particularly when those fixed ideas reflect a tendency toward self-aggrandizement or grandiosity.

My decision to include a separate chapter on the self/ego reflects my bias as a clinical psychologist. I am not referring to ego in the sense that Freud talked about it as part of the triad of id, ego, and super-ego, which has specific theoretical implications. I am using the term to refer to our sense of a separate self; the fragile thing we work so hard to inflate, protect, defend, and hold up. While I do not believe the Buddha ever used the term ego, we have adopted it in the West to connote the sense of self he described. As much as we try to believe otherwise, our sense of self—of who we are—is not fixed or permanent. Our experience is ever-changing as are we.

Over the many years of my professional career, I daily saw in my office the suffering caused by the ego. Much human suffering is a function of protecting the ego from shame and invalidation and seeking means to obtain admiration and aggrandizement. Both the teachings of the Buddha and the methods of ACT comprised the tool kit that I used to address the suffering of my psychotherapy patients caused by the ego.

Ego is a mental construct consisting of a lifetime of stories we tell ourselves, and internalize, representing the totality of our life experiences filtered through our lens. The filter with which we see and experience the world combines our genetics, brain chemistry, home life as children, conditioning, peer relation-ships, economic circumstances, and other experiences we accu-mulate in a lifetime. The ego internalizes all the successes and failures of our life including all the joys and sorrows. It is our conscious self and is how we interact with the world around us.

It is who we tell ourselves we are which is often distorted out of self-interest.

The ego can be either inflated as seen with narcissism, deflated as seen with low self-esteem and depressive disorders, or it can be balanced with a realistic sense of our strengths and weaknesses. It is never static or fixed. It is constantly changing, from moment to moment, depending on external and internal circumstances.

The ego seeks happiness, gratification, recognition, and the fulfillment of sensual desire. Everything that we identify with is part of our ego. It is our conscious experience of who we are from which we unconsciously try to edit and exclude the negative qualities.

The ego is where the shame-pride continuum exists. Simply stated when we feel adequate within ourselves the ego feels pride. When we feel inadequate the ego feels shame. Shame and pride exist on a continuum at opposite ends; we vacillate continually along the continuum. We feel inflated when we are filled with pride and deflated when we are filled with shame. We seek to meet the world with a pride-filled ego as doing so reveals what we consider to be our most attractive traits. We try to keep our shameful parts hidden from others and ourselves for fear of being judged or rejected.

This trait of humankind, this ego, has caused untold suffering in the world over the millennia. It is all about I, me, and mine. Ego is where emotional reactivity originates. It is where the Three Poisons of greed, hatred, and delusion manifest. The source of comparing ourselves with others and external standards is the ego.

The ego is not something to get rid of even if we could. We need a healthy ego to function in the world. We also need to see where it causes great suffering and alienation from others. Monitoring our ego with mindful noticing, pausing, and discerning, we learn where the expression of our ego needs is unskillful and causes harm and suffering. We have agency to manage our unwholesome ego needs only if we are aware of them.

A healthy sense of self lives in the present moment as much as possible and has relinquished fixed ideas, either laudatory or negative, about itself. It guides us toward seeing our interconnectedness to all things as part of a much larger context. We refer to this as self-as-context in ACT. A healthy sense of self becomes less about our selfish motives and more about the greater good.

We could not function in the world without a sense of self. It is the mental template that guides us every minute of every day. We must have preferences and make choices. Our impulse control, based in our sense of self, puts the brakes on our worst tendencies in what is known as our executive function. We seek to cultivate a healthy and honest understanding of who we are, warts and all; we do not deny the problematic attitudes and behaviors. Instead, we work to recognize and accept them—which we can only do when we honestly embrace and admit them. We cease seeking our happiness outside of ourselves and stop trying to make ourselves special in the world. No longer do we use avoidant, compulsive, or distracting behaviors to deny who we are.

It took me years of Buddhist practice and study to clarify this path and set a skillful means of walking it. While I have a way to go my awareness of where I need to go and where I trip up is more evident. It has been and continues to be painful to admit to and acknowledge my shadow side. By incorporating self-compassion and self-forgiveness in the exploration, I can do so with less shame and self-recrimination. I began to see the worse that I felt about myself, the harder I tried to look good and inflate myself with others, which only served to alienate them. Such is the imbalance caused by trying to fix a negative self-assessment.

The work with our egos is not that of renunciation of all earthly pleasures, self-denial, or asceticism. It does not mean denying the joy in our lives or not having fun. It is an honest and balanced reassessment of who and what we are, shorn of all the baggage we pile on to look good, reassure ourselves, deny our negative qualities, and support our self-delusions.

As my practice deepened over the years it became more apparent that much of the narrative that I had developed about myself was a fiction to cover and soothe the wounds of my early life. Yet I worried that I would collapse into nothingness if I gave up the story. The narrative is what we psychologists call the "false self," a concept developed by the British psychiatrist D.W. Winnicott in the 1950s. The false self is the persona we put on like armor early in our lives to try and overcome early trauma and defend ourselves in the world.

Psychologists distinguish between highly traumatic events like abuse and neglect and so-called everyday trauma to connote the normal, but painful, slings and arrows of the human developmental experience. But even everyday trauma is painful and we work diligently to protect ourselves from experiencing it.

My false self has many facets as they do. One of the more prominent ones growing up was that of the good boy. Outward appearances reigned supreme in my Southern, privileged, white, upper-middle-class family. No one asked, knew, or wanted to know, what my internal experience was as long I looked good on the outside for the world to see. The standard was perfect manners, grooming, behavior, and performance at school and elsewhere. All my basic survival needs for shelter, food, clothing, and material comfort were met by my parents. I wanted nothing regarding such needs. Yet, I was very lonely as the experience was of never being seen or understood for who I indeed was—that real person beneath all the outward appearances.

This was a source of great suffering throughout my early life and young adulthood. I did not understand why I was unhappy since I was following all the rules and striving to be the good boy. Had I been sold a bill of goods? Was it a massive fraud? I felt dead inside.

I knew no other way and no source of relief until a course of intensive psychotherapy in my 30s followed by discovering the Buddhist path in my early 40s. When I began to delve into Buddhist teachings I felt I finally had a way of understanding and confronting my suffering beyond what even therapy had provided. For more than thirty years that promise has held though the work continues. The transformation in me has been profound regarding my self-acceptance and happiness and the happiness of those I love.

I do not want to leave you with the impression that any of this is easy. Typically, we have to be in such a state of suffering that we are highly motivated to do what we need to do to start changing. It takes tremendous courage and tenacity to look honestly at our flaws and imperfections. We need a lot of self-compassion and self-forgiveness to navigate such tricky waters. A community of fellow travelers, such as a Sangha or a 12-step group, can be invaluable for the journey.

Western Buddhism as it has evolved has incorporated the therapeutic culture of the West which has been a positive trend. The addition of Western psychological theory, specifically ACT, fits well with Buddhist teachings. The result is a much more robust means of reducing or attenuating suffering. The ego and the work required to manage it sit at the center of the combination of the two approaches.

Reflection:

- How do you expend time and energy in the care and feeding of your ego? As you think about doing less so, what thoughts arise?

Chapter Ten

Reactivity

"Suffering can thus be seen in large part as a kind of resistance or reactivity to the pain of the present moment."

—Donald Rothberg

Have you ever thought about the evolutionary purpose of shame? As with many other innate responses shame is a vestige of our evolutionary past. It is an emotion hardwired into the species that evolved so our ancient ancestors were inhibited from exhibiting behaviors that would result in their being banished from their family, community, or tribe. Evolution selected those with a higher tendency for shame because banishment from the tribes of our ancestors 200,000 years on the savannahs of Africa meant certain death from starvation, predators, or hostile tribes. Those with a low capacity for shame were banished and did not survive when they behaved badly. Therefore, they did not pass their genes on to future generations. Humans evolved to be shame prone; it is considered a hard-wired emotion. In our lives, without mindful management, excessive or toxic shame is one of the primary causes of emotional reactivity. A primary challenge in practicing Practical Dharma is managing our emotional reactivity. Simply put, emotional reactivity is the problematic tendency to be controlled by our emotions.

Suffering almost always involves a degree of impulsive reactivity. Individuals living in a constant state of emotional reactivity are characterized as emotionally dysregulated, making stable relationships difficult and causing much suffering.

One of the basic tenets of Buddhist teaching is the need to learn to manage our emotions as we progress on the spiritual path. The fundamental challenge in reducing reactivity and achieving equanimity is acceptance of things as they are, not as we want them to be. Suffice it to say our mind is not at ease, nor are we at peace, when we are in a state of emotional reactivity.

Viewed from an ACT perspective we exhibit psychological flexibility when our unskillful emotions are not battering us. Instead, we cope with, accept, and adapt to difficult situations. Such flexibility requires self-awareness through mindful discernment and contact with our core values.

Emotional reactivity has multiple triggers and manifestations—individual (shame and guilt), relational (anger and conflict), and social (taking sides). The popular term for emotional reactivity is "hair trigger."

Reactivity involves our conscious mind so we can, with practice, make choices about our reactivity such that we are not prisoners of, and governed by, our emotions. Decisions made based on emotions rarely turn out well. We all have multiple triggers for our reactivity, the specific nature of which results from our individual life experiences.

In addressing our reactivity we first cultivate awareness by noticing and pausing. Then we can see with intention and discernment the pattern of our reactivity and how we become contracted in heart and mind. Each of us has unique recurring and predictable reactivity patterns based on our personal history.

The absence of reactivity is characterized by a sense of spaciousness and qualities of clarity and humility. We are calm, reflective, and experience equanimity. Our emotional stance is largely in balance. We are psychologically flexible in our dealings with the world and "look before we leap" in most situations.

The Three Poisons of greed, hatred/aversion, and delusion are significant contributors to our reactivity. Emotional reactivity is often characterized as bondage; its absence is characterized by freedom from suffering.

Shame is a primary human emotion and central to our understanding of reactivity. Psychologists' study and understanding of shame exploded 40 years ago and forever changed the field. Because it is so important we will examine it in more detail beginning with some definitions.

Guilt and shame are often confused though they frequently co-occur. Guilt is the result of a transgression against someone or something which typically focuses on external behavior. For example, if I break your lamp I feel guilty. Guilt offers redemption and reconciliation through corrective words or actions. If I replace your lamp my guilt is reduced or eliminated. If I disparage you but then apologize my guilt is lessened.

Shame is different. We feel shame when we violate an internal or external standard to which we subscribe. The focus is on our sense of self, our ego, and self-worth. With toxic unhealthy shame, we feel flawed, unlovable, and defective. For example, if I do not live up to perfectionistic standards in some aspect of my life I must be flawed or damaged. This is negative or toxic shame.

Healthy shame is an inborn emotion that helps govern our socially appropriate behavior. It is necessary for our acceptance in our social group as was true for our ancient ancestors. Embarrassment and feeling self-conscious are mild forms of shame while humiliation is an intense form.

Positive morality is a result of healthy shame. In anticipation of feeling shame I will avoid engaging in immoral, illegal, or socially unacceptable behavior such as taking all my clothes off in public or eating with my hands in a fancy restaurant. Healthy shame signals us to put the brakes on our unskillful impulses to inhibit our most offensive tendencies and prevent negative judgment or rejection by others.

Shame becomes a problem and triggers reactivity when we attack ourselves for not meeting an arbitrary standard. If the experience is sufficiently intense, suicide can be the response in highly shame-prone cultures.

Violence will likely ensue if we feel shamed or disrespected by others. For example, road rage incidents typically have shame as the source of violent or reckless behavior. The emotional response is shame if one feels small, diminished, or disrespected, such as when cut off in traffic. The angry reactivity, born of shame, is then directed outwardly toward the other driver.

Healthy shame is the guardian of ethical and moral behavior in Buddhism. In his more general teachings the Buddha called shame-like emotions a "Bright guardian of the world" in that it kept people from betraying the trust of others. He also called shame-like emotions a "Noble treasure" which is more valuable than gold or silver because it protects us from doing things we would later regret.

The suffering from toxic shame, and the triggered reactivity, come from our often unconscious clinging to the idea that we must live up to an unrealistic, if not perfectionistic, standard in all aspects of our life. Another trigger is the belief that others should recognize our importance and treat us with proper deference. We work hard to protect the false self we created and not have it exposed lest we feel shame.

Connecting meaningfully with others when we are gripped by toxic shame is not possible. We are voiceless and want to withdraw, hide, and not be seen. Neither do we wish to be exposed and humiliated for the imagined defects and flaws that seem apparent to us. We do what we can to avoid feeling small and defective often by wielding negative power over others, including abusive/aggressive behavior, or trying to inflate our external image with self-aggrandizement or the trappings of success. Again the ego comes into play as it is our sense of self that suffers shame.

In my work with shame, I discovered how feeling shame quickly triggered me to become reactive. A sign of my vulnerability to shame is feeling self-conscious around others. It is a red flag. When I felt self-conscious I would vigilantly monitor my words and actions so as not to violate my internalized standard regarding appearances, a vestige of my family's expectations.

When triggered in my youth I came to an emotional fork in the road regarding shame. One fork was an attack on myself in which my sense of self collapsed. I wanted to tuck my tail between my legs and slink away filled with self-loathing. The other fork, which became my default, was to feel rage toward whomever, or whatever, triggered me and from whom I felt judged or criticized. The bar for that feeling was low because my constructed false self was on a shaky foundation. Alternately, my rage was empowering unlike collapsing into self-loathing on the other fork. Other than feeling energized and self-protective, the rage fork was no less dysfunctional as it alienated others and I was again alone. I was filled with remorse for my behavior, triggering yet more shame. I could not find a way out of this dynamic and the pattern persisted.

With Buddhist practice, I began to see options by employing our good friends: noticing, pausing, and discernment. Once I could see the pattern I could bring Practical Dharma tools to bear on the problem. The cues to noticing were the feelings of rage that would start to arise in my mid-section when I felt ridiculed, criticized, exposed, and shamed. I learned to pause and name it, "I am having a shame attack." Only then did I have the option to respond more skillfully and inhibit my reactivity, letting go of the urge to react.

Invoking self-compassion helps immensely as does the recognition that "It's like this now." In other words, the situation in which I find myself is what it is, not what I wish it were. I can either accept it or fight with it and keep my reactivity and suffering going.

When I am reactive it helps to reach out to a trusted other for connection—to be open about my pattern of reactivity and to gain perspective. While I still get triggered—usually when I am tired, hungry, or stressed—it happens less often and less intensely.

What are some specific examples of our reactivity? They include flying off the handle, lashing out at others, angry withdrawal, speaking harshly to others, using self-protective mechanisms that further isolate us, self-judgment, and self-harm to name a few. If we dive deeper into reactivity we see that it is often a function of the forces of craving and clinging to an idea that things, or we, should be different than they are—the foundation of all suffering.

Often shame is about an old wound being reopened related to belonging, being seen, intimacy, or security. When we discover such wounds, we must respond to them with compassion toward ourselves and without judgment. Sharing our suffering with trusted others and receiving their compassion is also a powerful antidote. Our meditation practice is a refuge that offers us the quiet contemplation to recognize these wounds. All our early life experiences, especially with our caretakers and attachment figures, shape our patterns of reactivity.

As a little boy, I was ridiculed for crying if I hurt myself. I developed a heightened awareness about being seen as sensitive which was viewed as a weakness for a boy in the 1950s. If someone suggested that I was overly sensitive I lashed out defensively in the reactive way described. This has been one of the biggest challenges on my path. Growing up there was much scrutiny and ridicule in my family due to the emphasis on outward appearances.

I grew up feeling very defensive and hypervigilant, often perceiving ridicule by others where it did not exist. It was exhausting as I was always on guard and had no idea how else to be. I would get defensive, annoyed, angry, and withdraw if I perceived ridicule or even good-hearted teasing. It felt as though others did not care about me or know me. As a child, I never developed the ability to laugh at myself much less have others laugh at me. The experience reinforced my painful feelings of separateness from others, especially my siblings with whom I often felt at war. I reacted immediately without thinking, understanding, or processing my emotions. It was a vicious, self-defeating cycle.

Practical Dharma has helped me understand this process, including the ACT concepts of self-as-context and cognitive defusion. Together they have given me the tools to work with it. The process begins with pausing and noticing the effects of perceived slights on my subjective world.

My first challenge was to set an intention to notice my reactivity once I had insight into what was happening. I had to learn to distinguish between responding vs. reacting, which involved pausing, breathing into my body's tightness, letting go to release the pressure, and finally acting with intention and integrity.

Reactivity has physical correlates in the body manifesting as the release of stress hormones like adrenalin and cortisol, shallow breathing, muscle tension, and tunnel vision; it activates the sympathetic branch of the central nervous system known as fight, flight, or freeze. When this occurs our problem-solving and ability to interact constructively with others goes offline. Self-soothing and calming, taking a time out, breathing slowly for several breaths, and allowing the physiological responses to subside are all antidotes for the physical aspects of reactivity.

My ongoing challenge became meeting such reactive feelings with openness and compassion. Our path is always those aspects of life that most challenge us. Like the toothache that cannot be ignored, these triggers make us notice where we need to put our energy and effort to change. With practice, we move beyond reactivity to accepting our painful experiences and feelings without shame. Challenging emotions that are fully felt and mindfully held can be surmounted through wisdom and released—all the while remembering that the ground of the spiritual path we walk is the true nature of reality.

We learn to live our lives from an awakened heart and mind. A vital component of this journey is self-compassion which gives us the freedom, safety, and resolve to shine a light into the dark, ugly corners of our shadow selves. We move from reactivity to acceptance of all facets of who we are and all that we experience. Greater emotional regulation, psychological flexibility, and freedom follow.

I consider reactivity one of our biggest challenges as human beings given that we are nothing if not emotional creatures. Our emotions enrich our lives but they also can imprison us and take away our capacity for wise decisions and Wise Action.

Reflection:

- Which emotions are most challenging for you in managing your reactivity more skillfully? Which tools to better manage your reactivity resonate with you?

Chapter Eleven

Desire

"Desires are not killed by fulfilling them."

—*Hermann Hesse*

Given its prominence in our daily lives, I want to dig deeper into desire. As I have noted, all of the Five Hindrances disrupt our practice and impede our progress on the spiritual path. Any of the hindrances take us out of the present moment and alienate us from ourselves and others.

Desire is not a bad thing. We depend on our desires to survive—the desire for nourishment, water, warmth, shelter, and sex for procreation. Our challenge is to distinguish between healthy and unhealthy desires. Poorly managed or uncontrolled desires quickly become compulsions or addictions, or what the Buddha called "thirsts." Unmanaged desires create tension that accompanies the craving. We are constantly distracted and think of little else but the source of our craving like my Kellogg toy. We live only on the surface of our lives as everything else becomes secondary to our preoccupation with our unskillful desires.

Sensual desire is fundamental as it involves feeding our senses of sight, smell, sound, taste, and touch which are our windows to the world. The Buddha included a sixth sense of thinking. However, when the pull of indulging any of the senses becomes too strong we focus solely on satisfying the sense pleasure accompanied by the narrative that we create to justify it.

The story we create about a sense desire becomes repetitive and powerful, especially when we are deprived of the opportunity to indulge the craving. Desire, sometimes referred to in Buddhist literature as greed, is a compelling part of the human experience. During mediation and daily life, we strive to watch our desires arise and pass away like all impermanent phenomena rather than getting hooked into the story and gratification of the desire. Once the narrative hooks us we are on shaky ground. The further along we are on the path of indulging our unskillful choices the more difficult it is to recover, or pull back, with skillful means.

Let me reiterate that there is nothing inherently wrong with sensual pleasure which is called a hindrance only when it interferes with our ability to stay present and be skillful in our choices.

We depend on our desires to stay alive. By training ourselves to watch our desires arise we learn to discern between those which are healthy, those which are problematic, and those which cause suffering in our lives.

As we notice a strong desire arise, we pause. We ask ourselves: How strong is it? Where in the body is it showing up? What are the physical sensations accompanying it? What might underlie it—loneliness, sadness, self-criticism, and/or shame?

In my practice as a psychologist, I found with my patients that the desire and craving for sense pleasure could be a way of attempting to self-regulate painful or difficult emotions. In ACT terms indulging in sensual desire is a form of experiential avoidance. Included are compulsive eating when not hungry, compulsive sex, intoxication with drugs or alcohol, compulsive spending, addictive gambling, spending hours on the internet, obsessive exercise, or anything else done to excess. Engaging in any of these compulsive behaviors distracts us from our painful inner life.

When we become familiar with our tendency toward compulsive sensual desire freedom requires looking at the desire directly, naming it, and feeling how it is experienced in the body—only then can we successfully begin to set it aside. By learning to experience it without judgment the underlying painful emotion loses its grip on us.

When I compulsively eat chocolate I am not addressing my poor mood but am trying to distract myself. I pay the price by feeling bloated, putting on extra pounds, and causing a sugar crash. When I refrain from reaching for chocolate and instead bring mindful awareness to my unpleasant feeling state, I opt for the skillful route. The compulsion lessens when I resist and touch into present-moment awareness of what I am feeling. As I become freer of the compulsive desire for sensual pleasure, my confidence grows and the more likely I can decide wisely which desires or aspirations will govern my life. Not that I have given up my craving for chocolate. I do, however, indulge more mindfully and skillfully. If you have never eaten a Hershey bar mindfully, I highly recommend it. Just try not to overdo it.

When we approach our desires with mindful awareness the habit of staying present becomes stronger over time and allows us to make better choices. We must also be mindfully aware of our physical and emotional state when confronted with a potent desire. For that reason, as an example, I suggest avoiding meditation on an empty stomach or when exhausted. The desire to eat or to nap will prove too great a distraction from present-moment awareness. It is not skillful for us to ignore awareness of our environment, both internal and external, when we are dealing with desires. We use discernment to assure that we do not set ourselves up for failure when managing our desires.

Discernment is critical to skillfully managing our desires. Do we see the desire accurately or just on the surface? Where is the desire coming up in the body? Are we able, with discernment, to see what is underneath it—a lack of connection to others, loneliness, sadness, irritation, shame, or other difficult emotional states?

As noted, from an ACT perspective addiction results from experiential avoidance of uncomfortable and unwanted thoughts or feelings. Having too many drinks at a party to ease social anxiety, using opiates to ease the pain of failure or trauma, or stimulants such as cocaine to avoid boredom or loneliness, are all forms of experiential avoidance.

We next turn our attention to exploring the subjective experience of strong desire rather than focusing only on the object of our desire. How strong is the pull to act on the desire? Where do I feel it in my body? Can I stay with the exploration rather than pushing it away with aversion or indulging it? Again we implement the tools of noticing, pausing, and discernment.

Desires are addressed skillfully by accepting them in full relief and not avoiding/denying them. Denied or disavowed unskillful desires can wreak havoc on our spiritual progress. This is why mindful self-awareness is such a critical practice. Our challenge is accepting without judgment, rather than denying or eschewing, the parts of ourselves we deem shameful or unattractive including our unskillful desires.

Forgoing the gratification of our problematic desires requires self-awareness and the practices of restraint and renunciation which are not easy tasks. When treating patients struggling with compulsions or addictions the challenge was helping them look beyond the outward behavior, such as compulsive eating, to the underlying feeling states that they were feeding. Once they could identify and name, without shame, the deep-seated feelings, such as inadequacy or defectiveness, we were on fertile ground. Focusing solely on external behavior was a dead end.

Our unskillful desires are often beyond our awareness because we are too close to them; they are the water we swim in. Practical Dharma, including the methods of ACT, helps us pull back the cover so we can address them skillfully. When I was mindlessly stuffing chocolate in my mouth on autopilot I had no clue what was driving my behavior. I only knew that I later regretted having eaten too much chocolate given the costs associated with doing so. The painful emotions that I was trying to feed persisted. Using the tools available the opportunity for change became real.

Reflection:

- Over which of your desires do you feel that you have the least control? Which of the tools described can you enlist to help better manage your unskillful desires?

Chapter Twelve

Anger

"Anger leads to hate. Hate leads to suffering. When we hold onto feelings of anger, we do more damage to ourselves than the person we feel anger towards. The truth is, anger is a punishment we give ourselves for someone else's mistake."

—Master Yoda from Star Wars

Have you ever tried to meditate or be fully present when angry? The pull to indulge ill will and anger is very powerful. We ruminate about it, dwell on our perceived wounds, replay the triggering event over and over in our minds, and plan our revenge or retaliation. Our intention is to avenge the wound of our hurt pride, our shame, and our humiliation. We seek to even the score. We briefly looked at anger in the chapter on emotional reactivity. Ill will or anger is another one of the Five Hindrances and, as with sensual desire, is highly disruptive of our path, our equanimity, and our serenity.

Revenge born of anger is a powerful impulse. Think about the decades-long Israeli/Palestinian conflict. One country kills someone on the other side. That side then kills one of the opposing side in retaliation. On and on it goes with no end or solution in sight. Sadly, humankind has been reenacting this since we stood upright if not before. Our primate cousins, chimpanzees, engage in the same pattern. Our capacity for ill will and violence is endless as are the triggers for it in our world.

When we are in the grip of anger it is impossible to be calm, reflective, and settled. We are not free but are prisoners of our hostile emotions which obscure our ability to see clearly. From an ACT perspective, we are operating from emotional rigidity and our efforts to control situations and others; we lack emotional flexibility that helps us "roll with the punches" with equanimity.

Ill will or anger result in emotional reactivity and are its primary causes. It manifests as resentment, annoyance, hostility, irritation, and potentially, violence—all forms of emotional reactivity. People are killed because of ill will. Young men when fueled by high testosterone levels, inflated pride, and the need to save face with their peers may choose death rather than appearing weak or cowardly. When the easy availability of firearms is added to the mix we have an epidemic.

The emotional reactivity born of anger and ill will takes many problematic forms including flying off the handle, lashing out, angry withdrawal, speaking harshly to others, using self-protective mechanisms that further isolate us, self-judgment, and self-harm to name a few. If we dive deeper into reactivity we see that ill will is often a function of the forces of craving and clinging to an idea that things should be different than they are—the foundation of all suffering.

When we are in a state of angry ill will, we want to hurt, punish, attack, push away, turn away, or withdraw from the person or situation that triggered us. Ill will manifests on a continuum from mild irritation and resentment to extreme violence.

We suffer when we are in a state of anger or ill will. It is painful and we contract physically and emotionally. We do not see the world clearly as our perceptions are skewed toward the negative. We operate with a reactive hair trigger devoid of the noticing, pausing, and discerning that guide us toward a more skillful response.

Ill will is a great disrupter of relationships and our connection to others. We lash out, we blame, and we engage in alienating behavior. When we are in the grip of ill will we cannot interact well with others—others avoid us so as not to be subjected to our hostility or other unskillful emotions. Ill will can be the product of underlying feelings of being defective or unlovable so we preemptively strike out to avoid criticism and protect our ego, following the adage that the best defense is a good offense. We justify our anger by identifying with the role of a victim of the world's perceived unfair treatment of us. Ill will alienates others and we end up emotionally alone and isolated.

Before I embraced Buddhism people correctly perceived me as an angry person. My temper was always lurking just below the surface of my emotions, waiting with hypervigilance to come out if I felt misunderstood, mocked, mistreated, or short-changed. Those close to me walked on eggshells so as not to trigger an outburst. They suffered from my outbursts and I suffered from the shame and isolation that resulted from my tantrums. The pattern was a primary source of suffering for all involved. I am very grateful that this pattern is no longer present thanks to my Buddhist practice.

Ill will is about the ego. Is the ego threatened? Ashamed? Embarrassed? Feeling unseen or unheard? Disregarded? Is our fragile sense of pride hurt? Are we interpersonally triggered either real or vicariously? Am I being judgmental and annoyed because I am clinging to a fixed idea about how others should treat me?

Have others disappointed me in some way? The triggers for our ill will are everywhere in our lives.

The prescription is familiar. We start with noticing, pausing, and discernment. The pause is critical as it lets our nervous system relax giving us the option of continuing to calm ourselves and generating a more skillful response. We bring compassion to ourselves and the source of our ill will and try to imagine the suffering of the other person that resulted in their problem behavior. We do not establish preconditions for those to whom we direct our compassion and those whom we exclude.

We do not judge our ill will as a personal failing. Rather we confront the self-serving view that the world is unfair to us, replacing it with a more spacious view that stuff randomly happens to all of us. We let go of any sense of victimhood and understand that adversity is a normal part of the human journey which we address skillfully with our mindfulness practice and the insights it produces.

Modern life provides us with an endless supply of things about which to feel ill will and anger. We are not captive to our more reptilian or lower brain functions. If given time to come online we have a cerebral cortex that will help us respond more skillfully. First, we have to notice and then build in the pause since the lower brain functions are immediate whereas the higher brain functions take longer to activate. Our challenge is to employ the lessons of Practical Dharma and set an intention to act with wisdom and compassion when ill will/anger arises.

There are instances where collective ill will may create the illusion of connection with others who share our hostile outlook. Connection predicated upon shared anger or hatred is neither real connection nor is it satisfying. It is not skillful and is dangerous and divisive; it causes separation between people and groups. Sadly, this phenomenon is rampant in modern society.

One of the most effective antidotes to anger is the practice of forgiveness. Forgiveness is primarily for our benefit rather than for the person we are forgiving. When we forgive we set down the weight of our ill will which causes us much suffering. We decide not to retaliate against the person who we feel harmed us. That person need not even know that we have forgiven them. To be clear—forgiving someone does not mean that we let them off the hook. Rather, we eliminate their power over us which existed when we are consumed by ill will toward them.

Ill will/anger and their close cousin reactivity cause us individually, those around us, and society, tremendous suffering. We must bring all the tools of our spiritual path to bear on the challenges they present.

<u>Reflection:</u>

- How do you typically handle anger? What is the role of your ego in anger or ill will?

Chapter Thirteen

Relationships

"A family is a place where minds come in contact with one another. If these minds love one another, the home will be as beautiful as a flower garden. But if these minds get out of harmony with one another, it is like a storm that plays havoc with the garden."

—Bukkyo Dendo Kyokai

We are relational beings. All our unskillful feelings and behaviors show up in our relationships which is one of the most challenging areas of our practice. The tools of Practical Dharma, including ACT, offer multiple options for addressing the pitfalls we encounter in our relationships.

Human beings evolved to live in family and tribal groupings which is how we survived as a species. To be cast out or shunned by others in the group is one of the most painful experiences humans can have. Two hundred thousand years ago it meant death on the savannahs of Africa. Simply put, our ancestors either learned to get along or they would die. Yet we are still trying to figure out how to get along. Practical Dharma offers some answers.

Relationships are central to the human experience. We need them for survival, community, connection, intimacy, procreation, cooperation, and safety. Our relationships include our parents, siblings, mates, children, friends, bosses, and co-workers or anyone with whom we have interactions. We have many relationships each with varying degrees of intimacy from the closest to the most casual. It is an axiom in my profession that the more intimate the relationship, the more likely we are to get tripped up and behave or speak unskillfully.

Relationships are primarily where we get conflicted, triggered, challenged, humbled, hurt, and angry; they have the potential to cause great suffering. They are where we reenact patterns from significant early attachments where we bring, often unconsciously, all our old hurts and wounds, expectations, and longings.

Relationships are also where we experience exhilaration, validation, joy, closeness, safety, comfort, and a sense of belonging, of being seen, heard, and validated. They are indeed one of the great joys of being human.

Before addressing specific relationship challenges let me remind you that our relationships, in all of their complexity, are no less subject to the law of impermanence than any other phenomenon. Not only in the sense that they eventually end, whether through leaving, divorce, or death, but that they are ever-changing and not fixed from moment to moment, day to day, and year to year. It is essential that we not cling to a fixed notion of the nature of our primary relationships lest suffering be guaranteed. Instead, we must attempt to accept the ever-changing and ever-evolving nature of our relationships. The so-called honeymoon phase of a new, exciting, committed relationship with a partner bears little resemblance to the day-to-day relationship of many years.

To understand relationship challenges we must look at the primary areas from both a Dharmic and relational perspective that present the most challenges as we seek loving, intimate, and functional relationships. These factors are not separate or discrete but are interwoven and overlapping. You will recognize some familiar themes:

Ego. The fixed belief in a permanent solid self is a key source of suffering according to the Buddha. Many, if not most, problematic relationship issues are born of ego needs. These include competition and winning, self-importance and narcissism, moral superiority, privilege, selfishness, and entitlement among other needs. Driven by our ego we want to win every argument, have the last word, and be the alpha. All these issues are toxic to the goal of positive relationships as they are antithetical to compassion, empathy, and deep emotional connection. Conflict, anger, resentment, withdrawal, contempt, and other unskillful responses result from them.

Absence of Presence. This refers to not showing up for the other person including not fully listening, not trying to understand, and not "walking in their shoes." Absence of presence also includes judging, criticizing, dismissing, mocking, lacking understanding, and not offering our full and undivided attention when required—not being present for difficulties and challenges that arise. Instead, we withdraw or push the other person away.

Too often we are unwilling to stick around for the hard part of relationships which require a great deal of work. Do not think otherwise. We cannot just go through the motions but must show up by being fully engaged with significant others including deep listening, compassion, empathy, and kindness. True intimacy deepens our connection to others which provides security and safety and lessens our suffering. It provides a refuge from the challenges of life. It is one of the true joys of being human but we must earn it.

Relational grasping and clinging. I am intimately familiar with this one which involves the belief that others should act as we wish, not as they are. We have fixed expectations, outside of our conscious awareness, where we revisit old patterns of feeling rejected, not seen, not heard, misunderstood, and devalued, all of which we impose on others in our life. Attempting to control the other person is common in this situation. This is a huge source of suffering in our relationships, both intimate and casual—with our partner ("Why isn't she/he more supportive?"), with our children ("Why don't they do what I tell them?"), or with the bank teller ("Don't they know I am in a hurry?").

This type of relationship issue is an equal opportunity source of suffering. We suffer as does the other person. Tremendous strain is put on the relationship and withdrawal and/or avoidance by one or both parties ensue. Closeness and intimacy cease and distrust results.

Emotional Reactivity. In relationships, reactivity is born of the prior three challenges: (1) when our ego is threatened, (2) when presence is lacking, or (3) grasping and clinging to expectations are present.

This is not a complete list of relationship challenges but these are most often present when reactivity occurs.

It remains a formidable challenge for Right Speech to prevail in our family relationships as that is where some of our most challenging communications occur. It is where we most often get our buttons pushed. With wisdom, we enter family situations with the knowledge and expectation that lifelong patterns get triggered—forewarned is forearmed, so we can attempt to plan and implement more skillful means.

We cannot be completely free of reactivity as we are human beings and emotional creatures. Rather, we seek to manage our emotions more skillfully to reduce and attenuate them. To manage our reactivity, the underlying process with all four prior relationship challenges is to notice when something is arising, cueing us that we are uncomfortable. We are more vulnerable to reactivity when feeling insecure, alone, easily threatened, misunderstood, or marginalized. When we expect the old patterns to emerge, we shift into a hypervigilant mode for perceived relational danger, becoming guarded and distrustful. If we do not notice, there is a high likelihood of being triggered into reactivity.

Relationship dysfunction erodes trust and goodwill so, at some level, we are always on high alert. We avoid feeling vulnerable in such fraught situations so we become self-protective, reactive, and verbally defensive. Our reactivity energizes and emboldens us. We enter attack mode to hide our fear, emotional pain, lack of control, feeling misunderstood, vulnerability, and fear of humiliation or embarrassment. Any emotional connection is severely strained or broken.

Relationship challenges are good news/bad news situations. The bad news is that each of us acts in individually predictable ways when things do not go our way. The causes and conditions, past and present of our lives, result in our getting triggered in uniquely predictable ways. The good news is that we have agency so can employ the tools of ACT/Practical Dharma to learn to act less predictably since our patterns are well known to us. Again, it is about noticing, pausing, and discernment.

To build more satisfying and intimate relations we bring an open mind and mindful awareness to our conflicts and frustrations with others. We set an intention to pay attention to what is arising within both our body and mind and then build in the sacred pause between the trigger and our response. This is perhaps some of the most challenging work we will ever do as the ego will strongly resist in the interest of protecting itself and/or winning. The challenge is to bring mindful awareness, moment to moment, to our interactions with others as soon as we sense tension or discord.

There are four Practical Dharma/ACT antidotes to the problem areas we just covered. Initially, we must commit to non-judging awareness of the problem areas we bring and accept our unskillful means without self-condemnation. Understand that these are normal human challenges, the potential for which is within all of us. We resist the tendency to blame the other person for the conflict. We immediately hit a wall if we do not accept our contributions to relationship problems and blame the other person. Our ego wants to win, not feel small and defeated. Discernment includes accepting our role in the conflict, clearly and non-defensively, with compassion.

Wise Speech. An essential practice that is an antidote for emotional reactivity. By bringing an attitude of wanting to solve the conflict and not win, we set an intention to pause before we speak. This pause provides a break between whatever strong emotions we are feeling and the need to speak; this helps break the chain of reactivity which becomes tit-for-tat in a relationship conflict. I am continually amazed at how quickly a conflict quiets and moves into constructive speech whenever I can do this. Here again, the pause is the essential ingredient.

Mindful Presence. This refers to creating a container for discussion which fosters deep connection and builds trust. It invites the other person into a safe space wherein charged issues can be discussed. Our full attention is required for deep listening to understand the other person. This is not a time to formulate our counter-response while pretending to listen. Mindful presence requires our willingness to set aside our agenda, especially the need to win, for the greater good of the connection.

Hospice worker, Christine Longaker, says in her chapter in an anthology, *The Wisdom of Listening,* "You must listen with your whole being, not just your ears." That is to say listen with your body, heart, eyes, and energy, i.e., with total presence—turning toward and listening in silence to the other person without interrupting. Fill spaces of silence with compassion and/or loving-kindness, not with your counterpoint. Allow yourself to imagine the other person's suffering. Be aware of reactivity, especially in the form of defensiveness or wanting to hit back with words.

Humor. No discussion of overcoming relationship challenges would be complete without addressing the importance of humor—not sarcastic humor, not mean-spirited humor, not mocking humor. Instead, good-natured self-deprecating humor. This type of humor requires that we laugh at ourselves and our foibles. Humor breaks down barriers and helps overcome emotional obstacles. I find it most helpful in broaching difficult or charged topics. As one colleague told me, "Humor can be used to smuggle new ideas into people's hearts." Laughing together forges connection.

My wife and I go annually to the beach with our siblings and their mates. Historically, such gatherings were fraught and tense and something to dread because lots of old conflicts would arise. Tension would be in the air. Several years ago, after both my parents and my wife's parents were deceased, we siblings began spontaneously using humor to address old hurts, resentments, and grudges. Even longstanding sibling rivalry issues became the stuff of our amusement. The stereotypic ways we were each viewed by the others got addressed with humor. This meant that each of us had to be able to laugh at ourselves and our quirks, a challenging practice that pushes the ego, pride, and defensiveness into the background and fosters connection. The humor generates joy and deepens connection and is a wonderful gift for all of us.

When we gather annually we spend much of the time laughing, telling stories, and connecting on a deeper level. We make fun of all the dysfunction and pain that we endured while growing up. Our deceased parents are not spared but when we make fun of them we do so with warmth and love that was historically inaccessible behind all the old hurt, pain, and resentment. I know of no more effective way of overcoming family emotional obstacles than the introduction of skillful humor.

Wisdom. We seek to understand the land mines in our relationships by seeing them clearly and not through rose-colored glasses or avoiding them with denial. Understanding the trip wires fosters the development of relationship wisdom.

By cultivating wisdom we learn our triggers and those of our loved ones. Out of such wisdom comes greater compassion and empathy for ourselves and others. We cultivate the ability to put ourselves in others' shoes and to see their suffering with empathy. We acknowledge and respect their point of view. We unhook from our ego's self-interest and relinquish the need to win, to be correct, and be superior, which distorts our reality and alienates the other person. Finally, we seek to interact from a position of vulnerability even though it can be very frightening. We forgo the interests of our ego in the service of greater connection and intimacy.

The work in our relationships is essential to our well-being. A discordant primary relationship is antithetical to our happiness and creates great suffering for both parties. As so much of our practice on this path is about acceptance and letting go never are they more needed than in our relationships.

One of the greatest of many gifts that this practice has given me is the significant improvement in my relationships with my wife, my children, my family, and my friends. They will tell you that I am no longer the controlling, reactive, judgmental, and driven person I was twenty years ago. To everyone's benefit no longer is conflict always someone else's fault nor is every interaction and decision about me. I have learned to laugh at myself and enjoy it.

We must set an intention to bring Practical Dharma tools to bear on our relationships to experience a reduction in suffering in ourselves and those around us. It is one of the greatest gifts that Practical Dharma gives us and that we can give ourselves and our loved ones.

Rumi, the 13th-century Persian poet, wrote, "Your path is not to seek for love but merely to seek and find all the barriers within yourself you have built against it." Prescient advice for finding our way through modern relationship challenges.

I would like to share a story of a primary relationship in my life with which I struggled for many years and caused great suffering. My father, who died in 2008 at 89, was a second-generation German immigrant from Detroit who was the only child of a severely alcoholic mother and a largely absent salesman father. He went to Duke University and graduated in the middle of WWII so immediately enlisted in the Navy. He was a Naval officer in the South Pacific for the remainder of the war, commanding a landing craft, at the age of 23, transporting Marines to war zones.

While in New Orleans in 1943 for training he met my mother at a tea given by the young ladies of New Orleans for the new Naval officers. Sparks flew. My mother, who had one younger brother, was the only daughter of my grandparents. Her father was the scion of an old Louisiana family who owned Linwood, a 500-acre sugar cane plantation north of Baton Rouge where his father and grandfather had owned 100 enslaved persons before emancipation.

My grandfather was a prominent attorney in New Orleans who wanted nothing to do with my father. Nor did he want my mother to have anything to do with him. He was, in my grandfather's words, "A Yankee and not our kind of people." But he could not say "No" to his only daughter so my mother rode the train with my grandmother to San Francisco where she married my father in a civil ceremony before he deployed to the South Pacific. When he returned from the war he had a daughter and a wife awaiting him as my older sister had been born while he was away. To the best of my knowledge, my grandfather never spoke a word to my father for the rest of his life. My father never went with us on our annual trip to New Orleans to see my grandparents during Mardi Gras as he was not welcome.

After the war, my father started law school at Duke which he did not like so he left. He joined the corporate world and worked in public relations for DuPont and Dan River Mills. In 1954, when I was six years old, he resigned from his job and went to Seminary to become an Episcopal priest. My mother was very unhappy as it was not what she had signed on for. She now had to clothe and feed three children (soon to be four) on a salary two-thirds less than when my father worked at Dan River Mills. She was not living in the style to which she had been accustomed growing up.

Their marriage was not good due to cultural differences, money issues, and because they were both psychologically damaged and emotionally immature. I was my mother's favorite, a mixed blessing which meant I was an emotional extension of her and often at odds with my siblings. With this came expectations for perfect external behavior lest I bring shame and embarrassment rather than admiration on her. She had no idea who I was as a person and had neither the awareness nor the curiosity to find out. All that mattered was that I was perfectly behaved, well-groomed, and reflected positively on her.

My father knew nothing about how to be a father. His alcoholic mother was emotionally intrusive when she was drinking and emotionally distant when she was sober. His father was rarely home. Consequently, he was a deeply insecure and anxious man. He was driven by a need to do good deeds, a motive that I believe contributed to his decision to go into the ministry. Because of his poor relationship with my mother, he avoided being at home and was almost always in the community ministering to others.

He was, however, not just that person. He was also a deeply compassionate and empathic man even if he had difficulty showing those qualities to his children. He would spend hours every week taking care of everyone in his church and others in the community. He became involved in the civil rights movement in the '50s and '60s in addition to his parish duties as the only priest of a large congregation. He was a vocal advocate for improved mental health services in the state. Regarding his children, it was a case of the "cobbler's children having no shoes."

I longed for him to be different my whole life. I wanted his attention and interest. I wanted him to show pride in me—to be Ward Cleaver from the *Leave It to Beaver* show or Jim Anderson from *Father Knows Best*.

Before puberty, I tried to be perfect hoping to please him by following my mother's script which was the only one I had. But it was to no avail as he was rarely around to notice. When puberty happened my hurt and rage broke through. I started acting out both from anger and to get his attention. Imagine his humiliation when he frequently had to pick me up at school or, on one occasion, at the police department for misbehavior. All while living in a small town where everyone knew us.

I continued to suffer from wanting him to be different. I had fantasies of how he should be as a father and I was hurt that he was not. I desperately wanted him to take an active interest in my schoolwork, sports activities, and life and to be a hands-on father like those on television. It was a classic case of how clinging to fixed ideas of how others should be leads to suffering. The pattern continued in different forms until he died. The experience was cumulatively traumatic for me as I know similar experiences are traumatic for many people.

As an adult I avoided him. It was too painful to be around him as I was too angry and hurt. He was anxious around me as he felt my anger toward him and my judgment of him. He never asked about me, my work, my life, or anything. I experienced him as self-absorbed and seethed inside whenever I had to be in his presence. When we moved back to Virginia in 1989, after living in New Jersey for 11 years, I reluctantly saw him on occasion out of obligation. It was arduous to be with him—a pattern that continued for almost 20 years until he died.

My father had been in assisted living due to early-onset dementia for several years before his death. He had a bad fall at the assisted living facility in early June of 2008. He died in hospice two weeks later. While at the funeral home to make final arrangements (as the oldest son in my family I was the default person for all such tasks) the funeral director, a friend from childhood, asked if I wanted to see my father before they sent him for cremation. I declined as it seemed pointless to me. My wife, Kay, in her wisdom, encouraged me to do so. I reluctantly went into the back room of the funeral home where I was alone with him.

My father was lying on a gurney covered with a sheet except for his head and shoulders. I stood there for two to three minutes looking at him. He looked so serene and peaceful, something I was not used to seeing. In a moment of spontaneity, I went over and kissed him on the forehead and told him I loved him.

For reasons I did not then understand but now know are the result of my Buddhist practice, I had what I can only describe as a moment of grace. I was overwhelmed with the awareness that I had spent my entire life clinging to the desire that he be someone other than who he was or was capable of being. This was an insight that I never had when he was alive as I was too immersed in the dysfunctional emotions that had caused so much suffering. I now know that I suffered greatly by clinging to the desire that he should be different—by holding him to an unachievable ideal that he be other than who he was capable of being. I suddenly understood that his behavior toward me had not been intentional.

I realized how much I had suffered terribly for over 60 years because of that clinging. And how much suffering I caused him with my anger, withdrawal, and avoidance. I felt as though fifty pounds of weight lifted off my shoulders at that moment. Several days later at his memorial service, I wept as I had never wept before. I grieved deeply both for him and for myself. I was free of the lifelong struggle and suffering resulting from my clinging and grasping for a father that was never to be. I was free of the guilt over the suffering I had caused him from my avoidance and contempt.

All these years later, I feel the same. The burden has never returned. Nor has the anger, the hurt, or the frustration. I now have a greater understanding, empathy, and compassion for his life, his suffering, and his struggles. I have been able to recall positive interactions with him and feel proud of his work for social justice, civil rights, and mental health. I am grateful for the values that he imparted to me which informed my choice of profession.

The Dharma gave me gifts that nothing else ever had with my father including forgiveness, acceptance, letting go, and compassion; freedom from all the unnecessary suffering I had both caused and endured. All from clinging to the fantasy of how he should have been. Such is the power and freedom given to us by these practices.

<u>Reflection:</u>

- What fixed expectations do you cling to with those to whom you are close? What is the impact on your relationship with that person?

Chapter Fourteen

Regret

"The experience of regret is actually the message; it's the lesson, the dukkha that happens when we make a mistake. It's really important that we understand that, because otherwise it's like fighting ourselves. It's as though healing is taking place, but we are resisting it.

—Ajahn Munindo

Simply stated, we can never be rid of our regrets. Our challenge is to change our relationship with them. Practical Dharma, including the psychological flexibility offered by ACT, has much to offer in dealing with our regrets. Regret is generally defined as a negative state, both mental and emotional, in which we engage in self-blame about the negative outcome of a past event. It typically includes a sense of loss and sorrow at what might have been and may also include a desire to change or undo a past choice.

Regrets are pervasive in our lives. They are like heavy weights around our ankles that we drag around. While our regrets are always with us, not far from the surface of our minds, we rarely bring them to awareness and work with them skillfully.

Who among us does not have multiple regrets—both choices made and actions taken or not taken, or opportunities lost or not taken? We spend inordinate amounts of time going over and over our regrets due to our inability to let go of them. Are we not like a dog chasing its tail? I lost count of the number of regrets that I carry. Might our regrets be a function of our unskillful clinging to past actions or inactions, or trying to fix something, in the service of our wounded ego?

I struggled my whole life with regrets before Practical Dharma. Many of my regrets were focused on the parenting of my children when they were growing up. As is true for many of us I had vowed to be a better parent than my parents and not to repeat their mistakes. Never would I treat my children the way that I had been treated. Yet I found myself repeating many of the parenting patterns with which I had been raised. I swore that I would never focus on the small stuff like clothing choices and grooming, or perfect behavior in social situations, as my mother had—the very things about which I constantly bristled as a child. Yet I repeatedly asserted control over the very same choices and behaviors being made by both of my sons when they were young. They suffered as I had. This was the source of my self-recrimination and regret. Only with the tools of Practical Dharma was I able to begin letting go of my regrets and forgiving myself for my many mistakes as a parent. As a result, and with time, I became a better parent and more forgiving of my mistakes.

Think about how we hold onto regrets. What is the point? What about the guilt and shame that accompany regrets? The remorse? The sadness? The self-recrimination? What about carrying the weight of our regrets? How it can be such a burden? We revisit our regrets repeatedly due to the mistaken belief that by doing so we can somehow fix them. This is an impossible task that serves only to cause us greater suffering. What about regrets from our responses to how others treated us? Do we blame ourselves or others for how we did, or did not, respond at the time?

Our regrets isolate us. We do not want to share them and feel the shame of mistakes made; we would rather hide and lick our wounds in private.

As I reflected on my relationship with the regrets in my life, it became clear that the time and energy I spend thinking about regrets means that I am not in the present moment. And to what end? Nothing about the past is ever changed.

We cannot be fully present and emotionally open while dwelling on regrets, clinging to them, and feeling the guilt and shame accompanying them. Dwelling on them causes more suffering. There is nothing to be gained from regrets with the possible exception of reminding us that we once did something we do not wish to repeat.

The first step in changing our relationship with our regrets is recognizing when we are tangled up in them. Because we are rarely consciously aware that we are revisiting our regrets they are always lurking in the background like static that causes us to suffer—waiting to pounce and pile on with self-criticism when we do something that causes a new regret.

As with all the challenges to which we bring Practical Dharma we begin by noticing our focus on regret. Without knowing what the regret is we cannot address it. To confront our regrets skillfully we begin by noticing phrases that signal regret: "If only," "what if," "I should have," "I should not have," "they should have," or "they should not have."

Our task is to examine our regrets thoroughly. How tightly are we clinging to them? What, if any, function might doing so serve? Can we thoroughly examine them without judgment? Can we see regrets as one more of life's experiences that can be consciously known? I do not mean rehashing or ruminating about them. Instead, I am referring to looking at them fully and with mindful discernment and compassion and then letting them go.

What are the thought processes that accompany our regrets? Obsessional worry? Mental images? Where are we holding regrets in our body: Our stomach? Muscles of the face? Upper back? Clenched jaw?

ACT emphasizes the importance of awareness and contact with the present moment as critical to our well-being. We can defuse (de-identify) from our regrets, if the ego is heavily invested in them or if we define ourselves by them. Once we are aware that we are dwelling on regrets we are halfway toward letting them go.

We need to use awareness to recognize regret beyond just feeling a non-specific unpleasant emotion. A clue, as I mentioned, is to notice phrases that signal regret. Another indicator that we are caught in regret is an awareness that we are consumed by guilt, shame, or self-recrimination about a past action. Or we may notice that we allow our conscious and unconscious regrets to inform our self-worth.

The next step is to label it. "This is regret," or "This is what regret feels like." We recognize that the behavior that led to regret was unskillful. We then respond with self-compassion and self-forgiveness, a huge part of managing regrets and letting them go.

It is common for there to be a more significant issue underneath any regret. When we focus solely on the content of the regret and ruminate about it we cannot see the larger picture. For example, regret may be driven by an underlying identification with needing to be right about a past issue or the humiliation of having lost in the face of a challenge. Both are about our ego.

We ask if the issue about which we are feeling regret is still active in our life. If so, can we let it go? Can we set it down and lighten the load? Again, letting go means consciously choosing to challenge the regretful thought. Habits of mind can be stubborn so we enlist self-compassion practice to aid us in letting go of habitual thoughts that plague us. For example, we invoke phrases such as we might use to comfort a close friend; or we offer self-statements of forgiveness to ourselves, reminding ourselves that we are fallible creatures for whom perfection is not attainable. We remember that we did the best we could under the circumstances at the time.

Regret is like static in our lives interfering with clarity in the present moment. Each of our lives with its unique joys and sorrows can only be lived fully by embracing the truth of our experience including our regrets. We embrace life in all its ever-changing, impermanent, and never-perfect mystery. It is not about ridding ourselves of regrets but changing our relationship with them.

Often letting go of regrets includes grieving past mistakes or past decisions. Doing so requires we acknowledge what was lost when we behaved in ways we regret. Did we lose the sense of ourselves as the good person we aspire to be? Did we feel diminished by losing an argument or missing an opportunity? Do we feel guilty about how we behaved or treated others? Do we regret not speaking up to someone who mistreated us or others? The list goes on and on. We are rarely without abundant opportunities for regret. Suffering ensues. Grieving a regret means facing the painful emotions accompanying the regret—leaning into the feelings and accepting the emotions. Then we can forgive ourselves, invoke self-compassion, and let go.

I have benefited from seeing regrets as a teacher when I am able. Regrets are experiences from which I learned to be a better person who is more skillful in his choices and actions; a person who seeks not to repeat the same unskillful behavior going forward and who feels gratitude for the lessons learned.

Reflection:

- Do you let your regrets define your self-worth? How would it feel to give up some of your regrets?

Chapter Fifteen

Anxiety

"Could we take anxiety to be something that may be of importance, may even be meaningful? And it says something about your history, and could we learn to sort of hold it in a way that's more compassionate, to sort of bring the frightened part of you close and treat it with some dignity, and keep focused instead on what kind of life you want to live connected to what kind of meaning and purpose."

—Dr. Steven C. Hayes

We humans hate uncertainty. We want control and predictability and to know the future—uncertainty, a lack of control, and unpredictability make us anxious.

Human survival needs drive these tendencies as was particularly true for our ancient ancestors who needed to anticipate and plan, particularly regarding food supply. Planning anxiety goes beyond basic survival needs into nonspecific fears for our survival. This was particularly true in an ancient world where random events could pose a threat.

Humans, because of our capacity for imagination, experience fear and anxiety regularly. Because we have a thinking brain we experience fear and anxiety in ways that creatures without a cerebral cortex do not. Our experience of anxiety is part of our evolutionary heritage. A certain amount of fear and anxiety is necessary in life as they protect us from danger or threats which was critical 200,000 years ago with early humans. Since we first gained the capacity for thinking and language we have made up stories, created religions, offered sacrifices, developed superstitions, and worshipped deities in a futile attempt to explain the unexplainable and control future events to quell our anxieties.

All humans in evolutionary history have lived with fear and anxiety. They are an inescapable aspect of being human and have been essential to our survival as a species—as a critical alarm system—as is the case for all creatures. The Buddha recognized fear and anxiety as part of the common human experience. You will recall that worry and restlessness, i.e., anxiety, is another of the Five Hindrances that the Buddha taught.

Our challenge in modern times is managing fear and anxiety since being anxiety-free is not possible. We do not have to worry about the same physical threats to our survival that our ancient ancestors did. Yet we need to find ways not to be consumed by fear or anxiety when it arises in response to imagined threats or an uncertain future. Practical Dharma offers us the tools to do so. ACT asserts that we can never be free of fear and anxiety. ACT/ Practical Dharma teach that we can change our relationship with them and, thereby, reduce the suffering that they cause. The process begins with not seeing the experience as a weakness or something about which to be ashamed. This includes not seeing fear and anxiety as enemies. The most effective psychotherapy methods for dealing with anxiety require that we lean into our anxieties and meet them head-on. We do not try to avoid them which only worsens them and constricts our world.

As I say to individuals suffering from anxiety disorders, "Don't get in a wrestling match with your anxiety, as you will lose." This method of facing our anxiety is known in ACT as graduated exposure and corresponds to the Buddha's teachings on accepting all experience rather than avoiding that which is unpleasant. In graduated exposure one is exposed incrementally to that which they have avoided out of fear in the past. The path to facing our anxieties is broken down into small manageable increments or steps so we are not overwhelmed with anxiety or panic. The incremental steps are often done using imagination before moving on to actual live situations.

Anxiety and its close cousins come in many forms including worry, impending doom, physical anxiety, panic, anxious anticipation, and a range of physical symptoms. All these manifestations have arousal of the nervous system's sympathetic branch in common: fight, flight, or freeze. Feeling anxiety and fear is something we have all experienced as part of the human journey. No one is free of fear or anxiety though we each have different relationships with them ranging from easy acceptance to total paralysis.

To be precise we need to make a distinction between fear and anxiety. When there is a specific immediate threat or object about which we are afraid such as a noise in the dark, an immediate danger, the outcome of a negative medical test, or a truck veering into our lane we feel fear in response to that trigger. Fear occurs in real time. Anxiety, which has the same physiological manifestations as fear, is anticipatory. It is about future events and includes non-specific threats. We become anxious about growing older, our children getting hurt, becoming ill, dying, financial ruin, our marriage lasting, and a host of other concerns. Our capacity for imagination provides endless opportunities for anxiety. With anxiety, there is no current real-time specific object of alarm. Instead, we are responding to the frailty, uncertainty, and temporary nature of existence with anxiety. We project into the future, responding to our inability to predict or control the it. The nature of impermanence that the Buddha taught underlies all such anxieties.

To change our relationship with anxiety we must give up the fantasy that we will ever be absolutely safe. The Buddha taught that all things constantly change and eventually disappear—even that which is most precious to us. Loss, large and small, constantly happens despite our resistance to it. This knowledge motivates us to plan and take sensible precautions about future risks while necessarily giving up our efforts to control or predict the future— or holding onto the belief that we can avoid all future danger or loss.

As we deepen our spiritual practice we inevitably encounter anxieties some of which we did not know were within us. This often happens when we get quiet during mediation. Our anxieties can then become fuel for our practice and potential teachers on our path. Being alert and curious about our anxieties allows them to function as stimuli for us to notice. There are ways in which anxiety may be understood for us to work with it mindfully.

We may habitually view the world through the lens of our anxieties such that we are living an anxiety-based life. There is very little mental rest when this is true because life seldom seems even temporarily safe. We continually mistrust our judgment or question the reliability of others. Constant worry about the future plagues us. We often second-guess ourselves and others, continually seeking one more opinion or assurance. When our existence is anxiety-based our pattern is to move from one obsession or worry to another. We are rarely able to be present in the moment. Our only solution lies in changing our relationship with our anxieties.

I discovered early in my Buddhist practice that much of my daily behavior was motivated by anxiety. It included anxiety about failure, anxiety about disapproval, anxiety about disappointing others, anxiety about being judged negatively, and anxiety about being anxious. The anxieties were present for most of my waking existence which was exhausting and demoralizing; it was the source of much suffering.

I suffered until I moved more deeply into the Dharma augmented by the additional insights of ACT. Once I began practicing daily sitting meditation the awareness of how much of my life was anxiety-based became apparent. What was also clear to me was how much shame I felt about being anxious, a situation that resulted in my wanting to hide my anxiety from others. This exacerbated my anxiety as I was now also worried about being outed as an anxious person, a common experience in a judging culture that expects perfection.

Anxiety is subjective, happening inside us. Except in its most extreme forms, it is invisible to others. Given that it is subjective and internal how do we learn to live with it? The more established our mindfulness practice the less likely we are to escalate from apprehension to heightened anxiety and then panic and terror. We learn to be fully present with it as we do with any other experience. We cease identifying with it as part of our sense of self, as in, "I am an anxious person." Instead, we defuse from it and label it as we would any other transient experience, "Anxiety is happening now" or "Anxiety is like this now." We learn to lean into it and face it head-on. Though we do not like it we accept it and avoid getting into a wrestling match with it. The least skillful responses to anxiety are attempting to avoid it, suppress it, or distract from it because doing so only makes it worse.

One of the values of spiritual practice, augmented by perspectives from ACT, is that we can come to terms with our anxieties consciously. We welcome all phenomena as the Buddha taught: pleasant, neutral, and unpleasant of which anxiety is an example. Our life becomes more integrated because we no longer try to deny or avoid what is true in the moment even if uncomfortable like anxiety. We accept our anxieties without shame as another common experience everyone experiences at some point.

Often we compound the misery of specific anxiety we are experiencing with the general anxiety inherent in the human condition. With mindfulness practice, we see how the untrained mind is agitated by the human experience including vague perceived threats to our existence. We gain tolerance for the unpleasantness of uncertainty and the naturalness of our imperfection and we consciously and openly accept impermanence.

The Buddha asks us to develop confidence that life is what it is—we cannot know the future much less control it. We cannot, nor are we supposed to, miraculously fix or eliminate anxiety. Instead, we gain the insight that happiness and peace come from relating to life just as it is, anxiety included, not as we wish it to be. Once we accept it as unpleasant and as part of the flow of human experience our suffering lessens and greater freedom ensues.

There is no place for magical or wishful thinking when dealing with anxiety. To paraphrase a popular expression, "anxiety happens." When it does, hypervigilance occurs and all of our senses are scanning our surroundings and our internal experience for perceived danger. Challenging responses will likely present themselves at some point in our meditation practice or in our life in response to anxiety. Because it is unpleasant we try to distract the mind and avoid them. It has been my experience, personally and as a psychologist and Dharma teacher, that if we can simply be fully present with the uncomfortable experience it will eventually release its grip both physically and mentally as do all impermanent phenomena. One of the gifts Practical Dharma has given me is the ability to accept my anxiety.

Working with anxiety involves benevolence and goodwill toward ourselves, otherwise known as self-compassion, in the face of whatever arises. Yes, we are anxious but instead of fighting it we embrace and accept it rather than unskillfully fighting with it physically or mentally. Doing so only creates more turmoil in our minds and more anxiety symptoms in our bodies. We remember that anxiety is simply what is happening in the moment and does not define who we are. Working skillfully with anxiety involves accepting whatever we are experiencing.

Neuroscience has provided us with understanding regarding brain activity accompanying anxiety. When the amygdala, the brain's alarm system, senses a threat it responds in a split second to activate the flight, fight, or freeze response. The neocortex, the more highly evolved area of the brain where thinking occurs, is slower to come online in the face of a threat. The neocortex will try to make sense of the danger and evaluate it. We cannot think ourselves out of anxiety. We must address it at the source, which is the amygdala.

Often we develop anxiety about our anxiety meaning that we develop a fearful response to the internal physical cues that signal a heightened anxiety response. Trying to stop or escape these sensations is known as experiential avoidance in ACT and is responsible for many, if not most, anxiety disorders. The internal responses include a rapid heartbeat, subjective panicky feelings, and hyperventilation. The physical symptoms are accompanied by catastrophic thoughts creating a cascade response. Our challenge is whether we can just be with it? Watch it arise and pass away? Face it head-on? Trust that this, too, shall pass? Achieve a sense of mastery when we have successfully stayed with the anxiety response until it resolves?

Exposure to that which is fearful allows the brain, specifically the amygdala, to experience that which is producing anxiety and see that no harm comes to us. Graduated exposure systematically does this so that over time the amygdala becomes desensitized to the triggers, be they internal or external, which are causing anxiety. Research in psychology tells us that without an exposure component it is difficult to manage our anxieties more skillfully. Exposure by imagination and fantasy can be as effective as exposure to the actual trigger for our anxiety and is a well-accepted psychotherapeutic technique.

There is extensive psychological research and literature in ACT and other schools of psychotherapy on graduated exposure and similar methods, a thorough exploration of which is beyond the scope of this book. For our purposes, an example is a person who is terrified of enclosed spaces such as elevators, a disorder known as claustrophobia. Typically, anxiety is the result of a fear of being trapped in a confined space and is relatively common, affecting approximately 13% of the U.S. population. A program of exposure would have the person voluntarily enter into increasingly smaller enclosed spaces gradually so as not to be overwhelmed with panic. As anxiety arises in an enclosed space it is noted ("Anxiety is happening"), watched as it arises while accompanied by slow deep breaths. The person remains present with anxious feelings until they subside which they will. Nonetheless, a strong urge to escape or leave the space will arise as the person feels trapped. They are instructed to resist the urge to leave and to remind themself that they are in no danger despite what their thoughts and physical responses are telling them. Once the anxiety subsides they can leave the situation with a sense of mastery and confidence.

For example, a typical psychotherapy patient with an anxiety disorder would begin, per my guidance, gradually putting himself in situations that made him highly anxious knowing that he would initially be very anxious. A strategy of graduated exposure was implemented as described in Chapter 3. By not leaving or escaping the situation, as he would have done in the past, his anxiety peaked and then diminished, an important lesson in the impermanence of all experience. He reported that the experience was extremely unpleasant as his anxiety was very high. With knowledge of the research on graduated exposure from ACT, I assured him that his anxiety would subside. Once that happened several times he was no longer afraid of his anxiety and it no longer determined when, or if, he went into situations he had previously avoided. This was an experience of the freedom that Practical Dharma/ACT offers us.

I have not said a great deal in this chapter about noticing because anxiety and fear are hard to ignore. They grab our attention aggressively and force us to notice. The challenge of noticing anxiety arising is insignificant as it may be screaming in our face. At those moments the challenge is to produce a skillful response to anxiety which includes accepting it, being fully present with it, leaning into it, welcoming it, and watching it as it arises and passes away. Finally, we avoid self-judgment or shame for having anxiety. We remember that persistent anxiety is a sign that we are fighting it and not accepting it.

Reflection:

- How critically do you judge yourself when you experience anxiety? What do you imagine would happen if you simply accepted your anxiety?

Chapter Sixteen

Patience

"Do you have the patience to wait until your mud settles and the water is clear?"

——Lao Tzu

It would be difficult to put Practical Dharma to use without cultivating patience, one of the ten *Paramis* or Perfections, that the Buddha taught. The Perfections are virtues that we cultivate to live a life unobstructed by suffering. They are typically referred to as noble qualities. Of the ten, patience is of particular importance in Practical Dharma. For a deeper exploration of all of the Paramis please refer to the references at the rear of the book.

Patience is the ability to endure difficult circumstances with equanimity. It is perseverance when confronted with obstacles and tolerating provocation without reactivity. Patience is forbearance when we are faced with chronic challenges. It is a virtue in most of the world's faith traditions while impatience is an obstacle to spiritual advancement and reduced suffering.

Impatience is a cause of much suffering and is typically marked by one or more of the following: anxiety ("Am I in the right line?"), anger ("I don't have time for this"), envy ("I should be first; it's my turn"), ego needs ("What about me?"), or other negative mood states.

An impatient state of mind cannot co-exist with being fully present and awake as it is a barrier to our present-moment awareness. Instead, we focus on our frustration about a pending occurrence or obstacle.

Strictly speaking, the Buddhist concept of patience differs from the English definition of the word. In Buddhism, patience refers to refraining from returning harm, not just enduring a difficult situation. It is not just a frame of mind but is also about our behavior when confronted with a situation that tests our patience. It is the ability to control one's emotions and behavior even when criticized or attacked and is also characterized as a form of non-reactivity.

We cultivate patience because we seek both inward and outward peace. It is a function of our ability to accept things as they are in the moment. To return to an earlier example of being stuck in traffic—I can let impatience take over with all the attendant suffering or I can accept that there is nothing I can do other than be present with the fact that traffic is not moving. Simply put, whenever we want life to be different than it is we are caught in impatience so we suffer. We lose our sense of humor and indulge in self-pity. Despair, blame, and resentment arise in us as nothing changes with the situation in which we find ourselves and the frustrating circumstances persist.

Patience plays a huge role in our relationships. My complicated relationship with my father, which I described in Chapter 10, included chronic impatience with him whenever we were together. Acceptance, compassion, and forgiveness were lacking on my part. What I failed to recognize in dealing with him was that when we are impatient with others, bringing patient understanding to their challenges and their suffering (i.e., compassion) is the first step to being able to communicate, forgive, and begin anew.

The practice of forgiveness and acceptance happens when we realize the underlying cause of our anger and impatience. Doing so requires discernment about the other person's unskillful behavior as we understand it and seeing their essential goodness. Serenity and calm develop as we accept the unskillful aspects of others and ourselves. This does not mean that we tolerate being mistreated. Setting clear boundaries with those who seek to hurt or exploit us is Right Action. Discernment is the tool that guides us toward Right Action when we encounter a toxic interpersonal situation.

The Buddha taught three components to cultivate patience. Here, I am paraphrasing them. The first is forbearance, followed by calm endurance of hardship, and finally, acceptance of the truth as it is.

- Gentle Forbearance

Gentle forbearance is not exactly acceptance of how things are. But it is no less critical as it inhibits our speaking or acting long enough to determine the most skillful course of action given that with which we are dealing. It is putting in a sacred pause before we respond.

- Enduring Hardship

The second aspect of patience is enduring hardship with calm equanimity. We must remember that the Buddha taught that the world "Rests on suffering." Yet, we do not passively endure suffering and do nothing to lessen it as though we have no agency as individuals. Here again, discernment guides us on how to endure or respond to hardship to reduce our suffering. Patience is not passive. It signals us to accept and feel compassion for our suffering while recognizing that we cannot eradicate it but can only reduce it. When we feel impatient in our lives, relationships, job, or spiritual path we are resisting how things truly are. Noticing our impatience is the cue to let go of our resistance and relax into the situation as it is.

I find that humor and curiosity about what is going on at moments of impatience help me manage challenges more skillfully. At those moments impatience manifests both in our thoughts and our physical response and serves as a red flag. In such situations, it helps to ask, "What would being patient look like right now?" We use our present-moment awareness to explore what happens with the relationship to our experience at those times. When we do so, relief, gratitude, and contentment often follow, especially when we are rushing around trying to anticipate what is next.

In our over-stimulated, multi-tasking, gadget-obsessed, social media era we are doing so many things at once that there is little space for serenity or patience. Still, we wonder why we are unhappy and feel alienated. Our challenge is to remember, several times a day, to practice relaxing into life with all its joys and sorrows and relinquish the need to know what will happen next.

• Acceptance

The third aspect of patience requires we accept our experience as it is with all its suffering rather than how we want it to be. Our experience is continually changing due to impermanence so we know it will change if we only have patience. Accepting things as they are requires noticing and discernment, profound wisdom, and compassion which take time to cultivate as we walk our path. We are then less likely to get caught in being overly insistent, frustrated, and demanding, all of which are the wellspring of impatience.

Another benefit of patience is that it cuts through arrogance and ingratitude and lessens the power of the ego. When we think that we are the center of the universe impatience results when the world gets in our way. Patience helps us cultivate humility which is a characteristic that moves us from resistance to acceptance, spontaneous presence, and patience. We relax and our suffering diminishes.

Holding onto our judgments about others and ourselves is a significant cause of impatience and suffering. By accepting both the pleasant and unpleasant aspects of life, including the behavior of those to whom we are close, we cease wishing for life to be different than it is. We are freer of the demands that we constantly put on ourselves and others that are dominated by feelings of impatience. As a result, we are awake for all of life on its terms, not ours.

Do not confuse patience with passivity, reticence, or procrastination which are qualities made of resistance, avoidance, and low energy. Patience is intentional and purposeful and involves discernment and an intention to cultivate. It is best practiced in less challenging circumstances that are not in the heat of the moment, allowing us to learn the skills needed in more difficult situations.

As I have said, Practical Dharma is no quick fix and neither is cultivating patience. It is effortful and requires a robust and long-term commitment. I am not saying that we do not see benefits along the way. Our ongoing work results in less suffering even though our efforts are never done. Westerners want instant transformation and instant gratification because we are culturally impatient. There is no easy road to the struggles we face in our lives. The methods of Practical Dharma are incremental and cumulative and require an ongoing commitment. Without patience, the inclination is to abandon the practice which is why it is such an important part of the path.

I frequently notice. or a loved one observes. that I am responding skillfully and with more patience to challenging situations that used to cause me and those around me much suffering.

Such change is gradual usually appearing when we are not expecting it. The rewards of reduced suffering and greater freedom from cultivating patience are well worth the effort. We must work at it and pursue it with the intention to change as it will not fall in our laps. Practical Dharma is not a set of passive practices where transformation happens simply from sitting in meditation every day. We must implement the tools available to us in our daily lives for changes to occur.

Let us briefly review the enemies of patience. We start where we often do with the ego. Arrogance and a sense of entitlement, born of the ego, are attitudes in which a lack of patience is embedded. Though neither is the same as anger they are closely related. Impatience is a typical response to anger, waiting in the wings to arise when we are frustrated or thwarted. The "hurry-up sickness" and sense of urgency that is pervasive in our culture is ripe ground for impatience.

Who suffers when we are impatient with others? True, the person we find frustrating may suffer if we react to them but primarily we suffer. Can we use the suffering that comes from our impatience as a teacher? To remind us to address it skillfully with the tools available to us?

Equanimity, which is one of the four Brahma Viharas, is an antidote to anger that helps us cultivate patience. As with every aspect of our practice, we begin with noticing followed by the pause and tuning into bodily reactions that characterize impatience as our cues. We become aware when impatience arises and what it feels like and where it is occurring in the body. Accompanying thought patterns which will be idiosyncratic to us, predictable, and familiar, are additional cues. We are now halfway toward managing our impatience more skillfully as we are fully and consciously aware of it. Once we notice, and see clearly with insight and discernment the sources of our impatience, we pause and breathe. We then give ourselves the directive to consciously let go of what we are holding onto that is feeding our impatience.

All the tools of our practice and steps of the Noble Eightfold Path involve, either directly or indirectly, the cultivation of patience. Patient people are happy people—I am more at peace when I am patient as you will be.

Reflection:

- Think about the situations that predictably make you impatient. Is it because someone is not responding to your expectations? What other triggers can you identify?

Chapter Seventeen

Judging

"Comparison is the thief of joy."

— Teddy Roosevelt

Teddy Roosevelt's quote sums up an important dilemma and source of suffering we face daily on the Dharma path. Comparing ourselves to others while we judge them— both of which are unavoidable tendencies.

We compare anything and everything about ourselves—our behavior, our income, our mental health, our attractiveness, our relationships, our possessions, our status, our homes, our pets, and on and on. The result of all the comparing and self-judging is increased suffering.

The comparisons and judgments are going on constantly in the background even when we are not fully conscious of them. In our modern times where everyone's life is on social media, there has been an explosion of comparing. A recent phenomenon that is the product of social media is known as FOMO, or "fear of missing out." With FOMO, we judge our social lives. We try to determine if others are having more fun, leading more exciting lives, or going to more social functions than we are. This modern phenomenon is one of many that has increased the suffering that comparing and judging creates.

Evolutionary psychology tells us that we are hard-wired to compare ourselves to others, the technical term for which is "status-watching." Human thinking patterns evolved to detect our physical, social, and intellectual differences from others. The shame-pride continuum and access to the best food and breeding opportunities are involved in the process.

Social psychology reveals that when we use comparing to make ourselves feel better we compare ourselves to people we perceive as having lower status. Alternately, when we imagine our status is low we look to people of higher status for comparison and clues about that to which we must aspire to increase our status. If an individual's status is high or rising, they take steps to fend off rivals. High status engenders pride, an inflated sense of self, and respect from peers, all of which are ego-driven. On the other end of the continuum, the shame of low status creates feelings of inferiority, vulnerability, and fear of rejection.

Most species that function in groups have a pecking order or hierarchical group structure. Though different criteria exist in our modern times, such a pecking order also includes us, humans. We compare ourselves and judge others as a vestige of our human evolution.

We live in a competitive culture where status is determined by wealth, possessions, educational attainment, attractiveness, and winning. Motivating much of the pursuit is comparing, which often results in ongoing self-criticism. We struggle to "keep up with the Joneses" and judge ourselves as failures if we fall behind our neighbors in these areas, generating more suffering. Practical Dharma offer tools for lessening this distress.

Children are not born with comparing minds. Their brains are not sufficiently developed to respond other than to sensations of hunger, elimination, temperature, and comfort. As the child's brain develops it is exposed to a competitive culture hundred of thousands of years in the making. The cultural norms get internalized by the child. Comparisons such as safe/unsafe or tasteful/toxic are necessary for the child's survival and are usually the first categories of comparison for a young child.

The process expands during childhood fed by cultural messages and developing peer relationships. The cultural norms become more complex until by early adolescence teens are in full comparing mode. For this reason, adolescence is a very challenging time for teens. It is why peer pressure is so powerful and everything including experiences, clothing choices, appearances, friend choices, winning, losing, popularity, and family status is grist for the mill of comparison. The underlying threats of shame, unpopularity, and feeling inadequate are ever-present. Teens will take significant risks, sometimes fatal, to achieve or preserve high status. If we survive the teen years we bring into adulthood the template for a life of comparing and judging.

Advertisers and marketers exploit our comparing tendencies by convincing us that if we only drive the right car, wear the right clothes, and drink the right beer we will surpass others in our never-ending pursuit of status. A recent phenomenon in our culture is the role of influencers who are people with large social media followings who companies hire to showcase their products. What brand of sneakers are the influencers wearing? What car are they driving? What style of clothing do they wear? Being cool only requires that we emulate the influencer is the intended message.

We seek and then cling and grasp to those things that we believe will bring us status and, therefore, happiness. We create stories and narratives to support our pursuits but it is a fool's errand and an endless futile quest because of the law of impermanence.

We are on a treadmill from which we can never escape if we do not take steps to intervene with intention.

My college years were characterized by judging and comparing mind. I believed that my worth was a function of my status when compared to my peers. It was critical that I attend the right college, join the right fraternity, date attractive women from the right women's colleges, drive the right car, wear the most fashionable clothes, and go to the best parties. Though I did well academically (in part to avoid being drafted and sent to Viet Nam), grades were secondary to my social life. I firmly believed that if did everything right concerning status I would finally be happy. But I was never happy because someone else always outdid me in the categories that I deemed important. It was a hollow and meaningless existence, not that I let anyone know lest my suffering be exposed.

What are the tools that Practical Dharma offers to manage our comparing minds more skillfully and reduce our suffering? First, as is often the case, is noticing with mindful awareness where we are getting hooked. Noticing how often we compare ourselves and judge others and the forms it takes. See how comparing results in competition with others and envy of others. We begin to see how we feel inflated but vulnerable when we are winning and deflated when we are losing and the suffering that accompanies each. We notice that we worry about losing if we are winning and feeling like a failure when losing.

Second, as we become aware we label it with a simple reminder to ourselves like "Comparing mind" or "Judging mind." Labeling opens the door for us to let go of the comparison and rein in the ego's need to compete, win, and feel superior to others. I find it tremendously helpful at these moments to practice compassion for myself and those with whom I have been comparing myself.

Practicing sympathetic joy, one of the Brahma Viharas, which is the taking of pleasure in someone else's good fortune, is a powerful antidote to envying those with whom we feel less than. Doing so lessens the ego's power over our feelings in those moments and reduces our suffering.

Such practices broaden our perspective and create a sense of spaciousness that puts comparing in a larger context. We experience equanimity and are less reactive. When we are not in comparing mode we are more open and available for meaningful connection with others regardless of their perceived status. We manage envy, jealousy, and competition more skillfully. Contrary to what Teddy Roosevelt said, our joy is no longer stolen so it is available to us.

Reduced competition and envy open the door for more meaningful connection with others. Such emotional intimacy is an antidote for loneliness, isolation, negative self-judgment, and acceptance of all of who we are. It is one of the joys that life offers us if we avail ourselves of it. It is yet another experience for which we can feel gratitude for this path.

Reflection:

- Are you able to see where your self-worth, how you feel about yourself, is tied to comparing yourself to others or an external standard?

Chapter Eighteen

Gratitude

"These two people are hard to find in the world. Which two? The one who is first to do a kindness, and the one who is grateful and thankful for a kindness done."

—*The Buddha*

When I was a child, my mother always said, "Count your blessings" whenever I whined or complained. It felt like a guilt trip so her admonition had no resonance with me. Who would have imagined that her words would return to me as an adult and strongly inform my embrace of Practical Dharma?

Practical Dharma applied in our day-to-day lives reduces our suffering and the suffering of those around us. Gratitude practice is one of the simplest and most powerful practices from the Dharma that we can do to increase our happiness and reduce our suffering. We do not have to look far to practice gratitude and not just for the big things in our life. But also the small everyday simple blessings and beauty in our lives—the wonder in our lives. This is one of my favorite and most regular practices because it pays significant dividends in the form of greater joy and contentment.

We are constantly surrounded by the wonder, magic, and mystery of life and all creation. We only need to wake up and experience gratitude for the world in which we live. This means taking nothing for granted—unfortunately, something we do every day in our busy lives. The practice is as simple as engaging in the mindful cultivation of gratitude daily.

I begin each day with a gratitude practice for the many blessings in my life. As best I can, I presume nothing. I now view every day as a gift as are all the details of my life. The practice has profoundly increased my happiness and reduced my suffering.

Gratitude balances the mind's tendency to focus on the negative and on what we feel is lacking in our life. The practice frees us from our usual litany of dissatisfactions. We have greater clarity of thinking and feel more connected to life. Mental spaciousness occurs and self-centered ego concerns lessen in importance.

I always start with gratitude for the human birth of which I am the product. The gift of this singular life—a miracle in the vastness of time and space that randomly joined sperm and ovum to create a life. How can I not express gratitude for such a miracle?

Gratitude practice helps us see that everything is interconnected and none of us can survive independently. We depend on the natural world and thousands of others to meet our daily needs for food, shelter, protection, information, and safety. We think about the abundance in our lives and acknowledge the individual acts of others that produced such bounty. As is written in the *Holy Bible*, "We all drink from wells we did not dig and are warmed by fires we did not build."

For example, when I read my morning newspaper, I think about the reporter who gathered the news, the person who felled the tree to make the paper it is printed on, the truck driver who took the logs to the paper factory, the people in the factory who turned the wood pulp into newsprint, those who manufactured the ink with which the paper is printed, the typesetter who formatted the news, the printer who printed my copy, the distributor who brought the papers to my city, and the delivery person who delivered it to my front door every morning, rain or shine. With a feeling of deep gratitude, I bow to them all.

Our hearts open when we practice gratitude. Feelings of generosity—of wanting to express our gratitude by practicing generosity arise. Gratitude practice does not mean that we deny life's difficulties. We fully recognize and embrace our challenges and suffering. However, gratitude practice prepares us to face problems with greater equanimity and resilience.

Can we be grateful even for the challenges in our life? Seeing obstacles as teachers can help us use the gifts of the Buddha's wisdom to create spaciousness and perspective in our lives.

A benefit of gratitude practice is discovering wonder and awe about the world. We see the world with new eyes in what is called "beginner's mind" in Zen. We see the forest *and* the trees as well as all the living creatures therein. We stand in awe of the vast complexity of the world and the universe surrounding us.

Gratitude also derives from an appreciation for seeing that we learn from setbacks. Toxic emotions like anger, irritation, selfishness, envy, and greed are neutralized. Wonder and gratitude are antidotes to feelings of loss, deprivation, scarcity, despair, and hopelessness. Our heart is full and open and joy happens. The Chinese proverb, "One joy scatters a hundred griefs" sums it up nicely.

Gratitude need not feel like an obligation. Instead, it is an appreciation for all the gifts that this life provides. It is taking nothing for granted though not in the sense of owing a debt of gratitude. Instead, it is a deeply felt appreciation that evokes feelings of generosity, its close cousin. We want to be as generous to the world as it has been to us. Nor is it an attitude of giving up or despair like "My life is terrible but I guess I should be grateful for what I do have."

Gratitude brings us ultimately into the present moment. We are thankful for things that are right here right now because they are precious and impermanent. We appreciate them because we know they will not last. Gratitude practice costs us nothing but time and effort yet the rewards are priceless.

Reflection:

- Do you tend to focus on what is missing from your life? Or, on all the gifts in your life? Consider beginning each day by bringing to mind five things for which you are grateful. Does doing so bring you more happiness and appreciation for your life?

Chapter Nineteen

Death

"It's only when we truly know and understand that we have a limited time on earth – and that we have no way of knowing when our time is up – that we will begin to live each day to the fullest, as if it was the only one we had"

— *Elisabeth Kubler-Ross*

This book would not be complete without addressing the three-ton elephant in the room—death and our mortality which are the things we spend so much energy denying or avoiding thinking about.

Western culture has removed death from our intimate experience. Modern medicine has set a standard that death should be prevented by any means possible. What does Practical Dharma offer us to better prepare for this inevitable final chapter of the human experience? How does our practice support us in preparing for the loss of a loved one and the grief that follows?

The Buddha taught that the mindful acknowledgment of our mortality helps us live in the present moment, appreciating every day as a precious gift. We learn to live our lives without regret so that we do not spend our last days or hours suffering about past decisions and choices made or not made. Many people that I treated in my practice over the years had tragic deaths because they came to the end of their lives with many regrets and the resulting guilt. A death informed by multiple regrets is not a peaceful or good death.

The traditional Buddhist teaching about death was based on the belief system at the time of the Buddha primarily borrowed from Hinduism. The teaching was that death was temporary as rebirth occurs in an endless cycle called *samsara*. The process continues until one achieves enlightenment, called *nirvana*, when the cycle ceases. Practical Dharma does not consider metaphysical questions such as reincarnation. These questions are unanswerable and do not bear on the daily challenges of reducing our suffering and that of those around us. We will leave open the question of what happens to us after death. Instead, we will focus on our relationship to the impermanence of the bodies we have been given in this lifetime.

Before immersing myself in Buddhist practice I was frightened of death. I avoided thinking about it or about situations that would remind me of it. The concept of death for me was infused with qualities of uncertainty and a lack of control. I was preoccupied with health issues and tended toward hypochondria, imagining that I had, or would develop, every possible dreaded illness. I had no belief in an afterlife so the finality of death was very frightening. I did not see it as a normal part of life but as an enemy of my existence so I suffered.

With gratitude, Buddhist practice and the lessons of the Dharma have helped change my relationship with the certainty of death. Though I do not look forward to dying it is because I love life and not because of fear. I know that my endless curiosity about this life in all its beautiful complexity will someday be gone. I get so much joy from learning new things, going to new places, experiencing new adventures, and meeting new people it saddens me to think it will end before I am done relishing life.

Having learned to let go of a high need for control, to better tolerate uncertainty, and embrace impermanence I am no longer afraid of death. I experience anticipatory grief thinking about being separated from those I love and cherish but I am reassured that I will not know since I will be dead!

I have certain hopes regarding my death. I intend not to leave my family with the task of cleaning up the details of my life by doing as much planning as possible. I hope not to suffer great physical pain or disability while dying. However, I accept that I have little if any control over the process of my death. Death remains on my mind frequently but more to remind me to embrace each day as a gift that brings joy, wonder, gratitude, and meaningful connections to those I love. As I watch my body age and my abilities decline, I do so with acceptance and gratitude for all the gifts of this life.

Living a Dharma-informed life, including all the practices we have covered, provides the means to change our relationship with death. Death is not the enemy any more than our ever-changing bodies are the enemy. Aging and death are part of the mystery of life. Indulging the fantasy that we can live forever is delusional; it is not accepting the truth of life and its finality. An essential part of changing our relationship with death is cultivating wisdom; the antithesis of holding onto the fantasy of immortality.

Humankind developed elaborate belief systems and practices over the millennia to cope with death's uncertainty and unpredictability. While such practices and beliefs may bring comfort, I believe they lack the wisdom that requires that we accept things as they are with all the uncertainty—not as our imagination with its wishful thinking tells us.

A powerful Buddhist practice thought to have been developed by the Buddha is known as The Five Recollections. They are cold water in your face set of reminders about the impermanence of our mortality. While they may seem negative and depressing upon first reading they can motivate us to live fully every day and take nothing for granted.

The recollections are:

1. I am of the nature to grow old; there is no way to escape growing old.

2. I am of the nature to have ill health; there is no way to escape having ill health.

3. I am of the nature to die; there is no way to escape death.

4. All that is dear to me and everyone I love are of the nature to change. There is no way to escape being separated from them.

5. My deeds are my closest companions. I am the beneficiary of my deeds. My deeds are the ground on which I stand.

Including the Five Recollections in our practice, which initially may be difficult or upsetting will, over time, help shift our relationship to our mortality and that of those we love. We might think of them as an exercise in graduated exposure, from ACT, for any fears of death from which we suffer.

Death is not something strange or unusual. It is happening every second all over the world. Accepting the inevitability of death supports our leading a meaningful life because there is more spaciousness in our daily lives as we are not contracting emotionally from a fear of death. It is the ego that flails against the reality of our mortality because the ego cannot comprehend a time when it no longer exists. We cling to the idea of a permanent immortal self which is an exercise in futility and we suffer as a consequence. Ironically, embracing the certainty of death, whenever and however it happens, is a source of freedom.

Reflection:

- Rather than avoiding thinking about death are you willing to use awareness of your own mortality to appreciate every day?

Chapter Twenty

Grief

"To spare oneself from grief at all cost can be achieved only at the price of total detachment, which excludes the ability to experience happiness."

—*Erich Fromm*

Regardless of who we are or the life that we have lived grief and loss due to the death of a loved one will touch us. Because we are relational beings from our first breath we will be greatly impacted by loss. Our capacity for love, which affirms our interconnectedness, makes our experiences of loss profound. The deeper the connection the more profound the loss. The following story illustrates this truth very powerfully and is one of my favorite parables from ancient Buddhist writings, the *Parable of the Mustard Seed*.

During the Buddha's time, a young woman from a wealthy family was happily married to a man in her village. She had a son who became ill and died when he was a year old. Her grief was overwhelming. She could not bear the weight of it. She carried the dead child in her arms wailing and weeping throughout the village. She begged her friends and neighbors to help her bring her son back to life. No one was able to help her or offer her relief. Nevertheless, she persisted and begged for help all over the village. One of her neighbors was a follower of the Buddha and suggested that the young woman visit the Buddha and ask him for help. She took the dead child to the Buddha and told him of her loss and her grief. The Buddha responded to her loss with empathy, patience, and compassion. He told her, "There is a way to solve your problem. Go to each house in the village and obtain a mustard seed from any family that has not experienced death and bring them to me." The young woman left hopeful that the Buddha had offered a solution to her loss. She immediately began visiting every house in the village. But she soon discovered that each family she visited had experienced one or more losses from death and could not give her a mustard seed. She then realized that death comes to all families and is inevitable. With that, she was able to bury her child and give up hope of his returning to life. She understood that death is part of the experience of life and that no one is spared loss and grief.

I volunteer to facilitate bereavement groups at a local hospice organization for those who have lost a child and are grieving the loss. It is very powerful and satisfying, if difficult, work. My biggest challenge is convincing the group members to accept their grief in its many forms—not fight it, not pathologize it, not feel ashamed of it, not deny it, not push it away, or minimize it. The heart-opening, however painful, is impressive to behold when group members can fully embrace their loss and share their feelings openly with the other group members. It is why I find the work so satisfying and why the members find it so healing. Grief is one human experience that should never be done alone. As one group member said recently, "This is not a club I ever wanted to belong to, but I am so thankful that it exists."

Grieving a loss can be a very lonely and isolating experience as the parable of the mustard seed suggests. Unfortunately, most people not dealing with a loss are often uncomfortable with, and avoid engaging with, someone in the throes of grief. Group members often complain about how unhelpful comments from others such as, "She's in a better place" can be. Seeing the group members care for and support one another reinforces that we need connection and community when we struggle with life's most significant challenges. For those dealing with the profound sorrow of losing a loved one, particularly a child, there is no substitute for sharing that grief with fellow travelers. Relationships and connection are very beneficial for someone experiencing the pain of grief. Accessing the tools of Practical Dharma, especially the acceptance of impermanence, supports and eases the grieving process.

People also grieve when they are dying. In coming to terms with my eventual death I alluded to the sadness that I anticipate if I know my death is imminent—not only the losses suffered by dying but also the losses due to being seriously ill. I anticipate sadness at losing my facilities and opportunities to do the things I love if I am sick. My death will cause sorrow for my loved ones, a sorrow that I am helpless to spare them. My challenge is to let go and be fully present with the truth of what is happening.

Dying people often speak of the profound sense of presence they experience as death approaches and the wisdom and clarity they achieve. They lament that they did not experience such benefits earlier in life. Is this not another argument for following a path that offers such benefits? Loss is inevitable so why not use it as a catalyst for spiritual growth and to reduce our suffering? To add perspective to the journey that is this life?

Sadly, in the West, we have sanitized death and dying and eliminated many of the grieving rituals that brought our ancestors together in shared grief. There is often a rush to complete the memorial service or funeral so everyone can return to their busy lives. Members of my bereavement groups complain that after the last covered dish is eaten they feel alone and without support from anyone who understands their pain. The task of settling an estate and tying up loose ends in the deceased's life can be overwhelming and add additional stress to the experience of loss. Ideally, one's community can be a helpful resource in navigating the maze of details.

As with much that we emphasize in Practical Dharma, the practice of acceptance is primary though it is no panacea for the pain of loss. Spiritual practice cannot help us avoid the pain of grief. Yet, by employing the tools available to us the loss can be held with greater compassion, perspective, and spaciousness.

Acceptance takes both time and actively facing loss. Though grief comes in strong waves we welcome it as necessary and unavoidable. Someone I know, who recently lost a child, told me that something was wrong with them because they could not stop crying. They insisted that they just needed to stop crying.

I responded that they needed to cry more and not try to stop as the grief needed to be accepted, as painful as it was, and faced openly. Repressing it would only prolong the grief.

I could not adequately grieve my father's death until I let go of many residual emotions and faced my loss clearly without the confusion of strong feelings. When he was alive there was too much noise in the system in the form of unresolved emotions for me to gain clarity about my complicated feelings toward him. When he died I grieved not only his death but also the missed opportunities during his lifetime for a deeper connection with him—the result of my holding onto unrealistic expectations.

Grief is real, it is raw, and it is painful but it is also heart-opening like nothing else I have experienced. There are no shortcuts to grieving; we must show up for it and welcome it without trying to avoid or run from it. I believe that using the tools of Practical Dharma can be extremely helpful in facing our losses.

Notwithstanding the pain, I have grown emotionally and spiritually from every major loss I have suffered. Some of my most profound losses have been the death of pets—I often joke that I grieve more deeply over the death of one of my beloved dogs than I ever have for a person.

The heart opening and the development of compassion for myself and others as well as the wisdom I gained could only have come from experiencing loss. Every significant experience in our lives, loss included, is an opportunity to either learn and grow as opposed to withdrawing, avoiding, and hiding. Accepting impermanence while seeing suffering as a teacher and embracing the sorrow in our lives are not inborn dispositions. They must be cultivated and acquired, and Practical Dharma makes that possible—with the effort comes the promise of liberation and emotional freedom.

Reflection:

- Think about where in your life you have experienced grief. Did you accept your grief and face it or try to avoid it by distracting yourself?

Chapter Twenty-One

Putting It All Together

"The dharma is the most precious thing in the world and we should put it at the center of our hearts and transform our whole lives into dharma practice. Otherwise, at the time of death, we will look back and say, now what was all that about? If we truly want to benefit others and ourselves, we have to do it. No excuses."

—*Tenzin Palmo*

My intention for this book was to present a summary of the Buddha's fundamental and most practical teachings. I have combined these teachings with methods of modern psychology from Acceptance and Commitment Therapy. Together, I believe the integrated approaches have the greatest likelihood of helping us live our everyday lives with less stress and suffering and more joy.

This book only skimmed the surface of the vast Buddhist discourses. Likewise with the vast literature on ACT. The practices applied to the life challenges we discussed have been life-changing for me and many of my students. I never imagined that my life could be so different. Every important aspect of my life has been impacted by the Dharma including my relationships, my work habits, my priorities, and the joy and happiness in my life. Every day feels like a gift for which I am grateful. I am truly blessed and deeply appreciative and intend to live the rest of my life in the light of the Dharma. I invite you to join me.

The themes that recur in this book are those that I return to again and again in the interest of reducing my suffering, that of my students, and the people in my life. The result of this practice is that I live a more awakened and ethical life which has supported me in becoming a better person.

Life is hard and none of us escape the challenges and suffering it presents. One choice is to give into despair and hopelessness in the face of adversity; to dwell in negativity and bitterness. A wiser choice is to step fully into the reality of life and accept it as we encounter it in each moment. We are all the product of the causes and conditions of our lives but we need not remain prisoners of our past. We have choices and agency and learning and following the practices of Practical Dharma enable those choices.

I know no better example of the transformative power of Buddhist practice than my own life. Since beginning this path I have gone from being a driven, impatient, anxious, unhappy, angry, and controlling workaholic who made those around him miserable to someone who sees life more clearly and with greater joy and spaciousness. I feel more deeply connected to those I love and I see joy and wonder in the natural world. My reactivity has dramatically decreased as I now take more things in stride. I try not to control those things which I cannot control and more readily let go of irritation and frustration. I am grateful for the gift of each day.

My life is still filled with challenges and contradictions. I still get hooked by grasping and clinging to things that I know are impermanent. Nonetheless, I am grateful for the gift of both ancient wisdom and modern psychology which have been my roadmaps on this journey. My gratitude has spread to include the many other gifts of this life. I no longer take any of the blessings for granted. I acknowledge with gratitude how fortunate I am to have all the experiences of this difficult and joyful life.

I am not a misty-eyed Polly Anna. My long-term habits of the mind have not been an easy case for these practices. I say when teaching that if these practices can be transformative for me they can be life-changing for anyone. During the years when I was unhappy and feeling lost, I never imagined that there was a way out of the darkness. As the methods described herein have brought me into the light of awareness and joy, I greet each day with gratitude.

To help you begin finding more joy in your own life I leave you with a few reminders and takeaways:

1. Review and remember the basic teachings we covered in the early chapters. They provide the Buddha's prescription for healing the illness of suffering. With its robust pragmatism, the modern wisdom of ACT enhances the process. Together they guide us to better places in our lives.

2. The essential and common threads through all the topics we covered include noticing, pausing, and discernment. These require mindfulness, present-moment awareness, intention, and patience. They are essential to the path and must be practiced daily. This is not an easy practice and will not succeed if we are operating on autopilot.

3. Be mindful of where we get tripped up on our journey. The Three Poisons of greed, hatred, and delusion explain most of where and how we suffer and cause suffering to others. Subsumed under these challenges

are the denial of impermanence, the ego's siren call ("I, me, mine"), the reactivity we act out, and the shame and avoidance we experience.

4. Relationships, and our actions within them and in response and reactivity to them, make us human and are central to our existence. It is difficult to see our suffering without the mirroring of others. We do poorly when we are alone and isolated which are sources of tremendous suffering. Successful relationships require work and sacrifice and are never easy; they require acceptance that the best of them is imperfect. Yet the rewards are without parallel.

5. The positive practices of the Brahma Viharas (loving kindness, equanimity, compassion, and sympathetic joy), the Ten Perfections, gratitude practice, and cultivating joy are antidotes to the toxic emotions, attitudes, and behaviors that we addressed. Without making these aspects of the teachings a part of our daily lives we will not change. "Wishing won't make it so," as the saying goes. They need to be an integral part of our daily practice.

I hope you found this book helpful and supportive and that it resonated with your struggles. Additional volumes could be, and have been, written about other aspects of Buddhism and Buddhist practices. There is also a vast literature on ACT. I have tried to present a brief but accessible overview of the most effective and achievable practices from each to reduce our suffering and improve the quality of our busy lives.

The Buddha told the monks in this Sangha not to take his word for anything he taught. Instead, he told them to follow his teachings and see if they worked. I encourage you to do the same with Practical Dharma. Do not take my word for anything. Instead, trust your own direct experiences as you experiment and observe what reduces your suffering. Start your journey on the path now, find a live or virtual Sangha, begin a meditation practice, continue to study the teachings, and see for yourself. Doing so costs you nothing but time and effort and the reward will be a richer and more joyful life filled with compassion and gratitude for all your experiences.

I wish you many blessings in your life's journey.

Peace to you and yours.

Reflection:

- Where in your life do you want to apply the methods of Practical Dharma to improve the quality of your life and reduce your suffering? If you are reluctant, what is holding you back?

i. About the Author

Jeffrey C. Fracher, Ph.D., a retired Clinical Psychologist, was in practice as a clinical psychologist for 44 years in New Jersey and Virginia. He has practiced Buddhism since 1992 when he took the lay precepts, committing to the Buddhist path, in the Sangha of the late Thich Nhat Hanh.

In 2013 he completed a 2-year Buddhist teacher training program at the Meditation Teachers Training Institute in Washington, D.C. He was a senior teacher at the Insight Meditation Community of Charlottesville for 10 years, where he was also president of the IMCC Board of Directors, before his retirement in early 2022.

In 2022, he founded Serenity Sangha of Charlottesville, a far-reaching virtual community of Buddhist practitioners which emphasizes Practical Dharma, the synthesis of modern psychology and ancient Buddhist wisdom.

Jeff, a native Virginian, lives in Charlottesville, VA, with his wife of 50 years, Kay, and his two beloved rescued Golden Retrievers, Kaiya and Khema. He has two adult sons, Eli and Luke. In addition to leading Serenity Sangha, he is a Clinical Assistant Professor in the Clinical Psychology Ph.D. program at the University of Virginia. He is a volunteer bereavement group facilitator at the Hospice of the Piedmont. He also serves on the City of Charlottesville Police Civilian Oversight Board.

ii. Acknowledgements

The list of people to whom I am grateful for help and support with this project is quite long. Nevertheless, I apologize to those I may have overlooked and failed to mention.

First and foremost, my deep gratitude to my wonderful life partner of 50 years, my beloved, Kay. What began as an 8th grade crush many years ago, evolved into one of the great joys of my life. Her support and love through all my life challenges, including this project, are immeasurable.

The members of Serenity Sangha, who encouraged me to commit my teachings to paper, inspired this project. Their commitment to the path of Practical Dharma inspires me every day and brings me great joy.

Many thanks to the readers who reviewed my drafts and made suggestions that greatly improved this effort: Bob Paviour, Christina Platania, Kay Fracher, and Phyllis Gardner.

My fellow Dharma teachers who have taught me, supported me, and shared their wisdom with me include: Patrick Coffey, Tara Brach, Teresa Miller, David Silver, Helen Farrar, Sharon Beckman-Brindley, Susan Stone, Heather Karp, Phil Davidson, Kay Davidson, Mary Vandevanter, Clay Evans, Don Abrams, and Hugh Byrne.

Much gratitude for my personal teacher of many years, Lila Kate Wheeler, who has guided me, confronted me, supported me, believed in me, and helped me become a better person. She is a repository of great Dharma wisdom which she has generously shared with me.

Admiration and gratitude to Steven Hayes, Ph.D., who, with his colleagues, created the psychology school known as Acceptance and Commitment Therapy, ACT, which has done more to alleviate human suffering than any other school of therapy of which I am aware.

Many, many thanks to my brilliant editor, Amy Lemley, writer, and editor extraordinaire, who brought her special touch to the rough draft with which I presented her.

Finally, to all the teachers, therapists, mentors, supervisors, role models, friends, colleagues, pets, adversaries, psychotherapy patients, and family members, who have taught me, challenged me, supported me, and guided me on my life's journey. Thank you.

iii. References

American Bible Society. (1995). *The Holy Bible: Contemporary English version*.

Anderson, B. (2019). *The Buddha's Guide to Gratitude: The Life-Changing Power of Everyday Mindfulness*. IMango Publishing.

Armstrong, K. (2001). *Buddha: A Penguin Life*. Lipper/Viking.

Bach, P.A., & Moran, D.J. (2008) *ACT in Practice*. New Harbinger Publications.

Batchelor, S. (1997). *Buddhism without Beliefs: A Contemporary Guide to Awakening*. Riverhead Books.

Bernstein, W. J. (2021). *The Delusions of Crowds: Why People Go Mad in Groups*. Atlantic Monthly Press.

Bodhi, B. (2000). *The Noble Eightfold Path: Way to the End of Suffering*. BPS Pariyatti Editions.

Bodhi, B. (2015). *In the Buddha's Words: An Anthology of Discourses from the Pāli Canon*. Wisdom Publications.

Brady, M. (2003). *The Wisdom of Listening*. Wisdom Publications.

Brahma Viharas. Four Immeasurables. (2015, January 27). Retrieved September 4, 2022, from https://brahmaviharas.net.

Buddhist Publication Society. (1996). *The Dhammapada: The Buddha's Path of Wisdom*.

Buswell, R. E., & Lopez, D. S. (2014). *The Princeton Dictionary of Buddhism*. Princeton University Press.

Chodron, Pema. (1998). *When Things Fall Apart*. Shambhala.

Dalai Lama & Tutu, D. (2016). *The Book of Joy: Lasting Happiness in a Changing World*. Avery Penguin Random House.

Dalai Lama. (2007). *How to See Yourself as You Really Are*. Atria Press.

Dhammapala, A., & Bodhi, B. (1996). *A Treatise on the Paramis: From the Commentary to the Cariyapitaka*. Buddhist Publication Society.

Epstein, M. (1999). *Going to Pieces Without Falling Apart: A Buddhist Perspective on Wholeness*. Broadway Books.

Epstein, M. (2018). *Advice Not Given: A Guide to Getting Over Yourself*. Penguin Press.

Feldman, C. (2017). *Boundless Heart: The Buddha's Path of Kindness, Compassion, Joy, and Equanimity*. Shambhala Publications, Inc.

Fronsdal, G. (2006). *The Dhammapada: A New Translation of the Buddhist Classic with Annotations*. Shambhala Publications, Inc.

Fronsdal, G. (2008). *The Issue at Hand: Essays on Buddhist Mindfulness Practice*. Insight Meditation Center.

Fromm, Erich (1947). *Man for Himself: An Inquiry Into the Psychology of Ethics*. Rinehart.

Fundamentals of Buddhism: Wisdom. (n.d.). Retrieved September 4, 2022, from https://www.buddhanet.net/fundbud8.htm.

Germer, C. K. (2009). *The Mindful Path to Self-Compassion: Freeing Yourself From Destructive Thoughts and Emotions*. Guilford Press.

Gleig, A. (2019). *American Dharma: Buddhism Beyond Modernity*. Yale University Press.

Goldstein, J. (2016). *Mindfulness: A Practical Guide to Awakening*. Sounds True.

Goleman, D. (2004). *Destructive Emotions: How Can We Overcome Them? A Scientific Dialogue with the Dalai Lama*. Bantam Books.

Gunaratana, H. (1992). *Mindfulness in Plain English*. Wisdom Publications.

Hanh, T. N., & Kotler, A. (1996). *Being Peace*. Parallax Press.

Hạnh Nhất, & Laity, A. (1993). *The Blooming of a Lotus: Guided Miracle of Mindfulness*. Beacon Press.

Hạnh Nhất. (1998). *Old Path, White Clouds: Walking in the Footsteps of the Buddha*. Full Circle.

Hanson, R. (2020) *Neurodharma*. Harmony Books.

Hanson, R. & Mendius, R. (2009). *Buddha's Brain: The Practical Neuroscience of Happiness, Love & Wisdom*. New Harbinger Publications.

Harari, Y. N., (2018). *Sapiens: A Brief History of Humankind*. Harper Perennial.

Harris, Russ, (2019), *ACT Made Simple.* New Harbinger Publications.

Harris, Russ, (2012). *The Reality Slap.* New Harbinger Publications.

Hayes, S. C. (2005). *Get Out of Your Mind & Into Your Life: The New Acceptance & Commitment Therapy.* New Harbinger Publications.

Hayes, S. C., Strosahl, K. D., & Wilson, K. G. (2004). *Acceptance and Commitment Therapy: An Experiential Approach to Behavior Change.* Guilford.

Hesse, Herman. (1910). *Gertrude.* Picador Press.

Jung, C. G., & Hinkle, B. M. (2003). *Psychology of the Unconscious.* Dover Publications.

Junger, S. (2017). *Tribe: On Homecoming and Belonging.* 4th Estate.

Kabat-Zinn, J. (1994). *Wherever You Go, There You Are: Mindfulness Meditation in Everyday Life.* Hyperion.

Kubler-Ross, Elisabeth (1959) *On Death and Dying.* Macmillan.

Kyokai, Bukkyo Dendo (1997). *The Teaching of Buddha*. Japan Publications.

Ladner, L. (2004). *The Lost Art of Compassion: Discovering the Practice of Happiness in the Meeting of Buddhism and Psychology*. Harper San Francisco.

Lao-Tzu (1990). *Tao Te Ching*. Kyle Cathie, Ltd.

Metamorphosis. (2021). *The Mustard Seed of Grief and Rebirth*. Buddhistdoor Global. Retrieved September 4, 2022, from https://www.buddhistdoor.net/features/the-mustard-seed-of-grief-and-rebirth.

Moffitt, P. (2008). *Dancing with Life: Finding Meaning and Joy in the Face of Suffering*. Rodale.

Moffitt, P. (2012). *Emotional Chaos to Clarity: How to Live More Skillfully, Make Better Decisions, and Find Purpose in Life*. Hudson Street Press.

Müller, F. Max, & Maguire, J. (2002). *Dhammapada: Annotated & Explained*. SkyLight Paths Pub.

Munindo, Ajahn (1995) *Regret and Well Being*. Retrieved September 4, 2022. from https://www.budsas.org/ebud/ebdha029.htm.

Nathanson, D. L. (1987). *The Many Faces of Shame*. Guilford Press.

Nathanson, D. L. (1992). *Shame and Pride: Affect, Sex, and the Birth of the Self*. Norton.

Nyanaponika. (1993). *The Five Mental Hindrances and Their Conquest: Selected Texts from the Pali Canon and the Commentaries*. Buddhist Publication Society.

O'Brien, B. (2018). *The Three Poisons-in Buddhism, the Roots of Unhappiness*. Learn Religions. Retrieved September 4, 2022, from https://www.learnreligions.com/the-three-poisons-449 603.

Palmo, Jetsunma Tenzin (2011). *Into the Heart of Life*. Snow Lion Publications.

Pasha, R. (2020, April 13). *67 Famous Theodore Roosevelt Quotes*. Retrieved September 4, 2022, from https://succeedfe ed.com/theodore-roosevelt-quotes.

Richards, V. & Wilce, G. (1996). *The Person Who Is Me: Contemporary Perspectives on the True and False Self*. Karnac Books.

Rothberg, Donald (2006). *The Engaged Spiritual Life: A Buddhist Approach to Transforming Ourselves and the World*. Beacon Press.

Ruth, D. S. & Ruth, R. S. (1998). *The Simple Guide to Theravada Buddhism*. Global Books, Ltd.

Rūmī Jalāl al-Dīn & Barks, C. (2004). *The Essential Rumi*. HarperCollins.

Smedes, L. B. (1997). *The Art of Forgiving: When You Need to Forgive and Don't Know How*. Ballantine Books.

Staff, L. R. (2019, December 6). *What are the Five Recollections?* Retrieved September 4, 2022, from https://www.lionsroar.com/buddhism-by-the-numbers-the-five-recollections.

Yoda, Master. (1999). *The Phantom Menace*. Retrieved September 4, 2022, from https://www.starwars.com/news/the-starwars-com-10-best-yoda-quotes.

Treleaven, D. A. & Britton, W. (2018). *Trauma-Sensitive Mindfulness: Practices for Safe and Transformative Healing*. W.W Norton & Company.

Watts, Alan (1957). *The Way of Zen*. Random House Vintage Books.

Wikimedia Foundation. (2022, August 27). *Buddhist Ethics*. Wikipedia. Retrieved September 4, 2022, from https://en.wikipedia.org/wiki/Buddhist_ethics.

Wilde, O. (2014). *Oscar Wilde, Complete Collection*. Create-Space Independent Publishing Platform.

Working with the Hard Stuff: Courage to Open to the Whole Show. (2019, August 31). https://awakeningjoy.info/blog/working-with-the-hard-stuff-courage-to-open-to-the-whole-show.

iv. Index

KAIYA

KHEMA

www.ingramcontent.com/pod-product-compliance
Lightning Source LLC
Chambersburg PA
CBHW071155130626
46553CB00004B/1675